Time Trap

by

Jeanie R. Davis

The Somerset Series, Book 2

Time Trap

Cover Art by *Kim Mendoza*

The Wild Rose Press, Inc.
PO Box 708
Adams Basin, NY 14410-0708
Visit us at www.thewildrosepress.com

Publishing History
First Fantasy Rose Edition, 2020
Print ISBN 978-1-5092-2899-7
Digital ISBN 978-1-5092-2900-0

The Somerset Series, Book 2
Published in the United States of America

Christopher read over the short note he'd composed. "Ahh," he moaned. In his haste to finish it and depart, he'd caused the ink to blob and run. Blowing on the paper to hurry the drying process, he considered the best place to put the letter so his uncle would be certain to find it. Cedric likely wouldn't visit the guestroom once Christopher disappeared. And the jewels. Where should he leave those? He'd have to take both to his uncle's chamber. Hopefully, with only a few staff members on duty, he'd avoid being detected.

As he made his way through the guest corridor and toward the family's rooms, noises rose up from the kitchen of the cavernous mansion. He hoped Rachel was busy working below. However, she could be anywhere—members of a skeleton staff often filled many roles. He needed to give himself a tour in order to locate his uncle's bedchamber.

It turned out to be an easy task; two girls talked and giggled as they tidied the largest room—the only chamber which had been occupied in the family wing. Christopher quietly peered into the room. Rachel and a younger girl chatted as one dusted a chest of drawers and the other swept the already spotless floor.

"Christopher, is that you?" His heart squeezed. He'd hoped to escape her notice.

He faked a smile. "Yes, Rachel, 'tis I." He tucked the note into his pocket and made sure the diamonds were securely stowed beneath his coat. "I just came to bid farewell. I must be going now."

Rachel grabbed the other girl by the arm and tugged her forward. "Meg, this is him." She beamed his way. "This is my fiancé, Christopher."

Other TWRP Books by Jeanie R. Davis

TIME TWIST — Book 1 of the Somerset Series
CHRISSY'S CATCH — Book 4 of the Christmas Frost Series

Dedication

To my awesome husband, Rick—
my biggest fan and greatest support.

Chapter One

Arianna's heart constricted as the Somers' home came into view through the car window. The sunset turned the dove-gray Victorian mansion to a rosy pink. So beautiful, like a fairytale castle with its soaring turrets. Yet beneath the beauty—a house of horror. A low moan escaped her throat. She winced as fear embraced her again. Closing her eyes tight to stop the visions—the horrendous memories of her last experience in the mansion—she couldn't keep silent tears from falling.

"Arianna, are you unwell?" Christopher pulled the car off the deserted road. "I cannot call Mother because of the lack of cell service out here, but she will understand if we do not show. They all know what happened." He squeezed her hand.

The heat his touch usually induced failed to warm her icy heart tonight. Coming back to the house in which she'd literally shed blood, sweat and tears terrified her. She glanced at him. His intense blue eyes begged her to be honest. But she couldn't.

"No. I need to do this. It's been nearly two months. It's time I met with your family—minus your hovering father, that is. They are so much a part of your life now. I'll be all right."

Christopher didn't look convinced but drove back onto the road. "One word is all it will take to leave if it becomes too difficult, love. One word."

"Thank you. I'll be fine." She swallowed her apprehension. If she wasn't fine, she'd fake it.

They pulled up to the front of the house. "Stay put. I'll help you out." Christopher kissed her cheek, then exited the car.

Before he made it around to her side, a loud noise assaulted her ears and vibrations shook her. She clutched the seat. *It's my imagination, not the time-traveling device. The noise, the vibrations—they aren't real. Christopher is real. Our love is real.* She took three deep breaths, willing her thumping heart to decelerate. *I can do this*, she silently repeated.

She had the door open before he reached it. "Watch your leg. You have another week in that cast, and I'm sure it's still tender." Christopher pulled her up and out with little effort. He'd treated her like a porcelain doll ever since she'd nearly died at his father's hands.

She hated it. With everything he felt responsible for, she didn't need to be an additional burden. Nothing was his fault. Nothing.

"At least I'm in a walking cast now, so I no longer need crutches." She lifted her chin and bent her stiff lips into what she hoped looked like a smile. "Okay, let's do this."

A gust of cold air whipped through her hair, chilling her to the bones. *If you know about the time machine, you know I can take you anywhere in the world to kill you.* The familiar and hated words reverberated down her spine, causing her to shiver. "Did you say something, Chris?"

"No." He narrowed his eyes. "Must have been the wind. It is nearly November—cold and breezy out here." He slipped his arm around her waist to help her up the driveway.

The wind, my imagination, or, more likely, a ghost. This place will always be haunted. She shuddered at the memories replaying in her mind.

Raising her gaze, she gasped at the sight. So focused she'd been on the haunting words in the air, she'd failed to prepare herself for what had loomed ahead. How could this beautiful house—the same house she'd worked countless hours, days, weeks, even months, decorating—be so foreboding?

Christopher stopped. "It's too soon."

"No it's not!" The words tumbled out with more force than Ari had intended. She shook her head and tamped down her emotions. "Sorry. I'm struggling with the memories—I'm sure you understand. But to move forward—really move forward—with my emotional healing"—she lifted her hands—"I have to do this."

"I'm so sorry, love." His kind eyes warmed her, instantly replacing the chill she'd felt moments before. Yet she could also see a shadow of regret reflected in them.

Knowing him as well as she did, Ari could read his thoughts. He blamed himself for not only her physical injuries, but her emotional scars, as well. "It's not your fault. Stop blaming yourself for everything. Your father is the man who attacked me. You are the one who traveled back through time—risked your life—to save me."

He let out a breath, but she knew she hadn't convinced him. They'd had this talk before and could go around in circles all night long. But not tonight. Tonight, she was determined to put the past where it belonged and move forward. She hadn't seen Mrs. Somers, Sarah or Joshua since she'd been released from the Pueblo hospital nearly two months before. It was time.

She walked toward the door. Chris double-stepped to catch up. Her cast hit the concrete with a thud, after moving from gravel.

She froze.

The clomping behind her was close—too close. She looked back to see the monster chasing her down a New York alley. It was him. A trashcan rolled into her path, tripping her. Clunk! A sickening crack shot pain through her leg. But she had to run. The monster bore down on her. She could feel him, smell him—

"No!" Terror gripped her as more memories attacked.

In seconds, Christopher had both arms wrapped around her, shock and concern etched across his features.

She had to stare hard into his face to be certain he wasn't his father. Once Christopher's azure blue eyes came into focus, she let go of a ragged breath and sagged into him.

"What—what happened?" he asked.

If she told him the truth, he'd insist she go back to Denver, and he'd never ask her to face her demons again. Maybe that would be best. If the mere walk up the Somers' driveway put her into such a frantic state, what would the rest of the night have in store?

Dropping her head, she studied the traitorous concrete as she blinked back tears threatening to fall. She could do this. She must do this. "My leg. I must have twisted it. Sorry. I didn't expect the pain to be so

intense." *Or the memories to be so vivid.* "Come on"—
she held out her hand—"we're almost there."

"Wait." Christopher bent down and examined her
leg.

She didn't know what he hoped to discover
through the thick layer of plaster, but she indulged him.
Her gaze wandered over the house. Movement caught
her eye. A curtain in a main level window opened
slightly and a face appeared. She stiffened and sucked
in a breath.

Those black eyes. Mr. Somers was here. She had to
get out. The monster was here. Her pulse quickened,
and her breath came out in pants.

"Hey, there's Josh."

Ari jerked at Christopher's voice, then peered
closer at the face in the window. Josh. It was Joshua,
not Mr. Somers. She needed to get a grip.

Without waiting for Christopher's reassuring arm
around her waist again, she hobbled as quickly as she
could to the entry. *Like pulling off a bandage.*

The door flung open as she neared it. Mrs. Somers
and Sarah welcomed her inside, out of the chilly night
air and the ghosts lurking in the dark.

Christopher entered close behind.

The women's eyes were fixed on her. She realized
they knew it would be difficult to come back to the
house where she'd been brutally attacked.

She forced a smile, even though the very smell of
the house made her stomach turn. Feeling like a
spectacle, she bit down on her lip out of anxiety, but
she needed to push through it. After all, the Somers had
also felt like spectacles, having been unwillingly thrust
here from the nineteenth century.

Josh joined the group.

His eyes are black like his father's. Memories bubbled to the surface. Mr. Somers' face flashed in her mind—his wild eyes sending chills down her spine, just as in the nightmares she'd been having for almost two months now. Perhaps they would stop once the cast came off.

She realized she hadn't moved from the foyer as Christopher's warm arm came around her, urging her toward a seat. Her smile became genuine when she took in the formal living room with all the plastic removed. Her eyes roved over walnut-framed, floral-fabric-covered armchairs and the classic, cream-colored sofa. She'd spent her last working day here ridding the furniture of the protective coverings. "It's so beautiful, isn't it?" she whispered.

Mrs. Somers nodded. "The entire home is beautiful because of you." Her voice, still quiet, had a confidence Ari had never heard in all her months knowing the woman. Mrs. Somers narrowed her eyes. She looked intently at Ari's face.

The scar from his ring. Ari immediately wished to disappear. The Somers didn't need the reminder of what had happened any more than she did. While the bruises and abrasions on her face had healed, the remnant of a deep gash across her cheek, caused by several back handed slaps from Mr. Somers, remained. Doctors had assured Ari it would fade, but it hadn't disappeared yet.

"Is that"—Mrs. Somers' voice hitched—"is that from Benjamin's ring?" A mournful whimper escaped her.

Ari raised her fingers to cover the scar.

"I am so very sorry for what my husband put you through." Moisture filled the sweet woman's eyes.

Arianna lost the battle she'd waged against her own emotions as tears splashed down her cheeks. She'd been so preoccupied about protecting herself, she'd given little thought to the effect her presence would have on these kind people. They weren't like Benjamin Somers. If anything, they were like Christopher. Victims, all of them. "Please, Mrs. Somers"—she sniffed and accepted a handkerchief from Chris to wipe her eyes—"don't apologize. You lived with the abuse far longer than I did. I'm fine. I really am. And Christopher drives to Denver every chance he gets. He's taking good care of me."

Guilt hit her like a wrecking ball. All the time Christopher had spent with her was time away from his family—the family he'd fought so long and hard to be reunited with. She must renew her determination to fix this and come up with a schedule where his family came first.

"Mother." Sarah, who had disappeared earlier, entered the room. "Supper is on the table, if you are ready." The young woman's demeanor had improved, but her eyes still drooped. Ari wished to wrap her in a hug, but Sarah's stiff posture suggested she wasn't quite ready for an open friendship yet. Ari couldn't help but wonder how she'd not seen the resemblance between siblings before now. Sarah had the same brunette hair and intense blue eyes as Christopher. And like her brother, her features were striking. Beautiful.

"Thank you, Sarah," said Mrs. Somers. She turned toward Ari and Christopher. "The kitchen is this—" She threw her hands in the air. "You know where it is,

Arianna. You know where everything is. You have spent more time in our home than we have." A smile creased her face.

She looked lovely. In the five months Ari had worked here, she'd never seen Mrs. Somers smile.

As Ari trailed behind the others to the kitchen, a blast of cold air hit her like a winter gust. She stopped in her tracks. Glancing around, she saw no air vents nearby. Curious. Like a magnet, an unseen force turned her head. Her eyes bulged as she found herself staring into the study. Heart slamming against her ribcage, she tried to flee—to follow the others. Common sense told her to pick up her feet and move, but she seemed to be rooted in place. Though the lights were off in the study, Ari's eyes automatically searched out the stolen art hanging on the walls. Something was missing. Had someone rearranged the pieces? No. She must be remembering it wrong. Then her gaze dropped to the ground, where she knew evil lurked beneath a trap door. Her body shook. The cold air snaking around her didn't help. Before long her teeth were chattering.

Christopher, who had followed his mother into the kitchen, came back to find her in a total meltdown of nerves and anxiety.

"There's blood on the wall," she muttered.

"What? Where?"

"There." Ari pointed. "Can't you see it? The other police officer couldn't see it, either."

Christopher looked closely at the wall, then back at Arianna. His brows furrowed as confusion filled his eyes.

"Why can't you see it?" Her hysterical voice rebounded off the walls, summoning everyone in.

Chris embraced her. "Excuse us, Mother."

Mrs. Somers twisted her hands together and opened her mouth to speak.

"Mother, it's all right." Christopher tried to gently nudge Ari back to the living room.

His family took the hint and went the opposite direction.

Ari wanted to move, but her brain refused to do anything but recall events from months before.

Christopher picked her up and carried her back to the sofa. "I'm taking you home. Being here is not helping anything."

She blinked several times to clear her mind. What had happened? "Uh...no—I'm all right. There are just so many memories here, Chris. Please be patient with me as I process them." She clung to him like a life saver in the rapids. He was her rock. Without him, she was certain she'd be swept under by the river of memories.

"I'm not going anywhere." He held her close and massaged her back. "I love you, Ari. I know you can get through this. But if you no longer wish to try, I will take you home. No one will blame you." He cupped her face in his hands. "Tell me what you want to do."

"I want you to kiss me. Then never leave my side in this haunted house again."

He complied, his soft lips gentle at first, then growing more passionate, as if his kisses could somehow fix her.

Perhaps they could.

Caught up in his spicy-freshness and the heat of his lips, Ari nearly forgot where they were...and the family waiting for them. She kissed him once more, running her fingers through his dark hair. "I think it worked." She smiled. "I feel much better now, but I might need regular refills."

Christopher chuckled, his delicious dimples creasing his face. "Come on. You need food."

As they sat around the kitchen table, Ari began to relax. She'd gotten through the hard part. Still, conversation with people she hardly knew didn't come easy. Her entire relationship with Sarah had been built through journal entries. And Mrs. Somers...try as Ari might, she couldn't think of a single conversation they'd shared. Mr. Benjamin Somers had made certain his was the only voice ever heard in this house. And although Joshua had reminded her of Seth, her deceased brother, the more he spoke tonight, the more she realized he'd come from a far different place and time than her brother.

The awkwardness ebbed as the evening progressed, and welcoming warmth emanating from each member of the Somers family acted as a salve to Ari's emotional bruises. Besides Christopher, they were the only people who knew what she'd lived through. Not the story she'd fed the police and general public. The true story from the beginning—that Christopher and his family had been transported to Colorado from nineteenth century England by his evil, egomaniac of a father, via an incredible time-traveling machine he'd invented. He had brutally attacked Arianna when she'd learned of his felonious ways and his nineteenth century crimes. She hadn't even told her best friend Maggie about being transported fifty years back in time to New York City, where Mr. Somers had tried to kill her. She wanted to tell her. Maybe someday. Likewise, Ari was the only other person Christopher and his family could speak with openly. *It must be claustrophobic, living out here with nobody nearby and no one to share the truth with,* she thought.

"What was it like riding on the time machine?" asked Josh. His seventeen-year-old immaturity showed in his bright, innocent eyes.

"Joshua," both Christopher and Mrs. Somers said in unison.

Josh's face turned red. "Sorry. I have only been on that huge original machine. I was just curious."

"It's okay, Josh," said Arianna. "Honestly, I don't recall. I was unconscious most of the time. Thankfully, I'll never have to know. I asked Christopher to destroy the devices so no one else gets hurt."

Guilty glances passed between Josh and Mrs. Somers.

Ari turned to face Christopher. "You did destroy them, didn't you?"

He opened his mouth to speak—

"Dessert, anyone?" Sarah placed a tray containing bowls of dark pudding on the table. Everyone's attention shifted to the food. Everyone but Ari's. Beneath the table she reached for Christopher's hand. He squeezed her fingers, but something didn't feel right—so cold, so clammy.

Chapter Two

Transcending time had never been on Christopher's to-do list. Until now.

After Arianna's reaction to his family's home—and, well, everything about it—he knew his time to return the stolen goods was limited. He felt guilty for not destroying the machine, as Ari had begged him. Yet he knew full well he wasn't capable of doing so until he'd tried his best to right his father's wrongs.

He turned the dial on the time-traveling device backward twenty-five notches. Still a novice, he hoped he'd set it correctly and would soon find himself in the 1990s—not the 1700s. Now that Mother, Josh and Sarah were spreading their wings and embracing—or enduring, in Sarah's case—the twenty-first century, Christopher could use his time to rid the house of objects which reminded him of his criminal father, who had disappeared to who knows where—hopefully too far to ever make his way home. Perhaps one day, even the house—the mansion on the hill, purchased with ill-gotten means—could be sold, or donated. He wished to wash his hands completely of the evil genius' misdeeds.

After filling the vials with chemical solution, he pushed the button that triggered the device's mechanism. Vibrations shook the room around him, but he remained still. How his father had invented such a contraption was beyond Christopher's imagination.

Why he'd invented it—well, that had become painfully obvious. The perfect crime was an unsolvable crime. And all his father's crimes were unsolvable. No physical evidence could be linked to Benjamin Somers—a man who'd been born centuries before or after each transgression had occurred. Even an eye-witness couldn't finger a felon who'd disappeared into thin air.

It didn't take long to arrive in Boston twenty-five years in the past. His landing locale, the restroom in the Isabella Stewart Gardner Museum, made this delivery relatively simple. He popped his head out the door to confirm he was in the right place. He was.

Although it was past midnight, many displays were still lit, no doubt for security reasons. Father had been brazen to rob from a museum in the 1990s. After all, electricity was nothing new, and alarm systems were far more advanced than in his usual haunts. *Father must have really loved these paintings.*

He glanced at the disc-shaped device at his feet. For all of his father's criminal activity, Christopher still stood amazed at his genius. He'd created something that resembled a large plate that could travel through time—Christopher shook his head—incredible. The sleek disc measured approximately five feet in diameter. Christopher began extracting art from the padded bin. Minus the space taken by the art container and the control tower rising up near the center, the machine could hold three or four people—standing, of course.

His mind flickered back to his initial transport—the first one he was conscious for, that is. When vibrations had begun shaking the room, he was certain he'd tumble off of something so flat and land somewhere in oblivion—another dimension, perhaps. But quite the opposite had happened; he'd felt a magnetic pull from the device. And while the world had quaked around him, he'd remained standing eerily still.

Then there was the vest. Ahh. Christopher let out a longing sigh. He wished he still had it. Unfortunately, his father had escaped while wearing it. Gazing at the paintings, he realized all his efforts were likely in vain—with the vest in his possession, its inventor—Benjamin Somers himself—could very well be committing a heist at that moment. His shoulders slumped at the thought. He shook the idea away. *I cannot control Father, but I have the power to right some of his wrongs.* The notion propelled his actions forward.

He continued extracting the pieces of art from the compartment. He'd just leave them to be discovered in the restroom. No sense tempting fate by spending any unnecessary time in the museum. Ideally, upon his departure, the loud vibrations caused by the machine would call a guard's attention to the lavatory, where he'd discover the paintings. The guard would be dubbed a hero.

Arianna had begged Christopher to destroy the time-traveling devices. "Nothing good will ever come from using them," she'd said. And he'd agreed. However, spending time in the mansion while helping his family learn about the twenty-first century had changed his mind. Each time he passed Father's abandoned bookroom, he was reminded of the art, jewels, money, and rare coins hidden in a safe, masked by a purloined painting. How many times a day had he peered into the study? Countless. He'd get as many valuables returned as possible—it was only right. Arianna didn't need to know about it. His head said no, but his heart pinched at the thought of keeping even one more secret from her. After all, secrets had nearly destroyed their relationship in the past. He'd do anything to preserve it now. He glanced at the traveling device—*nearly anything.*

The lavatory door burst open as Christopher tugged the third and final painting from the bin.

He froze.

"Put your hands up where I can see them." The night guard brandished his revolver.

Christopher couldn't put his hands up when they were gripping rare art. "I don't wish to damage the painting, sir. I'll just put it down first."

"A conscientious thief?" The man rolled his eyes. "Don't move a muscle. How'd you dismantle the art, anyway? We've upped security ten-fold since the heist in '90."

"Oh"—he forced a laugh—"you thought I was a thief?" Christopher's heart hammered, but he needed to play it cool and not upset the man with the gun. He shook his head as he looked squarely into the guard's eyes and let out a scoffing noise. "No. I'm no criminal. I found these paintings and just wished to return them." *I found these paintings?* He obviously wasn't a good liar, either.

The guard narrowed his eyes. Keeping the gun trained on Christopher, he glanced down at the art. Unfortunately, Christopher had wrapped the pieces in padding and brown paper, so the man couldn't see that they actually were the very same paintings which had vanished from the museum a few years before. "You took the time to wrap the art you stole?"

Christopher, taking advantage of the guard's distracted attention, shoved the painting into the man's astonished face, hoping he'd grab it and not let the precious art fall to the ground. It worked. The guard nearly dropped his revolver as he caught the heavy painting—and his balance. Christopher pushed the button on the traveling device as he mounted the machine. In a matter of moments he transported away from the museum. Away from the 1990s. Back to his new life in the twenty-first century.

Chapter Three

Time stood still—for once.

No Somers family to make awkward conversation with, no mansion to spook her. Tonight, it was just Christopher and her, and that suited Arianna just fine. Three months had passed since her visit to the Victorian house on the hill, and she wouldn't mind if she never saw it again. Ironic, after all the work she'd put into making it elegant and beautiful.

Colorado Springs had become a solution for now. Meeting in the middle allowed Christopher time he needed with his family and time with Ari.

She stared across an intimately small dining table into his azure eyes—such an intense shade of blue. Echoes from the nearby kitchen, as well as neighboring diners, sounded faintly in the background, but his eyes held her captive. What she would give to know his thoughts when he gazed at her so tenderly.

"What are you thinking right now?" His voice, low and husky, shook her from her trance.

She smiled. "In fact, I was wondering what you were thinking. Sometimes when you look at me like that"—she shrugged, unable to find the best words to describe how this handsome man filled her with joy—"I like it. You make me feel special."

Christopher lifted her hand and kissed her fingers. Chills ran the length of her body.

"Here is your dessert. Enjoy." A waiter placed a ramekin filled with golden crème brûlée between them.

Ari's eyes widened. "Yum. My favorite." The delicious aroma of caramelized sugar wafted through the air.

Christopher took the spoon and scooped out some of the creamy custard. "Open your mouth," he motioned to Ari.

The decadent dessert melted on her tongue. Could life get any sweeter? She had Christopher *and* crème brûlée.

"This arrangement has worked out better than anticipated. Wouldn't you agree?" He gave her another bite, then took one himself.

"Absolutely. Meeting twice a week in the middle, here in Colorado Springs has been the perfect solution to our long-distance relationship. Now you can spend your weekdays aiding your family and your weekends at the precinct." Ari only wondered how long this arrangement would continue before the next step. With each passing week, she felt more prepared to make their relationship permanent. *Christopher is the one.* She'd forgiven his past secrets and loved him even more because of his dedication to his siblings and mother. And the fact that he'd been born and bred to be a nineteenth century gentleman—as strange as it sounded—was the icing on the cake. He shared her self-respect and high standards.

Though she loathed time travel because of the lives it had stolen from her, she had to admit that despite beginning as a deal-breaking secret between them, it had solidified their relationship in the end. That Ari had found Christopher despite the miles and centuries which had separated them was nothing short of a miracle. She would do anything to preserve and nurture such a rare and precious relationship.

"We talked about catching a movie on Thursday. Have you picked one you'd like to see?" Christopher pulled her from her musings.

"I think it's your turn to choose," said Ari. Their relationship, which had begun as anything but conventional—because of his secret identity—was continuing as such: A nice dinner out on Mondays, then Thursdays were Ari's favorite—they called it their "try-something-new night." Colorado Springs was a fun city and new to both of them—beautiful, with tall trees and mountains, yet smaller than Denver and larger than Pueblo. Thursday evenings had become their time to explore.

He leaned forward and kissed her, causing a tingling sensation to ripple through her.

"What was that for?" she asked.

He smiled, his dimples creasing his cheeks. "I couldn't help myself. You're so beautiful." He ran feather-light fingers along her jaw. "It's hard to believe your face was ever bruised and scarred so badly. It's now flawless."

"And since my cast was removed—which I'd begun doubting would ever happen—the nightmare we lived through last summer is just a bad memory." Except for the real nightmares she still experienced. But he didn't need to know about those.

Christopher's smile faltered.

Mentally chiding herself, she realized she shouldn't have brought up her leg. She knew he blamed himself for his father whisking her off to New York—fifty years in the past—where she shattered her leg, but was spared a broken neck, thanks to Christopher. "It's not your fault. And my leg doesn't hurt anymore. So, quit blaming yourself and kiss me again." She closed her fingers around his hand and tilted her head as he complied. "I'll never get tired of your kisses."

"That makes us perfectly compatible, because I'll never tire of providing them." He kissed her once more.

Laughing, he managed to pull away enough to grab her spoon and dig into the dessert.

When the waiter returned and cleared the empty dishes away, Christopher checked his phone. "It's getting late, and you must rise early for work."

She hated that speech. He always gave it at the end of their dates. She knew it was given out of concern for her, but how she wished to be married so the evening wouldn't end after the goodnight kiss. They'd been dating this way for weeks now—ever since her cast had been removed and she could drive safely. She understood the reason why their relationship must move at a snail's pace—Christopher's family still needed him to teach them about the modern era in which they'd been unwillingly thrust. His father had made certain they'd remained in the dark; kept them prisoners in their own home for over four years so they'd be completely at his mercy—as if he possessed any. Having witnessed Mr. Somers' abuse first hand, Ari waited willingly for them to become independent enough to not just survive, but thrive. For now, she'd be happy for any time she had with Chris.

Hand in hand they walked to the parking lot. The cold February air driving them closer together.

"Look at your tire, Ari." Christopher motioned to

her little red Subaru, tilting lopsided in the parking space.

"Oh no." She hurried to the trunk to retrieve the spare. Clapping a hand over her mouth, she groaned. "I never replaced the tire after my flat last year." She dug through her purse. "I've got a card in my wallet; a number to call for roadside assistance. You go on home and I'll just wait for help."

Christopher narrowed his eyes and lowered his brows. "I'm not leaving you here to wait alone. Let's go back into the restaur—"

The lights inside the restaurant flickered off before he finished his sentence.

"I guess we'll wait in your car."

"You don't have to stay with me, Chris. I'll be fine." Having faced similar situations on her own for several years now, she was unsure at times how to react to his chivalry. Of course she'd love his company, but he also had to rise early in the morning.

He leaned down and kissed her. "Humor me. Let me at least think you need me."

Ari shook her head and smiled. "You can take the man out of the nineteenth century, but you can't take the nineteenth century out of the man." She placed the call to request assistance, then they both slid into her car. Turning on the ignition, she flipped the heater to high so they wouldn't freeze while they waited.

Minutes later her phone rang.

"That must be the roadside service wondering where I'm parked." She answered. "An hour? I see. Okay. Thank you." She let out a groan.

"What did they say?" asked Christopher.

"There's been a big accident on the interstate. It

will be at least an hour before someone gets here. You should go. It's going to be late."

He reclined his seat. "I'm not going anywhere. But you should grab a nap. Sounds like a long night."

Unlike her encounter at the Somers' mansion, where she didn't want him to leave her side, she wasn't nearly as frightened waiting alone in a deserted parking lot. But having him beside her made it so much more pleasant. "Thanks, Chris." She reclined her seat, too, but didn't dare close her eyes and chance having a nightmare. They occurred nearly every time she slept. She'd not risk Christopher finding out and blaming himself for yet another thing he would feel responsible for.

Her eyelids drooped. She forced them open. Turning her head, she noticed Christopher staring at her.

"Why are you fighting sleep?" he asked. "You have work in the morning. I'll wake you when they arrive." He leaned over and kissed her.

"Maybe I was waiting for that." She gave him a sleepy smile.

He kissed her again.

"Yeah, I definitely needed that." Her heart thudded. Adrenaline would help her stay awake. *Keep the kisses coming,* she thought.

"It's probably good you have bucket seats." He kissed her one last time, leaving her lips tingling and wanting more.

She sat back and closed her eyes, relishing in the sweetness of his kisses. With his hand on her shoulder she'd just rest for a minute.

Chapter Four

The monster's thick fingers were wrapped around Ari's neck. She couldn't breathe. He'd as much as admitted to being the drunk driver responsible for killing her family. Now Mr. Somers would finish the job by squeezing the life out of her. She tried to jerk out of his grip.

"Arianna." Christopher was shaking her. "Wake up. You're having a nightmare."

"I'm awake." She sat up and hurried to wipe moisture from her face.

"What were you dreaming about?" Christopher peered down at her, his concern-filled face blurry from the tears still hovering in her eyes.

She shook her head. "It—it was nothing. Sorry to startle you."

"That was *not* nothing, love." He pulled out a handkerchief and dabbed at her face. "You were thrashing around as if caught by a demon."

He got that right. Mr. Somers was the devil himself. "Please, Chris, don't worry about it."

"Has this happened before? Was that why you resisted a nap?"

Ari said nothing.

"It's my father, isn't it? He tortures you in your sleep." He punched the dashboard.

"The doctor said the nightmares will go away with

time." She shrugged. "I just wish it would be time already."

"I can't help but wonder if seeing me is making it worse."

"No! You are everything right in my life. Please, Christopher, don't blame yourself for this. You carry enough guilt. Don't take on more." She could tell her words weren't getting through. He was adding her lack of sleep to his failings—which were not failings at all. Her heart constricted. Life without Christopher would be unbearable.

"Perhaps I should give you space—you know, take a little break. After all, I didn't allow you time to…process"—he ran his fingers through his hair—"all that had happened to you before we began seeing each other in earnest."

Before she could talk him out of his ridiculous notion, someone tapped on the window. "Did you call for roadside assistance?"

****

On the following Monday morning, Ari's phone chirped, signaling a text. Working onsite in a newly built model home, she spotted her bag and fished out her phone, grateful this particular job was in town, where she had reception, unlike the last.

Christopher's handsome face lit up the screen. *Late start today. Would you mind terribly if we canceled tonight?*

She wondered where he'd texted her from. Couldn't be his mother's home—no service there. He must still be at his apartment in Pueblo.

"Of course I mind," she mumbled, although, she had to admit putting in a few extra hours in on this project wouldn't hurt. And perhaps she could catch a late dinner with Maggie. She wrote back: *I'll miss you but do what you need to do.*

Thank you for understanding. I will miss you, too. Call you later. Much love, Christopher.

She let out a breath of resignation. It had been a long weekend without him, and now she'd have to wait three more endless days. Torture. She shook her head, attempting to keep her emotions in check. "What am I, fourteen? I can certainly live a few days without Christopher." Grabbing her measuring tape, she headed into the bedroom—back to work. Back to her life as an interior decorator.

On Thursday she worked at her office, ordering mid-century style furniture for an upcoming project. Christopher usually called or texted before heading to the Somers' house to confirm evening plans. Today, he'd done neither. She didn't know where to meet him. Perhaps he'd call en route to the Springs. The unsettling feeling that he might be easing his way out of her life— for her own good, in his mind—hung over her like a shroud. But she pushed the nagging thought away, refusing to acknowledge it.

The dinner hour came and went. No word from Christopher. Ari called him and got his voicemail. She left a message: *Where are you?* This wasn't like him. Worry ate at her like and ulcer.

Chapter Five

Christopher exited his father's lab—referred to as the "dungeon" by his family—in a rush. Time had gotten away from him and he had no way to contact Arianna. He couldn't tell her what had detained him, of course—she'd never understand.

"Christopher, is that you, dear?" his mother blocked his way to the door, her face etched with concern.

"Yes, Mother. But I'm late and must be going." He tugged car keys from his pocket.

"But you have been gone since yesterday. I've worried so."

Christopher paused in his forward motion, drew his mother into his arms and kissed her cheek. "I'll explain tomorrow." He looked earnestly into her crystal-blue eyes, understanding her anxiety. If for some reason he didn't return from one of his conscience-inflicted time-traveling missions, she and his siblings would certainly flounder in their challenging circumstances. "I'm sorry to worry you. Do you think I should not continue returning the goods Father stole?" He knew he'd inherited his mother's sense of right and wrong—she'd taught him integrity and self-respect. If she thought his actions misguided, perhaps they were.

Stepping back, Mother dropped her head and wrung her hands. Finally, she squared her shoulders and raised her eyes to meet his gaze. "Son, I support your efforts to right your father's wrongs. I only wonder if the risk is too great. And, while I understand your need to meet Arianna so often, I do not think you can keep up this pace. You rarely sleep."

Her tone, astonishingly strong, reminded him of her fortitude—the mother of his youth. Father had quashed her self-confidence over the years, but bit by bit it was creeping back. For that he was grateful.

"Thank you for your honesty, Mother. I will take some time to consider safer methods of returning the purloined goods. You know, however, I have tried a few alternative approaches already and failed." He lifted his hands, then dropped them in a gesture of defeat. "I'm sorry to have caused you such anxiety."

Some of the worry lines smoothed from her face.

"As far as Arianna goes…I love her. I wish to be with her every moment of every day, but I cannot. Not yet." With all his heart he longed to be finished with the whole time-traveling burden. "Unless I think of a better solution, I'll continue meeting her in Colorado Springs. Twice a week is hardly often enough." He frowned. He knew he sounded like a love-sick pup, but Ari was a beacon of light in his once dark and dreary life. She made living in the twenty-first century—something he'd initially loathed—wonderful.

"But it's la—"

He cut her off with another peck on the cheek as he made his way out the door.

As soon as he entered cell phone service range, he called Arianna. She answered on the first ring.

"Christopher, are you all right?"

"Yes. I—I just got detained. I'm on my way."

27

"Do you realize what time it is? It's too late for a movie, or even dinner."

He glanced at his watch. Nearly nine o'clock. He pushed out a frustrated breath. "I'm so sorry. I had no idea it was so late. Are you certain you don't wish to meet for a late supper?"

"I ate an hour ago. You didn't call me this morning. Where have you been?"

Think, think, think—I've been in Paris, France, one hundred and fifty-one years in the past. Only my calculations were incorrect, and I should have gone only one hundred and forty-nine years. He couldn't tell her the truth. What a mess he'd made of it. He'd shown up at the Louvre, only to discover that the paintings he'd come to return had vanished from the time-traveling device's storage bin and were instead hanging from their pegs at the museum—as if they'd never been stolen. He was then jolted with the realization that his father hadn't been there yet—he'd added a year backward instead of forward. From now on, he'd slow down and think through his calculations instead of rushing from one heist to the next so carelessly. As it was, he'd had to return to the present, reset and reload the machine and start over.

"Christopher, are you there?"

"Uh…yes. Sorry. I was taking care of some family matters this evening. Time got away from me is all." It wasn't really a lie. His father was still family, like it or not. And the reason he'd been time-traveling was a direct result of Father's criminal deeds.

"Family." She let the word hang for a moment. "Let's just meet for dinner on Monday." Her voice sounded   tired,   disappointed   and   maybe   a little…frustrated.

His heart twisted, never wishing to fail her. He didn't blame her, though. She'd been more than patient with his family's demands on his time—their absolute need for him to teach them how to exist in the twenty-first century. They'd done well, but to accomplish all he'd set forth to do required a couple more weeks…at least.

He wrapped the conversation up as quickly as possible, not wanting to answer further questions. "I'll see you Monday, then?"

Things went better on Monday—marginally. He called Ari in the morning to set up a meeting place for dinner, but he still grossly underestimated the time it would take to deliver rare coins eighty years in the past to Maryland. The problem came as a result of the establishment his father had robbed. It wasn't an establishment at all—it was a single collector. Christopher had no way to enter and exit the man's showroom discreetly. He waited until evening fell in Baltimore, which was two hours earlier than in Colorado. Then he was able to break in and replace the coins, get out and race home, and then to Colorado Springs—thirty minutes late.

To his relief, Ari quickly forgave his tardiness and sat patiently waiting at the restaurant. Mother was right, he couldn't keep up this pace. Something had to change. Plus, it really wasn't fair to Arianna.

"You look so tired." Ari frowned, gazing across the booth where he slumped in his seat. "Why are you so much busier now than when you first began helping your family? It seems backwards." She looked at him more intently.

Christopher pushed food around his plate. He'd eaten one supper already while waiting for night to fall in Baltimore. Of course, he couldn't mention that to Ari. Unsure how to answer her question, he pondered for a moment. In past months so many secrets between them had almost permanently damaged their relationship. He should just tell her the truth. Then again, her reaction to his time traveling could also break their bond.

Ari cleared her throat. "What's going on, Chris? Is there something you're not telling me?"

"I just need more time." The words came out in a loud jumble—not at all the soft answer he'd formulated in his mind. He mentally pummeled himself for his lack of tact.

Ari recoiled, looking as if she'd been slapped. "Time for what, exactly?"

"I'm sorry, Arianna. I didn't mean to snap at you." He ran his fingers through his hair, then rubbed his eyes. "You're right. I'm exhausted." He let out a tired breath. "I'm afraid things are going to be"—he shrugged—"crazy, as you would call it, for a while." He paused, debating his next words. "If we could take a break—"

"A break?" Ari's face crumpled.

His weary mind and body yearned to cheer her, but everything he said seemed to make things worse. "Just a short one. Two or three weeks? I think life will settle down and then we can move forward." Would she even want to move forward after that little speech—or after she found out about his trips to the past? "I—I think I've bitten off more than I can chew." He fumbled with his napkin. "It might be a good thing—the break, that is. We can see if your nightmares go away when I'm not around for a while."

Her face clouded and moisture gathered in her eyes.

A dull ache grew in his chest. He couldn't tell if she looked more hurt or angry. He'd sworn to himself after their last big fight—when she'd discovered the truth of his nineteenth century origins—that he'd never hurt her again, and here he sat, bruising her heart once more.

"Fine, Christopher. Take whatever time you need." She stood. "It's late. I've got to go."

A lump clogged his throat as he watched her throw money on the table and walk away at a brisk pace. He sprang from his seat to stop her from leaving. She couldn't walk out on such a sour note.

But she turned to face him, shaking her head. Her message was clear. "Don't even think about following me."

His shoulders sagged, wondering if she'd ever speak to him again, let alone share a future with him. Tired and frustrated, he tamped down his anger at himself for hurting the woman he loved and headed for home.

The road back to his apartment in Pueblo seemed endless. So many thoughts badgering him nearly had him making a U-turn and driving back to Ari. If he turned on his lights and siren, he could probably beat her to her apartment in Denver. The thought danced in his heart; would it put her smile back where it belonged or only be a temporary fix? He wanted to give up this whole idea of restoring stolen goods to their rightful owners right now. Tonight.

A large critter ran into the road—a dog maybe? He couldn't be sure. Christopher swerved just in time. *Whew. Close one.* His heart thudded at the near miss. Pulling over, not because of the animal scare, but because he needed to think carefully about his next move, he parked on the shoulder and deliberated his choices. One option would take him back to Arianna in Denver. The other would send him home. He idled on the side of the highway, mulling over the possibilities.

Arianna was his top priority. That fact was never in dispute. Sharing a future with her meant everything to him. He hadn't been completely honest about his family, using them as an excuse for his sloppy behavior. Such deceit went against every fiber of his being. In reality, Mother, Josh and Sarah still needed occasional help dealing with present day problems, but they'd come a long way and now only required minor guidance from him.

Washing his hands of Father's crimes. Another priority. He wasn't certain he could be his best self for Arianna with guilt from the ill-gotten goods dangling over his head, especially when he could do something about it. But could he do both—return the goods and give Arianna the time and attention she deserved? That was the question that needed answering. He wished he could honestly say he'd perfected time travel and could easily pull off the last half-dozen or so returns without complications. But if he'd learned anything over the past few weeks, it was that time travel never happened without unwanted surprises.

The question niggling in the back of his mind suddenly pushed itself into the forefront. Would Arianna forgive him for his trips to the past? The possibility that she wouldn't caused his heart to spasm. Had he jumped in without thinking about the consequences—again?

It might be too late. He'd made several trips to date for which he'd have to confess. The road before him seemed painfully obvious. Already having risked his future with her, he should finish what he'd started and pray—once he was completely done—for her forgiveness, then hopefully make her his wife. Why did he feel so uneasy? *Because such a grand outcome is easier imagined than accomplished.*

He swallowed down his insecurities about his tenuous future and drove back onto the highway headed for Pueblo, not Denver. Soon he'd pull into the parking lot of his lonely apartment and go to bed. Alone. With no assurance things would ever change.

Chapter Six

Ari pushed her apartment door shut harder than necessary. She hadn't been so angry with Christopher since she'd pieced together the secret of his nineteenth century origins—and worse, discovered that the evil Benjamin Somers was his father. His family had now had seven or eight months to adjust. What in the world was taking so long?

All the familiar emotions of hurt and betrayal flooded to the forefront of her mind. *But Chris had good reasons for what he'd done then. His father had banned him from his mother and siblings, who were in trouble. I'd been his path back into their lives.*

She flopped onto her bed without changing her clothes. Conflicting thoughts ping-ponged through her mind. There had to be more to the story. He kept something from her, she felt it in her bones. But after their history, would he really do that? *If he thinks he's helping me, he would.* She should have never told him about the nightmares. Or…it could simply be what he'd claimed—demands from his needy family.

Her nightmares were particularly bad that night. She'd hardly slept. What that meant, she didn't know. Perhaps the nightmares were related to her mounting stress levels. Taking a break from the one person she could talk to about everything wouldn't help. Would Christopher reconsider the pause in their relationship if he knew that?

She scanned her apartment for her phone. Nowhere to be found. Then she remembered the frantic state she'd been in last night. It must be in the car.

Retrieving it, she noticed she'd missed a call and several texts. All from Christopher.

She listened to his voicemail:

Ari, please forgive me for how badly I behaved at dinner tonight. It was inexcusable. Trust me when I tell you that taking a break is as difficult for me as it is for you. It is not permanent. We will be back together very soon...if you'll have me. I love you.

Hearing the pleading sincerity in his voice nearly broke her heart. She immediately called him, prepared to bite back any residual anger from the night before. She should have trusted him last year—she would trust him now.

"This is Christopher." His voice faded in and out.

"Christopher, I got your message. Sorry I didn't return your call last night—left my phone in the car."

"It's okay. I just wanted you to know how much I regretted the tone of our conversation. I apologize for sounding harsh."

So...he wasn't taking back the words he'd said, but the delivery. Ari gritted her teeth, not wanting the argument to flare up again.

"Are you still there? I fear I might lose you as I am nearing the mansion."

Was he speaking metaphorically, or literally? "I'm here and you're forgiven. I just hope the break you asked for isn't for too long. And...if you're doing this because of my nightmares, I really think not seeing you will make them worse."

No response.

"Christopher?" The line was dead. *Did he hear any of that?* She quickly dialed him back but only got his voicemail. She left a message: *It's all right, Christopher. I just hope your family adapts to their circumstances quickly and that the stress you seem to be under eases soon. Love you.*

She plodded through the next week like a turtle crawling uphill through maple syrup. If she'd learned anything from her relationship with Christopher, it was patience. His family came from two centuries ago—even before Dickens wrote serial novels and Queen Victoria ruled over one-fourth of the world. It could take years for them to completely adjust. Add to that adapting to the loss of a husband and father. Although Benjamin Somers was a tyrant, he did his part—though, using illegal and immoral methods—as the family's provider. The roles for women two hundred years ago—especially females born into an aristocratic environment—vastly differed from today. She couldn't imagine what changes Mrs. Somers was experiencing. Ari was being selfish and demanding to expect so much of Christopher's time. *I'll suck it up and wait. Christopher is worth it.*

Another week passed and another. She tried calling several times, but only his voicemail picked up. That night—or early morning, rather, three A.M.—he'd left a voicemail expressing his disappointment of missing her calls. She wondered why he was up so late. Perhaps his shift at the precinct had changed. That would explain a lot.

Another week passed.

Sorry I've not been in touch. Thinking of you often.

Yours, Chris.

The texts he sent her were always short and left little room for conversation. He must spend most of his time where there is no service. She wondered if something were seriously wrong with his mother or siblings. Perhaps an illness…

She rushed to engage with him. It was early; hopefully he could talk before heading to the mansion today. *Christopher, I've missed you. How are things going over there?* She pushed the send button and prayed he'd answer.

One heartbeat, two heartbeats, three—

Things are going much slower than I had earlier anticipated. Please forgive my absence.

Though it wasn't the response she'd hoped for, Ari smiled, happy to get one at all.

Any idea how much longer it will take? She hesitated. Too needy? Perhaps, but the emptiness without him threatened to consume her. She pushed send.

She watched her phone as if her life depended on his response. Finally, her phone buzzed: *Message failed.* Ari pushed out a breath of disappointment. Those were the words she'd grown accustomed to and learned to hate.

Her faith in Christopher and their wonderful— nearly perfect—relationship began to waver. And the nagging and all too familiar debate reared its ugly head again. Had he ever loved her? Maybe not, or he possibly loved her too much and felt that his presence in her life was causing her nightmares. The notion shot pain through her chest, piercing her heart. The loneliness nearly suffocated her. Now that she had experienced being in love with the man who seemed her perfect match, she didn't want to live without him.

Chapter Seven

Christopher agonized over his lack of all things Arianna. He'd worked day and night returning stolen goods so he could move forward with his hopes to propose to her. And in addition to time traveling, he coached his family on twenty-first century living and social norms or worked at the precinct. He couldn't remember the last time he'd slept a full night. His intentions had been to call Ari each day on his way to the mansion, but traveling to and from such a variety of time zones messed with his plan.

Another problem presented itself—the rare times he had connected with her—his inability to give her straight answers had made their conversations awkward, as he didn't want to lie but couldn't tell the truth. He'd settled on short texts whenever he had a minute—which wasn't often enough.

Today he would call her on his way to the station and pray he could manage a decent conversation—he longed to hear her voice. He only hoped it wasn't too early on a Saturday morning.

"Hello." Ari's voice sounded sleepy.

He'd probably awakened her. A mental debate ensued. Apologize and hang up, or have a conversation? Lately, he'd been sleeping at the mansion and going straight to work from there, which allowed for no texts or phone calls. It had been too long. He needed her—at least a few minutes of her time.

"Hi, love. It's been a while…are you still speaking to me?"

"Christopher. It's so good to finally hear your voice."

She couldn't know how hearing *her* voice blanketed his soul with warmth. "Sorry if I woke you. I just really needed—"

His police radio blared. He had to answer it. At the same time, his phone beeped, signaling another call. "Hold on just a second." He answered the phone first.

"Officer Flemming." It was his sergeant. "There was a mass shooting in Colorado Springs at 0400 this morning. Five officers down and two in critical condition. They need help. I told them I'd send you over, pronto."

"I'm on my way." He turned his cruiser around and headed in the direction of the Springs. Memories of his dates there with Ari flooded through his brain, reminding him she still waited on the other line.

"Ari, are you still there?"

"Yes. What's going on?"

"A mass shooting in the Springs. The radio is going nuts. Can you hear me?" The radio relentlessly barked out commands. He needed to respond and answer questions that the Colorado Springs dispatcher was asking him. His heart twisted into a knot. The conversation with Ari was once again doomed.

"I can barely hear you over all the police chatter. It sounds like you need to go."

He smothered a groan. "I'll call you back when I get a chance. Love you."

"Love you."

The crisis in Colorado Springs lasted longer than anticipated. A great deal of police work needed to be done, since two of the shooters had escaped capture.

His investigative work tracking the criminals took him through Denver the next Friday. He didn't have much time, but he'd make it for Ari. Stopping at a flower shop, he picked up a bouquet of roses—yellow, her favorite color. Perhaps he could surprise her at work.

Ari's little red Subaru wasn't in the parking lot of Johnson and Tate Design Firm. He ached to see her. He went into the cottage-style office anyway, in hopes he could be directed to her current job site.

"Arianna is out of the office until Tuesday. She took a long weekend," said the receptionist.

That wasn't like Ari at all. At least he didn't think it was.

He turned to leave.

"Christopher Flemming, is that you?" Tasha Tate, Ari's boss rounded the corner, nearly running into him.

"Ms. Tate." Christopher nodded. "It's nice to see you. I had hoped to surprise Ari."

"She'll be sorry she missed you. Maggie talked her into taking some vacation—girls' time out. They went to some ritzy resort in Scottsdale, Arizona. I guess Maggie needed a break from her toddler." She chuckled.

Deflated, Christopher left the roses on her desk. Wilted roses were better than nothing at all.

Chapter Eight

The summer months slipped away. Ari had dreamed of a winter wedding—Christmas themed. She didn't know why—maybe to offset the horrible events of that December four years before when her family was taken from her. With each passing day, she felt her dream withering. It would be too late to plan a winter wedding for this year. Perhaps next. *But if Christopher completely disappears from my life...* Tears burned her eyes. She refused to consider the possibility.

She sat cross-legged on the wilting, late September grass, contemplating her future. She let the autumn chill clear her head. Cemeteries were quiet—the perfect place to think, and Ari needed to deliberate her future. She'd thought she'd figured it out weeks ago, but no, things had changed. She pushed gold and red leaves away from the headstone and spoke to her mother.

"Look, Mom, I brought your favorite." She straightened the purple asters she'd arranged in a vase. Autumn blooms were hard to come by so late in the season in Colorado, but she'd managed to locate some in her mother's favorite color.

"There's something missing in my life, Mom. I thought I would feel better once your killer was found, but..." Her words trailed off. She knew exactly what was missing—Christopher. Months had passed since she'd left him sitting in a Colorado Springs restaurant.

Her heart thudded, remembering how warm, how wonderful and how absolutely happy he'd made her. Yet, after only a handful of texts, some wilted flowers, and a couple of phone calls over the past months, frustration ate at her. "I really thought he was the one," she whispered. He'd asked for a break, and she'd obliged, but without so much as a weak explanation concerning the pause in their relationship—only that it involved family—she worried something else kept him away. Had their relationship been one-sided? Her eyes burned.

A gentle breeze carried the scent of flowers from surrounding graves. Ari could swear she smelled her mother's perfume. She didn't hear a voice but knew exactly what Mom would tell her. "Be patient, Ari. Be patient."

"I know, and I'm trying. But it's been months, and I really miss him. I love him. I thought he loved me." She tugged one of the asters from the vase. "When I text him, he sounds happy to talk to me—that is, if I'm lucky enough to catch him, which is rare—yet he seems...I don't know...rushed, preoccupied. I think he's so busy with his family that he's basically forgotten me." She buried her head in her hands. The stem snapped, bringing her to her senses. "I need to move on and quit pining over a man too good to be true. He was probably just a dream, anyway." She looked at her cast-free leg. Perhaps it had all been a fantasy. Their evenings in Colorado Springs still warmed her heart, but had they been just another token of Christopher's overactive conscience—his need to make up for the secrets he'd kept months before? Without the cast as a reminder, she wondered if the memories would fade and she could eventually convince herself he had never existed at all.

"That's it. I won't cry over Christopher anymore." She wiped her eyes. "He isn't here. Unless he does something soon to change my mind, I'm moving on." Instead of a burden lifting from her heart, heaviness increased. She tried to ignore it, but the weight of her decision pinned her down like an anchor pressing on her chest.

"Do something…like tracking you down in a cemetery to apologize? And beg for your forgiveness?"

Ari turned abruptly at the sound of the deep British voice behind her, and the heaviness lifted. "Christopher." Rising to her feet, she tentatively moved toward him, unsure of where their relationship stood. He, however, wasted no time gathering her into an embrace. She drank in his spicy fragrance and the warmth of strong arms around her. She closed her eyes and let time melt away. "Is it really you?"

"I'm sorry it's taken me so long to get here," he said quietly.

Grateful tears burned her eyes. She kept her head buried close to his heart but couldn't stop her shuddering body. She didn't care. Christopher was here.

He held her back and looked into her eyes. The sun dipped behind him, setting his outline aglow. "Hey." He wiped her tears with his thumbs. "I'm sor—"

"It's okay. I'm just happy." She smiled, taking in his features as if she were looking at him for the first time. His azure eyes had never looked so intensely blue. She raised her hand and fingered his rich, brown hair. So soft. Closing her eyes, she breathed him in again, electric currents traveling through her body. She had ached for him—ached for his touch. Physically ached. But…she let her arms fall and stepped back. "Why *has* it taken you so long? I've hardly heard from you since last spring." Her emotions ricocheted from elation to frustration.

He reached for her again.

She stiffened, and he dropped his arms.

"I'm so sorry. I've gone crazy without you, Ari. I never stopped loving you."

"Then where have you been?"

"My family has consumed most of my time."

Ari tilted her head and gave him a skeptical look.

"You're right, there's more. And I'll tell you everything, but for now, can I just hold you?" The plea in his eyes was all it took for Ari to fall back into his arms. They remained in a silent embrace for several moments.

She soaked him in, her heart pounding like a pack of wild horses set free.

He caressed her cheek, stopping at her chin. Tipping it up, he bent his head until their lips met. His kiss, gentle at first, deepened as passion sparked between them.

Shivers electrified her skin. Yes, she would forgive him.

His kiss almost made up for the time without him. Almost. Ari closed her eyes and let the world disappear. Everything she needed was in her arms. Love and contentment replaced the empty longing she'd felt only moments before as her anger faded.

She nuzzled her face to his chest. "How long are you here? I'll be happy with five minutes or five days— just to see you, touch you, is more than I had hoped for."

Christopher ran his fingers through her hair, sending a mass of tingles down her spine. "I'm here until tomorrow; then I must return to work. I was hoping I could claim your evening, and tomorrow morning, as well."

She looked up, meeting his gaze. The blue of his eyes intensified with the dramatic reds and orange hues of the sunset behind him. "Consider them yours." She rose on tiptoes and kissed him again.

A chilly gust of autumn wind drove her tighter into his arms. He held her close, massaging warmth into her. "You're freezing. Let's get you home." They left the cemetery, driving separately to Ari's apartment.

All the way home she flip-flopped between feelings of elation and feelings of confusion.

Entering behind her, Christopher scanned the room, a grin spreading across his face. "As I said before, your apartment is so 'Ari'." His eyes danced from frames to furnishings, canvases to cushions, pinstripes to poplin. "You have exquisite taste and talent."

She didn't know why his compliment meant so much to her. Perhaps because this was her home, decorated with her taste in décor—not a house she'd been commissioned to decorate.

Pulling up a list of restaurants on her phone, she ordered in Chinese food, not wanting to share him with anybody—not even the wait staff at a restaurant. They huddled together on the sofa to eat.

"Don't forget your cookie." Christopher cracked his open and removed the tiny white paper.

Arianna laughed. "You believe in fortune

cookies?"

He lowered his brows. "Oh, yes. I take them quite seriously. Listen." He cleared his throat and read, "Someone you care for deeply will come to your rescue."

"Ha." Ari shook her head. "You must have opened mine. And that fortune has already happened. You came to my rescue—more than once." She leaned over and kissed him on the cheek.

He turned and captured her lips with his, holding her close.

Warmth traveled from her head to her toes. She couldn't imagine being happier. Christopher was back.

"We have rescued each other in my ways, love. However, fortune cookies are rarely wrong. Read yours."

Was he serious about fortune cookies? Ari humored him by reading hers. "Things aren't always as they seem." She rolled her eyes and tossed it in an empty food carton. "Some fortune."

"One never knows about these things." Christopher folded his and tucked it into his pocket. Interesting.

They cleared the dinner mess and began chatting. She told him about the new project she'd been assigned since she'd seen him last—a remodel for a sweet, older woman. "Very safe," she assured him. "How is your family doing, now you've properly introduced them to the twenty-first century?" Surely, they'd had long enough to adjust by now. Or perhaps new problems had arisen, demanding his constant attention.

He grinned. "It's as if Joshua had been born in the wrong era. He loves to drive, and gadgets—he's already a pro on computers. At my place, that is. Still no

Internet at the mansion. Finally allowed outside the box Father kept him in, he'll not let anything get in his way." Light flickered in his eyes as he spoke of his brother. "He even got a job."

"He what? Where?"

"At an electronics store."

Ari smiled at his enthusiasm—so happy the sparkle had returned. "Josh reminds me of my little brother, Seth. My parents went to him with all their technology questions." A twinge of pain flashed through her. How she missed that kid. "What about Sarah?"

His smile faded. "Things aren't progressing as well there. I think the damage Father inflicted on her will be much harder to repair. She needs a friend—someone outside the family to boost her confidence."

She sighed. *Ah, it's Sarah's struggles that are requiring his attention.* "I thought the same thing when I read her journal. I'd hoped she'd moved past those feelings by now. It's been over a year. I've wanted to call her, but"—she shrugged—"no cell phone service."

"Even with service, I doubt she'd answer. Sarah is intimidated by modern technology. Growing up, we paid our neighbors a visit when we wanted to chat." He chuckled. "Now we not only have phones, but smart phones. It's scary for Sarah. Father kept all forms of communication out of my family's reach. I'll have a talk with her. I know she'd love to see you. You've been the closest thing she's had to a friend since we arrived in the twenty-first century."

"I'll plan to visit her soon, then. She needs friends—she needs to build a life. I wish we could find a way for her to attend school, become a volunteer, or even nanny for someone."

"Whoa, let's not get ahead of ourselves." He gave her a lop-sided smile, then lifted her hand and kissed her fingers. "Thank you for your concern. What about your nightmares?"

Ari shrugged, unsure how to answer. She didn't want to tell him how much worse they'd gotten right after he'd disappeared—that would only make him feel bad. Her therapist had been helpful, however, and she could honestly say they had decreased lately. "I'm all right, now that you are here."

Conversation paused. Christopher looked at Ari as if he were contemplating his next move. Finally, he spoke. "I have a confession to make, Ari." He dropped his gaze.

She stiffened and angled her face to see his. "Do I want to hear it?"

He raised his head. "It's nothing so unpleasant. And now it is in the past."

She swallowed and allowed her shoulders to relax. "Then what is it?"

Chapter Nine

Christopher inhaled, then let out a slow breath. He needed strength to go on. What he was about to confess could damage their relationship. Ari had made it clear she'd wanted nothing more to do with the time-travel that had brought him to modern-day Colorado. She especially wanted nothing to do with the device they had both traveled on—his father's wicked machine. It had nearly cost Ari her life, and he knew she was still recovering from her ordeal—if not physically, then mentally and emotionally. The fact that she wouldn't confirm or deny that she still suffered nightmares had him second guessing their relationship—for her sake. Was he selfish to keep seeing her? He'd convinced himself that he wasn't, then prayed he was right about the matter. He'd wrestled with how to tell her about his time-traveling escapades for weeks now, but he realized there would be no future for them at all if he didn't come clean.

"Christopher?"

He cleared his throat. "The reason I asked for a break was not only because of the time I've needed to devote to my family." He paused to take another breath.

Ari narrowed her eyes.

"I've been using my father's device to return the goods he stole from various galleries around the world." He fidgeted. "If you'd thought the cell phone service sketchy at my family's home, you should try it from a hundred years ago." He forced a chuckle to lighten the mood.

She didn't return his smile, and he watched as her face paled. "Christopher, that is so dangerous. You mentioned possibly returning the stolen items, but couldn't you have just mailed them to their respective galleries anonymously?"

"That had been my original plan, but I felt that I could not avoid having them traced back to me. I decided I'd best hand deliver them. As you can imagine, there is no easy way to do that—the best of explanations as to how I'd come to possess the art would likely get me thrown in jail." He swallowed, then continued. "Therefore, I had to travel back before all the fancy alarm systems were developed, yet after the pieces had been stolen, so I wouldn't get caught." There. He'd said it. Now he'd pray for a miracle because he couldn't imagine life without Ari. The past few months had been his loneliest since arriving in the twenty-first century. She was not only intelligent, kind and beautiful—with her long, blonde tresses and her sparkling blue-green eyes—but since their unfortunate adventure in New York City last fall, she'd shared in his time-traveling history and knew everything about him. He didn't want to live one more day without securing a future with her.

He couldn't tell if she appeared more frightened or angry at his confession.

Finally, she said, "So, because you are the exact opposite of your father, you've been jetting through time to right his wrongs." She shook her head. "Your infamous father, Benjamin Somers, strikes again."

"I'm not so noble as that, Ari." He observed her hands twisting together and drew them into his. "It's just"—he squeezed her fingers—"I couldn't be in that house with so many constant reminders of Father's crimes, especially when I had the power to do something about it. And you're correct about it being dangerous. That's why I didn't tell you what I was about. It took some getting used to, as there was definitely a learning curve. Now I think I've got it down to a science."

She shivered but didn't pull her hands away. "Learning curve? What happened?"

He was afraid she'd ask that question. He'd only tell her about one of the disasters. No need for too many details tonight. "I had a little mishap in Italy. Nothing I couldn't handle once I'd found a glue substitute. It taught me never to leave home without my toolkit."

He held his breath, hoping she'd let it go at that.

After an interminably long pause, she did. "I'm just grateful you returned unharmed." Her face scrunched in concentration. "I should remember, but can you tell me again why you couldn't make a trip to the past and return home the day before, as if you never went at all?" She tapped her head, as if trying to recall what she'd learned about the device.

"By his notes, it appeared Father was attempting to tighten the parameters on the machines, but he was unsuccessful. The small disc and the vest only travel in real time—there and back, as if you were traveling on an airplane—or they travel in yearly increments. There are no settings for days, weeks or months. I wish there were—it would have vastly expedited the process. It has taken me months to do what I thought I could accomplish in weeks."

She nodded. "Oh yeah. That's it." She looked directly at him. "Are you finished? Is everything returned?" Her eyes pleaded with him to say yes.

"With everything I can do. The art was fairly simple to trace, as missing Van Goghs and such are headline news. However, there is no way to determine where the gemstones originated—except for the diamonds that began Father's crime spree. I cannot return the untraceable jewels, and traveling back to the nineteenth century would be foolish."

Her shoulders relaxed a fraction. "Why is that? If you ran into someone you knew, would you be guilty by association?"

"Most likely. Because I disappeared with my father after the heist, the unassigned blame would land on me. Someone needs to be held accountable for the crimes. That's how it would be viewed by the *ton*—London society."

"What about returning them now—in the twenty-first century?"

He shook his head. "I Googled it. The old Emporium no longer exists." He hesitated for a moment. "I hope it wasn't the robbery that put them under." He paused, then cleared his throat. "I suppose it doesn't do to dwell on what might have happened."

"So, no more trips to the past?" Ari's lips lifted into a hesitant smile. "You've thought through every scenario and can confidently leave the unfinished business unfinished?"

"No more trips."

Closing her eyes, she released a breath. "Thank goodness." She wrapped her arms around him. "I know you were doing what you thought was right. I can't say I understand the risk you took to do it, and I'll admit to being hurt by it, but I cannot fault you for moral integrity. After all, it's so much of what I love about you."

Relief washed over him, relaxing his tense muscles. "Thank you for understanding." He tightened their embrace, letting his fingers wander through her golden tresses. "I love you." He lowered his head and kissed her tenderly. She smelled so good. Her tropical-scented shampoo filled his senses, warming him all over. He deepened the kiss, and what had begun as passionate, turned fiery. He trailed kisses down her neck.

She let out a sigh and he felt her fingers in his hair, heightening his desire for her.

He stopped, then let go of Ari and squeezed his eyes shut for a moment. *Ari is a lady, maybe not in the nineteenth century sense, but in every other way imaginable. She deserves better.* "Please forgive me."

She looked dazed. "Forgive you for what?"

"I realize morals have drastically changed in the past two hundred years. But I haven't. Allowing passion to control my actions"—he shook his head—"I vowed I'd never compromise you that way." He hoped she understood his meaning and had no doubts about his desire. He tilted her face to look into her eyes. They were gleaming with unshed tears. "Are you angry? Have I hurt your feelings?"

A soft smile curved her lips. "I've been waiting so long for a man just like you. Thank you, Christopher."

She gave him a sweet kiss and ran her fingers through his hair once more, fanning the flame and nearly causing him to reconsider

"I'm not going to lie; it won't be easy, but I feel the same way." She blew out a slow breath.

Relieved, he hugged her again. He didn't think he could love her more deeply than in that moment. The fact that two people from such vastly different times and backgrounds could be so in sync with each other amazed him.

Glancing at his watch, he groaned. "It's nearly two o'clock. I hope your friend Maggie didn't wait up."

Ari narrowed her eyes. "Maggie? Why would she wait up?"

"Oh, right." He let out a low chuckle. "When I arrived in Denver and found you absent, I called her, hoping she could direct me. I was right—she knew you visited the cemetery on Saturdays. She then offered me her guestroom for the night."

Ari sighed, then nodded.

"I'll be back first thing in the morning. After all, you promised it to me." He held her close once more, then kissed her goodnight.

Chapter Ten

Leaving Ari felt like leaving a piece of his heart. Thankfully, Christopher had taken a piece of hers with him to fill the empty spot.

Just a few, short hours later he woke to his alarm.

The risk he was about to take grew from an anthill to a mountain as he rose and made preparations for the day. After a shower, he pulled his nineteenth century clothing from a dry-cleaner's garment bag and smoothed it, happy to see it had remained relatively wrinkle-free and in good condition. "Now, if I can remember how to tie one of these." He held up a cravat.

It took longer than usual, but the years eventually melted away as his fingers slipped into their old routine, tugging the white cloth into a dashing knot. He appraised his reflection in the mirror. "I look ridiculous." He glanced at the jeans hanging on the nearby chair and almost gave in to the urge to change, but the clock on his nightstand forced his decision as it flickered, moving the numbers from 7:57 to 7:58. "I just hope she still finds my century romantic." He took a steadying breath and dialed Ari's number.

"Hello." She sounded sleepy. Christopher smiled at the vision of her clearing the cobwebs.

"I trust you are still willing to give me your morning?"

Arianna's laughter tickled his ear and warmed his

heart. "Of course. I never go back on my word. Are you coming here? I'll make you breakfast."

"Let me oversee the food. Can you meet me? I'll text you the address."

"Okay. Uh…I'll need about thirty minutes to get ready. Someone kept me up so late last night, I overslept this morning."

The warmth in her tone caused his heart to accelerate. He wanted to rush to her apartment and abandon his plan, but instead said, "Excellent. I'll send you directions, as our destination is a bit off the beaten path." He ended the call and gathered his belongings.

Not wanting to answer any questions Maggie might pose, he ignored her raised eyebrows and put a finger to his lips. "Not a word to Ari. Thank you for the use of your room."

"But—"

"I'm certain she'll call you later. I'm sorry to be rude, but I must be going. Thank you again for your hospitality." He gave Maggie a quick peck on the cheek and exited.

His drive took him through some rough areas of Denver—the very areas he'd called home when Father had banished him from the family's house over five years before. It seemed like a lifetime had passed since then. Just the sight of his surroundings elicited a range of emotions. He took a breath to tamp them down.

Slowing his vehicle to get a careful look, he scanned a seemingly deserted park, searching for familiar faces. One man standing near a massive oak tree watched him with hooded eyes and a suspicious glare. Christopher pulled to the curb. The man took a step backward. "Stewart, is that you?" Christopher hollered.

The man squinted his eyes against the morning sun. His leathery skin scrunched into a dozen lines. "Who's askin'?"

That voice belonged to Stewart, all right. Warmth flooded his heart at the sight of his first American friend. The man who'd taken him under his own tattered wing and given him the basic tools needed to survive in the twenty-first century. "It's Christopher— or Flemmin', as you prefer to call me."

Suspicion fell away from the man's face as he approached the car. "Is it really you, Flemmin'?"

"Yes. I don't have much time, but I've got something for you and the others." He tugged a bundle from beneath his seat.

The homeless man looked at him through narrowed eyes.

"You will never know how much you did for me when I had nowhere to go," Christopher said.

"That was s'long ago I nearly forgot aboutcha. I see yer still wearing them odd clothes."

Christopher chuckled. "Only for today." He handed Stewart the package. "See that Jeb, Bags and the others get a share."

The man's mouth dropped open as he peered into a pile of twenty-dollar bills. No amount of money would be enough for Christopher to express his gratitude to his homeless friends; they'd helped him so much when he'd been tossed out of his family's home and disowned by his father in such a foreign land and time. By showing him the ropes—teaching him skills such as living off the land, and how he could obtain a Social Security number in order to work—they'd likely saved his life. He was glad he could do at least a little something for them to show his thanks.

"I've got to go." Christopher didn't wait for a reply. He could see the mix of emotions spread across Stewart's weathered face. He drove away, making a few more turns, then slowed to a stop.

The scene before him was breathtaking, causing him to pause before proceeding with his plan. Living on the streets five years ago had introduced him to this peaceful place. When he'd needed to be completely alone, he'd wandered until he'd discovered a grove of aspen trees. It lay hidden just beyond streets and a park that were filled with vagrants; thus, it didn't attract tourists. He'd come to think of it as his personal refuge—a calm in the confusion that was once his life. He felt as though God had dropped it there just for him. Now he wished to share it with Arianna.

The yellow, sun-kissed leaves on the aspens fluttered in the cool breeze. Many had fallen to the ground, carpeting the dirt below. Christopher pushed nostalgia aside to make room for new memories.

The chilly autumn air smelled clean and woodsy. He grabbed a basket from the back seat, as well as a quilt from the trunk.

Dropping rose petals along the way, he made a path beside a creek that gurgled and flowed over twigs and pebbles. The trees parted, and he stepped into a small clearing. "It's just as I remember. Perfect." He spread the blanket atop the long, withering grass and unloaded the basket. The food didn't consist of much— bagels, cream cheese and grapes.

Just as he finished putting what remained of the roses in a cup, he heard a twig snap. His heart began thumping at a rapid pace. He blew out a breath and squelched the urge to grimace at what he imagined he must look like.

This is for Ari, he reminded himself.

Chapter Eleven

Arianna picked her way through the trees and scrub oak following the trail of rose petals. At first, she'd been nervous about entering the cluster of vegetation, especially after driving through the dregs of Denver to get there. But then it occurred to her that Christopher knew something she didn't about this part of town, and her anxiety morphed into excitement.

It's like being on a treasure hunt.

She rounded a bend, keeping her eyes on the crimson-colored pieces of velvet, until bright sunlight blinded her, and she realized she'd entered a clearing.

Standing rooted in her tracks as her eyes adjusted enough to see, she sucked in a breath. There Christopher stood, wearing nineteenth century clothing. Her jaw went slack. She'd never seen anyone so handsome. "Wow." A tingle shimmied down her spine.

He smiled, making him even more gorgeous as his dimples creased his handsome face. He held out a hand.

Ari moved to close the distance between them, but before she was close enough to touch him, he dropped to one knee and popped open a small box. Sparkles of light twinkled in every direction.

Butterflies tumbled in her stomach. She wanted to pinch herself. Was this a dream? After all, only a day ago she'd been ready to force herself to forget Christopher had ever existed. Now this. Her heart thumped at an erratic beat.

"Arianna, when I am with you, I am so very happy. You make me wish to be a better person. You are everything I want, and everything I need. We've—*I've* wasted too much time hiding behind secrets. Too much time being apart." He swallowed and glanced down before continuing. "Will you marry me?"

Completely overcome, she opened her mouth, but the words were stuck in her throat. Her eyes burned with tears that began to spill.

The unanswered question still lingered in Christopher's blue eyes.

She nodded and choked out, "Yes."

His face relaxed as he stood and pulled her into his embrace. "That makes me the luckiest man in any century." He tilted her face and pressed a kiss on her lips. "I love you, Ari," he whispered.

She tingled all over as the butterflies took flight, tickling her every sense.

Still speechless, she watched as he extracted the ring—a sparkling diamond nestled in a white-gold filigree setting—from the box.

"Don't worry, the diamond came from Jameson's Jewelry—a very nice store in the mall." He winked. Sunbeams hit the gem, sending shards of light dancing across the trees.

She gasped. "I've never seen anything so beautiful."

He lifted her hand and slid it onto her finger, then kissed her.

Electricity coursed through her body. She held the ring aloft to admire. "I couldn't have picked anything so lovely."

Her eyes shifted to his attire. "Christopher…" He looked amazing, as if he'd walked out of one of her beloved books.

He stood motionless while she reached one hand out and touched his cravat. It was only a piece of cloth, yet she felt intimately included in his life from centuries past. Her other hand caressed his face. She raised her gaze to meet his. "Thank you, Christopher. Thank you. It will be an honor to be your wife. I love you, too."

Tears escaped his eyes, and her heart warmed at the love she felt for this man—this wonderful man who would soon become her husband.

"I never thought I would meet someone like you, Ari. Someone who I can speak openly about my background and my family. Someone so beautiful and kind." He pulled her in closer. "I had to travel through time to find you, but now that I have you, I'll never let you go." He gave her a slow, passionate kiss.

Eyes closed, Ari relished in the sparking electrical currents. They zinged from her head to her toes, then clustered in her heart. "I feel the same way. Finding you was a"—she shrugged—"a miracle." She allowed passion to steal her breath away as he kissed her again.

Wind rustling through the trees ended the trance. "I brought food." He motioned to the small buffet he'd laid out on the blanket.

She shook her head and let out a soft laugh. "After that, I don't know if I can eat. But since you obviously spent all morning cooking, I'll do my best."

His mouth curved into a lopsided grin. "When we're married, I will fix you a proper breakfast."

"I like the way that sounds." She pulled him by the lapels and gave him another kiss.

Sparks ignited with every touch. Firecrackers exploded with every kiss. Now she looked forward to an eternity of fireworks, sharing her life with the man she loved.

Just as they began to eat, Ari's phone buzzed. "That might be Maggie. She was pretty confused when I left this morning," said Christopher.

"It's on the blanket behind you." Ari pointed. "Will you turn it off, so we don't have any more interruptions? We don't have much time before you need to leave; I don't want to share it with Maggie." She shrugged. Her best friend would have to wait. Ari needed to savor every moment she had with Christopher.

He found the phone in the crumpled blanket. His fingers fumbled around, bumping keys, to locate the power button, but before he found it, something must have popped up on the screen, catching his eye. "Why is my father's name on here?"

"Oh." She let out a nervous laugh, "I was researching his original crime. I wanted to see if there was any mention of the London Diamond Emporium closing because of it. You seemed regretful about it last night. I'd hoped to give you closure." And make certain his time travel adventures had truly come to an end.

Christopher nodded, but his eyes remained fixed on the screen. His faced paled and then hardened.

"What is it?" His expression made her uneasy.

"It's my uncle. Did you read the article beneath the piece on Father?"

Shaking her head, she scooted in for a closer look and placed a hand on his arm. His muscles were rock-tight.

"The article is about a ruby stolen from the Royal Family's collection."

"What about it? Your father didn't steal the jewels from them, did he?" She tilted her head to read his expression but couldn't capture his gaze. Her former elation turned to nervous anxiety.

"No, but someone did, and then must have pawned it at the Emporium. I think I've seen that ruby. It's still in the safe in Pueblo." His strained voice weakened more with each word.

"What does that have to do with your uncle?" *Please drop it. Please drop it.*

Christopher pointed to the tiny words on the screen next to an artist's rendering of the uniquely cut jewel. "After a search for the missing ruby dead-ended at the London Diamond Emporium, it was assumed to be among the gemstones stolen in the Benjamin Somerset heist."

Ari shook her head, still confused. She read on and gasped.

"The Earl of Hemington—my uncle—was tried and hanged for my father's crime." Emotion cracked his voice. "I cannot let that happen. I must return the ruby and the other jewels before that date." He stretched the picture on the screen to see the numbers. "The fifteenth day of October in the year of our Lord one thousand eight hundred and fourteen."

"Christopher. Did they think your uncle stole it?" Her voice rose to a panic pitch. "You can't go back there." Tears flooded her eyes, making the picture—and the entire phone—blurry. She should have left well-enough alone. Her nosiness never failed to find trouble, and Christopher's sometimes overzealous conscience never failed to land him in the middle of it.

He dropped the phone and pulled her to him.

She cried on his shoulder.

"No," he said. "He was condemned by association. London society…back then, anyway, insisted on assigning blame. A crime was committed; therefore, someone must pay. In this case, it was my uncle. He played no part in it." He gently held Ari back and looked into her eyes, his hands caressing her shoulders. "A business closing because of my father isn't worth the risk; my uncle's life, however…I must go back." He tightened his hold on her. "I'm so sorry," he whispered. "If there were any other way…"

She pushed back. "There has to be another way. You can't go, Christopher. You said it yourself—traveling back to nineteenth century London is too risky." Wracking sobs shook her body. They'd finally come to a perfect place in their relationship, and now this. She'd been ready and waiting for months, only to have her dreams come true, then be dashed all in the same day. No, she was not okay with him going back to a place from which he might not return—even if it would save his uncle's life.

Christopher pulled her close again. As he cupped her face in his hands, his intense blue eyes misted. "It's just one more trip, love. We will be together soon. Nothing—not even two hundred years—will keep me away. Do you trust me?" Enfolding her in his arms, he gently rubbed her back.

Her body shuddered.

"I will ask again; do you trust me?"

A lump clogged her throat as she tried to speak, but the words couldn't hurdle the mass. Trust wasn't the issue. Unplanned, unforeseen and unfamiliar problems were. How could he ask her to exist on trust when there was no way to control the unknown? Squeezing her eyes shut, she shook her head.

"No? You don't trust me?"

"That's not fair, Chris. Of course I trust you. But trust won't save your life."

A dark cloud moved over the clearing, as if an omen.

He held her back to face her. "We are meant to be together. The tremendous odds of us finding each other in the first place should have proven that."

Ari had to admit the truth of his statement. Still… "What if something happens that is beyond your control and you don't—"

He cut her off. "Ari, I've spent countless hours thinking about you—about us. Trust me on this. I will come back. I love you. Life without you these past few months has been empty. No matter what happens, I will find my way back."

A clap of thunder sounded nearby, and rain began falling, mingling with the tears on her face. "I'm sorry, Chris. I'm not okay with this. I know you'll do it anyway, because that's the sort of man you are." She swiped at her tears.

He captured her hands with his and tugged her close again.

She buried her head next to his heart and finished her thought. "And, ironically, because you are this man—this man who will go to the ends of the earth to right the wrongs of the world—I fell in love with you." She couldn't give him her blessing, but she needed him to know her intense love for him would never change.

He dried her tears, then kissed her passionately—as if it were the last.

Stubbornness warned her not to give in to the warmth spreading through her body, but she found his touch, his strength, and, most of all, his character, irresistible. She let go of her hesitancy and melted into his embrace, ardently returning his kisses.

When they finally broke from their reverie, he peered deep into her eyes. "I love you, Arianna. I will return." He pointed to her ring. "I promise."

Chapter Twelve

Arianna's sofa pillows still smelled like Christopher. She closed her eyes and let the memories—good and bad—flood her mind. He'd asked her to marry him—a dream she'd nearly let go of. He was going to travel back to the nineteenth century—a nightmare she'd have to live through.

His admission that he'd been using the time-traveling device to weave through the ages, returning valuable items stolen by his father, hadn't been welcome news. However, she shouldn't have been shocked. After all, he was the most conscientious man she knew. She loved him for his integrity, but wondered why he hadn't destroyed the machine, as she'd thought he had, and moved on with his life. She knew the answer, though. *He won't destroy it until he has rectified his father's wrongs. It's Christopher.*

After a good cry, she pulled a blanket—which also smelled of Christopher—up to her nose and gave in to the exhaustion caused by too many rides on the emotional roller coaster.

A couple of hours later her phone chirped, waking her. A text from Christopher. Her heart twisted, caught between a thrill and an ache. She clicked it open.

On a break at the station. Just want you to know how much I love you.

A fresh wave of tears filled her eyes. No. She

suppressed them, refusing to let them fall.

If you truly loved me, you wouldn't travel back to the past again—ever. Her finger hovered over the send button. But again, no. She deleted the message and just sent a heart emoji instead.

Today should be the happiest day of her life. She'd become engaged this morning—and not to just anyone, to her perfect match; a man who treated her like a queen; a man she would love and cherish through eternity. The realization helped her shelve her stubborn feelings of foreboding. For the rest of the day, she would celebrate. Go shopping; eat junk food.

After returning home from her excursion—arms laden with clothing bags, stomach full of a greasy burger and fries—she turned on the oldies station and began deep cleaning her apartment. Tidiness always made her happy. Whenever she caught a glimpse of her diamond, a fissure of excitement zinged through her. Yes, she could do this.

Her phone rang just as she finished dusting. Maggie's face flashed on her screen.

"Hi, Maggie, what's up?" She'd wondered how long it would take her friend to ask about Christopher's visit.

"What's up?" Maggie repeated the question with much more emphasis. "Is Christopher still there?"

"Uh, no. He's at work."

"Then spill."

Arianna heard the tap, tap, tap of Maggie's fingernails drumming on a hard surface in the background. She'd seen her do it so many times at work, she didn't even have to imagine the look of anticipation on her face.

"It's a lot to talk about over the phone. I'd rather tell you in person." Ari held her hand up and silently admired the secret Maggie tried to extract from her.

"Seriously? A very handsome British man—the very man you've been pining over—leaves my house decked out in clothes only a book-lover like you would understand, and you're not going to tell me why?"

A very loud "humph" made Ari stifle a laugh.

"At least tell me if you two are good. Christopher gave nothing away before he left. For all I could tell, he was headed back to England."

All amusement diffused with those three words— "back to England." The sudden ache in Arianna's heart threatened to spill out in her words. How she wished she could tell Maggie everything about Christopher. She couldn't, of course. But Ari had vowed to be happy today. She'd shake off the darkness and concentrate on the ring donning her finger. It had come with a promise, after all. And she trusted Christopher to keep it.

She swallowed the hurt and took her voice up a notch to a happy pitch. "He probably didn't want you to call me and give it away."

"Give what away?"

"Uh...I don't know. I really should tell you in person."

"Ari. You're killing me. Literally. I think my heart has officially stopped and I shall soon collapse to my death. That is, unless you tell me."

Arianna rolled her eyes. "Wow, Maggie. Such drama."

"Well?"

"Okay, fine. Christopher decked himself out in my favorite genre's clothing because I find it so romantic."

"Romantic for what, exactly? What did he want to do in those clothes?"

"Ah, not much. He just came to propose."

Silence.

"Maggie? You still there?" Ari could hear commotion but couldn't tell if it was good or bad.

"Ari, it's Jason. Maggie threw the phone at me and went off blubbering something. They look like happy tears, but are you all right?"

Relieved, Ari silently congratulated herself for focusing on the positive and tucking the rest away. "Whew. I was worried Maggie was mad at me. I'm fine. I just told her that Christopher asked me to marry him."

"Congr—" A muffled "Oomph" followed.

"Sorry…sorry…Arianna." Maggie had obviously reclaimed the phone. "I'm ecstatic. You and Christopher are going to be so happy. And you're going to make the prettiest babies." Her voice cracked, and she paused to blow her nose. "I can't believe you were going to wait to tell me in person. You don't sit on this kind of news. It's like a mother hen sitting on her eggs too long—the chicks need out."

Ari laughed. She loved her quirky friend. "I think motherhood has changed you. Shouldn't I be the one crying?"

"Don't give me that. Come on, tell me the truth. How long did you bawl after he asked you? Remember, it's me—I'll know if you lie."

She wouldn't need to lie. She'd been sobbing most of the day, but not tears of joy. "Uh…you got me. I've been crying since he left." She tossed the dust rag in the washer, then forced herself to focus on what had happened that morning—Christopher had asked her to be his wife. Their future might hang in the balance, but as of this minute, she was engaged to the man she loved. She needed to sound the part and not let bitterness infect her mood.

"I knew it. We have so much to plan. I'm coming over right now. I can't wait to see the ring."

"Whoa, Mags. We haven't talked about a date yet, or anything." Not to mention the trip he would be taking to London that might swallow him up. She scowled at the thought, then shook herself back into the conversation at hand.

Maggie took a loud breath. "I'm still coming over. I can't wait to see the diamond…oh, wait, did he give you a ring?"

"Yes, he gave me a beautiful ring and I'd love for you to come over. Just not too many questions yet, because I won't have answers." A dose of her best friend could be just what she needed right now, although it could backfire, as well.

"Deal."

"Love ya, Mags. See you soon."

"You, too. I'm on my way."

Ari sank into her recliner, hand outstretched. The large stone shimmered under the lamplight. "I really am blessed. Christopher is a good man. How'd I get so lucky?" Her leg, which had been out of a cast for months now, chose that moment to throb. "Oh, yeah. I earned it."

A year's worth of nightmares rushed to the forefront of her mind. Memories of being dragged through time, stalked by a madman, then saved by his son. "I really am lucky—lucky to be alive, thanks to

Christopher. Even if he's going to turn around and risk his life for someone who lived two centuries ago." Her optimism made a U-turn as anxiety reared its ugly head again. *Stop it.* Clenching and unclenching her fists, she closed her eyes and mentally pushed the negative thoughts away.

The doorbell rang thirty minutes later, and Ari opened it to Maggie, loaded down with bridal magazines and wearing a huge grin.

"I stopped by the drugstore on the way over. We don't need to know the wedding date to start picking colors and a gown."

Ari chuckled. Just seeing the light sparkling in Maggie's eyes lifted her spirits. She led her to a table to relieve her burden, then wrapped her in a hug. "We also don't need to have a date for me to ask you to be my maid—or, I guess it's matron—of honor."

Maggie let out a squeal. "Of course I will. Now let me see that ring."

While Maggie oohed and ahhed over the diamond, Ari couldn't help wondering how she would explain the many things that were so…unexplainable. Things such as why Christopher had been absent all summer. "No big deal, Maggie. He just needed to visit the East Coast, Italy and a few other countries." That didn't sound crazy. After all, what cop didn't do some international traveling for work? She smothered a scowl. And why were the wedding plans left unsettled? "Oh, and he has one more trip to make; then we'll set a date. Where to, you ask? Just to London in 1814." She expelled a breath and took off her ring, so Maggie could try it on. She wished she could tell her everything. Maggie was her closest friend, after all. But Ari didn't want her to think she was nuts. Still…nah. Maggie knew Christopher belonged to the Somers family. That would have to be enough, for now.

"Ari?" Maggie waved her ring-bedazzled hand in front of Ari's face.

"Sorry. What did you say?"

"I said, now that Christopher has come clean about being a Somers, will he still go by Flemming? Or will you soon be Mrs. Somers?"

Mrs. Somers? The notion was cringeworthy. Somers, Somerset, Flemming. All the surnames of Christopher's family made Ari dizzy. "Flemming." Thank goodness. "It's his mother's maiden name. He never wished to be associated with his criminal father. That's why he dropped Somers in the first place. Actually, his family's surname is Somerset, not Somers. They dropped the e-t when they moved to America." Maggie would freak out if she knew Christopher was the grandson of an earl. Too bad she couldn't share that piece of information.

"What? Somerset sounds so regal. I wish he'd go back to it," said Maggie.

Ari shrugged. "I like Flemming."

Maggie held the ring up to the light and watched the prism effect burst through the room. "I don't think I've seen anything so exquisite. It's got to be like a carat and a half—maybe two. Tasha's going to flip."

Tasha *would* "flip." Ari was certain of it—being her boss and the closest person Ari had to a mother. "You have to promise not to tell anyone, Maggie. Especially Tasha." It was one thing to be plied with questions from Maggie, but she'd need time to come up with a better story for the rest of her friends.

Maggie's smile flattened. "I can't believe you'd even think I'd do such a thing."

Ari tilted her head and narrowed her eyes. "Who have you told, Maggie?"

Maggie's face flushed red. She dropped her head and studied her feet.

"Maggie?"

"You didn't say it was a secret on the phone."

"You told everyone, didn't you?" *And that's why I should have waited to tell you last.*

"Sorry...I was just so happy for you." Maggie handed the ring back to Arianna.

Ari shook her head at how Eeyore-like Maggie looked. "It's okay. Geez, you're just like a little kid. What'd you do—send out a mass text?"

Maggie's eyes widened, telling Ari that was exactly what she'd done. "Do you forgive me?" Her hazel eyes pleaded.

"Of course. I can't stay mad at my matron of honor, can I?"

Maggie let go of a heavy sigh. "Thank you, Ari. I'm a terrible friend. But you already knew that."

Ari rolled her eyes. "Let's get to work. It's late and there are so many magazines to look through." She closed her eyes and took a breath, willing away the worry gnawing at her.

I trust him. I promised him, and I do.

Chapter Thirteen

"One more, son," Beatrice Somers mumbled through the half-dozen pins sticking out of her mouth.

Christopher stood motionless while his mother pushed the last pin into the vest cover.

Since his father had escaped capture wearing the original time-traveling vest, he, with the aid of his younger brother, Joshua, followed their father's careful notes to construct a new one. Hopefully, it would function as well as the original. Josh assured Christopher it would.

"I do not understand why you must have the vest and the carrier disc," Joshua said as he pulled the vest from Christopher's broad shoulders, cautious to keep the pins from pricking him. He analyzed the details, comparing it to the pictures his father had sketched.

"I promised Ari I would return, and return I must. You know what happened on my last trip to Italy." Christopher fixed Joshua with a look.

"I repaired the vial and replaced the wiring. The disc is fully functional now," Joshua said, all innocence.

"Still, I'll be taking both the disc and the vest to ensure my return. I'm about to be married. I'll leave nothing to chance." Looking at Joshua, he realized his brother had matured tremendously in the last year. But he was still his *little* brother and probably didn't understand Christopher's feelings for Arianna. "Let's just say that having to spend several days in Florence, puzzling out a way to mend the device for my return home was more of an adventure than I had desired."

Joshua raised his shoulders, then let them drop. "I can't help it if I am smarter than you are at this stuff. Not to mention, it was you who left the repair kit in the lab instead of putting it in the storage container."

Christopher gave him a not-so-gentle slug on the shoulder.

"That's why you should take me with you." Josh set pleading eyes on his brother.

"Sorry, Josh. It's too risky. And Mother and Sarah need you here."

Joshua's face fell into a pout. "Fine, but you promised that someday I will get to go. Don't forget that."

"I cannot very well forget something you remind me of regularly." He smiled at his brother, who, now at eighteen, reached Christopher's own height over six feet.

"What if you come upon one of our acquaintances in London?" Christopher's mother, whose mouth no longer doubled as a pin cushion, wrung her hands.

He'd wondered the same thing and found no answer. However, he must calm her fears, which he understood all too well. He'd fought his way back into her life—into all of their lives—after his father had declared him dead when he'd refused to condone those nefarious crimes. Friends, acquaintances, and even enemies inhabited the world he was going back to.

Unbeknownst to his father, however, he'd done Christopher a favor by exiling him from the family, thus forcing him to pick up skills from living on the streets he wouldn't have learned any other way—some lifesaving. "Do not worry, Mother. I'll be prepared for whatever comes my way." He gave her a reassuring hug and kissed her cheek.

Her sad eyes looked doubtful. "It is evening here. When you arrive in London, it will be near daylight. Take care no one catches you with the jewels. Have you a plan?"

Christopher knew it would be risky to arrive in London so close to daylight hours as far as being recognized went, but he couldn't find a better solution. In early October the sun didn't rise until seven a.m., which would give him enough time in the dark to figure out where he'd landed and formulate a scheme.

"Yes, Mother. My plan is to arrive in the same year as Father's heist. It will be six months later, but evidently the scandal will not have died. I must get there as soon as possible to save Uncle Robert from perishing for Father's crime. As you know, Father constructed the machines to move forward or backward in real time. Otherwise, I'd have to jump a year in either direction."

Beatrice's forehead wrinkled. "I do not understand why you cannot just deliver the diamonds and push a button, bringing you back to the same day—or even the day before."

Christopher had often tried to explain the time markings on the machine and why one couldn't just pick any old time they wished to travel to and from. "It simply doesn't work that way—"

"The machine only moves in yearly increments," Josh interrupted. "Or it's like flying on an airplane in real time—only a lot faster."

"As if any of us knows what flying on a plane is like." Christopher nudged his brother.

Josh shrugged. "Not many people can say they've been on a time machine, but have never flown on a plane." He smiled and a dimple much like Christopher's appeared on his face. He turned his attention back to his mother. "So, Chris can either go there, drop off the jewels and come right back, which would still take a few hours and wouldn't save any lives since it's been over two hundred years, or do what he's doing—go back two hundred and *five* years." He looked around with pride twinkling in his eyes.

"That's right, little brother." Christopher patted his back.

"And one day I will be the one doing the time traveling." Josh looked at Christopher with a glimmer of hope.

"You'll never give up, will you?" Christopher shook his head. He hoped once he returned from this trip—this final trip—to be able to destroy the devices once and for all. However, he'd not dash Joshua's dreams just yet.

Beatrice sighed. "I will not feign understanding anything about that demonic device. But I trust your plan will be successful."

Christopher nodded. "Arriving just before the sun rises gives me time to stow the machine and leave the jewels in the Emporium. If I've cut it too close to operating hours, or if I'm at a distance from the shop, I can blend with the passersby until I deem it safe to leave the jewels, reclaim the device and leave. If I arrived in the dead of night, it would be far more dangerous, as I don't know where Father designed the machine to land. I do not wish to lug diamonds through the streets of London in the dark."

Beatrice blanched, clearly understanding the perilous risk he would be taking. "And that is why you are dressed in nineteenth century garb." She straightened his cravat, then appraised him.

He stopped her hand as it neared his head. He knew the look in her eye said, "I must smooth your dark locks, son." His childhood flashed before him.

"I am thirty, Mother. Do not worry over my hair." He kissed her hand before releasing it. "And you are correct about why I'm dressed as I am. On my other excursions, I was able to arrive in the actual galleries, leave the art, coins, or what-have-you, and depart immediately. It didn't matter what I wore. This time I must look as if I belong. Father did not include a setting for the Emporium—imagine that." He smirked. "I suppose he did not wish to return to the scene of his original crime. I'm not certain where I'll arrive in London."

Beatrice narrowed her eyes. "'Tis not worth the risk. Why go at all?"

Christopher let out a breath. He knew his uncle hadn't always been kind to Mother. Although her family had been wealthy landowners, they'd never held a title. To Robert, a title had meant everything. In public, he had pretended acceptance of Beatrice, while privately, he'd thrust her lack of aristocratic blood in her face with his not-so-subtle barbs. Christopher had sensed the tension between them at a very young age. Maybe he wasn't worth saving.

He shook his head, giving himself a mental

reprimand. "I must. Surely you do not think it's tolerable that Robert die for Father's crime? You know I wouldn't go if there were another way."

Beatrice glanced at her fidgeting hands and then back at him. "No, son, I do not think it's tolerable for Robert to die. Nor do I wish for *you* to die for your father's crime." Tears leaked from her eyes, and she choked back a sob.

Christopher pulled her into an embrace. He held her until her tears abated. "That's why I constructed the—"

"We," chirped Joshua.

"Yes, right. That is why we constructed the vest— to make sure I have two ways to get home if it comes to that. I need to do this, Mother. The streets are quiet before the sun rises, and the thieves dissipate so close to dawn."

Beatrice gave him an understanding nod, but her rigid posture told him she wasn't in full agreement.

He turned from her sorrowful gaze and addressed his brother. "Josh, is the vest ready?"

"Mother needs to put a few stitches in the outer covering; then you're set to go." Josh handed the vest to her. "You are going to look preposterous wearing that vest in public—like some kind of rocket-man. It's good Mother made a covering for it."

"I'll not be wearing the vest. It will be stowed with the gems. The vest is merely a second way to return home if the disc fails again."

Beatrice made quick work of sewing in the necessary side-stitches.

Christopher watched her carefully. He didn't like disappointing his mother and knew her well enough to see she longed for him to remain at home. His uncle's life would have been long over—two hundred and five years later—anyway. Still, his conscience nagged at him to right Father's wrongs, and this trip would be the last. Pulling her into his arms, he hugged her close once more. "I will return, Mother. Remember, I am engaged to be married. Nothing will keep me from Arianna. Not to mention I've only just been reunited with you, Sarah and Josh. Please do not trouble yourself worrying. I will return."

He looked up from his tearful mother to see Sarah in the doorway. He'd grown used to her somber moods, although he'd remembered her in London as a happy girl. If anyone were to return with him, it should be Sarah. Yet, it was still too dangerous.

"Were you going to leave without saying goodbye?" Sarah tilted her head and wrung her hands.

"Of course not." Christopher crossed the room and wrapped his arms around his little sister. Her blue eyes shimmered with unshed tears. "Sarah, perhaps you should have Joshua drive you into town and call Ari while I'm away. I'm certain she would love to come visit." He knew that, above all, Sarah needed a friend. She and Arianna already had a budding relationship and would now soon be sisters. Sarah only needed prodding. "I texted Ari to tell her you might be calling. You know how much she'd like to spend time with you."

Sarah stiffened. "She is expecting a call from me?"

"Sarah, it's Ari. You needn't be afraid." He rubbed her arms and offered a reassuring smile.

Her shoulders relaxed a fraction as she expelled a breath. "I know. I'm uncertain why I've become so insecure. I abhor it."

"Father put you—and the rest of us—through unimaginable trials. Don't be so hard on yourself. It will just require time before you will be back to your old self."

She sighed. "Old is right. I'll be old enough to be put on the shelf."

Christopher smirked. "Twenty-one is hardly old enough to be put on the shelf. Especially in this century. Remember, we no longer live in the 1800s. You are young and beautiful. You just need a friend to…you know…do whatever girls your age do." He pulled a confused face.

Sarah giggled, which eased some of the anxiety he had about leaving her. He'd worried about Sarah the most since they'd been reunited. The others were adjusting well, but Sarah's heart seemed blackened from the abuses inflicted by their father. Now that Benjamin Somers was too far away to hurt them anymore, she still suffered—as if her scars refused to heal. Unfortunately, on several occasions she'd expressed her discomfort in this modern world where there seemed to be no place for her. Christopher didn't have the answer.

He hugged Sarah, then loaded the vest and jewels into the storage compartment of the device. Giving his mother one last kiss, he said his final goodbyes, then turned the dials to engage the machine that would take him back in time.

Chapter Fourteen

London, England 1814

The sun had yet to rise in London. Christopher paused to let his eyes adjust to the darkness. The dank London air mingling with livestock and sewage odors assaulted his nose. Nostalgia temporarily paralyzed him. A streetlamp flickered, shedding light through the fog onto the establishment to his left. Sotheby's. Bond Street. Of all places to land. *I should think Father would wish to avoid the establishments from which he'd been evicted.* There had been several on this road.

Calculating in his mind, he realized it would take approximately forty-five minutes to walk to Hatton Garden, where the London Diamond Emporium was located. Extracting a flashlight from his toolbox, he checked his watch, which he had previously set ahead to London time. 6:30. He should have departed Colorado earlier. He'd supposed his father to have set the device to land closer to the jewelry shop, or in a park, such as he had in New York City. Hyde Park would have been a lengthier distance to the Emporium, however. Certainly, there were other green areas closer to his destination.

As his eyes adjusted to the dark, he scanned the area for hiding places. Although relatively light in weight, the machine was a clumsy burden. Relieving himself of it before sunrise was top priority.

Well-known as one of London's premier streets of fashion, Bond Street was the last place Christopher wished to be. In a few hours it would fill with people. Thank the stars above wealthy shoppers were also prone to sleep to a late hour. So busy with engagements of one sort or another deep into the evenings, they failed to rise with the sun. He glanced around, wondering what reason his father would have to choose Bond Street as his landing destination.

Interesting how nineteenth century Londoners resided among business establishments—so unlike modern America. His eyes roved from a millinery shop to a modiste/furrier, then settled on a private residence. A horse whickered as Christopher moved along the road. His heart warmed. *I do miss the horses,* he thought. Using his flashlight to locate the residence's barn, and thankful there was one, since many Londoners housed their horses and carriages in a communal mews, he found an obscure corner where a mountain of hay would hide the machine from view. Taking care not to damage the device, he hollowed out a spot in back of the hay just big enough for it to nestle. Then arose the question of how to get the diamonds back to the Emporium. Walking through London with the heavy pouch during daylight hours seemed his only option—safer than in the dark. If it were a bit later, he could hire a hackney. Having brought several old coins with him, he could afford it, unlike the years he'd walked to and from his job. After he finished this errand, he'd have no further use for them.

He reflected on the endless miles he'd been forced to trod just over five years ago—before being catapulted to the twenty-first century. His family had owned a carriage, but his father insisted it be left at home for those rare instances he might need it. As the principal wage earner in the family, Christopher had worked as an assistant barrister in the center of London. The walk from East London to his place of employment had kept many cobblers busy mending his shoes. That, he did not miss.

The pink sky warned him of impending daylight. He tucked the pouch inside his large overcoat, supporting it with his arm. As he crept from the corner of the barn past the livestock, he nearly ran into a large carriage. His eyes popped as recognition dawned. On the coach was a coat of arms he knew well—the Hemington family crest. *My uncle, the Earl of Hemington lives here*. And that was why his father programmed the device as he had. He knew he could take refuge in his brother's home, which sat vacant except for the months Parliament was in session.

Christopher's father, Benjamin, was the third son of an earl. His brothers Robert and Cedric both stood in the blood line before Benjamin for the coveted position. Christopher had known both his uncles well as a child, but after his father's descent from an up-and-coming scientist and inventor to an outcast of society, he'd not seen or heard from either one.

This must be Robert's home. He shivered. Robert had frightened Christopher as a youth. Loud and opinionated, he'd assumed his role as earl long before it had been bestowed upon him. Cedric, on the other hand, had been gentle and caring. A drastic contrast. No doubt Father favored Robert. Christopher let out a huff. No matter. He was there to return the ruby to clear

Robert's name. Kind or unkind, he didn't deserve to die for his brother's crime.

"Ho there." Christopher froze at the sound of a raspy, male voice. He ducked behind the coach, but it was too late.

A frenzy of ideas and explanations pranced through his mind, but none made it to his lips. An old stable hand had him by the arm and hauled him from behind the coach.

"What business do you have trespassing on the earl's property, eh? Were you trying to steal a horse?" The old man yanked on Christopher's arm, attempting to prod an answer from him.

Christopher didn't have an answer. He stumbled over words as his thoughts collided with one another. The only coherent thing he could muster was the question of why he hadn't thought through every possibility, so he might have an adequate response in an event such as this?

"Bertrand, do you have the coach ready?" Another voice pulled both his and the stable hand's gazes toward the home.

"I found a horse thief on the property. What shall I do with him?" The old man hauled Christopher forward a few feet.

The sun now blazed over the horizon and threw light into the stable, blinding Christopher as he tried to see who had spoken just a couple rods away.

"Christopher? Is that you?"

Shading his eyes, he squinted up to see his uncle. He blinked a few times. It wasn't Robert—it was Cedric. "Uncle? Are you visiting your brother?"

The stable hand loosened his grip. "Do you not

want to charge this horse thief, then, sir?"

"He's no thief. He's my nephew. Leave us, Bert. I'll take care of matters from here."

Christopher let out a puff of air and allowed his rigid posture to relax.

Cedric turned toward him. "Robert passed shortly after you and your family disappeared. 'Twas a fever."

Hadn't the article on Arianna's phone said Robert was hanged for Father's crime? Christopher thought for a moment. No, no, it said "Earl of Hemington." It was Cedric. *Cedric's life is in peril.* A cold chill seeped through Christopher's body. What if he hadn't come back? He had always loved and admired Cedric. He shouldn't die for Father's crime. No one should— except Father.

Cedric narrowed his eyes, waiting for a response.

"I didn't know. I'm very sorry," said Christopher.

Cedric tugged at a watch in his vest pocket. "Half past seven. I have but ten minutes to hear at least an hour's explanation of where you and your family have been and why you have come here today. Christopher, you know I have always favored you, so I will give you the benefit of the doubt, but please assure me I am not granting you something you have not earned. Tell me you've not been involved in your father's criminal activity." He paused. "And speaking of your father, where is he?"

"He's not with me, and I have never been involved, Uncle. I am here to make restitution to the London Diamond Emporium for Father's heist. But more importantly, I am here to save your life."

Cedric's face creased in confusion. "Save my life? What have I to do with it? And how do you think getting to the Diamond Emporium will be possible? Every Bow Street runner is on alert and looking for Benjamin. You cannot be seen on the streets of London. Should anyone recognize you and point you out as his son, you will be found guilty without so much as a trial."

"But I am here to return the jewels—"

"It will not matter to the authorities. You disappeared with your father. You are guilty by association. Having the jewels on your person only makes you guiltier." Cedric glanced from his townhouse to his coach. "For now, you must remain hidden. I will see you safely into my home, but then I must leave. We will speak again when I return. An emergency session at the House of Lords has been called—it will likely take the entire day."

Christopher mentally kicked himself for even thinking that returning to the scene of his father's crime had been a good idea.

Never mind. Once Cedric was gone, he'd simply slip back out to the barn, find the device and head home. He'd leave the jewels and a note for his uncle. Cedric could determine the best way to return them to the jewelry shop—or not at all.

Following his uncle, he entered the house, where he was instructed to remain until Cedric's return. "I know you will be tempted to leave, but, Christopher, I have much to tell you and I anticipate you have much to tell me, as well. Please, I urge you to stay. Whatever you do, don't venture down Bond Street. You will no doubt stumble into an acquaintance there." He paused and took a breath. "You will not find many friends left in London after what your father did. I may very well be your only ally."

Christopher frowned. Even more reason for him to make a hasty getaway.

"I must go. Give me your word you will stay until I arrive home this evening." Cedric eyed Christopher until he received a nod. "Very well. I have a skeleton staff on duty; they will show you to a guest suite and see to your needs."

Christopher watched his uncle leave the premises; his heart heavy from the promise he'd given to stay. He simply could not keep it. He'd put himself in a dangerous situation by coming, and, as much as he wished to stay and explain everything to Cedric, he couldn't risk delaying his departure.

Chapter Fifteen

Ari had run longer and harder Saturday morning than usual. Knowing Christopher had transported himself to a dangerous place and time the night before called for therapy, and for Ari, morning jogs fit the bill. "Running, chocolate and shopping—all great remedies for a troubled heart." She kicked off her sneakers, located a chocolate bar she'd been breaking pieces from, and took a bite.

As she prepared to jump into the shower, her phone rang. She nearly ignored it, then noticed the number began with a Pueblo area code. She turned off the water and wrapped up in a robe.

It surprised her to hear Sarah on the other end. "Hi, Sarah. I hoped you might call." Arianna warmed at the sound of the girl's timid voice. Countless times she'd thought about Sarah and wished to contact her, but without cell phone service at the Somers' mansion, there wasn't a way. She missed her communications with Sarah through her journal—although that hadn't ended well. She wanted to somehow draw her out of her bashfulness—and out of the despondency Christopher had told her Sarah struggled with.

"Josh drove me to town, so I could call you. As you know, Christopher left for London last night."

Did Ari detect a quiver in Sarah's voice? She no doubt missed Christopher already, too.

"He will not be gone long, but…would you care to come stay here until he returns? He estimated it will be tonight or tomorrow morning…so, I guess I am inviting you to spend the weekend." Her strained laugh resonated with nerves. "I know it is difficult for you to be in this house. We—we only thought—"

"Thank you, Sarah. I would like that," Ari answered hurriedly to relieve the tension she heard mounting in Sarah's voice. She would go, and she'd be the friend Sarah needed. Ari knew Sarah's unease resulted from the years of heavy-handed abuse from her father. "Thank you for inviting me. I'll pack a few things and get on the road right away."

She ended the call and twisted her hands together. Sleep hadn't come easy the night before, knowing Christopher had taken his father's time-traveling machine back to his own land and time. The last thing she wanted was to spend the weekend alone, worrying about his safe return. Yet, spending it with Sarah and her family meant staying at the frightening mansion. Her heart rattled just thinking about it. *It's okay. It will be worth it to be there when Christopher arrives back home.*

Doubts about his safe return shouldered their way to the forefront of her mind. *Christopher is brilliant. He wouldn't do anything that will keep him in London.* She'd told herself so repeatedly, but still, fears and misgivings picked at her. She would find comfort being with others who loved him and awaited his arrival home from his final globe-trotting adventure. It would also be nice to speak freely of the traveling device and the family's experiences venturing into the twenty-first century. Holding back the truth at work and around

Maggie had been more difficult than she had imagined.

She spent longer in the shower than she'd planned, talking herself out of various doubts and concerns. Then, tossing her overnight bag into the back of her little red Subaru, she headed south to Pueblo and beyond. It rained, slowing her travels. The weatherman had forecasted an early snow. At least this was only rain. She reached the Somers' fortress by mid-afternoon.

Familiar chills prickled her skin at the sight of the house, but she closed her eyes and willed them away. Today she didn't have Christopher with her to ward off the evil spirits that seemed to haunt her here, but it was time to get past acting so childish. These people were going to be her family. She took several deep breaths and stepped out of the car. *Mind over matter. Mind over matter. Mind over matter.*

"You are here. Welcome," said Mrs. Somers. She and Sarah stood on the porch, waiting, when Ari had toted her bag to the door.

Misgivings about being at the Somers' home had her nearly fleeing several times. But once the ladies spotted her, she knew it was too late for second thoughts. Under their scrutiny she felt like a one-year-old who had taken her first steps.

"We worried you might have decided against coming," said Sarah.

Very perceptive of them. She'd decided that very thing several times while packing, on the road, then again just now. "Sorry. No, I didn't. The rain slowed me down a bit." Ari had one foot on the threshold and the other poised to run. Rain continued to sprinkle down on her. She should have carried an umbrella to the door, but the showers had lightened up a lot, plus her hands were full with her purse and overnight bag.

"The rain. Of course, of course." Mrs. Somers shook her head. "I seem to have forgotten my manners. Please, come in before you get wet." She led Ari into the foyer, then turned and raised her arms as if she wanted to hug Ari—but dropped them to her sides.

Arianna couldn't take the awkwardness any longer. This was her era and her turf. The Somers obviously still felt like visitors here. They'd come from a society of rules and formalities. And still, five and a half years later, they knew little more of modern times than when they'd arrived. Christopher had done well teaching them survival skills—how to shop at a grocery store, use modern appliances, drive cars and employ other nonexistent-from-their-past devices, but they still lacked modern-American social skills. Ari wouldn't allow her own apprehension to add to their burden. They had as much—if not more—to lose than Ari if something happened to prevent Christopher's safe return.

She pulled her future mother-in-law into a hug.

Mrs. Somers' muscles, rigid at first, relaxed. Without words, Ari felt warmth and love from this woman she'd spent so little time with.

Sarah opened her arms for a hug, as well. The wall of anxiety Ari had built crumbled away.

Josh entered, calling out to everyone. Then Ari remembered he had a job in Pueblo. Good for him. He'd learn about this century by diving right in, as Christopher had. They congregated in the family room.

"So, you're expecting Christopher back tonight or tomorrow morning?" Ari asked.

"Yes," said Sarah. "Hopefully tonight."

The tension on Mrs. Somers' face did not escape Ari's notice. "Are you worried about him, Mrs. Somers?"

Mrs. Somers squeezed Ari's hand. "Call me Beatrice. And yes. I am worried. You see, although Christopher returned to London several months after...er...well, his father's crime took place, I fear if he is spotted, he'll be apprehended." Worry lines appeared on her forehead.

Ari looked at Sarah and Joshua, hoping to get reassurance. She needed to hear somebody say they were certain Christopher had taken every measure possible to ensure his safe return.

Joshua seemed to be reading her mind. "Don't worry, Arianna. We constructed a vest, so if the disc fails, he'll have it as a back-up."

Instead of calming Ari, his words caused her to feel woozy. She began wringing her hands. "Has the disc failed before?"

Josh glanced at his sister and then at his mother. Both looked at Ari with concerned eyes. "Oh...Christopher didn't tell you about Florence?" said Josh.

He'd mentioned it, but she hadn't pressed him for details. Arianna shook her head. She feared trying to speak might bring on tears.

Josh waved his hand in the air. "It was nothing, really. He just landed too close to a display case in an art gallery, and the device got a little...banged up is all. The main problem occurred when he'd discovered he left the repair kit here at home."

"Ahem...you took the repair kit out of the bin to

use and never replaced it, Josh. It was your fault." Sarah rolled her eyes at her brother.

Joshua's cheeks turned pink. "At any rate, he had to become creative. Turns out tree sap is a good bonding agent when you're in a bind." He laughed.

No one else did.

He cleared his throat and went on. "This time, besides constructing a back-up device, we made certain he had all the tools he would possibly need on board. He'll be fine."

"But what about your mother's concerns? What if he's discovered?"

The room fell silent.

"I'm sorry, Arianna," said Sarah. "Perhaps we should not have invited you to spend the night. I think we have troubled you."

Ari shook her head. "I was already troubled. I don't even know why—just a feeling, I suppose. We can worry together. Maybe play more of that game you taught me, Josh?" She knew very well why she'd been troubled. If Christopher's uncle could be executed for a crime his brother had committed, authorities surely wouldn't hesitate to punish Mr. Somers' own son. She tamped down her fears and forced a smile.

Joshua beamed. "I'll get the playing cards. Come join us, Sarah."

"And I'll fix refreshments," said Beatrice. "Three o'clock. Hmm, nearly teatime. Perhaps Christopher will be back in time for supper."

Just the thought of him arriving home in time for dinner helped ease Arianna's nerves.

Chapter Sixteen

Christopher closed the door to his bedchamber, tucked the bundle of jewels beneath the bed, then found a sheet of paper in the bureau drawer. Sitting at a desk, he contemplated the best and most succinct explanation he could pen to Cedric.

"Sir?" The door rattled as someone knocked. "Sir, Lord Hemington instructed me to have the cook fix you some breakfast. It is ready if you'd like to come down and dine."

Christopher's stomach rumbled, screaming for food. With all his time-travel preparations, he scarcely remembered his last meal. He was hungry, but also needed to get home straightaway. He debated while the growling increased. "Please have a plate sent up to me."

"Very well."

Christopher continued considering what to write. The urgency to compose the letter and get out nagged at him. He smoothed the paper and located a quill pen and inkwell.

Within a few minutes a servant's scratch at the door interrupted his concentration. "I've brought food to break your fast, sir," a female voice said through the door.

The woman's accent was a strange mix of cockney and refined English. He opened the door and pointed to the desk. Perhaps he could eat and write… Then leave.

Scooting a chair up to the desk, he waited impatiently for the maid to do her job and exit the room, so he could get on with his plan.

She placed the tray on the desk, then glanced at him. "Would you like a cup a rosie? I can be back wif a pot in a hurry."

Rosie lee. He hadn't heard that cockney term in years. "Tea. Yes, please." Between her speech and the smell of English food wafting around him, nostalgia hung thick in the air. Not long ago he'd wished only to return to the nineteenth century. Now he couldn't wait to escape it.

He waited, but she didn't leave the room. He felt her gaze resting on him and turned to face her.

She sucked in a breath. "Christopher? Christopher Somerset? Is it you?" He winced at the name Somerset. Indeed, it was his name, but his father had soiled it.

He studied her face. The softness of her cheeks had become hollow, lending her a sharp and more angular appearance, and her rosy coloring had paled. But those were the same hazel eyes he'd found enchanting in his youth. "Rachel?" A cautious warmth spread through him. He hadn't seen Rachel in years.

She wrapped her arms around his neck, pulling his head to her shoulder. "I knew you'd come back for me."

In reaction, he flinched and pushed her away. Arianna's face flashed through his mind—the only woman with whom he wished to be so intimately close. He and Rachel had been childhood sweethearts, but in the nineteenth century, a display of affection such as hers was highly inappropriate—especially in his bedchamber. He glanced around the room to make sure nobody had witnessed the embrace. The open door exposed an empty hallway. He let out a sigh of relief.

Dropping her hands to her sides, she stepped back. "Are you unhappy to see me after all these years?"

"No, of course I'm happy to see you. I've often wondered what became of you when I left for Cambridge. Did you marry?"

She let out an ungraceful snort. "Are you asking did I have my London Season?" She smirked. "No. I have been working for your uncle for the last seven years. There are not many men my age to choose from in a life of servitude.

Her sarcastic tone took him by surprise. He began to second guess if this woman really was Rachel Cartwright. The Rachel he knew had always worn a smile. Her quick wit had made him laugh, and her eyes…her eyes had sparked with mischief.

"When Mama died, I took her place working for your uncle." She pulled up a chair next to his, their elbows touching.

A feeling of uneasiness crawled up his flesh.

"Oh, Christopher, do you remember the fun we had?" She gazed up at the ceiling, as if all her childhood memories hung in a cloud above them.

"That was very long ago. We were just children." He moved his chair away a few inches, hoping she'd take the hint. Her actions were uncomfortably inappropriate. And had her cockney accent suddenly morphed to refined English? She had learned it while growing up in his uncle's home. The *cockney* was the mystery. She must have picked it up from the other servants.

"We started out as children, but I was fifteen when

100

you left for school. Nearly marriageable age." She dipped her chin coyly, as if she were still a teenager.

Christopher's lips quirked. Fifteen may be old enough to marry in the nineteenth century, but where he'd just come from—and where he must return—one could get arrested for cavorting with someone so young. Oh, how things had evolved. They'd been far too young to wed back then. He'd never considered it. Evidently, she had.

Rachel must have mistaken the amusement on his face for an invitation. She placed a hand over his, making him wince. "Do you remember the promise you made?"

He wished to jerk his hand from beneath her calloused fingers but didn't want to offend. "No, Rachel, I do not."

Her lip jutted out in a pout. "You said you were going to marry me."

He narrowed his eyes. "I what? We were children. I had not even gone off to university yet. I'm certain we never discussed marriage."

"Do not pretend innocence. You wished to marry me, but your father said I was not good enough for you."

Now *that* conversation he did remember. Father had made it crystal clear how he'd felt about Christopher being seen with a girl so far beneath his station. But he had never led Rachel to believe they would one day marry.

She let out a huff and her voice rose. "I still have the necklace you gave me." She put a hand into her décolletage and fished out a chain with a locket dangling on the end.

The memory floodgates opened. Christopher had saved his allowance for weeks to buy Rachel that necklace. It wasn't terribly valuable, but it meant something to a fifteen-year-old girl. She'd beamed with delight when he'd given it to her. However, she had obviously taken the gesture as something far more meaningful than he'd meant it to be. It was a trinket. A token of affection given in their youth. He'd assumed she had moved on with her life. Yet she hadn't. His heart went out to her. But at the same time, he was confused. There had been no question about the status of their relationship when he'd left for Cambridge. It was over. His father had made certain of that.

He couldn't take his eyes off the necklace. The silver locket seemed to mock him.

"I even kept a lock of your hair inside." She clicked it open, revealing curls of dark hair tied together by a thread.

A shiver ran down Christopher's spine. He ducked his head to hide a grimace. "How in the world did you get my hair, Rachel?"

"'Tis not important. But I assure you, the hair is yours." She stroked his head.

He jerked away.

An odd grin turned her lips up. "When you stayed at your uncle's manor, I often watched you sleep."

He felt blood draining from his face, picturing Rachel in his room. If they'd been caught, consequences for her could have been dire. However, she'd narcissistically deemed herself a lady—constantly inserting herself into the Somerset family's world, his world. In fact, she likely assumed he'd be forced to marry her. Delusional. A sudden thought sent ice through his veins: *had she wished to be caught?*

Tucking the locket back under her plain work dress, she patted her heart. "If the rumors are true, and your father has fled London, there is no one to stand in our way."

A weight tightened his chest as the pleasure of seeing an old friend dissipated. Now he saw it for what it was—an unpleasant coincidence. Of all people to run into, why her? Why Rachel? A happily married Rachel would have been interesting—even fun—to catch up with, but this girl who had carried a torch for him all these years—without his knowledge—threw a cog in the wheels of his plans. "Rachel, I am only in London for business. I must leave straightaway. I'm sorry. I'd thought you would have moved on with your life—be married with a houseful of children." He lifted both hands, then dropped them.

"Well, I am not, am I?" She speared him with a look. "'Tis as if you went off to college and never gave me a second thought."

"That isn't true. However, I do believe we both understood when I left, we were not destined to wed. In fact, as I recall, you cried yourself into a swoon that put you down for a week. I could not even say goodbye." He remembered being turned away when he had tried. "She has a terrible case of the vapors because of you" he'd been told.

Rachel's eyes misted. "You meant that much to me." Her hand once again found his.

He stood, uncomfortable with her nearness. Moving to the window to put distance between them, he fiddled with a curtain tieback. The fabric, woven with shades of blue, reminded him of Ari's eyes. The color of the sea on a clear day. He yearned for her now more than ever. Seeing his childhood sweetheart again caused him to realize how his life had taken a turn for the better, not worse—as he'd imagined it had five years ago. If he'd remained in the nineteenth century, he would have never known love the way he did now. He would never have known Arianna.

"Where are you going?" she asked, interrupting his thoughts.

Christopher tilted his head and narrowed his eyes in temporary confusion.

"You said you are leaving London. Where are you going?"

A good question. Colorado? Far away from her touch? "I am going abroad." He pulled his chair a few more inches away from hers before reclaiming his seat.

"Is that where your father ran off to? Did he go to the continent?"

You could say that. "I honestly do not know where my father is." Christopher took a bite of his sausage. The meat tasted bland and dry as he forced it down his throat. His appetite had fled, but he had to keep busy until Rachel left.

She lowered her voice and put her face very near his. "Did you help your father with the heist? That is what they are saying."

Christopher choked on his food and laid his fork down hard on the wooden desk. "Absolutely not! How can you even ask that question? You know me better than that… Or at least you once did."

"Oh, stop acting so righteous. 'Tis me, the girl you stole kisses from behind your carriage house."

"Stealing kisses and stealing diamonds are two

very different things!" He wiped his mouth with a cloth napkin and rose from his seat once more. "Please, Rachel, you must go now. It really isn't proper for you to be in my room."

"But, Christopher, you promised." She yanked out the locket from beneath her neckline again.

From his peripheral, he could see it, but pretended not to. The necklace meant nothing. Why she'd kept it all these years, he had no clue. And the hair? He began questioning her sanity.

Before he could wonder further, her arms came around him in a tight embrace. "Kiss me, Christopher. No one will know. Lord Hemington left his family at the country estate; it's only me, Meg and the butler here now. Cook and Bertrand never come up to the bedchambers."

He pushed her away—a bit more forcefully than he'd intended. "Stop it, Rachel, I'm sorry you thought I would return to London and marry you, but the truth is, I am betrothed to another."

Rachel reared back, as if she'd been slapped. "No!" Her voice sounded gravelly, foreign almost. "You belong to me!"

"I belong to no one, but my heart belongs to Arianna. Now please leave me."

She appeared to be simmering and simpering at the same time. Then the tears began.

He looked at her sympathetically, wishing he could help her—especially if he'd been the cause of her grief. But she was forcing his hand. He walked to the door and motioned for her to leave.

With a mighty huff, she turned and pushed past him. "You will regret this, Christopher," she ground out.

He closed and locked the door behind her, then heaved a heavy breath.

His head ached from the confusion. Had he led Rachel on? He thought back through a handful of conversations that had occurred twelve years ago for him—although only seven for her. Hazy at best, he still couldn't remember a time in which he'd made a commitment to or used her in any way. She'd blown their relationship to an unimaginably large proportion.

Pacing the room, he rubbed the back of his neck where a kink had formed. Rachel was smart. She might cause trouble. The sooner he left, the better.

The blank paper sitting on the bureau caught his attention. Words jumbled in his mind. He sat down, pushed his food aside, and contemplated the letter he'd planned to write before Rachel's interruption. Nothing too wordy, just a brief explanation. He needed to leave a warning about the jewels and how imperative it was for them to be returned immediately; a few words of farewell, and then he would return to his new life.

He uncorked the inkwell and scowled. *I do not miss these.* He twirled the quill pen around in his fingers before plunging it into the black liquid. There were many things he didn't miss from the nineteenth century. He wished he'd stayed in Pueblo instead of returning to this place where he was wanted—by both the law and Rachel Cartwright.

Chapter Seventeen

The Pueblo sky dimmed as the sun melted into the horizon. Still no Christopher. Determined not to be disheartened, Arianna challenged Joshua to a game of air hockey. When the large fixture had first been installed, she had shuddered thinking about the possible damage an errant hockey puck could do to the perfectly painted walls, but as a guest, she was happy to have the game as a diversion.

She jumped back when a disc slammed into the goal next to her. "You've obviously been practicing."

Josh laughed. "I might have been born in a different century, but I am a fast learner." He winked, which almost brought tears to Arianna's eyes. She hadn't thought Joshua looked like Christopher until that moment. How would she get through the night without knowing he was safe?

"Well, Mr. Fast Learner, take that." She slammed the disc back, scoring a goal in return.

Once they were all played out, Sarah led Ari to a guest bedroom. "You may sleep in here. I'm certain Christopher will arrive sometime during the night."

Ari knew she wouldn't be able to sleep. Adrenaline pulsed through her veins. "Are you tired, Sarah?"

A smile stole across Sarah's face. "Not in the least. Would you like to stay up and chat?"

"Yes. Let's have some good old-fashioned girl

talk…or…new-fashioned for you, I suppose." They giggled and found a sofa and some cozy blankets to snuggle up in.

"Now that you can speak freely, tell me all about life in England. I've always wanted to go there." Ari took a sip of hot chocolate Beatrice had brought in with a plate of cookies.

Sarah's eyes lit up. Once she began talking, it was as if she'd become a different person.

Ari couldn't help but let herself live through Sarah's memories of fancy gowns and handsome boys. Her own memory of Christopher proposing to her dressed in his nineteenth century clothing had taken her breath away.

"I only wish I'd had a London Season." Sarah let out a wistful sigh. "Then I could have come out in society and perhaps been courted."

"Was there someone special you would have liked to court you?"

Sarah's cheeks turned pink, giving away the fact that indeed there was a certain man she'd had her eye on. "Hudson." She lifted a hand to her face as if to cover her blush.

"Hudson. But you were so young in London. How was it you already had a…suiter?"

Sarah let out a shy giggle. "I was fifteen. Most girls were married by seventeen or eighteen. If I'd had a season at sixteen, Hudson and I could have wed soon after." She dropped her gaze to her lap. "Those were our plans."

A giddy excitement bubbled up in Ari. She clutched Sarah's hand. "You planned to be married to Hudson?" That explained so much of what Ari had read in Sarah's journal. Her early writings had been optimistic, excited.

"I'd known him since we were young. He was two years my senior and very handsome. His father was an earl, as my grandfather had been. In fact"—Sarah tilted her head up, her eyes sparkling—"Hudson was heir to his father's earldom. I wonder if that happened."

"I have a way to find out." Arianna punched letters on her phone, then remembered the lack of cellular service so far from the city. She sighed. "What's his last name? I'll look him up later."

"Drake. Hudson Drake the third," Sarah said. "There was this tree on Hudson's family's London proper—" She covered her mouth and her cheeks reddened.

"What about the tree?" Ari urged her on.

"You will think I am childish." Sarah squirmed as if she were bursting to let her secret out.

"Girl talk is all about sharing stories about boys— especially when there's a tree involved." Both girls laughed.

"Very well. I will tell you, but you must swear to keep it a secret. Only Christopher knows, and that is because he helped me."

"I promise."

"You see, the trunk of a large tree on Hudson's property had a hollowed-out area, just big enough to hide letters. I believe the tree was a plane tree. Common in England."

Ari liked where this was going. Sarah's eyes sparked with an energy she'd never before seen.

"Once my family had settled in London, Hudson left his country home in favor of the family's London residence. No one questioned his actions because his father had been ill, and all suspected he didn't have much longer to live; thus, Hudson would be needed to fill his father's shoes. Living in London with his father and learning his role as an earl made sense. However, I knew he really moved to the city to be near me."

"He told you that?"

"Yes. Well, he wrote it. We did not have many opportunities to see one another in London. And we did not have those." Sarah pointed to Ari's phone.

Ari was beginning to put the story together. "And that's where the tree comes in."

Sarah nodded. "Hudson wrote me letters and left them in the tree hole, then Christopher picked them up and replaced them with notes from me. He walked past Hudson's home on his way to work, so it really wasn't off his path."

Ari's heart swelled, thinking about Christopher on such a sweet errand for his little sister.

"I wish you could have met Hudson. He was kind and handsome. So handsome." She shook her head and sighed. "Even if we'd stayed in England, I couldn't have had a Season, since we'd become outcasts from society." She sipped her hot chocolate, then wiped her mouth. "I shall never forget the good times, however. The years we'd lived in the grand country estate—the Drake's neighbors." Her face fell into an expression of resignation.

Ari could almost feel the darkness stealing away Sarah's enthusiasm.

"I just turned twenty-one. Hudson surely found another girl to marry."

Mr. Somers had more than taken Sarah away from

her home and era; he'd ruined her plans to marry Hudson. He'd suffocated her hope.

"Hudson sounds nice. I wish I could have met him, too." Ari gave Sarah's hand a squeeze. "Do you like it here in the twenty-first century, Sarah?" she asked, recalling her promise to Christopher about becoming a true friend to his sister. A friend would help Sarah move forward, not dwell on the past—a place Sarah could never return. "Perhaps being here can serve as a fresh start."

Sarah shrugged. "Although society had shunned us, I still had friends, and though I doubt it could have happened, Hudson swore he would still marry me. I've just been so very lonely." Her voice had become reflective, sad. "Father made it difficult for me to like it here. I guess I should try a little harder. I just still feel…trapped. Limited."

"If you learned how to drive so you could get out and meet people and get a job, like Josh did, then perhaps you'd be more content. What do you think?" Ari knew she treaded on ice that could crack and break beneath her, drowning their friendship before it had completely firmed up. But Christopher had said she needed friends, and Ari was determined to try.

"You sound like my brother." Sarah laughed. "Perhaps you are both correct." She cuddled closer to Ari. "This is a good start, is it not?"

"It's a very good start." Ari let out a breath and allowed herself to sink into the blankets.

They talked late into the night until sleep finally came.

Pots and pans banging in a room below woke Arianna. A savory aroma wafted through the house, making her mouth water.

"It smells like Mother is cooking a full breakfast." Sarah's eyes twinkled, warming Ari's heart.

"And maybe Christopher is home in time to eat with us." Ari jumped up and folded her blanket. "I can't wait to see him." Her heart raced at Christopher possibly being so near.

They stumbled into the kitchen together.

"It smells so good, Mother."

"I haven't had a decent breakfast since…well…I can't remember when." Ari smiled, then thought, *since before Mom died.* She quickly pushed away the twinge of sadness.

She couldn't keep her eyes from popping at the sight of the breakfast spread: poached eggs, bacon, sausage and fried tomatoes covered the table. "This looks delicious." Her own mother used to make Ari's favorite waffles, covered in fresh strawberries and cream. This looked heartier and healthier—but nothing was as tasty as those waffles.

She glanced around the room—no Christopher yet. Disappointment weighed heavy on her heart. Soon. He'd arrive home soon.

Her stomach growled causing Sarah to laugh.

Beatrice smiled, but her red-rimmed eyes betrayed her inner concerns. She'd probably been cooking up a storm to keep from thinking about something.

Ari's mood darkened. "It's Christopher, isn't it? You're worried something's happened to him." Her voice rose and so did the panic she'd been holding at bay. "He should be here by now. I knew it; something's happened."

Beatrice crossed the room and pulled her into a

hug. She sniffled. "I am sorry, dear. I do not mean to frighten you, but yes. I am worried. He has never taken so long to return before—except for his trip to Florence."

Ari's eyes stung. The thought of something happening to Christopher, after all they'd been through, was unbearable.

Joshua materialized from who-knows-where. "Mother, give it time. Christopher is clever. He will return. He'll not risk getting caught. He told us as much. Arianna is his world now. He wants nothing more than to return and marry her."

Ari's face heated, but she appreciated Joshua's insight. "Is it true? Is that what he said?"

Beatrice nodded at the same time Sarah and Josh said, "Yes."

"He loves you ever so much, Ari." Sarah took her hand. "Josh is correct. Christopher will return at any moment." She gave Ari and encouraging smile.

Chapter Eighteen

Christopher read over the short note he'd composed. "Ahh," he moaned. In his haste to finish it and depart, he'd caused the ink to blob and run. Blowing on the paper to hurry the drying process, he considered the best place to put the letter so his uncle would be certain to find it. Cedric likely wouldn't visit the guestroom once Christopher disappeared. And the jewels. Where should he leave those? He'd have to take both to his uncle's chamber. Hopefully, with only a few staff members on duty, he'd avoid being detected.

As he made his way through the guest corridor and toward the family's rooms, noises rose up from the kitchen of the cavernous mansion. He hoped Rachel was busy working below. However, she could be anywhere—members of a skeleton staff often filled many roles. He needed to give himself a tour in order to locate his uncle's bedchamber.

It turned out to be an easy task; two girls talked and giggled as they tidied the largest room—the only chamber which had been occupied in the family wing. Christopher quietly peered into the room. Rachel and a younger girl chatted as one dusted a chest of drawers and the other swept the already spotless floor.

"Christopher, is that you?"

His heart squeezed. He'd hoped to escape her notice.

He faked a smile. "Yes, Rachel, 'tis I." He tucked the note into his pocket and made sure the diamonds were securely stowed beneath his coat. "I just came to bid farewell. I must be going now."

Rachel grabbed the other girl by the arm and tugged her forward. "Meg, this is him." She beamed his way. "This is my fiancé, Christopher."

He stiffened at her declaration, wondering why Rachel wished for his affection after so many years. And he, a criminal in the eyes of the *ton,* would not be considered a fortunate match—even for a servant.

Rachel once again extracted the silver locket from beneath her apron and dress. "See? He gave me this when he proposed marriage. I was but a girl of fifteen. Is it not the most romantic love story? A real-life fairytale." She gazed to the heavens, still clutching the locket. "Now, after so many years, he's home to make good on his promise." She turned to him.

He couldn't decide if her expression looked joyful or threatening. It made no difference. He refused to play her game, no matter how many tears she had shed in his room. "Rachel, as I explained earlier, I am only here on business and must leave—"

"Shh." Rachel moved toward him and pressed a finger to his lips. "You'll not leave me here. Take me with you, Christopher," she pleaded.

He took a step backward. "I have urgent business to attend to." Without waiting to hear her argument, he turned and fled the room.

Finding himself back in his bedchamber, he paced while he puzzled out his next move. He couldn't deposit the letter and the jewels in his uncle's bedchamber for obvious reasons. Then where? Perhaps the bookroom?

Peering out his door, he waited until he was certain Rachel wasn't lurking nearby, then fled the room and aimed for the study. The large home made his task a challenge. As a police officer, he kept himself in peak physical condition, but there were so many stairs. *Twenty-first centurions have no idea how easy they have it.* He panted as he approached the bookroom door. Glancing around, he twisted the knob. Locked. He let out a silent groan and headed back to his bedroom.

He'd wasted too much time looking for a place to stow the letter and jewels. Racking his brain, he could see no other solution than to leave them there in the guestroom and get to the stable and the machine. Hopefully, by the time they were found, he'd be safely back in the future with Arianna where he belonged— where he should have never left. Ari had been right. His overactive conscience caused him to sometimes act impulsively. The notion of Rachel finding the items crossed his mind, but he didn't care anymore. Perhaps she'd see it as recompense for the broken promise she'd conjured in her mind. He shoved both the jewels and letter under his bed, then crept out.

A stroke of luck got him to the front door undetected. He gave a furtive glance about the foyer before slipping out and making a dash for the stables to find his device.

"Where do ya think you're going?" The same crusty voice he'd been greeted with in the wee hours of the morning stopped him in his tracks.

"Oh, good day, uh…Bertrand, is it?"

"I knew ye were a horse thief. Who skulks around in stables before dawn? Horse thieves. And here ye are back again. No matter what the master says, ye ain't to be trusted—relation or no relation."

"I am not a horse thief. I only wondered if I could take a look at the...stallion?" Christopher had caught a glimpse of the horse in the dark morning hours and hoped he'd guessed correctly. He remembered his uncle's fondness for the breed and assumed he had paid a visit to Tattersall's Auction while staying in London.

The old man's wrinkled face brightened. "Oh, he picked a good one, he did." Then, just as fast, his face fell back into pinched suspicion. He looked Christopher up and down. "Nah, I still cannot trust a man I do not know."

Cedric has a champion in Bertrand, Christopher thought. He'd never remembered a stable hand so protective.

He regarded the man, sizing him up. Bertrand stood a few inches shorter than him, but the physical labor he performed on a daily basis was evident in his muscular build. Christopher was strong, as well, and he had the age advantage. Bertrand looked to be in his sixties, although working outside in the weather could have added premature wrinkles. He didn't wish to hurt the man, just get to the device.

"There you are." Rachel's voice oozed sugary sweet.

Startled, he whipped around to see her standing inches behind him. She skewered him with a "how dare you leave without me" glare.

His heart plunged to his feet as he saw his chance for a quick escape fade away. "I told you I needed to go, Rachel. I am only here on business." He attempted to make his voice firm—shake himself from this immature girl in a woman's body who continually thwarted his efforts to disappear.

Bertrand's eyes grew wide. "Was yer business to steal a horse?" His voice rose to an unhealthy volume for Bond Street. Though the stables were in the rear of the property, Christopher did not wish for Bertrand's accusations to reach the gossiping ears of the *ton*—or even worse, a Bow Street runner. Nor could he even pretend to have business on the busy street frequented by many of his acquaintances, for fear of being apprehended in his father's stead.

Caught between the glare of the crusty stable hand and the wanton eyes of a vixen, he opted to flee to his room. Again. Perhaps he could leave during the night. "Once more, it was never my intention to steal a horse. I have business on Bond, but suddenly do not feel well. I think I shall retreat to my bedchamber." He shot a warning look at Rachel and wasted no time hustling back up to his room.

Relief spread through him when he saw that his letter to Cedric and the jewels sat undisturbed beneath the bed. Fatigue made his eyes droop once he took a seat on the bed. He looked at his watch. "Three o'clock. What has become of this day?" He had thought to be back in Pueblo by now, but eating a late breakfast, being waylaid by a delusional woman, and attempting to execute an escape—and failing—had stolen precious hours from him. He felt hopelessly trapped. The bed beckoned. With the limitations Cedric's servants had imposed upon him, and the impossibility of walking the busy London streets, he gave in to the call and lay back on the pillow. He'd rest his eyes and work through a solution in is head.

A servant's tap at the door woke him from a deep sleep. Evening had fallen, plunging his room into darkness. Still in a fog, he reached to turn on the nightstand lamp, only to have his hand bump into a candle. Oh yes. No electricity. How easy it had been to get accustomed to luxuries of the twenty-first century, and how difficult he was finding it to function without them.

"Supper is being served," a voice on the other side of the door said.

Supper? He'd fallen asleep. For how long? He had no hope of avoiding his uncle now. He blew out a frustrated breath. "I will be down straightaway." He fumbled to light the candle. Without a change of attire, he couldn't dress for supper, and the clothes he wore were rumpled. Once the candle shed some light, brightening the room a bit, he did his best to smooth his clothing and comb through his hair.

"There you are, my boy. I feared you might never wake but decided against rousting you prematurely. You obviously needed the sleep. Are you well?" asked Cedric.

He'd missed it—his chance to escape to the future, and all because of a vindictive woman and a suspicious stable hand. Anxiety constricted his chest. His family and Arianna had surely panicked by now. If Father had been such a genius, why hadn't he created a machine that could travel in time increments less than a year, making it possible for Christopher to return the jewels at his leisure, then travel home earlier the same day? Or even the day before? He cursed the limits of the time machine.

Taking a calming breath, he set thoughts of the

people waiting for him in the future aside. He could get through dinner, then be on his way. "I'd no intention of sleeping so long. But I assure you, I am well." He forced a smile.

Cedric sat at the head of a long table. His grin warmed Christopher's heart. "I must admit I am happy to have someone to dine with." Cedric motioned to the empty chairs lining both sides of the table. "It gets lonely without Meredith and the girls along. They chose to stay at our country manor whilst I attend to business here."

Christopher, unsure of which seat etiquette dictated he occupy, hesitated to sit. The last time he'd eaten at his uncle's table, he'd been just a lad.

Cedric turned to the butler, who awaited his instructions. "Another setting over here." He pointed to a seat near him. "No sense in shouting across the room." His smile broadened. "I had Cook prepare a special meal for our…reunion."

Resigned to the fact that he'd not be leaving any time soon, and grateful once again he'd found Cedric and not Robert in London, Christopher put his anxiety on hold and prepared for the feast the wonderful smells wafting through the room promised. As the food came out with the butler instead of Rachel, he breathed a sigh of relief. Cuisine from his past he'd nearly forgotten appeared on one dome-covered dish after another, beginning with savory soup. Roast pork and potatoes followed, accompanied with rolls slathered in creamy butter, and sweet pickles. How he wished Arianna were sitting at his side. She would relish every moment dining in this glamorous room, enjoying this elegant fare. His heart warmed thinking of her. He missed her.

Finally, eclairs were served for dessert, and Christopher thought he'd entered the gates of Heaven.

"Christopher." His uncle's voiced pulled him from the trance in which the food and thoughts of Ari had put him.

He looked up, still chewing the pastry.

"We need to talk about your father." Cedric's voice, which had been jovial moments before as he spoke about certain members of the gentry and their unique idiosyncrasies, became serious.

He knew it was inevitable. The topic of his disappearing family had to surface. Christopher had weighed his options throughout the meal and decided he would try honesty with his uncle. After all, if anyone knew of Father's genius, it would be his brother. "Yes, about that. I wish to explain, but may we retire to the bookroom to do so?" He glanced around the dining hall, which, other than himself and Cedric, was empty. However, he knew servants hovered nearby. And at this point, besides his uncle, he trusted no one.

Cedric's gaze followed Christopher's. "You wish to keep your secret from my servants?" He chuckled. "I do not believe they will take an interest in your father's whereabouts, but if that is your desire, we can move to the bookroom."

Christopher let out a breath. "Thank you."

They finished the meal, then Christopher followed his uncle through a winding corridor and into a wood-paneled room. Once again nostalgia made it hard to breathe. Cedric had sent someone in ahead to lay a fire and light the lamps. The butler placed a chair before a mahogany desk. Christopher took it, sitting across from his uncle.

"That will be all, Lund," Cedric said in a tone that made it clear he wished for privacy. The butler bowed and left the room.

Despite the flames that crackled behind him, the chill in the air—another reminder of the bygone era—caused Christopher to miss the twenty-first century with its modern furnaces. *How many mornings did I rise early enough to lay the fires for my family?* He hadn't resented the extra chore ere his workday began; he had, however, resented his slumbering father—always too hungover to do much of anything productive before midday.

"So, your father?" Cedric interrupted Christopher's resentful musings.

Casting a glance at the door to ensure his story remained in the room, Christopher began to convey the tale from the time he'd been summoned home from Cambridge to the present.

"A time-traveling device?" Cedric's voice rose.

Christopher squirmed, knowing even the thickest of walls could not contain his uncle's loud declaration.

Apparently recognizing the discomfort on Christopher's face, Cedric lowered his tone. "Surely you jest—or have you lost your mind? Time travel"—he scoffed—"not possible. Is it?" Cedric arched a brow.

Chapter Nineteen

Cedric's questions came too quickly for Christopher to answer. He waited until his uncle had processed the information. "I assure you, I am quite sane. My family has been living in the twenty-first century in America."

"America?" Cedric's face puckered, as if he'd eaten a lemon. "Fitting. Many criminals are sent to America. But you—" He shook his head, obviously biting back his words. "And what do you mean by the twenty-first century?"

"I know it's hard to believe; but it's true. America is not the continent of criminals you might envision. 'Tis very modern and well-accepted—even by the British." Christopher narrowed his eyes, studying his uncle's face. *Does he believe me?*

Cedric's expression gave nothing away. He just motioned his hand for Christopher to go on.

"Father continued to use his device to trot across space and time, committing heists, and even murders. While I was finally able to extricate Mother, Sarah and Joshua from his grasp, he escaped the law and fled to yet another destination." Christopher pushed his hand through his hair. "I cannot restore a stolen life, but I have been returning as many of the purloined articles as possible by using his device. That is why I have come to London."

"What has happened to you, my boy? I fear you have lost all bearing on reality. No one can travel through time—not even Benjamin Somerset."

Christopher let go of a frustrated breath. Any amount of explaining he offered would not explicate the seemingly impossible. "I've spent five years trying to understand it myself. Look at this." He tugged a cell phone from his pocket. Of course it did nothing but light up, but that was enough. "This is called a telephone. I speak to other people on it."

Cedric's body jerked and his mouth dropped open, reminding Christopher of his own reaction to the future and all its surprises.

"I can also look up historical events and other information when I'm in the twenty-first century. I have a screenshot—er…picture—of the article about you." He flipped through his photos, grateful he didn't need internet or cellular service to access them. He handed the phone to Cedric.

His uncle eyed the phone suspiciously before taking it from Christopher. Instead of reading the article, he turned it over and over in his hands, his face lined in concentration. "I do not comprehend. How can it be possible?"

Christopher wasn't certain if Cedric spoke of the phone or of the time-traveling machine. He supposed he'd have the same answer either way. "I wish I could tell you, but I don't understand it myself. Nevertheless, my tale of being whisked away to the future is true."

Cedric returned the phone to Christopher as his gaze moved to the doorway. "What is it?"

"Your port, my lord." Christopher cringed at the sound of Rachel's voice, and he tucked his phone away.

He hadn't heard the door open. *I wonder how long she's been standing there. And what did she hear?*

Cedric motioned her in.

Christopher kept his eyes forward, preventing her from spearing him with one of her wicked glares.

She placed the port on the desk between the two men, dropped a curtsey and quit the room.

Cedric filled his own glass, then looked at Christopher, raising his brows in question.

"Thank you, no." He had to keep his mind sharp for his travel home tonight.

"How did you free your family, Christopher? What happened?"

He mulled over how much of the long tale Cedric needed to hear, desperately wishing to hurry and be on his way back to the twenty-first century—and Arianna. He settled on a condensed version, summing up his relationship with Ari, as well as his father's attack on her, which had resulted in both Father's escape and the family's freedom. "You see, I am anxious to hasten my travel back to America because that is where my family and Arianna await my return. We plan to be wed soon." He heard a hiss, which put him on edge. Glancing around the room, he saw no one other than Cedric. The fire cracked and fizzled. He tamped down his anxiety and continued, still unsure if his uncle believed any of his story. "The device is already set for my journey home. I need only to dig it from the hay in your stable."

"I see…" Cedric took a slow swallow of his wine. "I do not wish to prolong your stay here, but I fear I must. There is an important matter we need to discuss that has nothing to do with your father."

Christopher's chest tightened. The urgency to leave

caused his heart to beat double time. He fisted his hands in his lap. Did his uncle not hear him say that his loved ones anxiously awaited his return? "What is it we need to discuss?"

"I sense your desire to flee this place…and, if what you are saying is true, this era." He took another sip of port. "I've many questions still about that and how it is even possible. But right now, I must remind you of who you are."

Christopher lowered his brows and tilted his head. "What is it you mean?"

"As you know, I have four children. All daughters—not a son in the lot of them." He shook his head. "You and your brother are the only remaining males in the Somerset line. You, Christopher, will be the next Earl of Hemington. Therefore, you must stay in England to take your rightful place among the peerage." He paused, regarding Christopher with sober eyes. "Do not think on this casually; 'tis a solemn responsibility."

Christopher's quick-beating heart thudded to a halt. He felt blood drain from his face. The thought hadn't entered his mind about his remaining cousins being female. Bearing a title had never been important to him—not in the nineteenth century; not in the twenty-first century—but he knew people such as Cedric—and his father—viewed it as a profound obligation of privilege. Tossing the responsibility aside would be equal to trampling on something sacred to his uncle. He didn't wish to be disrespectful.

He massaged his temples as he contemplated an appropriate response. The candle flame nearest him danced a merry dance, mocking his discomfort. It sent shadows to and fro across his uncle's features, causing his demeanor to change with the light and dark. How appropriate. 'Twas both fortune and ill-fate to have found Cedric here this morning.

He reflected on his attempt to leave earlier. "You said my family's name has been ruined as a result of Father's crimes. I would never be accepted by the peerage or London Society. I daren't even walk down a city street for fear of being apprehended."

"That was true of today, but tomorrow I will attempt to persuade the members of Parliament of your innocence. We shall merely need to concoct a believable story of where you have been these past six or seven months." Cedric raised his brows, a flicker of hope shining in his eyes.

"There is more," Christopher said. "One of the jewels purloined in the London Diamond Emporium heist came from the Royal family. A ruby. I believe it had been stolen, then pawned at the Diamond Emporium."

His uncle grunted.

"You see, the officials will trace the jewel to the Diamond Emporium, deduce it was stolen by my father...and—" He shook his head and lifted his hands.

"What is it, Christopher? What's going to happen?"

"They will apprehend you for the crime. That is why I had to bring the jewel back."

"And you know all of this because of that thing?" He pointed to Christopher's pocket, wrinkle lines creasing his forehead.

"Yes, look." He pulled out his phone again and brought up the picture of the article once more. He handed it back to his uncle.

Cedric held a looking glass up to the screen this time and silently read the words promising his death. All color drained from his face. "This cannot be. How can such a fortune-telling contraption exist? 'Tis possessed." He dropped the phone.

Christopher plucked the phone up. "In the twenty-first century, history is easily accessed. I do not have time to go into details, but on the fifteenth day of this month, you will be hanged. That is, unless we get the ruby back to the Emporium before the officials investigate it." The words came out in a tumble. Christopher's heart shook in his chest. He had no idea how to read the blank look on Cedric's face. Did he believe him? Would he help him?

Cedric finally spoke. "Let us say what you are telling me is the truth. Once we deliver the ruby and pull my feet out of the boiling water your father so kindly put me in, will you consider staying?"

Christopher fidgeted before meeting Cedric's gaze. Finally, he stilled his hands and cleared his throat. "My duty to my family is of greatest concern right now. I fear leaving them to flounder in the future would be irresponsible, not to mention cruel, on my part." He ended it there but knew keeping his promise to Arianna was another primary motivator. He longed to be with her more with each passing minute. However, he doubted his nineteenth century uncle would understand love and family over title and duty.

Cedric let out a breath and took another sip of his port. "Then go back to…America and return here with them all. Your family does not belong in some futuristic world in which my brother forced you."

"What about my fiancée, Arianna?"

"You are not married to the girl yet. Surely she will understand the importance of carrying on the Somerset name." Cedric's face took on a sharpened edge Christopher had never before seen. "I am certain you will find a suitable match here in London equal to the chit in America." His eyes burned with determination.

Christopher stood, unable to listen to his uncle any longer. The anger which had been building below the surface reached a boiling point. "Arianna is no ordinary girl—certainly no chit. I cannot leave her. I do not mean to be disrespectful, but I never wished to be the next Earl of Hemington, and I will not marry anyone but Ari. I only came here to save *your* life." He strode to the door.

Cedric remained at his desk, but Christopher sensed an undercurrent of anger and frustration emitting from him.

"If you will excuse me, I must be going now. I fear I have tarried here far too long." He paused at the door, noting its angle slightly ajar. *If Rachel heard anything, all the more reason to leave immediately.* His pulse throbbed. Holding the door frame, he dropped his head, willing himself to calm down and get back in control. Anger was a trait he wanted nothing to do with—a trait Father's actions had taught him to loathe. But staying and becoming the future earl was not an option. He must leave—and leave now. He turned back to Cedric. "Will you accompany me to the stable, or shall I use force against your stable hand?"

A shadow of resignation crossed Cedric's face. He put his glass down and rose. "Very well, then. Let us not resort to violence against the poor man. He is one of my most faithful servants. He plays a good role, but you gave him a fright when you arrived this morning."

Some of the knots which had formed in Christopher's stomach untangled a fraction as he heard Cedric acting more like the kind uncle he'd known. Still, the urgency to leave prodded him to move along quickly.

"I must admit I shall be fascinated to see this traveling device you claim my brother created," Cedric said as they passed through the corridor and to the back door of the townhouse, grabbing a lantern along the way.

By his tone, Christopher was convinced Cedric still didn't have confidence in his story. He didn't blame him.

"If anyone other than you had presented me with such a fanciful tale, I would have had them sent to the madhouse. But you have always been honorable—despite the deplorable role model you had." He let out a derisive snort. "What is it constructed of? Did you employ a silversmith?"

"It is made of metal. You'll see." Realizing he could answer all of Cedric's questions and still not convince him of the device's reality, he rushed ahead, hoping to show instead of describe the machine.

As they entered the stable, the smell of horses and hay filled Christopher's senses. He strained in the darkness, expecting Bertrand to appear. "I guess your stable hand sleeps after all." He let out a low chuckle and watched as the air escaping his mouth turned a frosty white. When he pivoted back to face Cedric, he noticed worry lines forming on his uncle's forehead. "What is it?"

"Probably nothing. It is only…Bertrand does sleep,

but he is very protective of the horses, and his senses are heightened such that noises quieter than a rat on the prowl usually roust him." He scanned the stable, holding the lantern higher in front.

Bertrand didn't emerge.

Cedric sighed. "No matter. Let us see this device."

The mound had shrunk since Christopher had created it. He narrowed his eyes, suspicious, but set to work digging at it. "I carved out a spot right back—"

"Is there a problem?" his uncle asked.

A horse whickered in the background as if to answer Cedric.

The chilly air made Christopher's fingers numb, but that was the least of his worries. His stomach twisted, and his blood ran cold. "Someone has removed it. We must find Bertrand."

"I am certain Bert has not touched your machine." Cedric wedged in beside Christopher to help dig.

"It was right here." Christopher pointed to an indentation which looked to have been filled in haste by a scattering of loose hay. "If Bertrand didn't remove it, perhaps he will know who did." Panic rose, but he willed himself to remain calm. He took a breath of freezing air.

Cedric stood and commenced a search for the old stable hand. "I will look in the saddle room—he has a cot there." He entered, shouting for the man, but then came out of the room shaking his head.

"Perhaps the carriage house? Or the grounds?" said Christopher. I'll circle around the house in this direction." He motioned to the north.

"And I shall do likewise to the south. Surely, he will be found patrolling the property."

It was unusually cold for October. Christopher plodded through the withered shrubbery and bare trees surrounding the large manor, the ground crunching beneath his boots. Precious time ticked away with every beat of his heart. He must find his device and get out of London. Where was Bertrand?

"Ho there!"

Christopher startled at the sound of Cedric's voice. He stepped aside, avoiding a collision with his uncle.

"I found no one. You?"

Christopher shook his head.

"There is a room for him just inside the house." He pointed to the servants' entrance. "He sometimes takes his meals there. Perhaps the cold air drove him inside."

Christopher wrinkled his brow in question. "Why didn't you say so? Surely he's inside on such a chilly night." They'd wasted nearly thirty minutes tromping around the large townhouse and gardens.

"Bertrand rarely uses his room, unless Cook summons him there. She hates for her creations to be spoiled by the cold...and the smells of his regular environment. I daren't tell her, but I honestly don't think he tastes the food anymore. He lives and breathes horseflesh."

Christopher crossed the grounds and yanked on the knob Cedric had pointed to. It didn't budge. "Do you have a key?"

Cedric tugged a ring from his coat pocket and wasted no time finding the correct key to the door. He pushed it open. "Bertrand?"

Christopher followed close behind with the lantern.

Aha. There he was. The stable hand lay draped on his bed, snoring.

Cedric called his name again.

"I thought you said he was a light sleeper."

"He is. Something is amiss." Cedric gave the old man a not-so-gentle shake. "Bertrand!"

"Wh…what…what is it, m'lord?" Bertrand sounded groggy and gruffer than he had that morning.

Even at a distance, Christopher could smell stale liquor on his breath.

"Are you ill, man?" Cedric's voice rose in alarm.

"N—no, sir." Bertrand looked around the room, disoriented. His eyes landed on an empty glass sitting on a small table. He rubbed a hand across his face then gave his head a good shake. "I was just enjoying the port ye sent down for me."

"I sent you no port." Cedric crossed the room and picked up the empty glass. He stuck his nose in it and made a sour face. "Did you not notice the bitter taste, you fool? This drink was dosed with laudanum. Who gave it to you?"

Bertrand's face began to pale. "Cook gave it to me. She said one of the housemaids received instructions from ye to bring it thus."

Christopher's heart lurched, and a chill made its way up his spine. Only one housemaid would do such a thing. But why?

Chapter Twenty

Arianna knew her stiff smile didn't reach her eyes as she listened to Joshua regale her with his memories of London. She was trying to be attentive to his recollections and anecdotes of a bygone era, but worry gnawed her nerves raw. At one time she would have devoured his every word about nineteenth century London—a time and place she found enchanting—but today his attempts to humor her only added to her frustration.

She realized Joshua had quieted and was staring at her with dark, penetrating eyes.

"Would you like to play a game?" he asked.

Caught. She'd been rude to only allow him half her attention.

Giving his arm a sisterly squeeze, she shook her head. "I think I've played more games since arriving here than I've played in my entire life. Thank you for the offer, though." She patted his shoulder. "I know you're trying to keep my mind occupied, and I appreciate the effort. What do you suppose happened to Christopher? He has been gone far longer than any of you expected. By the looks you exchange with each other, I can tell you are all worried."

Beatrice and Sarah, who'd been busying themselves in the adjoining kitchen, dropped what they were doing and came in to join the conversation.

Beatrice pulled Ari into a hug.

She hadn't realized how rigid with apprehension her body had become until she felt soothing arms around her.

"My dear girl, you are correct. I believe we all wished to spare you our anxiety. I, for one, am relieved you brought it up. I can no longer pretend I am not frightened. He has been away far too long."

Sarah's head bobbed in agreement, and Ari saw her eyes fill with tears.

A lump grew in her throat. *What has happened to Christopher?* She covered her mouth to stifle a sob.

Joshua looked at the clock on the wall. "It is past two in the morning in London. It should have only taken hours, not days to accomplish his task." He looked as if he might cry with the others, but then cleared his throat and continued. "He was delayed in Florence for an equal amount of time. I do not think we should panic."

It might be too late for Ari; after hearing their admissions, she was already alarmed.

A rumbling noise made her jump.

She watched a smile spread across Joshua's face. "It's him! He's back!" He sprinted for the study, the rest of the family and Ari close behind.

Her heart thudded. A giggle reverberated through her, imagining herself in Christopher's arms again. Now they would be free to plan their wedding—free to plan the rest of their lives. The trips to the past had finally ended. No more worries. She exhaled, and her heart felt lighter than it had since he'd proposed marriage. An invisible weight had been removed. A weight she hadn't realized had grown into a heavy burden. The mass had now lifted, and she couldn't keep the smile from her face.

The ground continued to shake in the study. Arianna reflected back to the time she'd been in that very room when Mr. Somers had employed the use of the device, which had been frightening, but paled in comparison to when he'd overpowered and kidnapped her. She shuddered at the memory but didn't let it quell her excitement to see Christopher.

"Christopher!" Joshua yelled through the trapdoor.

Silence.

The vibrations had stopped, and they all waited, impatient to hear his deep, comforting voice. Especially Ari.

She crowded in beside Joshua and hollered down through the opening in the floor. "Christopher. We've all been waiting for you."

More silence.

"I'm going down there." Joshua descended the ladder.

Ari couldn't help but follow, Beatrice and Sarah trailing close behind her.

The lab's chemical odor assaulted Ari's senses. She almost turned back as bile rose up in her throat, the memory of her last visit through the trapdoor, nearly paralyzing her with fear. Again, Beatrice's comforting arms came around her.

"You do not need to stay down here. Christopher told me what you went through at the hands of my husband. It is unforgivable."

Ari trembled within Beatrice's embrace, then remembered why she was down here—Christopher. She shook herself to rid her mind of the memories that plagued her and put her fears aside. "Thank you. I think I'm all right now."

She turned to face Josh and Sarah who both wore confused expressions. Her eyes dropped to the disc—the empty disc. She gasped. "Where is he? Where is Christopher?" Her hands flew to her mouth.

Joshua shook his head. He looked up at Ari, brows furrowed and eyes full of fear. "Why would he send back the machine…empty?"

Panic clutched Arianna's heart.

"What about the vest? Perhaps he sent the disc and is returning with the vest," Sarah said, climbing onto the disc to investigate, careful not to touch any dials that might send her to another place and time.

Another vest? Ari dared to take a breath and let go of a fraction of the alarm she'd felt. "What are you talking about? Christopher sent your father away wearing the vest," she said.

"Remember what I told you earlier, Ari? Christopher and I constructed a new one in case of emergency. He said he'd leave nothing to chance this time," said Josh.

"That's right, but this time?" Ari tilted her head.

"Yes." Josh lifted a shoulder and let it fall. "Because of you. He said he'd stop at nothing to return to you, Arianna."

Tears burned her eyes. "Then he must be coming home in the vest?"

"I'm certain he is," said Joshua. "Check the bin, Sarah."

Sarah complied. Her face fell into a frown. "Oh no. It is still in here. And it appears he sent a note."

Arianna's heart froze again. If the disc and the vest

were both here, that left no possible way for Christopher to return. She twisted her fingers together.

"What does it say, dear?" Beatrice's shaking voice cut into Ari's thoughts.

Sarah began to read aloud. "My dearest family, Providence has truly been my companion on this voyage, as I have had the good fortune to find my dear uncle, and now earl, Cedric. He has reminded me of the obligation to king, country and family that now rests on my shoulders. I am to be the next Earl of Hemington. I have thought long and hard about this and feel it most prudent to rid myself of any temptation I may have to return to you; thus, I am sending this evil contraption back to where it came from. I am sorry I cannot come in person to explain, but I am certain you will understand."

Sarah paused. She looked up, a perplexed expression tugging at her brow. "Why would he do such a thing?" Moisture filled her eyes and spilled over her lids. "He cannot leave us here to fend for ourselves in this horrid time. We will perish without him. Surely he knows this to be true."

Arianna felt her own tears coursing down her cheeks. None of it made sense.

"Please continue," Beatrice said in a watery voice.

Sarah lowered her head and read on. "I have also had the good fortune to be happily reunited with Miss Rachel Cartwright. We have rekindled our love for one another and plan to be wed shortly."

Sarah squinted her eyes while she scanned the note. "There must be some mistake. It is unbelievable. I cannot comprehend why he would—" Her voice hitched. She dropped the note and brushed past Joshua, leaving her words dangling.

Complete numbness took possession of Arianna. She couldn't move or speak.

Joshua picked up the letter and read the rest in silence.

"This is impossible," Ari said, her voice barely a whisper.

"What does it say, Josh?" Beatrice moved closer to her son.

"It says he is happy with his decision and we should all be happy for him, as well. He says to tell Arianna—"

Ari finally found her voice. "What does he say to tell me?"

Joshua's gaze met hers and then dropped again. He shifted his weight from one leg to the other.

"What does he say to tell me, Joshua?" She reached for the paper, but he pulled it back.

His voice cracked as he read the remainder of the letter: "Tell Arianna I'm very sorry, but I had forgotten what true love really is. Now that I have found it again, I daren't leave Rachel's side, lest I lose her once more. She is and always has been my one true love. Yours, Christopher"

Ari's knees turned to rubber. She steadied herself against the wall. Her stomach twisted into so many knots, she knew it was only a matter of time before she vomited.

Beatrice must have sensed her distress. She grabbed the nearest pot and handed it to Ari.

It reeked of chemicals. The smell was all it took. Ari retched and retched some more, until there was nothing left in her stomach. Tears fell into the pan, mingling with her vomit. Her entire body shuddered in wracking sobs. The odor of old memories combining with new, painful information—a lethal mixture.

She fell to her knees and buried her head in her hands. Warm arms encircled her, but they couldn't remove the chill in her heart.

Chapter Twenty-One

"Rachel!" Christopher knew the servants were asleep but didn't care about disturbing anyone. He'd had enough of Rachel's games and needed to retrieve his device before something untoward happened to it. Thoughts of Arianna and returning to her propelled him forward. He would knock down every door in the servants' quarters if he must to find Rachel—the person standing between him and getting home—and, more importantly, to find the device.

"Christopher, who is Rachel?" Cedric asked. His breaths came out in pants, having to trot in order to keep stride with Christopher.

"It is a long story, but she is working in your employ and I am certain she is the housemaid that dosed Bertrand, as well as the person who stole my device. I must find her. It's late. I can take care of the problem from here."

"I will help. I cannot leave you until the matter is settled."

Christopher nodded and pushed open a door.

A girl shot to a sitting position in her bed.

Christopher held the lantern up to see if it was Rachel.

"Why are you in my room?" The housemaid who'd been working with Rachel earlier squinted against the light and pulled her blanket to her chin.

"Where's Rachel?"

The girl looked to her right at the empty bed next to hers. "That is her bed. I've not seen her all evening. I thought she might be with you…since you are to be married."

Christopher blew out a frustrated breath. "Rach…Miss Cartwright lied; we are not to be married. Do you have any idea where else she might be?"

The girl's eyes widened, and she shook her head. "She…she said something about making certain the wedding happened sooner rather than later."

"What did she mean by that?"

Even under the small beam of the lantern, Christopher could see the girl's face redden. His stomach twisted as her meaning became clear. "Never mind. I will find her." He exited the room and the servants' quarters, fists clenched.

Cedric trailed behind him. "Why does the girl think you are marrying her?"

Christopher turned to his uncle. "That's a tale from a childhood misunderstanding. Miss Cartwright's mother worked for you before she passed. I knew Rachel as a youth."

Cedric raised his eyebrows. "I see."

"Please, Cedric, let me handle it from here."

"Very well. But if you need further assistance, I will be in the bookroom." Cedric pivoted and headed toward the study.

Christopher wasn't surprised to find his room unlocked. Somehow Rachel had access to every part of his life here in this house. He wondered when she had become so manipulative. Perhaps she always had been, and he'd been blind to it. His disgust for her intensified.

He threw the door open and looked around with wild eyes. She wasn't in the front room. He entered the sleeping quarters and pulled the curtain around his bed. He scowled at the sight of her.

Rachel's lips turned up seductively. She patted the empty spot next to her. He felt anything but sympathy for her now. "Get out of my bed," he ground out.

"You mean *our* bed?"

"Get out of my bed and tell me what you've done with my device."

Rachel's mouth fell into a pout. "Come now, Christopher, we're no longer children."

"Where is my device, Rachel?" Anger heated his face like a roaring bonfire. "If you weren't a lady, I'd throttle you." He narrowed his eyes. "Come to think of it, you aren't a lady." He advanced toward her.

Her eyes bulged, clearly frightened by the anger that now sparked from Christopher's very being. She raised a hand to ward him off. "Stop! I will leave!"

"Where is my machine?" He emphasized each word, lest she misunderstand his meaning, or his intense frustration.

She scooted out of bed and adjusted her nightgown. Moving out of Christopher's reach, another wicked smile curled her lips. "You will not be needing your *machine* any longer."

He took a step closer.

She put up a hand to stop him. "Think before you do anything foolish. One cry from me and everyone will believe you have ruined me. Then you shall be forced to marry me. In fact, I thought to seduce you, but since you seem to be unwilling, letting everyone believe it happened will have to do. H—"

Christopher clapped his hand over her mouth. She was of the working class, which made her threats hollow. Still, he didn't need undue attention. "Tell me what you have done with my device. I do not wish to hurt you." He knew he could never truly harm her, but if she screamed, he'd restrain her somehow. "I will release your mouth, but if you so much as speak above a whisper, I will wring your neck. Do you understand?"

Rachel nodded.

He slowly moved his hand from her mouth to her shoulders. "Speak."

"'Tis hard to draw air with your hands so near my neck." She made a forced choking noise.

"Speak!"

"All right, all right. I sent your device back to whence you came. Or so I assume."

He stiffened. No, that would be impossible. "How would you know how to accomplish that?" He glared at her.

She rolled her eyes. "I may have overheard you talking to your uncle about where you stowed it and that you had already set it to return to America. All it would take was the turn of a dial, you said."

Abhorrence built in Christopher with every word he heard her spew. He tightened his grip, inching his hands toward her neck. "And the vest?"

"What vest? I didn't rummage through your belongings. I am not a snoop." She let out a snort and tried to push his hands away.

When she gagged, he realized his fingers were dangerously close to squeezing the life out of her. He loosened them a fraction. "What will my family do? They need me," he said more to himself than her.

"Do not fret, I sent a note."

His heart froze. "You what?"

"I said, I sent a note from you explaining that you were to become the next earl."

Christopher was so angry he didn't care what she did any longer. She could yell or scream—life as he knew it had ended when she'd cut off his transportation home. He pushed her onto the bed. "Tell me every word you wrote in that letter."

She rubbed her throat and hauled herself into a sitting position, then pulled her knees to her chest, looking like a frightened mouse on the big bed. Her voice was small as she recited the letter. "I did my best to imitate your writing. I've kept all your love notes. So, you see, Christopher, you are now free to marry me."

Christopher pointed to the door. "Get out."

Rachel scrambled to her feet and fled to the exit. She stopped and glanced back at him, perhaps hoping he would reconsider.

"*Get out!*"

She disappeared, slamming the door behind her.

He sat on the edge of his bed and buried his face in his hands. Thoughts of his family believing he'd deserted them when they needed him most shot pain through his head. Thoughts of Ari believing he'd not return to her, and worse, believing his declaration of love for another woman, shot pain through his heart.

Chapter Twenty-Two

Josh tossed the note into the trashcan.

Ari thought she saw a tear escape, but he quickly swatted it away. She wasn't the only person devastated by Christopher's actions.

Christopher's actions—something didn't fit. Or was it that she didn't want it to fit? Moments passed while she attempted to digest the unfathomable.

"Would you like help up the ladder?"

A voice jolted her from her thoughts. "…Uh…ladder?"

"The others have gone. I asked if you'd like help up the ladder." Joshua's face had become a blur.

She squinted at him to force his features into focus.

He cleared his throat, which had sounded clogged. "You need to get out of here." He motioned to the lab. "So do I. Would you like help?" He held a hand out to her.

Fog filled her head, and she thought she might be dreaming. On wobbly legs she made it up the ladder and into the study. Numb from head to toe, she stood beside the heavy desk, her eyes following the pattern on the rug beneath her feet.

They replaced the rug; it's very nice. She tilted her head and began to hum. The pattern swirled in subtle tones of creams and browns. Round and round they went. The room dimmed as the swirls contorted into odd shapes. They morphed into angles with jagged edges piercing her consciousness. The room began to spin. Ari ducked to avoid a sharp edge aimed at her head. Where she dodged one, three more came at her. She put a hand up, knowing the effort futile. The saw-like figures exploded into thousands more. The room had become a whirlwind of lights. She lost her balance and the funnel opened, swallowing her whole.

"Arianna."

"Christopher? Is it you?"

"Yes, I am here." Christopher caught her just in time. He cradled her in his arms, stroking her hair.

Tingles shimmied down her spine.

He still wore the same clothes he'd worn when he'd proposed to her—buff-colored pants met his leather boots, and a black waistcoat and jacket that starkly contrasted with the white cloth wrapped around his neck. So handsome.

She gazed into his azure-blue eyes and the chill in her heart began to thaw. "I had the strangest dream."

When he moved a fraction, a sunbeam hit her face. A gentle breeze whispered through the shrubbery nearby, carrying the soft scent of barberry through the air. Strange, she thought she'd been inside. No matter. All was well with Christopher's strong arms holding her.

He looked away.

"Is everything all right?"

He turned back to peer down at her. "Oh, yes. I am happy you came."

"Came?"

Bells jangled in the distance, and a smile stole across his handsome face. "Are you well? Can you stand on your own?"

Ari loosened her grip on him as he steadied her on her feet, but she remained clinging to his arm. The bright rays made her squint. "Where are we? Is that a church?"

"Of course, my dear. Where else would we hold a wedding?"

Chills zinged up, down and sideways through her body. Her skin tingled with excitement. "So, it's true. The day has finally arrived?"

"The day *has* arrived. Come, my love. 'Tis time for us to be wed."

Ari's eyes darted to a female standing behind Christopher; she wore a pale pink gown with a shimmery overlay. Her hair, piled atop her head, looked to be held together by tiny, white roses.

The woman placed a gloved hand on Christopher's shoulder. He turned toward her, putting his free arm around her waist.

Ari let her arms fall lifeless to her sides.

"Yes, love. It is time." He crooked his arm for the woman to take.

Nausea curdled Arianna's stomach. Her knees buckled, forcing her to the ground. "Christopher?"

He glanced back. "I am so happy you came to share in our joy." He continued walking to the church.

The contents of Ari's stomach heaved. She attempted to stand, but the ground below jerked her back down. Grasping the bush nearest her, she clung tightly so she could vomit without notice. Her body shuddered and shook. "Why? Why? Why?" She lifted a hand to wipe her face, stopping short when she saw pricks of crimson dotting her palm. They grew into great drops until forming a pool in her hand. *The barberry. There are thorns in the barberry shrubs.* They were not only planted for their pleasant appearance, but also to keep out the wildlife.

She laughed aloud at the thought. *I'm the wildlife.* Murmurs from the wedding goers met her ears, but only caused her to laugh louder. She couldn't stop. She clapped a hand over her mouth to quiet the noise.

A woman shrieked, "She is a demon!"

"No...I'm not a—" The metallic taste of blood hit her tongue. She cringed, then laughed again. "Maybe I am a demon." Her laughter morphed into something foreign to her ears, then settled into wracking sobs.

"Ari." A hand gently nudged her. "Arianna, wake up."

Ari sat up bolt straight and looked at her palms. "Where...where is the blood?"

Sarah stared at her through swollen eyes. "Blood?"

"Where is Christopher? Is he married?"

A moan escaped Sarah's mouth. Tears spilled down her cheeks. "You were having a nightmare."

Ari let out a great sigh. "A nightmare? That explains everything." Her shoulders sagged. She smiled at Sarah, but Sarah looked pained. "What is it? Did Christopher come home? How long did I sleep?"

Sarah's hand shook as she lifted a handkerchief to her own bloodshot eyes.

"Sarah?"

Between her sobs, Sarah spoke, "Do you remember nothing about the letter Christopher sent to us?"

Shaking her head, Ari lowered her brows. "No...no, that was a nightmare." How did Sarah know about her haunting dream? Christopher must be downstairs—*her* Christopher. Surely he'd made it back by now. To be in his arms again... She smiled with anticipation. Her mind at ease now she'd awoken to realize her nightmare hadn't been at all real.

"You have been asleep for hours. You...uh...swooned in the bookroom and Joshua brought you up here to your bed. I only woke you because of the strange laughter we heard." Sarah tilted her head and narrowed her eyes. "Will you be all right?"

She shouldn't worry about me, Ari thought. Sarah was the one who looked out of sorts... Why? The letter... Fear picked at her consciousness like a partially healed scab. "But...no, it must have been a dream. Christopher would never—"

The hollowness of Sarah's puffy eyes cut her off short. Cold dread spread through her body. Not a dream, then. Christopher *had* found someone in the nineteenth century he loved more than her.

Something shattered inside—she was certain it was her heart.

"I will get you some tea." Sarah turned to exit the room.

"No, Sarah. I need to go. I'm sorry I fainted...or, swooned. I just need to leave." Although her mouth felt like cotton, she feared putting anything in it would come right back out.

Sarah stood in the doorway while Ari gathered her belongings. Her movements felt wooden, but at least the room no longer spun. When she was satisfied she'd packed everything, she looked up to see that Beatrice and Joshua had joined Sarah.

"Please don't leave like this." Beatrice walked

toward her and pulled her into her arms.

The comfort she expected to feel didn't come. Beatrice was kind, but she wasn't Ari's mother. Her mother was dead—because of Beatrice's husband. Ari held no malice toward Christopher's mother—she had been a victim of her husband's cruelty, too. But she couldn't pretend to feel reassurance that wasn't there.

So many thoughts tangled in Ari's mind—thoughts of her history with the Somers family. Thoughts of Christopher. *I'm stronger than this. Why can't I pull myself together?* This wasn't her first breakup…yet, somehow it hurt so much worse than the others. Why?

Because Christopher is the man I've waited for my whole life. The man sent through time to love me and share my hopes and dreams, as well as my ideals. The man I've pledged my heart and soul to.

She needed to clear her head. She needed air.

"I'm sorry. I really can't stay. Everything about this place reminds me of Christopher. He's made his choice and"—her voice cracked into a sob—"it's not me." She backed away from Beatrice and walked as fast as her wobbly legs would carry her down the stairs and out the door.

The cold autumn air slapped her face. Reality stung, but she needed to confront it.

Confusion and a foggy brain had her driving erratically. She knew she was pushing on the accelerator too hard but didn't care. Didn't care if she sped, didn't care if she crashed, didn't care if she died.

Flashing red lights forced her to slow to a stop.

"License and registration," the officer said through her open window.

His uniform caused a tremor in Ari's heart.

When she supplied the requested documents, he narrowed his eyes. "Have you been drinking, miss?"

"No. I've been crying because of a man like you—a man who pledged to protect and serve. Only he didn't—"

"Ma'am, I need you to step out of the car."

Ari pushed out an angry breath, then shoved open her door and stood in front of the officer. "I'm not drunk or high. Please, officer, I'm just tired and I want to go home."

Despite her pleadings, the officer still insisted she walk a straight line, then gave her a breathalyzer test. "Looks like you're clean." He ripped a speeding violation ticket from his pad. "Slow it down."

Somehow she made it safely to her apartment in Denver. It hadn't been easy to focus through the tears that had continually filled her eyes, clouding her vision.

She nudged the apartment door closed behind her with her foot and headed straight for bed. She shouldn't have been tired after her long nap, but the exhaustion was undeniable. Weaving through the room, she found her bed, crawled between the covers and let sleep take her away.

Morning rays of sunshine entered her room uninvited. Ari pulled the comforter over her head, unwilling to face reality just yet. A few moments later, she realized it was no longer the weekend. She managed to locate her purse, which had fallen to the floor, spilling its contents, and let her fingers drag through the scattered items until they stumbled onto her phone.

It blinked "low battery" at her.

"Hopefully there's enough for this call."

"Johnson and Tate Design Firm, this is Brittany." The high-pitched receptionist sounded every bit as perky as Ari knew she acted.

Ari stifled a groan. "Brittany, it's Arianna. I'm not feeling well and won't be in today."

She didn't know what Brittany's response was; she hung up before she'd have to listen to her chirpy voice again.

Burrowing into her feather pillow, she closed her eyes. *I wish—I wish I'd never met him.* She blew out a puff of air, allowing her muscles to loosen and meld into the bed. Every inch of her body gave way to fatigue, seeping into the mattress until there was nothing left of her—nothing left to hurt.

Chapter Twenty-Three

Christopher paced the room.

With both the disc and the vest gone, he could find no solution. The lantern he'd carried into his bedchamber earlier, guttered. He barely noticed. *I must find a way to get a message to Ari.* He continued to walk, occasionally knocking into a piece of furniture—the room so dark and unfamiliar. He remained unfazed and concentrated on the problem at hand.

Certain he'd worn a hole in the rug and weary from the miles he'd trod across the floor, he fumbled around and located a wooden chair. The thought of even sitting on the bed made his skin crawl. Rachel had ruined the bed. Rachel had ruined his life. And by now, Rachel had probably told anyone she could roust that he had ruined her. No, tonight the discomfort of a hard chair to rest on would suffice.

While he allowed his fatigued limbs a break, his mind continued to puzzle a way out of the predicament in which he found himself. A good portion of the time centered on self-condemnation for thinking it had been a good idea to travel back to nineteenth century London. Oh, to have a second chance; to reconsider that idea. Without a time machine, there would be no second chances. Ironic.

Another portion of time he'd spent reconstructing the machine in his mind. However, without Father's notes, or Joshua's help, there were gaps in his knowledge. *But I must try. There is no other option—unless…becoming the next Lord Hemington—*"No. That would not help. I must return to the twenty-first century now." He pounded the arm of the chair. "I must return to Arianna." His heart felt as though it had shattered into a million pieces, imagining Ari reading the note Rachel had sent. He groaned.

It would be a risk, but he'd need to leave his uncle's townhouse in the morning to go in search of the chemicals necessary to get the machine to work. He was fairly certain he could recall which ones were needed. The device itself, however, would be more difficult. Having helped Josh construct the vest, he had a general understanding of the science behind its success; however, the vest was made of an extremely light metal alloy. Material that did not exist in the nineteenth century—to his knowledge. He pictured the large steel plate that originally transported him to the twenty-first century and blew out a long sigh. How would he duplicate that?

The questions buzzed around his mind—rapidly at first, then slowed into a blurry zigzag of random thoughts. Finally, he could no longer keep his head upright or his eyes open. He'd just rest them for a moment. He let his body slouch in the wooden chair, certain he wouldn't fall asleep in such an uncomfortable position.

A rap at the door brought him to his senses. The sun spilled bright rays into his room, causing him to squint. He jerked to his feet at the realization he had fallen asleep. Moaning at the crick in his neck, he shook his head in an attempt to clear the fogginess. The knock came again, this time louder, demanding his attention.

"Come in." Christopher hoped Cedric was on the other side, but to his dismay it was Rachel. He wondered how she dared approach him again after what she'd done.

"Thought you might be hungry. You did not come down to break your fast, so I've brought toast and tea." She put the silver tray on a small table in the dressing area, then pulled up a chair and sat.

Nothing she did shocked him any longer. How had he ever fallen for her charms in the past?

"Well?" She arched her dark brows.

Food was the last thing on Christopher's mind. And seeing her made his stomach turn. "Thank you, no. Leave me." He walked through the room and gazed out the window, folding his arms across his chest. The gardens were within view but had withered to an ugly brown from the cold weather. *They are as wilted as my heart.*

"You look as if you haven't changed your clothing since yesterday."

Like a lingering illness, the woman persisted.

Christopher had his back to Rachel, but her voice increased in volume, warning him she was moving closer. He took a calming breath to squelch his urge to lash out at her. The anger he'd felt the night before gave him pause. Only his father had ever unleashed Christopher's ire. Normally quite temperate, he didn't like his reaction to Rachel and wouldn't repeat it. It achieved very little to storm about—he'd learned that at a young age from Father. Still, her very presence put him ill-at-ease.

"What is so special about your little American

paramour—or whatever she is? What does she possess that I do not? Does she come from a titled family—are we back to that? Because I thought you were above such small-minded reasoning."

He shook his head but continued to stare out the window. "She is not my paramour—we are not lovers. You wish for me to list her virtues. They are lofty when stacked against your own."

A humorless laugh escaped her lips. "Oh, I see. Poor Christopher is brooding. He spent all night attempting to discover a way out of his predicament." Her voice reeked of sarcasm.

She moved beside him, but he refused to look at her.

He could imagine the mock pout she wore. He'd seen it often—whenever she didn't get her way. Memories from his past welled up. Rachel had been his childhood sweetheart, but she'd also been manipulative. It took being on the receiving end of her exploitation to remember.

He felt fingers stroke his arm.

Her touch repulsed him. He jerked away from her.

"There is a way out." She spat the words. "But only one, and you know what it is."

He finally turned to face her and narrowed his eyes. "You honestly think I would marry you after everything you have done to ruin my life?" He wouldn't marry her even if Arianna weren't waiting for him in the future.

She tilted her head and raised her chin. A look of defiance lit her eyes. "You made a promise, Christopher. I intend to see you keep it."

"I'd sooner die than marry you, Rachel."

Her face blanched. Motionless, she waited, glaring at him. Perhaps hoping he would change his mind. When he didn't speak, her lip curled into a sneer. "You would rather die?" She snorted. "So be it." She turned and pushed past him, exiting the room.

Christopher waited only a few moments before he stepped out, locking his door behind him—as if it even mattered—and set off in search of his uncle.

"Lord Somerset had an early meeting today, sir," the butler said as he examined a spoon. The young housemaid Christopher had woken the previous night sat across the table from the butler, polishing a knife. The butler turned to the girl. "You must be thorough, Meg. It appears you missed a spot." He pointed to the handle of the utensil and handed it to her.

Frowning, she muttered, "Yes, sir." She inspected it, turning the spoon over and over again, but never seeming to locate the spot.

Christopher realized she never raised her eyes to his. Either he'd embarrassed her last night, or Rachel had concocted a story about him. Whichever it was, it made him uncomfortable being in his uncle's townhouse with people he didn't know or trust. He'd have to take his chances on the streets of London.

He pulled his coat up high around his neck, and tipped his hat down to hide his face, grateful for the chill in the air. Bond Street was uncharacteristically quiet. *Most upper-crust shoppers must still be asleep.* He didn't waste too much time wondering where everyone was; he knew he didn't have time to waste. Walking straight to number 143—Savory & Moore—he paused, taking a deep breath before entering. He was certain he would be recognized there; the company had once employed his father. It hadn't lasted long and had ended poorly, as Father had been more interested in using the chemicals for his own inventions than for Mr. Moore's or Savory's. Christopher scowled. It was a risk, but he knew of no other place to find the needed chemicals.

He rubbed on the frosty glass, then peered in to see if he recognized anyone.

A face peered back, startling him.

He jumped backward as the door opened.

"Christopher Somerset? Is that you?" A smile spread across the man's face.

Christopher let his stiff frame relax a fraction. "Yes, Mr. Moore, 'tis I."

"Come, come." Mr. Moore pulled Christopher through the door and to the crackling fire.

Christopher took a furtive glance around, ready to bolt if he had reason to.

"No need to be so cautious. 'Tis only me. Haven't you heard? There is a hanging at Newgate Prison. The whole of society is there to witness it."

Christopher's stomach knotted. He knew it wasn't his uncle ready to hang, but if things didn't change, it would be soon.

Moore shook his head. "I cannot fathom why folks wish to witness something so brutal." He dragged two chairs to the fire and motioned Christopher to sit. "I imagine you haven't many chums left in London, after what your father did." He inclined his head and raised his brows.

"No. I don't imagine I do. It was a risk coming to see you, I will admit."

Mr. Moore chuckled. "I never thought you played a

part in the heist, though disappearing with your family did not help your case." He craned his face to the rear of the shop. "Mavis, bring some tea. Service for two."

Christopher froze. He'd learned the hard way that he couldn't trust anyone—especially the help.

Mr. Moore must have sensed his hesitation. He said in a low voice, "Mavis is recently here from Scotland. She knows nothing about the heist. So, tell me, what *did* happen all those months ago?"

A graying, middle-aged woman appeared bearing a tray with the requested tea for two. After filling the cups, she dropped a curtsey and left the room.

Once he knew she was out of earshot, Christopher recited the story—including the time travel—pausing in his telling to allow Moore to express his doubt.

Moore waved his hand, motioning him on. He was, no doubt, the only person apart from his family who would believe his father could actually create a time-traveling device.

In fact, Christopher thought, *he'd probably inadvertently helped Father.*

Moore's eyes widened as Christopher spoke. He lifted the cup to his lips and took a slow swallow as he appeared to be digesting the story. "Chemicals, when used correctly, can be mighty powerful. One can never be too careful." He took his glasses off and rubbed his eyes. "But time travel? I never thought I would see the day. Your father is a genius—I'll give him that."

"You believe me, then?"

Moore put his spectacles back on his nose. "I witnessed Benjamin tinkering with some odd chemical combinations while in my employ. I shall never forget how he had the store vibrating one afternoon. He would never tell me what his end goal was. And then"—he shrugged—"it was necessary to let him go because of the missing items—again, chemicals potent enough to create powerful propulsion. And to think all that time he'd been working on a time-traveling machine."

"I am very sorry for the materials he stole from the store. I have some coins. Please allow me to repay you." Christopher yanked a pouch from his jacket pocket.

Mr. Moore waved a hand. "Bygones. I wish to hear more of your adventures. You say you have traveled back from America—two hundred years in the future? All this to keep your uncle from hanging?" He gave his head a slow shake. "I always knew you were a man of honor. So unlike your father."

Christopher let out a breath of relief. He'd liked and admired Mr. Moore in the past, but after some of the shenanigans his father had pulled, he didn't know how well he would be received at Savory & Moore. He took a sip of tea, letting the warmth spread through his body before he began to explain the reason he'd come. "I fear that trouble follows me. My device—rather, my father's device—has been stolen, sent back to America, and I've no way to return. That is why I'm here. I don't know if I can do it, but I must try to recreate the machine my father built. May I purchase chemicals from you?"

A bell jingled, signaling a customer. Moore stood immediately, and Christopher tugged his hat down to hide his face. He felt his arm being pulled and realized it was Moore. "I believe what you are looking for is back here, sir," he said, loud enough for the customer's benefit. Christopher followed Mr. Moore to an unoccupied, small room. "Have a seat. I'll return shortly," he whispered.

Christopher nodded and sat on a stool to wait. His gaze floated across the room, landing on shelf after shelf of labeled bottles. He rose back to his feet and began perusing the vials, reading each chemical name. *I wish Josh were here. He is far more adept at chemistry than I'll ever be.* He squinted to read the tiny longhand, surprising himself when he located two of the chemicals right away. He continued looking for the rest.

"Mr. Somerset." A large man wearing a constable's uniform and a scowl filled the frame of the tiny room. His loud, bass tone nearly shook the bottles out of Christopher's fingers.

Christopher met his intense stare but said nothing.

"Are you Mr. Christopher Somerset?" The deep voice caused the room to quake, right along with Christopher's heart.

Christopher looked for Mr. Moore but could see nothing beyond the massive officer. "Yes, I am Christopher Somerset."

"Then you are coming with me." The burly constable yanked Christopher past a dumfounded Mr. Moore, who held both palms up. An apologetic expression on his face.

Two Bow Street runners waited near the entrance of the shop. Christopher overheard one say, "Judge'll have him swinging before he can say not guilty." They both laughed. The constable never broke stride, pushing him through the room and out the door.

Chapter Twenty-Four

A loud knock brought Ari out of her trance. She'd spent the last few days in a haze.

"Ari. It's me, Tasha." The voice on the other side of the door was loud enough for the entire apartment building to hear.

Ari gave herself a mental shake. *Why would Tasha be here?* Her boss didn't generally make house calls. She shuffled to the door and cracked it open. "Tasha? Is everything all right?"

"That's what I came here to find out. Are you going to invite me in?"

"Oh, yeah. Sorry." She opened the door wide enough for Tasha to enter.

"You've been out all week." Tasha furrowed her brows and appraised Ari. "What do you have? Is it contagious?" She lifted a hand to Ari's forehead. "You don't feel warm."

"I've been out all week? What day is it?" Ari closed her eyes to conger up the date, or even the month. How long had she been living in a daze?

Tasha led Ari to the sofa, then took a seat next to her. "It's Friday. You really must be sick." She glanced around the disheveled room, a confused expression on her face.

"Why didn't you just call, Tasha?"

Tasha's lip pulled into a tight line. "I did. Where's

your phone?"

Ari looked around until she spotted it on the table. She began to rise, but Tasha gently nudged her back down.

"I'll get it." She retrieved the phone and pushed some buttons. "Just as I suspected—it's dead. I've called you every day this week. What's going on? This isn't like you."

Ari shrugged. "I think it must be a virus—the flu, or something." Or, more accurately, heart problems— *it's broken.* Her gaze dropped, and she began to wring her hands, unaccustomed to lying. "I'm feeling much better today. I'll be in on Monday." She'd wasted far too long wallowing. Tasha was right; it wasn't like her—none of it. Always conscientious, she'd never skipped out on work because of a heartache.

Tasha narrowed her eyes, looking unconvinced. "Are you sure? You're pale. Don't rush back to work on my account. I was just concerned. I'll bet Christopher has been going out of his mind trying to reach you. Where's your charger? I'll plug this in." Tasha held up the phone.

Hearing Christopher's name sent a tremor through Ari's body, and her eyes burned. She located the charger and gave it to Tasha.

"Thanks. Now I'm going to fix you some lunch. You look like you haven't eaten in days."

In truth, Ari couldn't remember the last food she'd had. She mumbled something about being too sick to eat, while Tasha jumped into action. She closed her eyes and willed the tears away. Her feelings were too raw to expose. She'd need time to collect her wits, now that she'd been awakened to how pathetic her situation was.

"Do you think you can handle some chicken noodle soup?" Tasha's voice floated above the sound of pots and pans clanging together.

Ari expected the notion of eating to make her stomach sour, as it had been doing all week, but she was happily disappointed. "Soup sounds perfect. Thank you."

"I'm not leaving until I know you've eaten. I don't know what you've got, but the only time I've seen you look worse was when you were in the hospital in Pueblo."

Ari winced at the reminder. Memories of her bruised and swollen face drifted through her mind—Mr. Somers' handiwork. Hopefully she didn't look *that* bad.

Tasha watched as Ari sipped soup from her spoon.

The hot liquid burned her tongue and throat, but somehow soothed her soul.

"Can I get anything else for you? Does Christopher know how sick you've been?" Tasha asked.

She treated Arianna like a daughter, and Ari loved her for it, but she couldn't bring herself to open up about Christopher just yet. "The soup hit the spot. Thank you, Tasha. And Christopher...he's been in Europe for...work." It really wasn't a lie. He'd initially gone to London to work on freeing his uncle. Tasha didn't need to know the details. "I'm sure he'll be by when he returns to the states."

"Hmm, I didn't know he traveled for work." She shrugged. Seemingly satisfied with Ari's progress, Tasha cleaned the dirty dishes and prepared to leave. "Promise me you'll call if you need anything?"

Ari nodded.

"Don't come back to the office until you are completely well. There are plenty of germs lying in wait to get us now that the weather has turned. You'll only get sicker if you return before you're ready." Tasha pulled on her black parka. "I've sent Evan out to check on your project. I hope that's okay. I couldn't reach you to ask about it."

Ari squeezed her eyes shut. How could she have been so irresponsible? She'd never left a job hanging. "Of course. I'm so sorry, Tasha. I'm certain I'll be better by Monday."

Tasha gave her a quick hug, then exited.

Ari was grateful for Tasha's visit. She'd been numb to reality long enough. Why had she let Christopher completely disable her? "This isn't me. I can rise above this heartache." She couldn't keep the tears from falling, but she could stand by her resolve to move forward. He hadn't given her a choice.

Retrieving her partially charged phone, she dialed Maggie's number.

"Ari, is that you? I've been trying to reach you for days," said Maggie.

"Yeah, well I've been...under the weather." The real reason for Ari's absence from life was eating her alive. If she couldn't tell Maggie the truth, who could she tell? She needed to confide in someone. "Actually, can we meet for dinner tonight?"

Ari heard a puff of air hit the phone. "I'm so relieved. I've been worried about you. The Grille at seven?"

"Sounds good."

Arianna arrived early for dinner. What did she have to detain her? Certainly not a toddler to ready for bed, or a husband to kiss goodnight. After Tasha had left, she'd spent a fair amount of time cleaning her musty apartment, which had gotten stale and a bit untidy from total neglect. Cleaning had energized her but did nothing for the ache in her heart. A thirty-minute shower had helped a little. Her determination grew.

"You look horrible, Ari." Maggie scooted into the booth seat adjacent her. "Should you be out of bed? Are you still sick?"

"I'm fine, Maggie, but thanks." Ari knew the sarcasm in her voice wasn't called for, but sometimes Maggie was too honest.

Maggie's brow creased. "Sorry. I've just been worried."

Arianna shook her head. "It's all right. I'm not sick—or, at least, not contagious."

"Then where have you been all week? And"— Maggie yanked Ari's hand up to examine her finger— "where is your engagement ring?" Her eyes widened. "Did you and Christopher have a fight?"

Despite her resolve to keep her emotions in check, Ari couldn't keep the tears from spilling. "No, we didn't fight, but we did break up." She swiped at her tears with a napkin.

Like a revolver, Maggie's questions shot out one after another, piercing Ari's heart. Perhaps it was too soon. After all, Ari hadn't thought through a plausible explanation… Because there wasn't a plausible explanation.

After every question had gone unanswered, Maggie cocked her head and studied Ari's face. "I'm gonna kill him."

"Well, good luck finding him, Maggie. He's gone."

"Gone? Gone where?"

"Uh...to England. He decided he missed London too much."

"But, his fam—"

"His family misses him, too, but somehow we will all survive without Christopher," Ari said, her voice sounded flat. If Maggie only knew how much his family needed him. Arianna had told her only the most basic details—that the family had relocated from London; his father—the very man she'd spent the previous year working for—was a criminal who'd nearly killed Ari and was now missing; and that Christopher had been nothing but a faithful defender of his family through his father's misdeeds...and a literal savior to Ari.

Until now.

"That makes no sense at all. And it's completely out of character for him to up and leave." Maggie shook her head before taking a sip of her soda.

Maggie was right. Nothing about the situation made any sense. It certainly didn't fit with Christopher's character. Yet she'd been there when his note had arrived. *It is what it is.* She lifted a shoulder, then let it drop. "I agree, Maggie. But can you just help me get through it? There's not much I can do with him in England." Two centuries ago.

"Call him. Or better yet, let me call him and give him a piece of my mind. It's just been a few weeks since he proposed to you! You were so happy." Maggie began punching numbers on her phone. Ari thought of stopping her, but knew her call would go straight to his voicemail, and that would save her an explanation.

An hour later, Ari didn't feel much better, but said

goodbye to Maggie and made her way to her car. Telling the truth—the real story—might be the only way to move forward. She'd thought about it tonight, but no matter the phrasing in her mind, it never sounded believable.

"Wait, Maggie!" she hollered across the parking lot. "Maggie!"

Maggie closed her car door and crossed the lot to where Ari stood next to her Subaru. "What is it?"

"I need to tell you something." Ari motioned to her car, and Maggie slid into the passenger side.

"What? Did Christopher text with an apology between here and the restaurant?"

Arianna wished he had. Better yet, she wished she'd wake up and find the whole thing had been a nightmare. "No. But I need to tell you where he really is."

Chapter Twenty-Five

Maggie's eyes shone with a mixture of curiosity and confusion. "Christopher's not in England?"

"He is. That part is true, but he's in England"—Ari swallowed hard and took a deep breath—"he's in England two hundred and five years ago."

Maggie's face creased in further confusion. "What?"

"You don't have to believe me, but please let me tell the story from the beginning."

"Please do. This I'm dying to hear." The sarcasm in Maggie's voice did nothing to reassure Ari, but she'd opened the door now, there was no turning back.

She began with all the secrets Christopher had kept from her and his fascination with the house.

"Yes, you told me that before, but you said it was because the Somers were his family and he didn't want you to know so he could stop his father from criminal activity without you getting hurt. Not that it worked." Maggie huffed and shook her head before going on. "Now you're saying he was looking for a time-travel machine?"

Ari shrugged. "I told you it would be hard to believe."

"Sounds like a long story. Start the car so we don't freeze to death."

"Really? You'll listen, then?" Ari turned on the

ignition, aiming a vent at Maggie.

"Of course I'll listen. I'm your best friend; I'll always listen."

It was true; Maggie always listened. Ari doubted, however, that listening would translate to believing.

Like a corked fountain finally unstopped, the entire story rushed out of Ari's mouth, fast, as if she'd have burst if she didn't let it go. "And now he's back in London with his childhood sweetheart, planning a wedding."

The expression on Maggie's face was unreadable. Ari had seen surprise, shock and doubt display in her eyes through the telling, but now that she'd finished—laid bare all her secrets—Maggie's face looked blank. Just blank.

"Say something, Maggie."

"I—I don't know what to say."

"Say that even if you don't believe me, you'll stand by me and let me cry on your shoulder. Christopher is marrying somebody else." Hot tears burned Ari's eyes.

Maggie pulled her into a hug. "I'll always stand by you, Ari. You know that. I just need time to process everything you've told me. I want to believe you. I do. But you've been through a lot, and that can really mess up your mind. I mean, being attacked by the man whose fortress you spent months decorating, then getting engaged to his son." Maggie shook her head and let out a breath.

"…But?" Ari arched her brows. Maggie had more to say. It was written in the pensive expression etched on her face.

She took one of Ari's hands in her own and gave it a gentle squeeze. "Just give me a few days. To process everything, you know?"

Ari nodded. Maggie wouldn't believe her. Why would she? The whole thing sounded crazy. But voicing it *had* helped—a little.

She barely heard Maggie shut the car door and then drive away in her own. Something Maggie had said in the restaurant had wormed its way through Ari's consciousness and remained. *It's not in Christopher's character to desert his loved ones.* The past five years were proof of that. Could the note have been some kind of hoax? A spark of hope flickered.

Ari had allowed shock and hurt to completely smother her. Now that she'd come up for air, she knew Christopher would never betray her trust. A sudden urgency to prove he hadn't left her rejuvenated her. Wherever he was, she'd find him and fix this.

Instead of driving home, she aimed her car south and pressed on the gas. She arrived at the Somers' house in record time, hoping to find someone still awake. After a timid knock went unanswered, she sagged down to the ground against the door. If only she'd kept her key to the house after the decorating had ended, she'd be able to sneak in and blast off to 1814. She needed to repair this.

The door opened, throwing her off balance. "Arianna? Why are you here?"

"Josh." She stood and clutched the door frame. "Sorry if I woke you."

He ran a hand through his hair. "I haven't been sleeping much lately."

Ari thought of her week of nothing *but* sleep. Josh must handle shock differently. Well, she'd had enough sleep. It was time for action.

"Why are you here?" Josh repeated as he motioned for her to step in.

The house was dark. Only a candle burning atop a sofa table shed a tiny beam of light. "You still use candles, Josh?"

"Sometimes." He lifted a shoulder and let it fall. "Old habits." He sat down and motioned for her to follow suit. "So?"

"Oh, right. I'm here because…well, I can't accept that Christopher is gone for good. I'm going to use one of the devices to find him." The speech, which had sounded better in her mind, didn't appear to impress Josh.

He shook his head and expelled a breath. "You are in denial, Arianna. You must acknowledge what he did and move on."

How could he think that? Didn't Josh even care enough to discover the truth? "No one needs to go with me, but the more I think about it, the more certain I am that Christopher didn't write that note."

"Then who did? Arianna"—Josh put a comforting hand over hers—"the note named *you* specifically. Who else would know about you besides Christopher? It has to be real." Joshua's voice had risen and then cracked. He regained his composure and spoke more softly. "I am not going to let you use one of those machines. They are dangerous."

"What is—" Beatrice entered the room. "Oh, Arianna. Are you well? 'Tis very late." She rushed to Ari's side, her kind eyes appraising her.

"I'm sorry, Beatrice. I'm having a difficult time accepting Christopher's actions. I want to go find him—bring him back home. But Josh doesn't agree."

Maybe Beatrice would see reason. She wouldn't be risking anything by allowing Ari to take one of the devices.

Tears filled Beatrice's eyes. "Sweetheart, Christopher is dead."

A cold chill slid the length of Ari's spine at her words.

"He chose to live out his days in the nineteenth century; therefore, to those whom he left behind, he is dead."

Ari realized for the first time that both Beatrice and Joshua's clothing—even Bea's nightgown—were black. Were they in mourning? How had they accepted Christopher's disappearance so readily?

"It would be best for everyone if you accepted this and moved on. Would you like to spend the night here?"

"No." No to accepting Christopher as dead and no to staying the night.

Beatrice's already teary face crumpled. Ari winced inwardly at her harsh response.

"I'm so sorry. I didn't mean to upset you, Beatrice. It's"—she shrugged—"I guess you're right. I apologize for bothering you both." Ari hugged Beatrice, then fled. She needed air. The Somers' mansion was beginning to feel like a morgue.

As she closed the door behind her, she heard Beatrice call out, "Ari, think about what I said. 'Tis unhealthy to deny the inevitable."

Tears gathered in Ari's eyes as she slid into her car. She pounded the steering wheel. "Christopher isn't dead! He might be detained; he might have even decided to stay in the nineteenth century to become an earl…and marry someone else." She sobbed. "But he's not dead."

Her drive home was a noisy one—in her head. Irritation with the Somers for mourning their son ping-ponged with thoughts that they might be right. Then there was the possible betrayal by the man she'd pledged to love—and trust—forever. Everything collided in her brain.

Sleep refused to come as thoughts and feelings about her situation continued to haunt her. After her parents and brother had been killed, she had experienced similar feelings—overwhelming grief. She was all too familiar with the stages. Yet, this felt different—even worse, somehow. She didn't think anything could be worse than losing her family—they were gone forever. A chill in the room had her tugging her comforter up to her chin. So was Christopher. Not only was he gone, but he was with another woman. Betrayal hurt worse than death. When her family had died, consoling arms had wrapped around her, cards of sympathy had arrived in the mail, and flowers covered every surface in her home.

She ached to be held, to be consoled, to be told things would get better. "But things won't get better." She sat up, grabbed a water bottle on her nightstand and threw it across the room.

Chapter Twenty-Six

Fate had either dealt Christopher a stroke of luck or misfortune. With only eight trial sessions held per annum, having one scheduled only five days after guards had first dragged him through the doors of Newgate Prison, felt like a blessing. To escape his filthy cell—even for a short time—lifted his spirits. However, it likely brought him several steps closer to the gallows, as well.

The Old Bailey was full of spectators, as numerous people crowded into terraced, wooden pews that stepped up to meet massive pillars. Christopher wondered how so many so-called witnesses had appeared to finger him for a crime he did not commit. Then the reason became clear. The constable who had arrested him plunked the bag of jewels in front of the judge.

"Is this what you have been looking for, Your Honor?" He held up a large ruby.

"The very stone." The judge glared at Christopher. His nasally voice didn't fit his distinguished demeanor. "You've many accusers. I will hear their testimonies first; then you may speak in your defense." He let out a snort, which Christopher knew meant the trial was over before it had begun.

He needed his uncle. Surely an earl would carry some weight in proceedings such as these.

A slovenly dressed man approached the judge. "Sir, I am John Wainsworth, Senior. This man killed my son. My only son." He sniffed and brought a handkerchief to his eyes.

"No. I did not kill anyone!" Christopher blurted out. His nerves sparked and sizzled. To be accused of theft was one thing. But murder? Unthinkable.

"Silence!" The judge rubbed the back of his neck, just beneath his wig, in an apparent effort to calm himself down. He proceeded to speak in a quieter voice. "I will tell you, Mr. Somerset, when you may speak." He pelted Christopher with a dagger-like stare.

Clenching and unclenching his fists, Christopher's heart dropped, sinking deeper with every accusatory word. It didn't matter what he had or had not done. Thanks to his father, many people were happy to put a noose around his neck, just to make someone pay. He couldn't let that happen. His family waited for him in the twenty-first century. Arianna awaited and trusted him. He glanced at the door he'd been dragged through wondering if he had the strength to push his way back out. The glare of the armed guards standing between him and the door suggested he not try.

Mr. Wainsworth's raspy voice interrupted Christopher's desperate scheming. "I've no one left to care for me in my dotage."

Cries of sympathy rose in the courtroom.

After he finished his tale, the owner of the London Diamond Emporium spoke. "I do not know why Mr. Somerset has kept the jewels all these months. One would expect a thief to rid himself of the evidence against him. At the very least, sell them for profit. But I can say for a certainty that these are the jewels stolen

from my establishment on April seventh of this year."
He shot Christopher a hateful glower. "How the king's
ruby came to be at the Emporium, I cannot say." He
stepped back, allowing the next accuser the floor.

"Your Honor."

Nausea twisted Christopher's gut at the sound of
Rachel's voice. Deep down he'd suspected her to be at
the crux of this fiasco.

She continued, "After having his way with me"—
disapproving murmurs rippled through the crowd and
Christopher was speared with murderous glances—
"this man told me he had committed the heist at the
Diamond Emporium, and he begged me to escape with
him. He said we could live like royalty from wealth the
jewels would bring us." She paused as if trying to
remember her rehearsed lines.

Christopher's skin crawled at the sound of her
deceitful speech, spewing poisonous lies on all who
would listen.

"I must admit to having been momentarily tempted
by his velvet words," she added, "but being a lady of
honor, I declined."

Christopher closed his eyes and shook his head.
She was far from a lady, and honorable? He snorted in
disgust.

No longer mixing cockney into her dialect, she
spoke in the perfect diction she'd learned, having
grown up with his own cousins. Her voice unnaturally
doleful, she continued, "He would not take no for an
answer, so when he left the premises to make plans for
our future, I informed the authorities. I was horrified
when the Bow Street runners located the gems beneath
his bed." She wrinkled her face in dismay and blew her

nose. "I had hoped he'd fabricated the tale to impress me." She batted her wide, hazel eyes at the judge, her lips turned down in a pout.

Such theatrics. Christopher wished to throttle her. How had he ever fallen for Rachel's charms? Even a boy in his teen years should have sensed her deceitful ways. Such a contrast from Arianna.

The judge rubbed his neck again. "Are there any other accusers?"

A rumble rose from the crowd.

"I mean to say, are there any more accusers directly affected by the actions of this man?"

The crowd quieted.

Somewhere in the courtroom a chair toppled over, the sharp thud sounding from wall to wall, echoing anguish in Christopher's heart.

He longed to be back in the twenty-first century, where even if he had committed the crimes of which he'd been accused, he'd receive a fair trial. His word against the whole of London gave him very slim odds.

"Mr. Somerset, what say you?"

Christopher flinched. Finally allowed to speak, words failed him. He couldn't very well tell the Judge the truth about his father transporting him and the jewels through time. He'd have to settle on some form of it. "Your Honor, it was not I who committed these crimes. Nor did I have knowledge of them until it was too late—"

"Hang him! Hang him! Hang him!" the crowd erupted. Several pieces of debris sailed through the air, aimed at Christopher—an overly ripe tomato nearly hitting him.

The judge quieted the taunts. "Do you have anyone

to stand up for you?"

Mr. Moore shouldered his way to the dais. "'Twas his father who committed the crimes, not Mr. Somerset. This man somehow risked his life escaping with the jewels in an effort to return them and make amends. His father, Benjamin Somerset, should be the man standing before you today."

By the hissing noises, jeers and flying debris, Christopher worried for Mr. Moore's safety. He appreciated his testimony but knew it would not go far to help him.

"I'll speak for the boy." A hush fell over the crowd as Cedric materialized. He stood as erect and confident as the Archbishop of Canterbury.

"My Lord?" The judge's eyes widened.

Christopher held his breath. Could his uncle perform a miracle?

Cedric nodded and held his head even higher as he addressed the judge.

"Mr. Moore speaks the truth. Christopher Somerset is a man of honor and integrity. I will vouch for anything he claims to be true," Cedric said.

The judge cleared his throat. "My Lord, I have great respect for you, but we all know how your family name will be soiled if this man is found guilty."

The crowd made a loud hoot of assent.

"For that reason alone, I shall be forced to take anything you say with a grain of salt." The judge turned to face Christopher. "Where is your felonious father?"

Cedric cut in. "Your Honor. My brother, Benjamin, has already soiled the Somerset name. My nephew has come to London only to redeem it by returning the jewels. He risked life and limb to do so."

"Let the boy speak." The judge scowled at Cedric.

"I do not know." Christopher met the judge's steely gaze directly. "If it were possible, I would deliver him to you myself."

"But since your father has disappeared, you took it upon yourself to bring the missing jewels back to London and return them…because you are so *honorable*?" The judge waved his hand and shrugged his shoulders.

Christopher winced—his world caving in on him. "Yes, Your Honor." Nobody would believe his story about coming to save his uncle's life. Why would they?

"Have you more to say—perhaps something of merit?" The judge spat out the words.

Christopher flushed, the anger he'd felt moments ago turning to despair. "No…only that I am innocent."

The judge shook his head. "You have been accused of many crimes, Mr. Somerset—most are punishable by death. You say it was your father's deeds that landed you here, but your father is nowhere to be found to defend himself. You stand here alone; therefore I find you guilty." He brought the gavel down hard. "You will hang in three weeks' time."

The crowd cheered.

Cedric leaped across the room and clasped Christopher's arm. "I will continue to do all I can to get you out of this." Worry lines creased his stricken face.

Guards pushed Christopher away from Cedric and through the throng of angry faces.

Rachel moved close enough to whisper, "You should have married me." An evil smirk bent her lips up, but no mirth lit her expression.

Bile rose in Christopher's throat at the sight of her.

He had never experienced such hatred. It tore at his soul.

"You do not think these will be missed, do you?" She opened her hand just far enough for Christopher to glimpse several diamonds peeking out.

Before he could say anything, he was jostled out the door and into the transport.

Within minutes they shoved their way back through the entrance of Newgate Prison. He blinked several times in order to adjust to the heavy darkness. Darkness so thick he could feel it enshroud him like London fog. He nearly tripped over something, which squeaked as it skittered out of the way. He shivered. Passing the cell he'd occupied while awaiting his trial, he realized he'd had it easy then; the dank air only thickened as they plodded along. The deeper into the belly of the prison they walked, the stronger the stench of sewage became, until it nearly choked him.

The guard pried at a cell door. It let out a strangled creak as it opened. "Enjoy your new home, chap." He pushed Christopher to the ground. Several rats scattered. "Oh, does the wildlife frighten you? Well, they be your only chums around here, they do." He shackled Christopher's leg to a large steel ring, then closed the door with a resounding bang.

Christopher sat up and moaned. The foul odors were suffocating, and the crazed voices ricocheting off the walls made it hard to concentrate. He closed his eyes and conjured up Arianna's smiling face. A lump formed in his throat. *I must get a message to her, but how?* Thoughts of his impending death didn't hurt nearly as acutely as the vision of Ari reading Rachel's letter…and believing he'd chosen someone else to love.

Never. Never would he do that.

"Christopher." Cedric's strong voice broke through the odious noises surrounding him.

"Uncle?" Christopher rose so he could look through the small grated window of the heavy cell door. He took three steps toward the voice when the chains shackling him to the ground jerked him backward.

Light from a candle Cedric held barely illuminated the room. Christopher took in his surroundings, then wished he hadn't. The ground moved with rodents weaving through mounds of human and animal waste and moldy hay.

"Christopher, can you hear me?"

"Forgive me, Cedric. Yes, I hear you. I cannot reach the door, but I hear you."

"Do not think on the tales you have heard about Newgate, my boy. You must believe you will get out with your life."

Christopher shuddered, knowing exactly what his uncle spoke of. Everyone did. It was told that residents of Newgate—even prisoners not sentenced to hang— rarely came out alive. If the gallows didn't get them, disease was sure to—prison fever. He didn't know what to say in response. The evidence surrounding him authenticated the rumors.

"I have paid and will continue to pay for this cell. 'Tis better than the dungeon beneath the Keep where prisoners sentenced to die share their space—like cattle. Here, you at least have some amount of privacy."

"Thank you," Christopher choked out. He assumed Cedric paid for the honor of visiting him, as well. Prisoners convicted of murder did not receive visits from anyone other than the abusive guards.

"I will plead your case with Parliament. Trust me." Cedric rattled the door. "Do you trust me?"

"Yes." Christopher's voice was just above a whisper. He recalled saying those very same words to Ari. *She trusted me. I let her down.*

"You are imprisoned because you traveled here to save me. I will do my level best to return the favor. Just…just do not give up."

"I will not give up." He swallowed back emotion. "I am eternally grateful for your efforts on my behalf."

Cedric hesitated. "Godspeed, Christopher."

The light disappeared.

Chapter Twenty-Seven

The next morning Arianna braved the supermarket. It was a baby step but felt like a leap. Her debate about going had been settled by her growling stomach.

Rounding the corner to the canned foods aisle, she nearly ran into someone. "I'm sorry, I wasn't watching—Zach?"

"Arianna. It's been, what, a year and a half?"

It had been, and it hadn't ended well between them. Ari's initial excitement at seeing a familiar face ebbed, while memories of her ex-boyfriend—cheater that he was—replayed in her mind. It seemed more like decades had passed since she'd seen him; so much had happened between then and now.

The two clogged the aisle with their shopping carts full of groceries. Luckily, store traffic was light this morning.

The smile dropped from Zach's face as understanding registered. He cleared his throat. "Actually, I'm happy to see you. Ari, I need to apologize for the way I treated you. I could tell you I've changed and that you are the reason, but I doubt you'd believe me. Anyway, again, I really am sorry."

He sounded sincere, but Ari had fallen for his charm before. She appraised him intently. He looked even more handsome now than ever—same face, but something had altered...a look of maturity, perhaps?

"It's all in the past, Zach." She exhaled, releasing the hurtful memories of their failed relationship. "What's new with you?"

"Well, after being served a slice of humble pie—much deserved, I'll admit"—he shrugged as a sheepish grin tugged at his lips—"I spent some time evaluating my life."

Ari tilted her head, amazed at his words and more than a little skeptical.

"You see, I had taken for granted that you would always be there for me. I had even planned on proposing to you."

Ari coughed. She'd had no idea.

"Of course, you had that 'hands off before marriage' rule, which I foolishly decided was fine for you, but not me."

A blush heated her cheeks. In the beginning, she'd set strict moral guidelines for herself to honor her late mother's wishes. Now she did it for herself. She knew her old-fashioned values had kept many men away—except for Christopher. No. She couldn't go there. Mentally wiping Christopher's image from her mind, she shook her head and brought her thoughts back to the present. Still, to think it was okay to cheat on her because of her standards? That wasn't acceptable.

"Are you all right, Arianna?"

She nodded. "Sorry, go on."

"Once you were out of my life, I realized how much deeper, more meaningful, our relationship had been than any I'd ever experienced."

Wait…what did he say? This was not the same Zach she'd dated.

Her confusion must have shown on her face

because he chuckled at her expression. "I know what you're thinking, but it's true, you changed me. That's when I began an evaluation of my life and the standards I'd set for myself. I've gotta tell you, I came up pretty short. I had money, a fast car and women aplenty…but I didn't have the one thing—make that person—I wanted most—you."

A shopper squeezed past, forcing them to move closer together.

Zach had always worn expensive cologne, costly apparel and pricey shoes. Today his jeans looked worn, his shirt—a pullover—was devoid a name-brand logo and his sneakers looked like any other shopper's. Perhaps he *had* changed. She sniffed, certain he hadn't given up his designer fragrance. Nothing—just a clean scent.

"So, I sold my car and my condo and joined Dentists Without Borders."

"You what?" Now she'd heard it all. Shallow, worldly Zach had done something completely unselfish?

"Yeah. I'm sure you've heard of Doctors Without Borders. It's like that, only dentists."

"I know what it is. I—I'm just surprised, that's all." And now embarrassed to be acting so surprised.

"I've only been back in Denver for a few weeks."

"Where were you?"

"I spent a little over a year in El Salvador. The experience—helping others in such dire circumstances—made me see things in a whole new light."

"Huh." She had no words beyond that. Could someone like Zach truly transform into such a complete opposite of his former self?

"How about you? Did you get married while I was on the other side of the world?"

"I'm—" She glanced at her ringless finger. Her eyes burned. *I'm no longer engaged...or even seeing anyone.* The emptiness felt like death. "No." She blinked back threatening tears.

"Would you like to grab lunch and catch up sometime? Just friends, of course. No pressure."

It was all so surreal. The man who had cheated on and lied to her was now some kind of saint, and Christopher, whom she thought so honorable, had become...she wasn't sure what, but his status had plummeted. She could hardly wrap her mind around it.

"It's okay if you can't forgive me, Ari. I don't deserve you." Zach dipped his head and turned his cart. "I really do understand." He shrugged. "It was great see—"

"Wait. Yes, sure. We can grab lunch sometime." If Christopher was with another woman, Ari should be with another man. Yes. This felt right.

He let out a breath and his stiff posture relaxed. "Great. I'm just getting back into my old dental practice and it's kind of crazy, but I'll text you and we can set something up."

Ari nodded.

He closed the gap between them and pulled her into a hug. "It's really great seeing you."

His embrace warmed her. Nothing compared to the fire she'd felt at Christopher's touch. Perhaps she'd never experience that sort of sensation again.

****

"You're on the rebound, Ari." Over the phone

Maggie's voice sounded urgent, as if she needed to stop a train crash.

"He's different, Maggie."

"Leopards can't change their spots, and cheating men like Zach can't change their character. Mark my words, Ari. It might not happen overnight, but eventually Zach will return to his old cheating ways."

"Or is it that you've just never liked him?"

Maggie's voice rose. "For very good reason, may I remind you."

Ari knew Maggie was right, but she felt she'd been tossed a lifesaver, running into the changed Zach as she had. She wanted to cling to it until she was safely ashore. "It's just lunch. And I need a diversion—something that will keep my mind off Christopher."

"Be careful, sweetie. Your heart is fragile right now."

Ari's heart was beyond fragile. She'd hit that milestone and cruised right through the light to angry. "I need to go. My other line is ringing… I'll be careful. Thanks, Maggie."

Arianna hung up but was too late to catch the incoming call. Checking the phone log, she saw the missed call had come from Sarah. *She probably heard about my late-night visit Friday and wants to jump on board with everyone else and tell me to move on. Well, I am moving on.*

The heaviness she'd been fighting hovered once again at seeing Sarah's missed call, threatening to enshroud her. While she contemplated returning her call, her phone began to buzz, startling her. Sarah…again. A mix of emotions had her debating. She'd finally taken a step forward—away from the

Somers family. Did she really want to look back—even for sweet Sarah, whom she'd tried so hard to befriend?

No.

The phone continued buzzing. Ari watched it until it went dead, and Sarah's pretty face disappeared. Guilt made her heart heavy, realizing Sarah must have had Josh take her into town to make the call.

Before Ari could put the phone away and forget about her lack of manners toward Sarah, her voicemail notification beeped. Sarah had certainly come a long way. Just a few months ago she'd been afraid to use a phone, let alone leave a message. Christopher had done well tutoring his family about the twenty-first century. Perhaps that was why he'd felt he could return to nineteenth century England—his roots, his home, his lost love.

Ari began to feel sick all over again—heartsick.

She wanted to delete Sarah's message; pretend she'd never seen it, but concern for Sarah trumped her own pain. After all, Sarah was hurting, too. She pushed play.

Ari, this is Sarah Somers. Mother, Joshua and I are planning a memorial service for Christopher.

Shock vibrated from the phone to Ari's heart. A memorial service? She swallowed hard.

Sarah's voice sounded wobbly. There was a pause, then she continued: *We will be holding the service this Saturday at noon. Please join us.*

****

Arianna cursed her overactive conscience for guilting her into agreeing to attend the service for someone she knew wasn't dead. Well, maybe he was, but it felt more like he was living—and loving—in a different dimension.

She'd read enough books from the Somers' era to know she could only wear black to the service. However, she'd not be wearing it after today. The rules of London Society dictated that those in mourning wear black for a full year. Ari had thought a lot about that after her family's tragedy. Already depressed by their deaths, dressing in black for so long wouldn't have helped her dark frame of mind.

Beatrice led her to the parlor, which was draped in black satin. Ari flinched at the macabre atmosphere it created. Only candles burned for light, adding to the sinister air.

Josh read some verses from the Bible, then Sarah sang "Amazing Grace." Her voice, a beautiful, clear soprano, gave Ari chills. She had no idea Sarah was so talented.

"In lieu of a burial, we will erect a cross in remembrance of Christopher in the garden. Everyone, please follow me." Joshua's somber voice, so much like Christopher's, reverberated through Ari's soul. He walked out of the room and through the back doors.

She wished to escape through the front door instead and never come back, but with only four people in attendance, she'd surely be missed. Out of respect for the Somers family, she followed them out.

Josh and Sarah each lifted a side of the wooden cross and shifted it until it sank into a pre-dug hole. Beatrice let out a loud wail. Ari would cry, too, if Christopher were really beneath that cross. Instead, she found the whole affair ludicrous and unsettling. Christopher had made his choice to stay in the nineteenth century. And as an earl, she was certain when he'd actually died there had been a grand funeral service for him.

Immediately, contrition riddled her conscience. *This is for the family, not for Christopher. It's their closure. I only wish I had mine.*

The Somers family stood around the cross with somber faces, silent—perhaps in prayer.

Ari couldn't look at the pieces of wood without her gut twisting.

Beatrice let out another moan. Ari couldn't take it any longer. She refused to grieve, celebrate, or even acknowledge that Christopher might be dead. If he'd deserted her and his family for true love and the chance to become an earl, he wasn't the man she'd thought he was at all. And he certainly didn't deserve a ceremony.

One more wail curdled her stomach.

"I'm sorry, but I have to leave." Ari tried to be discreet, but again, in such a small assembly, found it difficult. She couldn't even come up with a good excuse. Grief, anger, disgust, anxiety. She felt them all, but couldn't pinpoint which propelled her away from that symbolic cross and out the door.

Chapter Twenty-Eight

Days and nights blurred together for Christopher; so dark it was in his prison cell. His only measure of time was when food arrived—if one could call it food. The scraps and parcels he'd been given under the guise of a meal wouldn't feed a dog.

A chorus of moans rose and fell—prison music, Christopher had declared it. And to him it was music, for in the silence, rodent chatter, gnawing and scurrying became deafening. He knew vermin were present; could feel and smell them, but it somehow worsened when he could hear them, as well. The moans came from human beings—a small comfort, yet a comfort just the same. Rodents, however, awaited the prisoner's death so they could dine on his flesh.

"Christopher."

Somewhere within the fogginess of his brain, Christopher heard his name over the choir of wails.

"Who is it?"

"It is I, Cedric." A small beam of light appeared through the tiny, barred opening on the door.

Knowing he would not be able to see his uncle even if he stood, Christopher remained on the ground, embedded in a small patch of moldy hay.

"Forgive my tardiness. I had hoped to have secured your release before now."

Hope surged through Christopher. "Do you have

news, Cedric?"

"Yes, although, it is not the news for which I had wished. Parliament is not easily persuaded to spare your life, Christopher, now that you have materialized with the jewels."

He slumped deeper into the hay and let go of his earlier anticipation with a low, mournful sigh.

"I confess I am not a persuasive orator such as my late brother Robert; however, I was successful in attaining a delay in your execution. We have three additional weeks—two fortnights from today—in which to work out a solution."

Two fortnights. That meant he'd been imprisoned only two or three weeks. It felt more like a year. Christopher's mixed emotions gave him pause. Even a minute longer in this purgatory was too long. And if he was destined to die here, the sooner the better. Yet, he'd promised Arianna. She trusted him. Didn't he owe it to her to continue fighting for his life? He swallowed his disappointment. "I thank you, Uncle, for speaking up for me."

"I am truly sorry, Christopher. I must make this right." Cedric's voice hitched, and the door rattled as if his uncle were trying to break it down.

Christopher needed to assuage Cedric's mounting frustration before he did something reckless. "It's not your fault. Please do not put your life in jeopardy for mine; you have a wife and daughters. I—I have no one." Thoughts of his family, struggling through their unfamiliar existence in the twenty-first century, weighed heavily on his heart. Thoughts of Arianna nearly broke it.

"Still, to die for your father's crime. And all for

trying to save me. 'Tis not right, Christopher. 'Tis not right. I will use the time we have been granted to formulate a plan. And I'll continue negotiations with Parliament."

Something skittered over Christopher's foot, pausing for a nibble. He kicked the rodent away. "Not yet. I'm still breathing," he whispered.

"I cannot hear you, Christopher."

He cleared his throat. "I shall look forward to your return. Oh, and Cedric, the girl…Rachel…Miss Cartwright—"

"I've not seen her since your incarceration. I have heard, however, she traipses about London, spending large sums of money, while professing to have a wealthy fiancé. If I am to understand it correctly, it was Miss Cartwright's accusations which landed you here."

"Yes. Between her fabricated tale and discovery of the jewels in my room, there was little to recommend my innocence."

"'Twas most unfortunate for you to have found her in my employ. I do so apologize."

"You couldn't have known. I do not hold you accountable for Rachel's actions against me."

Cedric released a breath, as if allowing a small portion of guilt to lift. "I had Cook prepare you a roast chicken. The guard would not allow me entrance with it but assured me you'd receive it for supper." He paused. "Keep the faith, Christopher."

The light dimmed with his uncle's retreating footsteps.

Christopher fell into a stupor. His well-intentioned uncle's visit nagged at him. Nothing Cedric could do would change Christopher's fate. Delay it, possibly, but not change it. The *ton* would not be satisfied until he was hanged for the crime. The crime he did not commit. Once again, Father had won.

His dark musings were interrupted by something hitting the ground near his foot. He felt the rush of rodents moving toward it. Another item landed, then another. Finally, one of the foreign objects hit his arm and Christopher picked it up. Small, hard. Smelled like…chicken bones.

"Your uncle paid me handsomely to deliver your supper." The guard belched and rumbled a loud guffaw.

****

Something was different in the belly of Newgate today. Christopher knew immediately what it was—his howling neighbor had quieted. In the absence of a guard hauling him off, silence meant only one thing—death. He strained to hear proof otherwise, but only rodents, which were no doubt feasting on the man's carcass, could be heard. Soon the already foul odor would increase.

He ran his fingers along his jawline. Stubble from weeks ago had grown into a beard. Without means of tracking time; without people in his life besides the neglectful, cruel guards, he felt his sanity slipping.

Out of the darkness, a bright beam of light hit his eyes, blinding him. He hadn't seen anything so bright since…the twenty-first century. But who?

"Christopher."

"Cedric?" The voice sounded a lot like his uncle's, but had a brash quality absent in Cedric's smooth timbre.

"I had to see for myself."

Father. Bile rose in Christopher's throat at the

sound of Benjamin Somerset's voice. "What are you doing here?"

"The real question is: what are you doing here? For the son of a genius, Christopher, you really are not overly bright. All you had to do was go on with your life; leave well enough alone, but that wasn't good enough for the honorable Christopher Somerset. No, you had to prove just how principled you are through your self-righteous acts. Look where it landed you." Benjamin hit the cell door.

"Is that why you came here—risked being seen by…anyone in London—to come berate me, Father? Do you not think I have enough self-rebuke? Leave me."

Benjamin grunted a laugh. "If you could see me, son, you would know I risk nothing by coming here. I am wearing the vest. My vest. The vest you, my very own flesh and blood, used against me, forcing me to escape with my life." His voice rose with each sentence. "I can disappear in a moment's notice." He let out a scoffing snort. "Such a pity you're not wearing it. A pity indeed."

"Again, Father, why are you here?"

Benjamin paused before he spoke. "Christopher, I came to you with many offers to share in my wealth—to work alongside me as a son should his father. But being the honorable man you think you are," he spat the words out, "you rebuffed my every proposal."

Christopher lifted his arm in an attempt to shade his eyes from the intense beam of the flashlight and hide from his monster of a father. "Is there no hope for you? How is it you can be so unfeeling toward your own flesh and blood?—to observe your eldest son suffering for *your* sins. I don't know what your plan is, but—"

"Haven't you had enough of this hell-hole?" his father interrupted. "Listen to reason, man. If these circumstances have not sufficiently humbled you, nothing will."

Christopher said nothing.

"Speak up, boy. With my help, you can leave this place forever; be with your mother, Josh and Sarah—even see the designer again."

To see Arianna again, Christopher would do nearly anything…

The flashlight suddenly turned off. Shuffling noises outside his cell made Christopher believe a curious guard patrolled the area.

"I must go. Think on it, Christopher," said his father.

Chapter Twenty-Nine

Ari, Mother is locked in her room. She's been there for days. Sarah has been cooking, but Mum has barely touched her food. I do not know how to help her. I thought the memorial service would give her closure— help her move on, but the depression into which she has fallen captive has only worsened. I am sorry to bother you about this, but I've nowhere else to turn. You alone know of our unique circumstances. Josh.

A lump formed in Ari's throat as she read and reread the text message from Joshua. Engrossed in her work, she hadn't seen the message arrive. "Three hours ago." She scowled at herself. "He sent the text three hours ago and is probably no longer in town to receive my reply." No matter; she'd write one anyway.

Josh, I didn't see your text until just now. Yes, I'll help. I'm on my way. But could she help? Her last attempt hadn't worked out well and only served to anger her instead. *I must. They have no one else.* She pressed the send button, then cleared off her desk to leave.

After she'd been driving for thirty minutes, her phone rang. Josh. She pulled off the freeway to talk to him. "Josh, I got your text. Sorry—"

"It's all right; I was at work. When I returned home and told Mum that I had begged for your help, she came out of her room. She really doesn't want to bother you further. She feels badly for what we have put you through already, so I drove back to town to call you."

Ari let go of a breath of relief. "Is she okay? Will she eat now?"

"I don't know. Last time she did. Sorry to alarm you—"

"Last time? You mean she's done this before?" Ari wondered how the family had accepted the letter so readily. Perhaps they hadn't. Maybe they'd been suppressing their true feelings. *And now Beatrice has cracked.* Ari recalled once reading about rules of Polite Society in Regency London. Most women didn't even attend funeral services for fear of becoming overemotional. Why hadn't Ari remembered that? Her era and the Somers differed in more ways than just the obvious. The people differed, too. Displaying emotions was viewed as weakness.

Josh continued, "It happened one other time. After *I* tried to go find Christopher myself."

"You did what?"

"Ari, I realized you were right, but I did not want to admit it. The note doesn't sound like Christopher. I decided, being the man of the house now, it was up to me to bring Christopher home." His tone rose.

Ari could feel his helplessness through the phone.

"Sarah said Mother shot out of her room like ball from a cannon when she felt the device's vibrations. They caught me before I could get away on the machine." He sounded disappointed for failing.

Ari, however, was relieved. "I'm sorry, Josh. How'd you get her to stay out that time?"

"I needed only to promise never to try it again without a plan in place that would ensure my safe return." He paused. "We thought we'd taken those same precautions with Christopher." His voice hitched, tearing at Ari's heart. "Where are you?"

"Just about to Colorado Springs. I'll be there in an hour, or so."

"No, don't… I mean, you needn't come. In fact, I think Mum would feel ashamed if you made the trip on her behalf. It might send her back to her room."

"Are you sure?" Relief and disappointment warred with each other. After the memorial service, Ari had vowed to keep her distance from the entire Somers clan. Each visit brought nothing but heartache. On the other hand, if Joshua and Sarah were both questioning the letter, shouldn't they investigate?

"I am sure." Then, as if he'd read Ari's thoughts, he answered her. "I worry that if we even bring up the letter or talk of going after Christopher, she'll sink into another bout of depression."

"I understand," Ari lied. If there was even a remote possibility that Christopher's letter had been faked, wouldn't his mother want to know?

"Thank you for your willingness to help her. It means a lot."

She ended the call and headed back to Denver.

****

Arianna didn't need to be riding a time machine to know things were moving too fast.

After she had agreed to lunch out with Zach, he seemed to think he'd been given the green light to plunge head-first into a full-on romantic relationship. A combination of her shattered heart and his relentless spirit urged her to agree to his requests for dates evening after evening.

Now and then memories of the old Zach muscled their way into the forefront of her mind, but Ari had become proficient at seeing what she wanted to see and ignoring the rest. Unlike Christopher, Zach treasured her. She grew more and more sure of it every day. Then again, it was all moving at lightning-speed—careening a bit out of control. Perhaps tonight she'd know if Zach was the man who would help mend her broken heart.

Seventies music played in the background of the hole-in-the-wall restaurant she had discovered on the outskirts of Denver. She twisted her napkin, contemplating.

"A penny for your thoughts." Zach tilted his head, his deep brown eyes exploring Ari's.

"I'm thinking about you...and me."

"That sounds intriguing." He covered her hand with his, calming her restless fingers.

She let out a nervous laugh. "I mean, I'm wondering about the two of us. As in, am I foolish to keep going on dates with you? We have a history, you know. And it's nothing to be proud of."

"We've been out what, five, six times now since running into each other at the market? Have I crossed any lines?"

"No. You've been a perfect gentleman." Such a different man from the Zach she'd dated a few years ago. At what point, however, would she fully trust him? And, although Christopher would never know Zach, somewhere in her subconscious she wondered if she only dated him to get even with Chris. She had most definitely moved through the stages of grief from shock and disbelief to anger. How does one retaliate against an offender living in the nineteenth century?

"I developed patience working in El Salvador. I had to; nothing comes quickly or easily for those people—or their caregivers." He lifted a shoulder then let it fall.

He'd brought that up every time they were together. She admired him for what he'd done in El Salvador, but why must he constantly remind her of it? Plus…patience? Patience is what she and Christopher had earned through a year of testing their relationship, not a couple of weeks of going out to dinner every single night. "It's just—"

"You're on the rebound? You've made that clear. And I hope I've made it clear that I'm not going anywhere. Lonely nights in El Salvador brought me to my senses." He leaned in and placed a sweet kiss on her lips. "Take all the time you need."

A tiny shiver ran through her body, then quickly fizzled out. She had to stop comparing Zach to Christopher. "It may be a while. I'm kind of a mess right now."

"That guy really did a number on you." He twirled a few strands of her hair through his fingers. "Must have been a real jerk."

She pulled away, her insides cringing. It was okay for her to think of Christopher as a jerk, but Zach had crossed a line. "He did. Right after you did a number on me. I guess the joke's on me." Blinking back tears, she reached for the check. "It's late. I've got work in the morning."

Zach intercepted her hand, grabbing the check. "Don't be like that, Ari. We had a nice time tonight."

"But this is what I'm talking about. I'm not ready and I'll make you miserable if I jump in too soon."

She paused, tilted her head and narrowed her eyes. That was the old Arianna; the girl who'd been cheated on by one boyfriend only to be jilted by another. Wasn't it time she started playing by her own rules, instead of letting the men in her life lead? "On second thought, Zach, you're right. Let's get out of here."

Zach paid the waiter and ushered Ari out of the restaurant. He tugged her to his car with some urgency, as if he were afraid she'd change her mind.

Ari jogged along beside him, nothing but anger fueling her actions. Anger toward Christopher and anger toward herself for allowing him to shatter her heart so thoroughly.

She turned on soft music and lowered the lights in her apartment. Images of Christopher sitting on her couch the night before he'd proposed made her want it as dark as possible.

Zach, no doubt, believed her motivation in doing so came from desire instead of painful memories. He cozied up to her on her sofa. "I've waited so long for this, Arianna." He tilted her chin up and lowered his head. Ari closed her eyes and imagined she was somewhere else…anywhere else. He kissed her with the same urgency with which he'd rushed her from the restaurant.

"Slow down, Zach. I'm not going anywhere," she said when he let her take a breath.

"Sorry." He nuzzled her neck, peppering her collarbone with kisses.

It felt good, but it didn't feel right. She was using Zach.

He worked his way back to her mouth, and at the same time gently nudged her to lay back on the sofa.

No. She pushed his chest, forcing him to stop. The hurt in his eyes nearly caused her to reconsider, but an inborne self-respect took center-stage. "I can't, Zach."

He moved to her neck again. "Yes, you can, Ari. Just trust me." His voice was pleading, but it wasn't Zach's she heard. It was—

Ari jerked back, shocked. "What did you say?"

"Do you trust me?"

The room began to spin around her. "I'm sorry, Zach, but you need to leave."

He bent toward her again. "But we're just getting start—"

"Now!" She pushed back and pointed to the door.

Zach muttered something undiscernible as he shrugged into his jacket and stomped outside. "Call me when you've grown up," he said before closing the door. Now *that* was the Zach she remembered.

Breathe, Ari, breathe. She didn't trust him, but that wasn't the truth of why she'd pushed him away. In fact, exacting revenge and proving she could move on from Christopher were her reasons for letting him get as far as he had. But those four words: "Do you trust me?" were last spoken by a man she had once undeniably trusted. Christopher. What had changed?

Ari splashed cool water on her face and scrubbed at her mouth. She needed to wash Zach off her skin. "I'm sorry, Christopher. I'm so sorry." Burying her head in a terrycloth towel, she sobbed.

Lying in bed, she cringed as a debate ensued between her heart and her head. She had promised Christopher she'd trust him no matter what. However, people change—perhaps he had. But it was one thing to change his mind about Ari, and it was quite another to have changed his character, to act in such a cruel manner toward her and his family. Yet, the letter said it all.

If only she'd been more insistent he not go back to London.

If only she had gone with him.

If only...

Chapter Thirty

Christopher squinted up at the light. He couldn't believe what he was hearing from his father. Benjamin had returned to the prison, prepared to persuade Christopher to aid him in his scheme. As always, his designs were self-serving and deceitful.

"Am I to understand that you have concocted a plan that will place all blame of your crimes on your brother Cedric, clearing your own deservedly tarnished name, thus designating you as the new Earl of Hemington?" he asked. Anger sparked in his chest.

"Do not forget, you will succeed me as heir to the earldom when I am gone."

Did his father not know him at all? When had Christopher ever expressed a desire to become an earl…or bear any title? Never.

"I came here to clear Cedric's name." Christopher stood and walked toward the door until his shackles stopped him. "Not send him to the gallows. I don't know what sort of help I could offer from a prison cell, at any rate."

"Once I plant evidence on Cedric, I need you to testify it was he, not I, who committed the heist. That you only took the fall to spare him but realized what an error it had been to let a criminal such as Cedric roam the streets of London."

Cedric, a dangerous criminal. Christopher closed

his eyes and shook his head. Taking deep breaths, he attempted to tamp down his anger. Caged and shackled as he was, there was no outlet for his fury.

Father's tone became gritty, like sandpaper scraping against Christopher's skull. "Do you not see? Cedric is the perfect man to hang for the crime. He has no heir to succeed him. And you must admit, his docile manner does not command respect. An earl should command respect."

"I respect him." It was his father Christopher had no respect for. And it was his father who should hang for the crime. He yanked on his restraints, wishing to throttle him for even considering such a plan. From his vantage point, however, he couldn't even see him through the blinding light.

Father either didn't hear or chose not to acknowledge what Christopher had to say. Nothing had changed—Father rarely considered anyone's opinion. He went on, "We can combine my acquired riches *and* wear the badge of honor." Which Christopher knew meant the title of earl—the one thing all of Father's riches could not buy him. "We can bring your mother, Sarah and Joshua back here, too, where we will lead the lives in which we were destined."

"And Ari?"

"Who?"

"Arianna Miller. You know, the designer." Christopher's whole reason for even giving audience to this madman—that, and as a prisoner, he really had no choice. "You said I would see Arianna, as well."

"And see her you shall, when we return to collect the others. Then you can tell her you've more important work in your own time."

Christopher stomped his foot and let out a snarl. Rage seethed from him. If only rage could break his restraints.

"Surely you know you can do better than that…girl. You will be groomed to be an earl; she's hardly your equal. Why would you waste time with that interloper anyway? She has been nothing but an insubordinate upstart from the beginning."

"I've heard enough," Christopher growled. He'd heard enough after Father's first vile sentence. But past experience had taught him he needed to hear Father's plans out—no matter how appalling—in order to stop him. He still regretted having shut him down so quickly when he'd come to Christopher for help with the jewelry heist—the original crime. Had he listened, he could have prevented all of this, but would never have met Arianna.

Before he could deliberate overly much about the "what ifs," his father pulled him from his ping-ponging thoughts. "Think on it, son. Just think on it. When the day of your execution draws nigh, you will change your mind."

I'd rather die than help you! He thought it rather than said it. He couldn't enrage Father too much; Cedric's life was in danger. Benjamin Somerset usually found a way to get what he wanted, with or without Christopher's help. He must be stopped. This time for good. His muddled brain began buzzing again. He must come up with something before Father left.

An idea sprang to mind. "Where are you lodging?" If he knew the location, he might persuade his uncle to find and steal the vest, thus preventing Father's escape. It was a long shot, but perhaps then, the noose would eventually bind the neck of the guilty man.

"Why do you ask? Are you wishing to pay me a visit?" He let out a loud laugh. "I am not staying in this century, if that's what you're after. But 'tis easy enough to travel here. Do not worry—I will return." He flicked a switch and the blinding ray from the flashlight vanished.

Christopher paced two steps one direction, then two steps back. He needed to warn Cedric. He needed to stop Father. But in this cage, he was completely useless to everyone.

Chapter Thirty-One

December brought gusty winds and a dusting of snow to Denver, but weather conditions had never stopped Ari from visiting the cemetery. The solace she gained from talking with her family was worth braving the storm.

Moisture on the ground made it too cold and damp to sit cross-legged near the graves, as she usually did. Instead she walked...and talked. Every emotion she'd experienced since Christopher's departure spilled out—from denial and isolation to her angry rebellion, and now severe loneliness and confusion.

"I should have stuck to my gut instinct and insisted the Somers let me use the device and search for Christopher. But their persuasive arguments convinced me the letter was real. I might never know for sure. He just hurt me so badly. Or maybe it wasn't him. It's not like him. He's so kind—he'd never do something like that to me. But what if he did?" She babbled on, making little sense, but feeling better for getting it out of her system.

The clouds parted, and the sun peeked through, drawing Ari's attention to a shiny object on her mother's headstone. A quarter. Strange. She removed her gloves, then picked it up and squeezed it between her hands, hoping to get some kind of direction from the heavens. So often she had brought her troubles to the cemetery, where her burdens had been lifted. She wanted—no, she needed—that now.

"Ouch." She let the coin drop. Somehow it had shocked her. She studied her palms, realizing she'd held the quarter so forcefully, it had left an indentation of George Washington and some of the words surrounding him. One word stood out—"Trust."

A chill made its way from her head to her toes. And it had nothing to do with the frigid weather. She knew what she needed to do. Slipping the quarter in her pocket, she headed to her car.

Before turning on the ignition, she reached for her phone. *Josh, I'm coming to talk about Christopher. I know your mother is fragile, but we must* do *something.* Arianna waited until she was well into the drive to push "send." She didn't want anything or anyone to stop her.

By the time she pulled up to the Somers' mansion, her resolve had only strengthened. But what about Beatrice? Ari didn't want to say or do anything that would spiral her further into depression. She'd need to tread lightly.

Before she could knock, Josh pushed the door open. "What are you doing here, Ari? I told you Mother is fine." His tone of voice and the look on his face reflected irritation and fear.

"I need to see the letter, Josh. I have a feeling Christopher is in trouble. Please, may I come in?"

"Mother is finally recovering. I don't think—"

"Who are you talking to, son?" Joshua's mother materialized behind him. "Arianna, is that you?" Beatrice nudged past Josh, pulled Ari through the door and wrapped warm arms around her. "I feared we might never see you again after the memorial service." She loosened her hold on Ari and appraised her.

"I'm so sorry. The service was—" Morbid, horrifying, were just a couple of adjectives which came to mind. She looked into Beatrice's eyes and saw longing, grief and fear. "The service was lovely. I—I'm just not ready to concede defeat." She took a deep breath, then let it out. She needed to execute her plan without sending the woman into another bout of despair. "How are you doing? Are you all right?"

Beatrice dropped her gaze. "It has been difficult." She sniffed. "Sarah and Joshua are holding up, and both are a great comfort to me, but all of us are woefully unprepared to live on our own in this century." She ushered Arianna into the parlor, where they sat on the same sofa she'd occupied during the service. Today, however, the sun shone through the windows. Ari was grateful the black cloth had been removed. Still, Beatrice wore the mourning color. "Christopher knew of our reliance on him better than anyone. I do not understand why he would have intentionally left us to fend for ourselves."

"That's why I'm here, Beatrice."

Josh, who stood nearby, sucked in a breath and placed a hand on his mother's shoulder. "Mother, are you weary? You did not take your afternoon nap. Would you care to lie down?"

Beatrice raised her head to meet Josh's concerned gaze. "Joshua, we have company. I'd like to visit with Arianna." She returned her attention to Ari. "Please, go on, dear."

Josh shot Ari a warning look.

She closed her eyes for a moment to contemplate her words, then took one of Beatrice's hands in her own. "In my heart, I think"—she cleared her throat and spoke with added confidence—"I *know* Christopher needs my help. I feel it in my bones. But I can't do it alone. Will you allow me to see the letter?"

Beatrice shook her head. "Sweetheart, the letter caused all of us so much pain, we destroyed it."

Ari's heart plummeted. She was certain a clue lay hidden in its words.

"Mother." Sarah had entered the room so quietly, Ari hadn't realized she stood next to Joshua. "It is true I tore up the letter, but it is still in the trash bin in the laboratory. Perhaps we can piece it together—if it's okay with you."

Beatrice's countenance drooped. She freed her hand from Ari's and twisted her fingers together.

"Please, Mother." Sarah dropped to her knees before Beatrice. "If we find no evidence of foul play, we'll speak of it no more." She glanced up at Josh then Arianna. "Right?"

"Right," both agreed in unison.

Beatrice raised her chin. "And if something does look amiss? What will you do?"

Ari, Josh and Sarah exchanged questioning looks.

"We will cross that road when we get to it," said Josh. He rubbed his hands together. "I've thought the letter was off from the minute I read it, but it caused you pain to discuss, Mother."

"Very well," Beatrice relented. But Ari thought she saw a spark of hope enter her eyes.

"I'll retrieve the letter." Josh rushed from the room, determination etched on his face.

The Somers family and Arianna gathered around the kitchen table where Josh laid the shreds of paper.

As he worked at fitting the puzzle together, he talked, his pent-up frustrations spewing out like lava. He'd gone from a timid, protective son to a super-hero on a mission.

The note, torn in many pieces, kept him busy while he spoke. "We are Christopher's only allies, Ari. We must help him. I am prepared to travel to the nineteenth century and find him, but Mother insists I should not." He said it with so much zeal, Ari wondered how long he'd pondered taking action, but hadn't because of his mother.

Ari gave Beatrice a sidelong glance, worried about her reaction.

Beatrice's face blanched, and then her brows drew together in concern. "I'll not risk losing both my sons."

Josh threw his hands in the air. "But if Christopher needs help, we cannot leave him there."

Ari and Sarah laid hands on Joshua's shoulders to calm him. They couldn't risk upsetting Beatrice now. Things had just begun to progress. "Shh, Josh, calm down," whispered Ari.

Beatrice cleared her throat. "What makes you think he's in need of our help? He sounded quite content in the letter." She motioned to the tattered paper.

Sarah spoke up. "For one thing, Christopher hadn't seen or spoken of Rachel in years. I do not believe this sudden affection toward her is genuine."

"Neither do I," said Josh, his voice calm now. "You must agree that Arianna has brought more happiness into Christopher's life than we all thought possible. Even he has said as much."

Ari's heart squeezed. "Who is she? Was he in love with her?" It hurt to ask, but she needed to know.

Beatrice placed a warm hand over Arianna's. "He'd thought he loved her once, even saved his money to buy her a locket—a token of his affection."

Ari gasped.

Beatrice patted her hand and continued. "But they were children."

Ari reflected on Sarah's admission of her love for Hudson Drake. At fifteen, she'd only been a child, as well. Yet she'd said it was normal for the time.

Ari stopped questioning and began listening again.

"It all happened so long ago. He broke things off with her before he left for Cambridge. So much has transpired since then, we had all long forgotten about Rachel."

"But the necklace." Ari shivered. "Why did he break up with her?"

Sarah scowled. "Father forced him to. Rachel hadn't been up to Father's standards."

"'Tis true enough; however, it was society's way— our way—back then, of course," said Beatrice.

"So, love…unrequited. It could be his motive for staying," Ari whispered.

"There," said Josh, pointing to the taped together letter on the table.

The words now nestled together in a legible fashion. Ari eyed the old-fashioned vellum with quilled-ink writing, unprepared for the reaction that seeing the actual letter would have on her. *I can't do this.*

Joshua studied her, waiting for her response. "What do you think? Should we read it together?"

A shock jolted Ari. Her pocket felt hot. She reached in and touched the quarter she'd removed from her mother's headstone. A not-so-subtle reminder of why she was here. *Thank you, Mom.* Taking a deep breath, she swallowed her anxiety and began to read aloud.

My Dearest Family,

Providence has truly been my companion on this voyage as I have had the good fortune to find my dear uncle, and now earl, Cedric. He has reminded me of the obligation to king, country and family that now rests on my shoulders. I am to be the next Earl of Hemington.

"Christopher never cared about power. I've never once heard him say he wished to become the Earl of Hemington," Sarah said.

Beatrice shook her head. "No, but he has always been conscientious about fulfilling his duties. If Cedric is the earl now, that means something has happened to his brother Robert. Neither of them had a son. In Benjamin's absence, Christopher would be the rightful heir. Please continue."

Ari agreed with Sarah; Christopher wasn't the sort of person who sought power. However, his mother likely knew her son better than either of them. She read on.

I have thought long and hard about this and feel it most prudent to rid myself of any temptation I may have to return to you. Thus, I am sending this contraption back to whence it came. I am sorry I cannot come in person to explain, but I am certain you will understand.

"He wouldn't leave us—even to become an earl." Joshua's voice cracked on the last words. Sarah pulled him into a side hug.

I have also had the good fortune to be happily reunited with Miss Rachel Cartwright. We have rekindled our love for one another and plan to be wed shortly.

Ari's voice wobbled.

I am happy with this decision and you should all be happy for me, as well. Tell Aryanna—

She stuttered to a halt, then narrowed her eyes at her name.

"Is it too painful, dear? Would you like someone else to finish reading?" asked Beatrice.

The heartbreaking words were difficult to read, but that wasn't what had stopped Ari. "Christopher knows how to spell my name," she blurted out. If she'd read the letter the day it had arrived, she would have spotted that immediately... Unless he'd forgotten. Men don't always remember things so trivial as name spellings. *Christopher would.*

She tamped down her confusion and cleared her throat to continue, feeling more and more confident Christopher hadn't written the words. Yet, he may have dictated it. All eyes were on her. She picked up where she'd left off.

I am very sorry, but I had forgotten what true love really is. Now that I have found it again, I daren't leave Rachel's side, lest I lose her once more. She is and always has been my one true love.

Yours, Christopher

There were many inconsistencies between the letter and the man Ari knew and loved. How had she not noticed before? "I don't think this is his handwriting." She tugged the birthday card he'd written so long ago from her bag to compare the script. "Sarah, he wrote a note to you, as well. Do you still have it?"

"Oh, yes. I'd completely forgotten about that."

Sarah sprang to her feet and headed to her room. She returned with the note in less than a minute.

Laying all three samples side by side, the group examined every word.

"No, they do not really look the same," said Beatrice. "The 'Y's' curve different directions." She lifted up the nineteenth century letter. "But, if not Christopher, who would have written this and why?"

Arianna began shaking uncontrollably. She rubbed her hands up and down her arms in an effort to calm her nerves, but it was to no avail.

"What is it, dear?" asked Beatrice.

Ari nodded her head back and forth in slow motion. "I know Christopher is in trouble. I must help him."

Chapter Thirty-Two

"What are you saying, Arianna?" Worry lines creased Sarah's forehead. "What do you mean to do?" She met Ari's gaze across the table, an earnest look in her eyes.

"I—I must go to the nineteenth century and find him. There's no other way." She glanced at Josh, who had tried to go but had been stopped by his mother. He was needed here. His family couldn't risk losing him. "I have no family counting on me here. But Christopher needs me in the nineteenth century. I should have gone sooner." Ari looked toward the study, where she knew the trapdoor leading to the time-traveling machines lurked beneath the rug.

"No!" Several voices stopped her before she was able to leave the kitchen.

"It's much too dangerous," said Beatrice.

"How would you even find him? London is a big city?" said Sarah.

"Not to mention, it isn't safe"—Joshua shrugged— "or proper for a lady such as yourself to be wandering around London alone."

"Josh is right, Arianna," said Beatrice. "Times have changed very much in two hundred years."

Ari should have realized that from the many romance novels she'd read from the British Regency era. But she must help him. A sense of urgency panicked her.

She took a calming breath, needing to think through this rationally. After all, Christopher might not need saving; it could very well be her overriding desire to have him back that fueled her thoughts and actions. "Will one of you accompany me?"

The kitchen became silent. She shouldn't have asked.

All eyes were on Beatrice. The decision, after all, would be hers. With her eyebrows drawn downward and her face pointed at her fidgeting hands, she looked thoughtful.

Ari hoped she was actually considering the idea. Otherwise, she'd have to risk it all and go alone. They'd done nothing for too long. Chris needed them.

Finally, Beatrice raised her head and cleared her throat. "If Christopher is in trouble, it is most likely because he was recognized." Beatrice looked at each of her children.

Ari couldn't help noticing the spark of determination growing in her eyes as she took command. So different from the woman who'd locked herself in her bedroom.

"Sarah and I would, quite possibly, be recognized, as well. Joshua, you have grown several inches in the past five and a half years. You've become a man, in fact. Perhaps you would not be so familiar." She narrowed her eyes. "I would not let you go before because you hadn't a sure plan. That was selfish of me, but I still do not negotiate this century well. Maybe, with Arianna, you can come up with a plan now. You shan't be going otherwise. I refuse to lose two sons to that dreadful device."

Josh perked up immediately. "I am certain I can, Mum." Just as fast, his excitement waned. "However, it would not be acceptable for me to be with Arianna unaccompanied on the streets of London."

"Unless you were married." A glint entered Sarah's eyes. She studied Joshua, as if discerning how to make him look like a married man.

"Can you do it, Sarah?" asked Ari. "Make him look older?"

Beatrice wrung her hands. "I don't know. 'Tis risky."

Ari could see Beatrice's insecurities reappearing in her downcast eyes and bent frame. Her heart went out to her. The notion of Beatrice and Sarah stranded in the twenty-first century gave Arianna reason to panic. The thought of being stuck in the nineteenth century for some untoward reason made her cold with fear. But the vision of Christopher being in trouble with no one there to help him drove a knife through her heart, making her audibly gasp.

Beatrice raised her eyes to her. "What is it, dear?"

Ari folded both of Beatrice's hands in her own. She needed to reassure her. "I know you risk losing Joshua. I can only imagine what that would do to you. Losing Christopher has hurt us all so badly. But we must take this chance to get him back. I feel it in my heart; he needs help. We can take both the new vest and the disc. Josh can wear the vest at all times; it will make him look older to have some meat on his bones." She nudged Josh with an elbow. "That way, if anything happens—anyone recognizes him who might harm him in any way—I will insist he disappear. Then I can get home on the disc." She hoped.

The important thing right now was to make certain Joshua made it back. Neither Sarah nor Beatrice knew how to drive, and, living miles from civilization, would have a difficult time working things out.

Beatrice's hands relaxed a bit. "Very well, but we must consider everything as we plan for your journey."

Ari let out a breath. "Thank you. We will." She looked to the other two who both wore expressions of relief, as well.

"I'll get started," said Sarah. I think I can make you a mustache, baby brother." She nudged Joshua.

"I'll examine the devices to make sure they weren't damaged in any way." Joshua turned toward the study.

"Beatrice," Ari stood, but didn't go anywhere, "do you happen to have a key to Christopher's apartment?"

"I do. Why?"

"I'm not sure. I just need to go there and see if there are any clues." She shrugged. "I feel like I need one of Christopher's belongings with me."

Beatrice walked across the kitchen and pulled a key from a drawer.

"I'll be quick." Ari brushed a kiss on Beatrice's cheek and left the house.

This may have been a mistake. Tears stung Ari's eyes when she entered Christopher's apartment. A hint of his scent was in the air. She bit down hard on her lip. She needed to compose herself and locate whatever she had felt the compulsion to find. Her eyes traveled over the sparsely furnished living room. Nope, nothing in there. Nor did she see anything in the kitchen. The bedroom, however, nearly undid her.

She zeroed in on a framed picture sitting on the nightstand. It was a photo of Ari and Christopher from their double-date with Maggie and her husband. They looked so happy and glamorous—Christopher in his dark suit and Ari in her red dress. Maggie had made them pose for pictures, as if they'd been headed to the prom, then emailed copies to Arianna. She must have sent them to Christopher, too. A lump grew in Ari's throat. "This was the night of our first kiss." He'd framed it and kept it by his bed. Tears splashed down her cheeks.

Next to the picture was a small paper. She picked it up to examine it through her teary eyes. The words caused an electric current to travel through her body: "Someone you care for deeply will come to your rescue." She clapped a hand over her mouth. The fortune cookie from a few months before. She instantly remembered Christopher's silly fascination with the cookies and his unrealistic belief in the fortunes. What had hers said? She tapped her head. It was short; some kind of cliché—"Oh my gosh! I remember," she nearly screamed. "Things aren't always as they seem."

Her heart rattled in her chest. She had to find Christopher. Still, there was something she felt she needed from this room—besides the heart-wrenching memories. She opened the drawer on the nightstand. There lay his service revolver and a pair of handcuffs. She didn't know what compelled her, but for whatever reason, she grabbed them both and stuffed them into her purse.

Before leaving Pueblo and cell phone service range, she made a couple of calls. She dialed Tasha first to let her know she'd be taking some time off. Then she called Maggie. "I know you don't believe me about Christopher being in nineteenth-century London, but he is. And I'm going there to get him."

A moment of silence passed before Maggie spoke. "Where are you, Ari?"

"I'm in Pueblo with the Somers family. They need my help. Christopher needs my help. I only wanted to let you know…just in case." Tears threatened to fall again, but Ari swallowed and willed them away—mostly.

"Just in case what?"

"In case something goes wrong, and I never see you again." Her voice hitched and she knew she'd better end the call right away.

"Ari, I'm coming down there. Stay put."

"It's too late, Maggie. We're leaving as soon as possible. I just need you to know how much you mean to me. You're my dearest friend."

"Wait, Ari!"

"I've got to go now. Love you, Maggie." She hit the off button before Maggie could respond. Hopefully, Maggie wouldn't send the cavalry in to save her.

By the time she returned to the Somers' mansion, Sarah had Joshua looking like a man nearing his thirties. "Wow, Sarah, you're really good at makeup and…"—she touched his realistic mustache—"what is this made of?"

Sarah laughed. "Father used to wear powdered wigs in England for formal events. You know, like George Washington. I cut one up, used a brown marker to dye it, and, behold, Joshua now has a mustache." Sarah's eyes sparkled.

"That's genius, Sarah. But what is holding it on? It looks secure." She gave it a tiny tug.

Sarah cheeks flushed, but it was Josh who spoke.

"She used superglue. I'm going to have this mustache for the rest of my life."

"Don't be silly, Josh. It will fall off eventually—probably even before you really are thirty." Sarah giggled.

Joshua glared.

Ari smiled at them, happy for the brief respite from the heaviness they'd all been plagued with. "We should get moving. What time do you think it will be in London when we arrive?"

Josh moved his mouth, silently counting. "It should be early to mid-morning. Hopefully we will land in an obscure area, so we won't be noticed."

Ari dressed in one of Sarah's nineteenth century gowns and bonnet, then packed a few more dresses in the bin on the device—just in case. She also added food and water. Without knowing what to expect, or how long it would take to find Christopher, food and clean water made sense.

"Take this reticule, dear." Beatrice handed her a pretty drawstring bag with a floral design embroidered on it. "Your purse is much too modern for the nineteenth century."

Ari thanked Beatrice and tucked the gun and handcuffs inside the reticule.

"And you'll need this, too." Beatrice opened a smaller pouch, which contained nineteenth century currency. "Otherwise, you will be on foot and without lodging."

It looked like a lot of money, but Ari didn't really know.

"Josh." Sarah tugged a letter from her pocket. "If you happen down this street"—she pointed to an address scrawled across the envelope—"would you put this in the hollow of the tallest tree on the property?" Sarah blushed. "Ari can explain why after you've gone."

Josh narrowed his eyes at his sister.

"I'll see that he does, Sarah." Ari took the letter and tucked it into Joshua's pocket.

Beatrice made sure Josh wore the vest beneath his old-fashioned clothing. "Vow to me you will come right back if you run into trouble." She looked pleadingly into his eyes.

"I promise." His words sounded like a grumble.

She embraced him fiercely, then hugged Ari, as well.

"I will bring him back," Ari whispered.

"Bring them both back." Tears rolled down Beatrice's soft cheeks.

Chapter Thirty-Three

Christopher broke a piece of hay from the mound he slept on and tossed it into the growing pile in the corner of his cell. After he forced down the slop the guard had delivered, he'd count them. He'd been doing this since his last three week stay of execution—adding a piece after the first, and sometimes only, meal arrived, in an attempt to track his final twenty-one days of life.

Today the food looked even less appetizing than usual. Even after he broke the green fuzz from the cheese, it still didn't taste right. His stomach soured when he swallowed it. But what else could he do? He'd starve if he didn't eat. Each time his uncle had brought real food, the guards devoured the meal, then taunted him. He finally told Cedric to stop wasting good food on the brutes.

He'd learned quickly about guard etiquette: ask the guard for help, get whipped. Ask the guard a question, get beat with a pole. Ask the guard where the food your uncle brought was, get garbage dumped in your cell, right after your beating. Pay the guard—well, Christopher didn't know everything the guards could be bribed to do since he had no money, but he did know Cedric had paid a hefty sum for Christopher's upgraded room and treatment. He shivered at the thought of being imprisoned in the cellar beneath the Keep, where men on Death Row were generally housed. There, the prisoners sat together, some shackled to the same ring, and the guards were even more abusive. At least here he had a modicum of privacy.

Scooping up the pieces of hay, he began to count. A wave of nausea hit him, and his vision blurred. "Seventeen, eight—" Bile rose in his throat, and before he could finish the pile, he had to retch. Tugging more hay from his bed, he mopped up the vomit and pushed it to the far side—not far enough. His head throbbed. No longer concerned with how long he had left to live, he lay in what remained of his bristly bed and gave in to sleep.

It was a fitful rest, interrupted by chills, sweats and bouts of nausea. Added to that were nightmares, which always began with Arianna's beautiful face morphing into Rachel's evil smirk.

"Christopher." A bright light hit his face. "Christopher! What are those splotches on your skin?"

He heard the voice, but couldn't will his eyes to stay open; nor could he speak above a moan.

"I've come for your answer, son."

Father. Christopher's already aching body quivered at the sound of Benjamin Somers' voice. He covered his ears, the noise making his head pound.

"You've less than a week remaining. Did you hear me? You will hang in days."

Christopher opened his mouth but couldn't make the words come out. He wished to tell Father to beg the judge to expedite the date of his execution—death would be a welcome release from this agony.

"Guard! See here!"

Christopher heard gruff mumbling but couldn't make out any distinct words from the guard.

"The lad is sick," said Benjamin, suddenly sounding like a concerned father. He needed Christopher now; who else could he find to point a finger at Cedric? The sudden realization hit with resounding force, nearly bringing Christopher to full consciousness.

More mumbling from the guard.

"*Gaol* fever?" Father's voice boomed. "He'll die from that!"

"He is going to die anyway." the gruff voice said with finality.

Good. Let me die and leave me in peace, thought Christopher.

"Not if I have anything to say about it," said Father. Retreating footsteps indicated that one or both men had left.

"Do not fear, Christopher," said Benjamin in a hushed voice. "I can get medicine. The twenty-second century has quick cures, even for typhus... But saving your life comes with a price. Be prepared to stand with me against Cedric, when the time comes."

Chapter Thirty-Four

Arianna had wondered how a disc with no sides could contain its passengers while traveling through time. This wasn't her first trip on the device, but it was the first time she'd been fully conscious. She had worried when the rumbling noises started, sure she and Joshua would tumble to their deaths. But once the journey began, they were pinned to the disc—in a sort of frozen state. The world spun around them, but they remained stationary. Amazing.

Landing, on the other hand, was not so pleasant. They hit the ground with a thud, nearly mowing over a pedestrian. The man blanched, clearly startled and confused. Peering down at the device, he cocked his head, then raised his gaze to meet Joshua's. His pale face made it clear he was frightened by the odd device and its passengers. "Sakes alive. In all my born—"

Ari cut him off. "Good morning, sir." She gave him her brightest smile.

Instead of finishing his sentence, the man shook his head and rushed into the nearest shop.

"If I am calculating correctly, it's nine o'clock in the morning, too early for most shoppers to be out, but not for the business owners." Josh straightened his cravat and stepped off the device. He looked at a nearby establishment. "Sotheby's," he said, reading the sign on the store. "I believe we're on Bond Street."

Arianna stepped off the machine and found her balance. Remnants of the London morning fog added a chill to the air, which smelled of—was that horse manure? She wanted to soak nineteenth century London up—roam around and explore. But the urgency to find Christopher had her heart beating like a snare drum. "Bond Street. I don't think I've read a British novel that doesn't mention Bond Street. I feel like I know where I am." She gave Josh a half smile. "Sotheby's is an auction house, right?"

Josh chuckled. "Something like that. You may know London better than I do." He picked up the device. Though relatively light in weight, awkward to carry.

The sights, the smells—everything about nineteenth century London—mesmerized Arianna. In a million years she would have never thought she'd be experiencing cobblestone streets, the clippity-clop of horse-drawn carriages and Bond Street in the 1800s. What a shame to be in the era she was most obsessed with under such terrible circumstances—a rescue mission for the man she loved. Or even worse—witnessing the man she loved happy in the arms of another woman. The thought shattered her confidence again. No matter how strong her instincts were that Christopher was in trouble, her doubts and insecurities lurked nearby.

"The question is, why did Father program the device to land here?" Josh scanned the area. "I thought we would end up near the store he robbed."

"Let's think for a minute. Is there anything here you remember your father mentioning? Benjamin Somers doesn't do anything unintentionally. There must be a reason."

Another passerby nodded as he approached the pair, then tilted his head, a question in his eyes.

Ari looked to where his gaze rested. The disc in Joshua's hands. They had to hide it—now.

"Good day," Joshua said to the man, rotating the bulky disc so the back faced out. They turned away and walked from the man before he had a chance to speak.

"We've got to hide it," whispered Ari.

Perusing the area, they realized there were no parks nearby. A private residence surrounded by bushes and trees would have to do. Unfortunately, the chill of the season had stripped most plants of their foliage.

"How about that townhouse?" Josh motioned to a manor across the street.

Ari's eyes widened, surprised at the size of the place. "That's a house? The British sure have a different definition of 'townhouse' than we Americans do."

"It probably belongs to a member of the peerage."

Careful no one watched them, they crept around the gate, locating an evergreen bush. "Perfect hiding place…unless a gardener prunes it," Ari said.

"At our country estate, the gardener rarely showed up during the colder months."

Finally free of the disc, Ari stepped back onto the cobbled granite street, Josh close behind. "If you can't think of a reason your father would designate this as a landing spot, what's our next move?"

"We need to find Uncle Robert." Josh kicked at a dead tree branch sitting in his way.

"Your mother said it's not Robert, but Cedric."

"Oh, yes. Then we need to locate Uncle Cedric."

"How do we do that? I wish you'd had phone books in your era."

"If he is in town, it's because of Parliament. I think we should head to the Palace of Westminster. We can't go in, but maybe we can catch him entering or exiting."

Ari stopped and looked at Josh. "You think we should spend all our time watching men walk in and out of a building? Christopher is here somewhere. We can't just take our chances on you possibly recognizing your uncle, who may or may not even be in town." She knew she sounded impatient with Josh, but now that the machine was stowed, the urgency to find Christopher had intensified.

He nodded. "You're right. I just don't know how to find him without Cedric's help. Perhaps we should make a path to the palace, shopping as we go."

"What?" Ari scrunched her face. "You want to shop? Now?" Her voice had risen, and several heads turned in their direction. She lowered it again. "Sorry. But we don't have time for souvenirs. Or am I missing something?"

Josh chuckled. "Sometimes the best way to garner information—at least in London—is to be among society. You'd be shocked at what you can learn from the ladies of the *ton*."

"Oh. I see."

He crooked an arm. "Shall we shop, then, wife?" He winked at Ari, reminding her so much of his brother, it made her heart hurt. She tamped down her rising emotions and took his proffered arm.

Foot traffic on Bond Street had picked up. Ari, captivated with people watching, occasionally tripped over the slightly uneven terrain. Josh, acting ever so husbandly, always steadied her.

"Let's go in there." She pointed to a store to her right. "It looks like a popular place. Lots of ladies."

They entered a millinery. The clerk, busy helping a customer—a woman wearing a gold dress—didn't look up. *Perfect*, they could mingle among a few members of society.

"I will take all three bonnets," said the woman to the clerk. She spoke so loudly, Ari suspected she wanted everyone in the shop to know she was wealthy enough to buy so many hats.

Josh stiffened. "That's Rachel," he whispered in Ari's ear. He immediately turned his back to the woman, so as not to be recognized.

Arianna's stomach dropped to her toes. *Rachel.* The Rachel Christopher had professed to love more than he loved her—assuming he'd written the fateful note? Ari remained close to her, feigning interest in a cream-colored bonnet with purple plumes sprouting from the top. It took all the self-restraint she could muster to not glare at the woman.

"Those are very good choices, very good, indeed," said the clerk to Rachel. "They will look lovely with your dark hair."

"I sure hope my fiancé agrees. He is the only man who matters." Rachel fluttered her lashes at the clerk. Ari didn't know if she could do this. Her stomach began to contract. But maybe Rachel was talking about another man. Ari could dare hope.

"Are you to be married soon, then?" the clerk asked. He tugged three round hatboxes from a shelf.

Rachel gave him a slanted look. "We haven't yet set a date. But he is rich and has given me plenty of pin money already."

She sounded a bit defensive to Ari. Was she making it all up? If so, where did the money come from? Christopher wouldn't use the stolen diamonds. He'd never cashed in a single one, even when he'd been living on the streets of Denver. Granted, if he were truly engaged to this woman, he had become a different person entirely. The unpleasant and unanswerable questions nagged at her.

"He sounds generous. It is not customary to give the bride pin money before the wedding. You are very fortunate." The clerk finished tying the last box with a string and handed it to Rachel.

"Indeed, I am. My Christopher would do anything for me."

Chapter Thirty-Five

Arianna's heart stuttered and nearly failed to beat at hearing Christopher's name. Here she stood—the flesh and blood proof of his letter. It was true, all true. Bile rose in her throat. She needed to exit—now. But her feet froze—plastered to the ground. Then the thought occurred, *Christopher might be here, waiting on his dear betrothed.* Her body jerked in reaction to her thoughts. For her to find him waiting outside would put both an end to their hunt and a dagger through her heart.

"Come, dear." Someone tugged at her arm. Joshua. Her temporary paralysis lifted, and she hesitantly followed him through the door.

"But Christopher must be here somewhere. We can't leave. He's here!"

"Shh. We must be discreet and follow Rachel. Let her lead us to him." Josh looked back to see if Ari had attracted any attention with her outburst. No one had looked up.

Ari lowered her voice. "Sorry. You're right." She exhaled, grounding herself once more. Still, her nerves zinged, imagining Christopher so close. She glanced around. No. Not yet.

"She's coming," said Josh.

Rachel exited the millinery as Ari and Josh pretended to window shop at a nearby store. Keeping an eye on their mark, they furtively tailed her at a safe distance.

A modiste, furrier, then shoe store later, Ari stopped, shaking her head. "She's clearly alone. This is ridiculous. Let's just ask her where he is."

"It's very peculiar for her to be shopping without a servant or companion. She's even carrying all her own packages." Josh shrugged. "She might be in there for a while." He motioned to another dress shop Rachel had entered. "It appears we have wandered to Gunter's. Let's get a lemon ice while we wait."

"Lemon ice? You can get something like that in December?"

"Yes. In here." He pulled Ari into a tea shop boasting its refreshments. "Lemon ice is even more plentiful in the cold months, because of the snow."

With all the walking she'd done, weighted down in the layers of clothing Beatrice had insisted she wear, Ari was tired and happy to stop for a treat.

"We should eat these, too." Josh opened his satchel and tugged out the sandwiches and water they'd packed.

"What is that?" A man sitting near Ari pointed to her water bottle. "I've seen nothing like it."

It took a moment to realize what had puzzled the man. "It's a plastic bottle." Should she tell him plastic wouldn't be available for another hundred years?

"And your food wrapper—plastic, as well?" The man's eyes were huge. "May I touch it?"

Josh took over the conversation. "Sir, the wrapper and the bottle are from America. You cannot find it locally.

"America?" His mouth turned down.

Ari handed the man her water. "You can have it. I've got more."

He took the bottle and squeezed it in, let it pop out, then repeated the motion. He chuckled. Soon he was entertaining everyone in the store with the bottle, then moved to the road with his treasure.

Ari's stomach growled. It had to be long after lunchtime by now. Famished, she devoured the food but savored the lemon ice. "Can you still see Rachel?" she asked. "We can't lose her."

Joshua turned slightly on his seat. "I see her. She's across the street, batting her eyes at the clerk." He shook his head. "I don't understand why she is alone and why she flirts with all the men."

Anger burned in Arianna's chest. "Something's not right." So many things were not right. Everything about this situation was absolutely wrong. She'd stolen enough glances at Rachel—the woman she'd come to despise—to see the glint of deception in her eyes. The girl was pretty, but also looked tired—older than her years. Ari swallowed another bite of lemon ice. *Whatever,* she thought. *If Christopher chose Rachel over me, it wasn't for her beauty.* The shallowness of her thoughts instantly pinched at Ari's conscience. But the bitterness infecting her heart threatened to spill out at some point. The sooner they pinned Rachel down and located Christopher, the better. Mystery solved. They could return to the twenty-first century and get on with their lives.

…Unless Christopher's in trouble. She swallowed the last of her lemon ice along with her anger and resentment.

Josh sprang from his seat.

"What is it, Josh?"

"She's gone! Two carriages passed by, blocking my view—only for a moment—and she disappeared." His eyes bulged, and his lips pulled tight. Sheer panic.

Alarmed, she hurried after him. Searching both directions on the road, they saw shoppers, but none wearing a gold dress. They peeked into the shops on both sides of the dress store in which they'd last seen her, but no Rachel.

"Now what?" Ari asked, deflated. Her hope of finding Christopher had begun to dwindle.

"Uncle Cedric. He's our only prospect now. Perhaps we can catch a hackney to Westminster. I don't think it is far from here."

"If he's even in town, right? That's what you said earlier, that he might not even be in London." Ari's frustration mounted. They'd had their chance and lost it. Rachel gone, and Christopher seemingly invisible gave her little hope. Her aching feet competed with the pain in her heart.

"I am sorry, Arianna. But we knew this would be difficult when we set off. If you'd rather, we can quit now, retrieve the machine and leave this century.

"No. We need to see this through. But we'd better move along. Parliament's meetings surely won't last much longer. We've been at this for hours." She glanced at the sinking sun.

A lamplighter, toting a ladder, nodded their way.

Ari stood transfixed, watching him perform his nightly duty, whistling a jaunty tune as he worked.

Josh gave her a gentle nudge, breaking the spell. He pointed to a large house. "I think that is the manor Sarah wished for me to deposit her letter. See that tree there? It's not but ten paces from the road and looks to have a hollowed out area in the trunk. Shall I investigate?"

"Yes. Let's check it out." They walked to the tree.

He extracted the letter from his coat pocket to put into the hollow, but stopped before letting it drop. "There's something in here." He pulled out a letter with Sarah's name on the front. Then another and another. "There's over a dozen letters in here. This guy must really love Sarah."

Ari's heart warmed at seeing the many notes, then immediately morphed to an ache for Sarah's loss. "I hope they help Sarah feel better," she said. However, she suspected they would more likely cause the poor girl to feel worse.

Josh tucked them all into his large coat pockets.

They walked on until Josh was successful at hailing a hackney cab. "I have always wanted to do that." He grinned as he helped Ari into the carriage.

It hit her then how this experience was not only new for her, but for him, as well. Even though this had once been his home, he was just a child then. "How old were you when you were"—she shrugged—"transported?"

"Five and a half years ago I was twelve. I'm now eighteen." He straightened in his seat, as if to prove his maturity. "Back then in London, we—mother, Sarah, Christopher and I—came to town regularly; however, Christopher led us about, hailing cabs and whatnot. He always looked out for us. That is why I refuse to believe he'd willingly leave us in the twenty-first century to fend for ourselves. It is not in his character."

With force, memories of Christopher's fierce

determination to find his father's machine and rescue his family bombarded Ari's mind. Her body jolted in response. "You're right. He wouldn't desert you."

"Nor you."

A sudden urgency to find Christopher's uncle made Ari's heartbeat accelerate. The clickety-clack of the horse's shoes hitting the granite setts reverberated through her already jittery bones.

Westminster loomed surreal before them. So many times today, she'd wished she were in London during this era for any other reason—or even better, no reason at all—so she could absorb her surroundings and enjoy the experience. She'd read numerous books about Regency Era London, and actually experiencing it could be a fantasy fulfilled. But, no, the pressure to find Christopher far outweighed her desire to relish the moment.

Josh helped her exit the cab. "Come this way." He motioned to a corner in which they could stand without being seen by anyone leaving or entering Westminster Palace.

Several minutes passed without so much as a stray dog crossing their path. "This place is deserted," said Ari.

Josh frowned. "Let's give it a bit longer. We really haven't another plan... But"—he shuffled from one foot to the other—"do you mind if I...uh...find a place to relieve myself?"

Ari would have smiled at his strained expression if her nerves weren't so raw. "No, I don't mind. Do what you need to do, but hurry, it's fully dark now."

He disappeared, and Arianna paced. What would their next move be? She had no idea. A streetlamp flickered, and she realized she'd wandered from the safety of their dark location. Taking a few steps toward the corner, she saw a shadow cast by the lamplight move behind hers. It had to be Josh, although he'd left in the opposite direction—she thought. She turned to see if someone followed her.

Chapter Thirty-Six

No one. Nothing but an empty street. She must have imagined the shadow. Then shuffling noises and sounds like footsteps had her trembling all over again. Though the trees and shrubbery were mostly bare, they were plentiful in this area—ample thick brambles and branches for hiding in the shadowy night. Her nerves soared to high alert. It wasn't safe for a woman—or even a man—to be wandering the streets of London alone past dark. Everyone knew that.

She debated calling out Joshua's name. He must be somewhere nearby. Doing so, however, could either alert the person following her of her companionless state, or make him aware that she indeed had a partner just ahead.

Realizing the obvious—that the person following her surely knew she walked alone—she tamped down her fear and called out, "Where did you go, dear?" She hustled forward a few steps. "Oh, there you are." She nearly sprinted to the black corner where Josh had left her.

He wasn't there.

She strained to hear noises. Had her ruse worked? And where was Josh?

Silence. But only for a moment. A dark figure moved toward her.

Her legs turned wooden, rooting her to the ground.

If she didn't get out of there, she'd be cornered. Taking a breath, she willed herself out of her temporary paralysis and took flight, running in the direction Joshua had gone—no easy feat in a long petticoat and dress.

Loud clomping sounded behind her. He was chasing her.

Something about this felt eerily familiar. It hit her—New York. Only, this couldn't be Benjamin Somers after her…could it?

Her skirts twisted around her ankles. She hiked them up but tripped on the cobblestone. Righting herself, she pressed on, not chancing a glance behind her. Where was Josh?

The sound of the heavy footfalls grew louder. She rounded a corner, heart thudding like a dozen wild horses on the loose. A light flickered in a shop dead ahead. She aimed for it. Surely, whoever chased her wouldn't follow her inside. She reached for the door handle, but a hand gripped her arm, stopping her. Oh no.

"Arianna?"

She shrieked. "Let go or I'll scream!"

Her captor dropped her arm. "It's me, Ari."

"Josh!" She sagged against him. "I—I was being chased! Did you see him?" Her breath came out in pants, and her body trembled.

"Chased by whom?" Josh craned his head this way and that.

Ari grabbed his arm for security and to quell her shaking limbs. "I don't know." She dared a quick look back. "He's gone now." A few more pants escaped her lungs. "He must have seen you." She turned to face

Josh. "What took you so long? Where have you been?" Her mood morphed from fear to concern, then irritation.

"I am really sorry, Arianna. But I found—"

Ari gasped and clapped a hand over her mouth. A man standing in the shadows behind Josh—was it Mr. Somers?

He stepped forward, spiking terror in her chest. Before she could react, he cleared his throat. "Cedric Somerset. Joshua's uncle." He bowed slightly to Arianna.

She let out a ragged breath of relief, then motioned to Josh. "I thought you were his father for a minute." Cedric's eyes still spooked her a bit, so dark and piercing like Mr. Somers. Yet they lacked the hollowness and evil glint of the man's—the man whom she'd come to loathe.

Cedric chuckled. "As lads we got that a lot. We both have our late father's eyes, as does Joshua. And you are?"

"Arianna Miller. Joshua's..." She turned to Josh for help.

"We'll fill you in," Josh said to Cedric. Then he turned to Ari. "Uncle Cedric has offered me—and you"—he glanced at Cedric, a question in his eyes.

Cedric nodded.

"He has offered us a place to stay while we're here. Ari, Christopher is in prison. That's why we could not find him."

The words tumbled from Joshua's mouth so fast, she took a moment to process them. "Wait. This is your uncle—the uncle we've been searching for?"

Both men nodded.

"And Christopher's in prison?" A lump formed in

her throat. For the better part of the day she'd harbored less than kind feelings toward Christopher. At least he wasn't with that horrid woman. But prison—

"Yes. I will explain everything on the way home," said Cedric, interrupting her thoughts. "My coach is this way." He motioned to the right.

Rustling in the bushes stopped them.

Cedric flung an arm out. "Shh. First, we should look for the scoundrel who chased you, Miss Miller," he whispered. Cedric had obviously overheard Ari's frightening tale. "Joshua, you must never leave a lady alone—especially at night." He kept his voice low.

Josh's cheeks reddened under the beam of a streetlamp. "Yes, sir." He didn't bother to explain his need for privacy.

Cedric and Josh rummaged around the bushes, with Ari sticking close to Josh.

"There are footprints here in the dirt." Cedric pointed to the ground. "He must have fled. Dark city streets are no place for a pretty girl such as yourself, Miss Miller."

After they'd scoured the path twice, they gave up the search and climbed into Cedric's coach, where the driver had patiently awaited his master's arrival.

Cedric recited what had happened with Rachel—as far as he knew. Josh and Ari connected the dots, explaining what had occurred in Pueblo.

Ari's heart nearly burst. All the horrible thoughts she'd entertained about Christopher betraying her trust were false. How could she have fallen for that nasty girl's lies?

Christopher had asked her to trust him. She hadn't—not really.

Chapter Thirty-Seven

Christopher lay motionless; awake because of the extreme ache in his head. His father had come earlier in the day with medication. His brain, too foggy at the time to register what was happening, had finally cleared enough to sort things out. But if he moved, the relentless pain shooting through his head intensified.

Father must have paid a hefty bribe to get medication past the guard. The serum Benjamin had forced down his throat was already healing him. He moved his head slightly—enough to see that the purple splotches on his skin were fading, and he no longer felt feverish. Father had told him treatments from the twenty-second century for typhus fever had eradicated the disease and saved countless lives.

Christopher didn't think he'd spoken a word to his father at the time of his visit, but he couldn't be certain in his deranged state of mind. He hoped he hadn't agreed to anything. It wouldn't matter, however. Whatever Father's plans were to oust Cedric from his title, Christopher would never be a part of. He'd rather hang.

What had Father said? Something about their scheme coming together very soon. Christopher forced himself to sit up. Rubbing his temples, he tried to recall the conversation he'd had with Benjamin the previous week. *Think, think, think. How did he say he would strip Cedric of his title, thereby taking on the title himself as the Earl of Hemington?* Whatever it was, he'd needed his son's help. Otherwise, why be so willing to cure him of his fever?

Christopher knew it was not due to fatherly love.

Words from his father's visit days before bled into words from today's visit. He couldn't puzzle out what his delirious brain had never processed in the first place. But the one thing he *could* remember—that Father had promised Cedric's imminent downfall— caused him to worry for his uncle all the more.

Had Christopher alerted Cedric? He vaguely recalled his uncle recently visiting him. But he scarcely remembered anything beyond a few incoherent sentences. *I must warn Cedric.* He closed his eyes and willed his uncle to materialize. *Though it might be too late.*

Chapter Thirty-Eight

Though dark when they rode up the street Cedric had announced was near his home, the surroundings were familiar. Ari nudged Josh, whose eyes narrowed in recognition.

"This is where we landed this morning," said Josh. "We stowed the machine just behind those bushes." He pointed to the evergreens at the side of Cedric's townhouse and looked to his uncle.

Cedric raised his brows. "'Tis curious. Your brother hid the…er…machine in my barn. Retrieve it and bring it inside. Let us keep it under lock and key, lest something untoward becomes of it, as it did before." He then called for Bertrand and handed over the horses and coach to his care.

Cedric took his time inspecting the device, marveling over its every aspect. "Remarkable. My brother, brilliant inventor that he is, created a machine that travels through time." He blew out a breath. "Did he transport your entire family on this plate? It does not look large enough to carry more than, perhaps, three— what with that box in the center."

Josh shook his head. "Oh, no. The disc we traveled on is much larger. Father created more than one device."

"Three, to be exact," added Ari. Memories of the night she had discovered all three devices, Mr. Somers' weapons stash and his secret laboratory made her shudder.

"And Christopher and I created one, as well." Josh tugged at his shirt, exposing part of the vest he wore.

"You are wearing a machine?" Cedric peered closely at the small portion of the vest.

"Supper is served, my lord," someone said through the closed study door, interrupting Cedric's inspection.

After stowing the device beneath his desk, Cedric led Ari and Josh out and locked the door behind him.

Ari dug into her meal—a pie with mashed potato crust and some kind of meat. Lamb, she guessed by its texture. Brown gravy and onions gushed onto her plate after she took the first bite. Though different from anything she remembered her mother serving, it was good, and she was famished. "How soon can we visit Christopher?" she asked Cedric between bites. She'd go right away if he agreed to it. Now that she knew where Christopher was, wild horses couldn't stop her from seeing him.

Cedric tilted his head and narrowed his eyes. "Christopher is in prison. Females cannot visit male prisoners—especially prisoners sentenced to die."

She choked on her food. "He's been sentenced to die?" Her tasty meal now soured in her stomach.

Cedric gave a single nod. "I assumed you had perceived as much. Murder as well as theft from royalty are capital offenses. A shadow darkened his countenance. "Now Christopher will die all because he tried to spare me from a similar fate."

Panicked, Ari glanced from one man to the other. "How can we save him? We have to get him out!" Her voice rose in volume with each word.

Cedric shook his head. "I've been puzzling it out for weeks and haven't found an answer. I've convinced Parliament to delay his execution thrice, but I fear the patience of the peerage is growing thin. The *ton* is screaming for blood. He is set to be hanged in just two days."

Ari gasped. This couldn't be happening. She pushed her plate away, the very smell of food now making her nauseous.

"There is more." Cedric continued, "When I saw him last, he was ill—prison fever. Any plan we formulate must be executed straightaway. Sickness will likely take him before the noose does."

Ari dropped her head. Shame and self-condemnation fell over her like a wool blanket—scratchy, stiff and suffocating. If only she'd come immediately instead of waiting so long.

Cedric tapped his chin. "He tried to tell me something, but weak, and I'm afraid, delirious as he was, I could hardly make it out."

"What? What did he tell you?" Josh pushed his plate away with force. The flames lighting the candelabra in the center of the table waved to and fro.

"Some gibberish about Benjamin. He seemed to wish to warn me—" He lifted his hands and shrugged. "As I said, gibberish."

Ari felt the blood drain from her face. "If Christopher said to beware of his father, that means Mr. Somers—I mean Somerset—is here." She shivered. "I am sure he was the person chasing me earlier."

Cedric furrowed his brows, looking skeptical. "There are plenty of ne'er-do-wells about the streets of London past dark."

"No"—she shook her head, feeling queasier by the minute—"I've been chased by him before. I'll never forget the sound of his feet hitting the ground behind me."

"I would think one pair of boots sounds much like another. 'Twould have been difficult for you to tell up from down in the state in which we found you." Cedric bit into his bread.

"Don't you see? Benjamin Somers got away from us. He could be anywhere!" She knew she sounded hysterical. But this man had killed her family, tried to kill her and was now responsible for Christopher's impending death.

"Hold on, Arianna. Cedric knows nothing of what Father did to you." He turned his attention to Cedric and regaled him with the tale, including the specifics of their chase through New York City, which had resulted in Arianna's broken leg.

Christopher had relayed the tale to Josh, who described it in precise detail. Hearing it again after over a year had passed still struck a fearful chord in Ari's heart. Benjamin Somers was a criminal. A criminal on the loose—the worst kind.

"Ah, yes. Christopher gave me the fine points of the story. I am certain he would have elaborated, but he wished to deliver the jewels and make a hasty return to you." He motioned to Arianna. "I apologize for my brother's severe treatment toward you, Miss Miller. As for Benjamin's whereabouts"—he shook his head—"he would not come here where he is hunted."

"Unless," said Josh, "he wants something from you. Father never stops until he gets what he wants. What could that be?"

"Money and power. Same as every other egomaniac. Only, he has means of stealing it from any century he chooses." Ari said each word with a bitter edge, then immediately regretted taking such a harsh tone in front of Cedric. "I'm sorry. I"—she swallowed—"I got to know him a little too well."

Josh spoke up. "You are partially right, Ari. He can steal money and possessions; however, he cannot steal power."

Cedric angled his head and narrowed his eyes. "As the youngest of three brothers, Benjamin always did feel cheated out of the possibility of attaining a title." His mouth pulled down to a scowl.

"He wants to be an earl?" Ari widened her eyes in disbelief. When would enough be enough for that greedy man? "You yourself said he is being hunted here. How could he possibly serve as an earl?"

The butler placed a bowl of golden pudding in front of Ari.

"No thank you." She pushed it away. Even the smell repulsed her. The current topic of conversation had her stomach souring more by the minute.

"Lund, I believe we shall all decline the butterscotch custard. We've had quite enough food." He rubbed his stomach. "Give my apologies to Cook." Cedric waited for the butler to exit the room, then turned back to Ari and Josh. "I suppose if he found a way to absolve himself of the crimes which have been laid at his feet, he could assume a position of authority. But that would be difficult."

"He's planning something. I just know it," said Ari. "Christopher might have been speaking gibberish, but he wasn't delirious." Her body jolted as an idea sprang to mind. "I don't know how, but his father is planning a way to steal your title."

Josh pushed his hand through his hair. "But Christopher is already in prison for the jewelry heist. Why is Father still being hunted?"

"Everyone knows it was Benjamin who committed the heist and the murder, but you know how Londoners are, Joshua. They want someone to pay. When Christopher showed up here with all the evidence in his possession, that was good enough for society. And I am ashamed to say my housemaid not only alerted the authorities, but led them right to the goods." He rubbed a hand over his face. "All because Christopher refused to marry her. And now he's a dead man."

Tears blurred Ari's vision. Cedric had made it sound so final. "We can't give up. There must be something we can do for Christopher."

A moment passed, then Cedric jerked, sitting up straight. "Joshua, if we can get Christopher to the twenty-first century, can physicians cure him?"

"I—I don't know, Uncle Cedric. My time there has been spent at home where Mother educated us. I know very little about modern medicine."

"Well, I do," said Ari. "My mother was a nurse. There isn't much that can't be cured in our century. I don't know what prison fever is, but I'll bet there's a treatment."

They'd circled back to the original question: how would they free Christopher? And since they suspected Benjamin's presence in nineteenth century London, how could they nab him before he did something dangerous to declare himself eligible for the title of Earl of Hemington?

"Wait, I nearly forgot. I brought Christopher's revolver and his handcuffs." Ari located her bag and pulled both items from it. "Maybe they'll come in handy."

"As when you were being chased, Ari?" said Josh, giving her a pointed look.

"Oh my gosh. I had a gun the whole time!" She put a hand over her face to hide her embarrassment.

"Let me see that." Cedric's eyes widened as he handled the gun. "I've seen nothing like it."

"Christopher is a police…er…a constable. It's his," said Josh. "We should probably get back to our plan." Ari thought Josh might be worried Cedric would accidentally fire the gun, as he never took his eyes off the old man's fingers.

"Very well." Cedric handed the revolver to Ari.

She placed both items back into the reticule.

"If you'd like, Miss Miller, you may retire. My butler has prepared a room for you. Joshua and I will devise a plan."

Arianna blanched. "Oh no. I don't want to miss anything." Typical men—of the nineteenth century, that is.

Cedric tilted his head, appearing confused. "As you wish. But we should at the very least retire to the bookroom, where there is a divan on which you can stretch your legs. You must be exhausted from your long day."

Long day was an understatement. Once settled in the bookroom, Ari listened to the men, chiming in when she had something to contribute, but try as she might, her eyes refused to stay open.

Joshua roused her early the next morning, anxious

to implement a plan hatched the night before. "We'll leave right after we eat," he said.

His optimism gave Ari hope. "We…all of us? What's the plan? I can't believe I fell asleep, but I'm glad you and Cedric came up with something." She began pulling on her walking boots.

"Sorry, Arianna. Uncle Cedric and I couldn't think of a way to get you into the prison. As it is now, he pays the guards to allow him entrance. He's not certain they'll even let me pass."

The ache in Ari's heart returned. She couldn't just sit idly by while Christopher rotted in jail.

"It is a good plan, Arianna. Please, stay here and let us do this. Christopher's my brother; I'd do anything for him." Tears gathered in Joshua's eyes.

Ari pulled him into a hug. "I know you would."

Breakfast foods were spread across a French Louis XV sideboard. *Oh, to transport a few items back to the twenty-first century,* she thought for the hundredth time. The bacon and trout with butter sauce she recognized, but the meat smothered in horseradish looked disgusting. She filled her plate with bread and bacon and took a seat next to Josh.

"You have a guest, my lord." The butler seemed to have materialized from thin air.

"We are dining," said Cedric. "Who is it?"

"It is I." A woman pushed the butler aside and stood with a smirk on her face.

Arianna stiffened. Why would Rachel come here? She glanced at Joshua. He hid his face behind his napkin. Ari breathed a silent breath of relief. Rachel would surely recognize him, although, at this point, did it really matter? The harm had been done.

"Miss Cartwright. How dare you show your face in my home." Cedric stood.

Rachel took a backward step, and her smirk faltered. "I have come to collect my belongings." She seemed to gain strength with each word.

"You've been without your belongings for weeks. Why retrieve them now?"

"There are"—she paused and ducked her head demurely—"personal items I find I cannot do without."

Cedric didn't budge. "I'll have your things delivered. However, they might possibly have been used as kindling to fuel the fire. Heaven knows my regard for you and your possessions is lower than refuse on the street." He said it as calmly as a conversation over tea.

Rachel narrowed her eyes, then just as quickly dropped her gaze and pouted. "I do not know why you are so unkind, my lord. Your nephew made a promise to me long ago. We were engaged."

Arianna flinched, wanting to charge right up to the girl and yank her hair out. Her innocent act made Ari sick.

Beneath the table, Josh nudged her with his knee.

She remained seated and held her tongue but wished to ask if getting one's fiancé killed was a tradition in this century.

"Miss Cartwright, where did you get that gown? I like to think I am a generous employer, but I know you never earned enough for such an extravagant frock."

Ari examined Rachel's attire for a moment. Other than the color, something differed from the day before. The wrap she wore was the same, yet seemed...bulkier.

"It is none of your business where I got my dress."

Angry darts leapt from Rachel's eyes. "I only came here to retrieve my belongings, and that is what I intend to do." She spun on her heel and exited the room.

Cedric turned to the butler. "Follow her. Discreetly. Her actions smell of something foul."

Rachel didn't take long to gather her belongings. In fact, after only minutes passed, she fled the house without a word.

"Ahem." All eyes turned toward the butler, who stood holding a large satchel. "The girl planted this beneath your bed, my lord."

Cedric took a quick look in the bag, then sprang to his feet. "Our plans have changed. Miss Miller, may I take your hand restraints and gun? I must catch the person responsible for this." He dropped the bag, the contents making a loud clinking noise. "Let us hope these old legs are faster than the housemaid's."

"I'll come with you, Uncle." Josh jumped up, ready to run.

"I think it best if you remain here with Miss Miller."

Josh huffed and sat back down.

"The maid took a hackney, sir," said the butler. "I will get a head start. She went that direction." The butler pointed to his left as he took off in a sprint.

"I will take my coach, then, so I can drag the architect of this crime to the authorities." Cedric shrugged into his coat.

Ari produced both the handcuffs and the revolver.

Cedric tucked them into an inner pocket and darted out the door. He reappeared and picked up the large pouch. "Evidence."

With the events of the morning moving at breakneck speed, Ari had barely had time to grasp it before Cedric and the butler disappeared. As the minutes ticked by, she worried more and more for Christopher. He needed help. But Cedric—the only person able to aid him—was gallivanting all over London, looking for Rachel and whoever had sent her to plant the jewels.

She let out a breath of disgust. That woman continued twisting the knife, and it was about to sever vital organs.

Chapter Thirty-Nine

A guard removed Christopher's empty plate. Glancing from the dish to Christopher, then back to the dish again, he narrowed his eyes. "First time ye've eaten in a week. Thought ye'd be dead by now. Are ye some kind of spirit? Goal fever doesn't take prisoners—it takes lives."

"I suppose I am fortunate," Christopher said. More than fortunate. Whatever Father had dosed him with had improved his health almost instantly.

"Scheduled to swing tomorra'. Shoulda let the fever take ye."

Another guard came to the cell, key in hand. "It seems you are wanted at the courthouse."

"Ah." The first guard smirked. "Get yerself healt from the fever, only to have your execution date moved up, have ye?" He sniggered.

The guards led him out to the transport, poking and jeering at him the whole way. Christopher didn't care. To be lucid and walking away from his rat-infested cell—even if it was temporary—felt divine.

He stumbled into the Old Bailey, guards on both sides of him. His eyes popped at whom he saw. There stood Cedric, flanked on one side by Father, his hands bound in front of him with…modern handcuffs? *Did Cedric manage that?* And on the other side stood Rachel, head hanging down, fingers twisting together.

Fresh disgust for the girl made his heart pound.

The judge cleared his throat. "It seems we are at an impasse and need information from you, Mr. Somerset."

He cleared his throat again, and Christopher realized the judge was speaking to him, not his father.

"Yes, Your Honor?"

"Lord Hemington here has produced whom he claims to be the real London Emporium jewelry thief." The judge motioned to Benjamin. "Mr. Somerset—your father, I have been informed—claims, however, Lord Hemington is lying to cover his own guilt, and that he"—he pointed at Cedric—"in fact, is the robber. More diamonds have been produced by Lord Hemington"—he nodded to a pouch on the dais— "which he declares were planted in his home by this woman." He motioned to Rachel.

Christopher glared at Rachel. A more manipulative, deceitful person he'd never known. And to be party to such an egregious crime—framing the man who had treated her so well. He shifted his gaze to his father. Nothing. No feelings of surprise or compassion surfaced for the man who had once served as his role model. The man had become despicable.

"Who committed the crime, Mr. Somerset? Both men have assured me that you alone know the truth of the matter."

Benjamin turned his eyes to Christopher, then tilted his head and scowled, sending a non-verbal message— or threat. Christopher knew exactly what it was: *I brought you medicine, saving your life. You owe me.*

The unspoken threat did nothing to change Christopher's mind about the man. If anything could be accomplished through his ill-fated attempt to right a wrong and save Cedric's life, it was this: his father would finally pay for his original crime. "Your Honor, Lord Hemington had nothing to do with the heist. My fath—Benjamin Somerset is the guilty party."

Benjamin lunged forward but was restrained by guards. "You are a liar, Christopher! Who saved your life just yesterday?" Spittle flew from his mouth, and his face turned crimson red.

Christopher didn't flinch.

"Take him away," said the judge.

"You'll pay for this, son!" Benjamin hollered as the guards dragged him out.

"Your Honor," Cedric said, "now that the issue is resolved, surely young Mr. Somerset can be freed."

Christopher dared hope for a miracle.

The judge looked as though he were considering the matter. He paused, then shook his head. "No, my lord. I am not convinced father and son were not working as a team. After all, young Mr. Somerset, as you refer to him, was caught first with the jewels."

The wind, which had just filled Christopher's sails with hope, blew out, leaving him as deflated as a featherless pillow. Rough hands yanked on his arms, and before he knew it, he was back in his rodent-infested prison cell.

He moaned. One more day and it wouldn't matter anymore—none of it.

Chapter Forty

The townhouse door creaked open. Ari's heart lurched, then stilled when Cedric entered...alone.

"Joshua, come with me."

"I'm coming, too." Ari stood and began walking toward the door, not even pausing to find her coat.

Cedric turned to Josh. "I thought you had explained prison matters to her, Joshua."

"He did." she blurted out. But she didn't care. She needed to see Christopher. "If I'm not permitted into the prison, I'll wait in the coach. Just don't make me stay here and wonder—"

"'Tis not a good idea to be alone near the prison—even in a carriage. Come, Joshua. I have additional clothing for you in the landau. Arianna, these have been trying times for you. I suggest you take this opportunity to rest. If we are successful, I shall return with Christopher by suppertime. Perhaps you can arrange for a meal to be prepared for him." Cedric turned on his heal and exited the manor.

Josh shrugged. "I'm sorry, Arianna," he whispered. "Just pray our plan works." He hurried to catch up with his uncle.

Ari watched the door close behind him. Pain spasmed through her body. How on earth did Cedric expect her to rest?

Her heart heavy, she longed to at least see

Christopher before he died; to tell him she loved him and plead his forgiveness for not trusting him. If she had ignored her broken heart and listened to her head when the devices had first arrived in Pueblo, perhaps she and Josh would have come to London in time to save him. Dark gloom enshrouded her. She'd never felt so helpless. Two gongs sounded from the clock in the main hall. With every passing minute, she was certain Christopher's life was slipping away.

She couldn't stand idly by while Christopher suffered in prison.

Without further thought, she left the townhouse through the front door. *I have no clue where the prison is located,* she realized. Surely a hackney cab would come along, and she could catch a ride. She headed in the same direction she and Josh had gone when they'd first landed in the nineteenth century. It was freezing out and she hadn't brought her coat. No matter. Christopher was suffering, and she would suffer, too.

Wide-eyed shoppers on Bond Street watched her trudge along. Many wore disapproving expressions. Were they concerned about her coatless state? Or her companionless state? She didn't care. Snow began to fall, making her trek even more difficult. Victorian skirts were hard enough to walk in without the added moisture on the ground.

Several long minutes passed. She'd seen hackney cabs but none stopped despite her wild waving. Her dress was soaked through and her teeth chattered. She knew the prison wasn't on Bond Street but had thought she could direct a hackney driver to deliver her there. However, the more she walked, the colder and more disoriented she became. *Am I still on Bond?* Perhaps this wasn't such a good idea after all. Her extremities turned numb and tingled. If she could find her bearings, she needed to make her way back to the townhouse before she froze to death.

Making a U-turn, she looked for familiar shops—anything that would give her a sign she was headed in the right direction. How had she become so turned around?

A man bundled in a long coat and tall hat approached her. He looked like Abraham Lincoln. "Are you well, miss?" He eyed her up and down. "You will catch your death exposed in this weather, dressed as you are."

"Please"—her teeth chattered so hard, the words had a difficult time making their way out of her mouth—"can you tell me if the Prison is nearby?"

"The prison." Disgust shone in his eyes. "I should hope not. Are you with someone—a husband or companion?"

"I—I must have turned myself around." She wouldn't mention that she hadn't known where the prison was in the first place. Wandering through London in search of Newgate hadn't been her brightest idea. "Then will you direct me to Lord Hemington's townhouse? It's on Bond Street."

"Oh yes. I know the place. 'Tis on the street parallel to this one. Not far at all."

Then she had been walking in circles.

The man gave her the simple directions, then motioned to the store behind him. "My wife and daughter are shopping in there. I fear I am in for a long wait—"

Too cold to hear the rest of his story, Ari thanked

him and made her way back to Bond Street and the familiar shops near Cedric's home.

By the time she stumbled into the manor, her goosebumps had goosebumps. Her face was numb and her nose runny. A warm bath sounded nice, but there was no time for that. Thank goodness Beatrice had insisted she pack a change of clothes in the storage bin of the traveling device.

The traveling device. She wanted to cry when she remembered its whereabouts—Cedric's locked study. She gave the doorknob a turn, just in case he had left it unlocked. Futile. She dropped her head, deflated—and still freezing. She needed dry clothing—*any* dry clothing. Her teeth continued to chatter as she walked through the manor, opening doors to see if she could find someone or something to help her. Where had the staff gone?

She pushed open a door, revealing a room shelved with labeled and organized boxes. A crate marked "Meredith" jumped out at her. *Meredith. Cedric's wife.* Bingo. Opening the crate, she immediately covered her nose, as a musty smell rose up. The clothes were stored in mothballs, but beggars couldn't be choosy.

Picking a dress, she closed the crate and stood to leave the room, but another label caught her attention.

Vicarage.

****

The clock chimed five times and Ari heard the front door open. Low tones of male voices rumbled through the room. Hope surged in her breast. She rushed through the main hall to meet them. "Christopher?" She couldn't tell who stood next to Cedric.

"We failed." Joshua threw off his coat and hat. "The guards would not let me past the front gate."

Ari's heart sank to her feet.

Cedric shook his head. "I offered a large sum of money. My bribes have not been turned down until this day. The day we needed success most desperately. We had planned to make a switch. Joshua would take Christopher's place."

That explained Josh's strange get-up—a hat that covered most of his face and a high-collared coat that covered the rest.

Cedric went on, "If it had worked, Christopher would be here, and Joshua would transport himself home with that traveling vest he is wearing."

The plan sounded risky. Too many things could have gone wrong, leaving Josh in the nineteenth century—in prison.

"I am sorry we failed. I've no other schemes to try." Cedric laid a consoling hand on Ari's shoulder, then narrowed his eyes at her dress. Perhaps he recognized it as his wife's, but he said nothing.

Ari didn't bother to explain. She only had one concern, and it wasn't the dress she had borrowed. The ache in her heart intensified with each beat as she thought of Christopher. He needed help. "Christopher's execution is tomorrow—" She choked on the words. They hadn't come all this way to fail.

Joshua's dark eyes teared up, and Cedric dropped his gaze to the floor in defeat.

She knew they'd done their best, but their best hadn't been good enough. She'd have to put her own plan in motion—that is, if she could come up with something—anything.

Cedric motioned her to follow him. "I do have a bit of news about Benjamin. Perhaps you would like to hear it over tea?"

The only news Ari wished to hear about Benjamin Somers was that he had fallen off the planet, never to be heard of again. But maybe it would be a diversion to talk about something other than Christopher's impending death. "Sure," she said, and followed Cedric and Josh into the drawing room.

Cedric explained the events of the morning, including the court proceedings that had landed Benjamin in prison.

"So, it was Benjamin who sent Rachel here with the jewels to frame you?" Ari asked.

"It was, indeed. But he is now a resident of Newgate Prison, where he belongs. Seems you were correct; Benjamin had concocted some ploy to blame me for the missing jewels. But Christopher failed to cooperate with him." Cedric sipped his tea. "Unfortunately, I was unable to persuade the judge to release Christopher. Seems His Honor believes both father and son are equally guilty."

Ari clutched the arm of the sofa as her heart thudded against her ribcage. "Did you see Christopher?"

"I did."

"He was at the courthouse? How did he look? Is he healing from his illness?"

"Yes, the judge summoned Christopher to the Old Bailey. Curiously enough, he seemed much better. Odd that."

Relief spread through every limb of her body. Many times today, she had envisioned Christopher dying alone in a dirty prison cell. The notion sickened her. To hear his health had improved was a comfort, although now he was surely aware of his impending execution. Perhaps it would've been better if he'd died from prison fever.

"Benjamin has yet to have a trial, but I am certain he will hang for the crime." Cedric's voice pierced through Arianna's contemplations.

Hearing of Mr. Somers' capture should have quelled a portion of her anxiety, but right now she only cared about Christopher.

Cedric continued. "And unlike Christopher, he'll not have an advocate pleading his case in Parliament."

At this point, it didn't really matter. She should be more grateful to Cedric, but if they failed in the end, what good had his sway been with Parliament? She needed to move away from the subject before her bitterness infected her words. "What about Rachel?"

"That I do not know. Once the judge sent Benjamin away and Christopher back to his cell, I left the courthouse, anxious to collect Joshua and implement our rescue attempt. I cannot say if they will respond to my allegations against her. She, of course, took no responsibility, but blamed everything on Benjamin and Christopher."

Of course she had. The awful woman.

Lund, the butler, entered the room. "Supper is served."

****

Ari twisted in her sheets after a short night of little sleep. Execution day had arrived. Cedric had failed. Joshua had failed. Even Benjamin had failed—which Ari now had mixed feelings about. Wasn't it better that

Christopher live, even if he couldn't be with her? Perhaps, but he'd never be happy knowing he'd traded his life for an innocent man's.

No one had come through for Christopher. Arianna tried to imagine the thoughts running through his mind this morning. To know his life would end in a matter of hours—her heart ached for him.

"It's not fair. Not fair! That's how it feels—at least to me." She shuddered and pushed the images from her imagination. "It's time someone saved you, Christopher. Heaven knows how many people you've put your life in jeopardy for. I can do the same for you."

While the men had been away, attempting to free Christopher, she had found and gathered a few items from the storage room. Cedric would surely stop her if he knew of her intentions, so she'd kept them to herself. She recognized that the chance of her own success was miniscule, but she had nothing left to lose—and Christopher had *everything* to lose. Then, during last night's somber supper, she'd plied Cedric with questions. He'd been a wealth of information.

"You see, I was born the second son, behind Robert, and did not think I would serve as the Earl of Hemington—at least so soon. Therefore, it was necessary for me to find another occupation. The clergy has always been a respectable profession for untitled members of the aristocracy. Therefore, I studied for the Priesthood." He had turned to Joshua. "I shouldn't be surprised your father never told you this. He didn't approve of my decision and has always considered me weak."

No doubt to avoid speaking of Christopher's impending doom, Cedric had droned on and on about his profession as a vicar. Arianna had hung on every word—and even used her phone to secretly record some of his statements so she'd remember the details.

Now, to pull off a miracle.

Long after the men had retired, she'd stayed up to copy and forge papers of ordination. She could be imprisoned for what she was about to do.

So be it.

The men had made no mention of attending Christopher's execution, but Ari was certain they planned to go. She doubted they'd wake her this morning, thinking she'd not wish to witness her fiancé's death. Cedric treated her as if she shouldn't do anything but rest, wait and rest some more. She half expected him to arrange for needlework to be supplied, so she'd have something to busy herself with. *Nineteenth century men.* She rolled her eyes.

But she hadn't rested yesterday. And this morning wild horses couldn't stop her from seeing Christopher one last time, and—with a massive amount of luck— saving him.

She shrugged into Cedric's billowy robes. They were so enormous on her, she felt like a mouse in a circus tent. She pulled the hem into a knot, in order to walk without tripping. With her black boots beneath the layers of flowing fabric, the knot was hardly visible. Stored with the robes, she'd found both a large top hat and a flat cap that resembled something a sailor would wear, except it was black, not white. After pinning her hair atop her head, she tried both hats on, then opted for the flatter one—less chance of it falling from her head. To top off the ensemble, she hung a chain bearing a large cross around her neck. Following Sarah's example, she'd created facial hair from one of Cedric's powdered wigs. No one would know the hair on her head wasn't white from beneath the hat. She attached it to her face using tree sap from the evergreen which had covered the traveling device outside—something she'd learned from one of Christopher's misadventures.

Having anticipated being in London longer than the life of her cell phone battery, she'd packed a wireless charger—on a hunch. Of course she'd known she wouldn't be placing any calls in Regency Era London, but there were many other uses for a cell phone. Today her phone could possibly save a life.

She tested the voice changer app she had downloaded weeks ago while playing with Ryder, Maggie's toddler. It took her voice down a couple of octaves but sounded so unnatural. Besides that, she'd have to say everything in her regular voice, then find the button to play it back. Too risky. While in the storage room, besides the box of Cedric's priesthood garb, she'd happened onto something that looked like a cross between a band instrument and megaphone. She lifted it to her mouth and spoke in the deepest tone she could muster. Her voice rang out loud and clear. Perfect. *I'll look foolish, lugging this thing around, but if it can save Christopher…* She shrugged into a long overcoat, then appraised herself in the mirror. The person staring back at her didn't look remotely familiar. Maybe she could pull this off. But if she couldn't… Chills prickled her skin at the thought of her possible fate—and Christopher's.

Bending the collar of the coat up to meet the hat, she slipped out the front door. Dressed as a man, she had no trouble hailing a hackney cab.

Chapter Forty-One

Someone rattled Christopher's cell door. He took a deep breath. There were no more stays of execution left for him. He would die today.

He'd slept oddly well the night before. Perhaps because he had given up hope for a miracle and allowed his mind to rest—to linger in a place with a beautiful golden-haired woman with eyes the color of the sea on a clear day. Thinking of Arianna was the only way he'd survived two months of imprisonment. His memories were the only things left to his name. No judge, no guards could take them away.

"'Tis time." The guard unlocked the chain that tethered him to a ring in the ground, but kept his legs shackled. "Follow me." Another guard stayed close behind him, no doubt to keep him from making a break for it. After three days of only bread and water, Christopher had no strength to do more than drag his feet.

Like a dirge, prison music oozed through the maze of chambers—men groaned awaiting their fates, rodents squalled over a crumb of food. Sounds Christopher would never have to hear again.

Odors of death, dirty bodies and vermin assaulted his senses, but he pushed them away. Newgate Prison and Arianna could not exist together in his mind.

He chose Arianna.

Christopher recognized the sheriff and the prison chaplain, who relieved the guards of their duty. "We will take the prisoner from here," said the sheriff. They led him outside.

He hoped to see daylight one last time, but the hour was early, and the morning overcast. A gentle breeze of bitter-cold air both chilled and refreshed him.

A silversmith removed his leg irons, but, in turn, his wrists were bound in front of him. The men pushed him across the yard, through the hangman's lodge, and out the debtors' door. No one spoke.

Climbing the flight of steps up to the gibbet took every ounce of energy Christopher had left in him. He glanced skyward to his fate. The gallows loomed overhead more than ten feet high. Two other prisoners stood in place, ready to be hanged. Before he could get a look at the congregation gathered to witness the executions, a sack was drawn over his head and he was tugged toward the structure, where a heavy rope tightened around his neck. He attempted to fill his lungs with air, but cold moisture had become trapped beneath the hood and nearly suffocated him. Even more suffocating were the regrets which slogged through his mind: Ari, Mother and his siblings would never know the truth of his disappearance. He hadn't willingly abandoned them—he'd never do such a thing. His chest constricted and his heart spasmed with pain for his loved ones.

"Forgive me, Arianna, Mother, Sarah, Joshua. God keep you all."

"Hats off! Hats off!" the crowd jeered. Christopher knew they didn't call for the removal of hats out of respect. Rather, those in the back hollered "hats off" so they could get a better view of the execution. Disgusting.

He swallowed and prepared to take his last breath. All his concentration went to thoughts of Arianna.

"This man is my parishioner. I demand he get the Benefit of Clergy," came a strange voice that pierced his numbness.

Indiscernible mumbling followed.

"Check his thumb for the mark," rang out yet another voice.

Someone clutched Christopher's bound hands and held them up.

"Is there a brand?"

The man holding his hands grunted. "No, sir."

"Don't matter. He's a murderer and a thief; no clergy for him," called out a voice behind him. Christopher assumed it was the principal hangman speaking. But what were they arguing about?

Think, think. Benefit of Clergy. Ah. It only took seconds to puzzle out. Having worked as a barrister's assistant in London, he'd become familiar with the term that procured many prisoners a release to the care of their vicar—or priest. But Christopher had no vicar—at least not in this century. Then once a prisoner had used the Benefit of Clergy, his thumb was branded so he would be ineligible the next time he was arrested.

The crowd, which had been jeering him and the other prisoners only moments before, fell silent. Then someone hollered, "Neck verse! Neck verse!" The congregation joined in the chant.

Neck verse. Christopher squeezed his eyes shut in concentration, hoping to recall what it was the crowd demanded. The stale air under the sack warmed as his breathing increased.

"His father, Benjamin Somerset, is now incarcerated and will swing for the same crime. This man is innocent. If he can read the verse, he should be entitled to the Benefit of Clergy," said the person who had put a halt to the proceedings. His voice, unnaturally loud, resounded through the chill air.

Christopher had no clue who had professed to be his priest. The voice was unrecognizable, but very distinct. He wished to uncover his head to see who had spoken up for him.

"Go ahead, then. Recite the neck verse, boy," called out the principal hangman.

Christopher's mind raced. The Bible. The neck verse—referred to as such for by reading it, a convict could get a lesser sentence, or even be released. Hence, saving his neck. Found in…the Old Testament. He'd studied the Bible with some intensity, but time had passed as had his focus of late.

"Benefit of Clergy states the prisoner must be able to *read*, not recite the fifty-first Psalm," said the priest.

A pause followed. Christopher longed to remove the hood. He coughed and gasped for air.

The restless crowd grew so silent, even the wind seemed to hold its breath. He sensed someone new had arrived on the scene.

"This man has been convicted of crimes he should have died for months ago. If he can recite—*not read*—any of the fifty-first Psalm, I will release him to your custody, Father. Otherwise, we shall proceed with the executions—all of them." Someone had summoned the judge. Christopher would know his nasally voice anywhere.

A collective gasp erupted from the congregation. Either they feared he *could* recite the verse, or worried he *couldn't*. By their alternating cheers and jeers, Christopher wasn't sure where the audience stood. Their loyalty fluctuated by the minute.

"Can you do it, son?" The priest's voice sounded hopeful, pleading.

He must remember. For Ari. He took a cleansing breath and cleared his mind. "Have mercy upon me—"

"Speak up." the judge demanded.

He cleared his throat and spoke his loudest. "Have mercy upon me, O God, according to thy loving-kindness: according unto the multitude of thy tender mercies blot out my transgressions."

The crowd broke out in a cheer.

He knew more: "Wash me thoroughly from mine iniquity, and cleanse me from my sin." His memory failed him from there. He held his breath and prayed it would be enough.

"Free him! Free him!" the mob demanded.

With his eyes still covered by the executioner's cap, he depended on his other senses to know what was happening around him. He strained, but only heard mumbling, with all the yelling from the crowd.

Finally, the mob quieted, apparently also trying to discern what the judge, the principal hangman and the priest were saying.

"Very well, then. I release him to your custody, Father. I trust you will deliver an appropriate punishment."

"Yes, Your Honor."

Another cheer arose from the onlookers. London Society—so labile.

The rope was pulled from his neck, but his arms remained bound.

"I have a transport waiting, Mr. Somerset. Come this way," said the priest.

"May I have the hood removed?" Christopher asked, hopeful.

"Not yet."

"Father." A voice stopped them. It sounded like the warden.

Christopher's heart stopped. His release had been too good to be true.

"Here are the prisoner's personal effects."

Relief. He expelled a breath under the suffocating executioner's cap.

He stumbled along, the priest clutching his arm. For such a resounding voice, the man seemed small in stature. Once he was helped into a carriage, the leather restraints were removed from his arms, then his head covering. He gulped the frigid air, filling his oxygen-deprived lungs. He wanted to speak, but his throat closed and dizziness overcame him.

Daylight burst through the clouds, piercing his vision. He blinked several times to adjust. After months of dwelling in darkness, he welcomed the intense rays. The priest sat across from him, his head bowed. He wore a black robe that looked several sizes too large for the man's small frame. His collar turned up to meet his hat, and a large, silver cross dangled from his neck. Thick, white whiskers covered his chin, indicating advanced years. His aged body must have been much larger at one time to have such a forceful voice.

Christopher owed his life to this man—this stranger sent by God.

"Thank you," he choked out, his gratitude filling him with emotion. "Thank you, Father."

"Shh," the priest pressed a finger to his lips, head still lowered. "You must be still until we are safely away," he whispered.

Christopher had many questions for the vicar, but he focused instead on staying conscious. He'd wait until they reached safety, which he assumed would be a church.

The old vicar motioned to a carriage blanket beside him. While Christopher relished breathing fresh air, the winter climate bit through his thin prison garb. He pulled the blanket around his shoulders. The priest then reached across and clutched Christopher's hand reassuringly. His gloved hand had a surprisingly firm grip.

The carriage came to a halt on Bond Street. Cedric's townhouse.

"Did my uncle send you? Of course. You must be his vicar."

The priest only hushed Christopher again and motioned for him to exit the carriage.

Still weak, the priest supported him inside and to a seat in the parlor.

The old man then began tugging at his beard. Why, Christopher couldn't fathom. Had he been in disguise?

In a haze of confusion, he began searching the manor for Cedric, stumbling as he walked. He needed to thank him for his brilliant scheme. His weak legs only carried him as far as the foyer.

"Christopher." The priest caught up to him.

"Did Cedric tell you to bring me here? Maybe he's at the church. Should we go to the church?" He paused in his search… Had the priest just called him by his Christian name? And his voice—the volume had lessened considerably. Then he spied a discarded speaking trumpet. Ah. "Who are—"

"Christopher." Once again, the priest's hand clutched his, demanding his attention. "Christopher, it's me."

He flinched. That voice. He stopped and looked closer at his rescuer. Those eyes. "It's impossible." Christopher's heart hammered against his chest. His knees wobbled.

"Ari—Arianna?"

"Yes. It's me." She took another step toward him.

He jerked, shocked. "It cannot be." He peered closely at her, then lifted his hand to touch her face— now free of facial hair. His voice broke into a sob. "Arianna? Y—You were the priest?" He pushed the hat from her head. Her hair broke free from the pins and fell around her shoulders. His lip quivered. Spent of his strength, he sank to the ground and wept.

God hadn't sent a priest to rescue him, He'd sent an angel.

Chapter Forty-Two

Ari, overcome with emotion, as well, lowered herself to the ground and wrapped her arms around Christopher's shuddering frame. They melded together in one form, wordless and clinging to each other, huddled in Cedric's foyer.

She shivered at Christopher's nearness. Months of separation had only intensified her love for this man. He wept in her arms, his head on her chest, and she longed to be even closer—no distance between them ever again.

Several long moments passed. He lifted his head and with trembling hands, he once again touched her hair and face, his eyes never leaving hers. "Can this be? Are you real, or just one of my hallucinations?"

More tears welled in her eyes. She grasped both of his hands. "I am real," she choked out, her heart swelling.

He pulled her into his arms again. "Arianna…Arianna. I can't believe it's you." His grip suggested he'd never let her go. And she didn't want him to. "Seeing your face again is all I have dreamt of for the past two months." He tightened his hold.

They clung to one another. His bent physique was fragile beneath her touch, and she could feel his ribs protruding through his thin shirt. He had suffered hardships she could never comprehend. It sent an ache straight to her core. But it was Christopher. Miracle of miracles. His bearded chin and scraggly hair didn't deter her in the least. He was alive, safe and in her arms. Emotion overtook her as wracking sobs shook her body.

"I'm so sorry, Arianna. I'm so very sorry." His hands stroked her back, soothing her. "I should have listened to you." He kissed her ear and cheek, then hugged her to him once more.

Ari returned his embrace with all the energy of her soul.

When they finally loosened their holds on each other, she looked into his watery eyes. The vibrant blue had dulled, and sores marred his face. By the discoloration of his skin and hair, not to mention his soiled clothes, she understood how much he had suffered in prison. A lump clogged her throat and fresh tears began to fall.

The butler entered the room, startling them. His expression turned from stoic to surprised. "Excuse my interruption. I thought I heard Lord Hemington." He gave them a curious look, no doubt at the sight of Christopher, not to mention the strange clothing Ari still wore. Then he straightened, remembering his role. "Mr. Somerset. I am happy to see you have returned to us safely. May I offer you my assistance?" In spite of his attempt at formality, Ari heard emotion choking in his voice.

She longed to remain in Christopher's arms, but he needed nourishment. She must take care of him—make up for lost time. "Yes, Lund. Thank you. Have the cook prepare Christopher some soup and bread. He hasn't had a proper meal in months."

"Perhaps I should bathe first," said Christopher.

His hollow cheeks caused Ari to physically ache. She shook her head. "Lund, bring tea and biscuits now." She turned to Christopher. "You can bathe after you have eaten something."

Christopher closed his eyes and dipped his head in assent. Ari thought he looked relieved.

"I will bring tea, sir, then speak to Cook about serving you a proper meal after your bath." Lund left, then reappeared only minutes later with a tea service. Ari read the deep concern in his eyes. He, too, acknowledged Christopher's dangerous state.

Christopher's eyes widened at the spread—mounds of biscuits on tiered serving platters surrounded glass dishes filled with decadent clotted cream. His hands shook as he lifted the bread to his mouth.

Ari rushed to pour the tea. "I think the cream will be too rich for your fragile digestive system. Perhaps you should stick to dry biscuits and tea.

He devoured them without speaking. The satisfied look on his face said it all.

"Sir," Lund had re-entered the room, "your bath is ready when you are."

Christopher wiped his face with the cloth provided and stood, with Ari's help, to follow Lund.

She trailed them both. The butler stopped and narrowed his eyes. "Miss, I will see Master Christopher gets properly bathed."

"I—I just need...I want to help." She couldn't watch Christopher leave, even for a bath. Proper or not, she would wash his filth, clean his wounds, care for him. She sorely wished to nurture him.

Christopher turned to face her, eyes misting again.

"It's all right, love. I promise to return." His voice was gentle. He kissed her forehead, then took the butler's arm and walked away.

It took every ounce of self-restraint Ari possessed to stay put. Parting with him for even a few minutes sent spasms through her heart. *He will come back. He promised.*

She changed out of the priestly robes and into her nineteenth century garb, which had dried, then carefully replaced the borrowed items in the room where she'd found them. "I'll have to apologize to Cedric for ruining his wig." She closed her eyes and sent up a prayer of gratitude. The ruse had worked. They only needed to get back to the twenty-first century now and get on with their lives—together.

She had so much to tell Christopher. They had exchanged precious few words—she being preoccupied with his care, and he struggling to hang on to reality. She reflected on his skeletal frame and new tears burned her eyes. Had she arrived at the gallows a few minutes later, Christopher would be dead. A shiver snaked through her body.

The front door opened, sending December air whooshing through the manor. Cedric and Joshua entered. Their energetic chatter ended upon seeing Arianna.

Josh beamed. "Ari, you'll never guess what happened."

"A priest showed up and freed Christopher." Cedric shed his coat. "But we do not know who the priest was or where he took him. We have sent out teams to search every parish in London, because he seems to have disappeared."

That explained why they had taken so long to return from the prison. They'd been looking for Christopher. Ari was grateful she'd had the time alone with him.

Joshua, also taking off his coat and hat, paused when he caught Ari's eye. "You've been crying."

She had been. Just the thought of Christopher being under the same roof with her brought waves of emotion.

Before she could reply, Joshua, his brows knit together in a look of concern, tugged a handkerchief from his pocket and gave it to her. "Please don't be angry with at us for leaving you here this morning. We could not bear the thought of you witnessing the gruesome hanging of your beloved. I nearly stayed at home myself. But cheer up. Did you not hear our news? Christopher is alive!" A smile spread across his face. "We just need to find him."

She wiped her eyes. "No worries, Josh, they've mostly been happy tears."

Josh narrowed his eyes but continued removing his gloves.

"I have good news, as well." She waited until they had their winter wear stowed. "You couldn't find Christopher...because he's here!"

Both men's faces blanched. "What?" they said in unison.

"Christopher is here," she repeated.

"Here? But how?" Cedric glanced around the room.

She opened her mouth to divulge the incredible tale, but a sudden realization stopped her. The authorities may be investigating Christopher's last-second rescue. And by forging documents of ordination—using Cedric's papers as her model—and impersonating a vicar by wearing Cedric's priestly garb, she might have put him in danger. However, if Cedric didn't know what she had done, he could plead innocence. She'd tell Joshua once they were safely back in the future. "A coach dropped him off over an hour ago. He said a vicar had rescued him?" She tilted her head and furrowed her brows, hoping for a confused look.

"True enough," said Cedric. "Saved him just before his final breath, I might add."

Joshua stepped in front of Cedric, elation radiating from him. "Ari, I wish you had been there. Christopher was brilliant. The priest asked him to recite a verse in Psalms. I doubted he could do it, especially having been ill, but he did. After all he has been through, he can still recite Bible verses." He swiped at a tear. "Where is he?"

"He's bathing. You might see if he needs help dressing. He is very weak."

Josh sprinted toward the guest suites.

Ari looked up to see Cedric scrutinizing her. Guilt pinched at her, and she wondered if he could see through her feigned innocence.

He motioned to her chin. "You have something on your face."

She felt her skin. Tree sap. A whoosh escaped her lungs. "Oh." She forced a laugh. "Breakfast. I'd better go wash." She fled to her room.

Chapter Forty-Three

A bath had never felt so heavenly. With renewed strength, Christopher scrubbed himself raw, washing away every bit of prison grime from his body. Stepping from the bath, he relished in the soft towel provided. He secured it around his waist, then reached for his smelly rags.

"These clothes should work. I believe you are about the same size as Uncle Cedric."

Christopher jerked toward the voice. "Joshua? Is it you? Did you come with Arianna?" He blinked away sudden tears at seeing his brother.

Josh laid the clothing on a dresser and pulled Christopher into a hug. "We came to save you. I went to Newgate Prison with Cedric yesterday to switch places with you—you see, I'm wearing the vest and could have blasted out of there—but the guards wouldn't allow me in."

"I cannot believe my good fortune." Christopher wished to say more, but a lump lodged in his throat. He hadn't thought he'd see Joshua ever again. He held him back to inspect him. Other than some fake facial hair on his lip, he looked the same. It had only been two months but seemed like a lifetime since he'd seen his family. Swallowing down the lump, he found his voice. "How are Mother and Sarah?"

"We held a memorial service for you." Josh buried

his head in his hands. "Mother cried in her room for days. Sarah and I didn't know what to do…" His voice hitched, and Christopher's heart went out to his brother.

"It's all right, Josh. I'm here. I would never willingly leave you and the others to languish in the twenty-first century. Never!"

"Ari tried to tell us that, but"—Josh slumped down on a chair—"eventually, we even had her convinced the letter was real. I am so sorry it took us this long to reach you."

"What happened to convince you of Rachel's deceitfulness?" He'd never forget the anger he'd felt when Rachel had admitted to her scheme.

"Arianna. She was determined to prove the letter was a forgery."

Of course Arianna had been the one. Christopher dressed quickly, with Joshua's help. He had been away from Ari too long. "Where is the device? We must be on our way immediately. I don't wish to risk another delay." His heart bruised at the thought of the worry and grief he'd caused his family. Coming here had never been a good idea.

"It's locked in Cedric's bookroom."

Cedric. Christopher needed to thank him for all his visits to Newgate and for persuading Parliament to delay his execution. He tied his hair neatly back and had Joshua give his beard a trim. A thorough shave would have to wait. He hadn't had the strength before his bath. Remembering the sharp razors of the nineteenth century, he'd feared in his weakened condition, he'd slip and slit his throat.

"Josh, you said you're wearing the vest?"

"Yes. Arianna made me promise to wear it always,

so I could escape if we were ever threatened. It was the only way Mother agreed to let me come."

Again, warmth spread through his chest at Ari's thoughtfulness. After the trials he'd put her through, he hoped she still wished to marry him. At present, he didn't feel worthy of her love. He'd put his entire family through a terrible ordeal. What had seemed necessary at the time had turned out to be selfish— selfish to leave Arianna immediately after asking for her hand in marriage, and selfish to leave his family at all in an uncertain future. *That stops now.* "I think you should transport home to present-day Colorado immediately, and let Mother and Sarah know I am all right. Then Ari and I will come as soon as possible."

Josh opened his mouth—

"Please do this for Mother, Josh. I know we have only just been reunited, but the sooner someone gets home, the better." He once again clutched Josh to him. "What you did, coming back in time to rescue me"—he had to pause to compose himself—"thank you, little brother. Thank you."

Josh sniffed. "Should I at least tell Cedric goodbye?"

"If you wish, but I think it's best you just leave now. Ari and I will be along shortly."

"Very well. But if you take too long, I'm coming back after you." As Josh twisted the appropriate dial on the vest, the room began to vibrate. In seconds he was gone.

Christopher regretted sending him away so soon. It would have been nice to eat a leisurely supper with Ari, his uncle and his brother. But thoughts of his mother and Sarah had urged him to send Josh on his way.

Still weak, he took timid steps, walking through the great hall and the dining area, expecting to locate Ari or Cedric. He found neither. He leaned against the wall for a brief rest. A wrap at the front door startled him. Lund rushed past him. Christopher stopped the butler long enough to ask if he'd seen Ari.

"I believe she has gone that direction." Lund pointed toward the bookroom.

"Thank you."

As Christopher neared the study, he saw her standing outside the room, her hand covering her mouth.

"Ari—"

She put a trembling finger to her lips, hushing him, her face as white as snow.

Chapter Forty-Four

Ari couldn't believe what she was hearing. With the bookroom door slightly ajar, she could see a woman's back. But she could hear the voices clearly as they argued.

"What's going on?" whispered Christopher.

"It's Cedric and Rachel. Listen."

"I'll not pay you until the job is complete," said Cedric in a voice so tinged with venom it was nearly unrecognizable.

"I have done everything you asked of me since I rid the place of that devilish contraption months ago," Rachel shouted back.

"And if you hadn't sent the machine away, I could have dispatched my nephew and taken it into my possession right away instead of dragging out this whole ordeal." A loud thud sounded; Ari knew Cedric had slammed his fist onto his desk. "As it stands, the boy's alive. I must kill him yet."

His voice bellowed so loudly, Ari wondered if all of Bond Street heard.

"And that blamed priest who saved him"—a guttural roar made Ari quiver—"I'd have killed him on the spot, had I found him today."

She felt Christopher's arms enfold her from behind, lending the comfort her anxiety-ridden soul hungered for. How close she had come to telling Cedric of her ruse. She turned and buried her head in Christopher's broad chest. His arms tightened around her.

Rachel's volume matched Cedric's, only higher and piercing. "If you recall, I needed to remove any temptation Christopher had to leave because he promised to marry me! I wanted *him*, not the machine! It wasn't until after I sent that thing back to America that you approached me with your scheme. How was I to know you would turn on your own nephew?"

Ari's stomach soured more with each poisonous word. She glanced up to see Christopher's mouth agape.

His gaze met hers, a glint of hurt and betrayal in his eyes.

More yelling drew their attention back to the conversation.

"And if you only planned to kill him anyway, why bother talking Parliament into delaying his execution?" Rachel spat out.

Cedric let out a huff. "I could have cleared his name had I wished to, but I needed to keep Christopher in prison long enough for someone to come searching for him, so I could gain possession of the machine. And, as you saw while delivering your performance here yesterday, it worked—Joshua and Christopher's American chit delivered the machine right into my hands. However, now I shall have to kill the lot of them."

Christopher sucked in a breath.

"Somehow we will escape," Ari whispered. "I didn't come all this way to fail." She tried to gain eye-contact with Christopher, but his attention was riveted on the conversation in the study, his eyes in a trance. Ari faced forward, holding his arms securely wrapped around her.

"And while I did not know it would work so well," Cedric continued, "keeping Christopher alive for as long as I did flushed out his father—my conniving brother. Now he shan't be in my way when I employ the machine."

From her periphery, Ari saw that someone else had joined them at the door. Probably Josh or Lund. Good—the more witnesses the better. She put a finger to her lips so they'd keep quiet.

"Are you saying you do not intend on paying me for my services until after you have killed Christopher…and his entire family?" Rachel's voice rose like the screeching of a violin. "You are more abhorrent than both of your brothers. Robert and Benjamin were monsters, but in comparison to you"— she paused—"at least they did not feign kindness."

A wicked laugh rumbled from Cedric. "I suppose you believed my story about poor Robert dying of a fever." A moment of deafening silence filled the air. "There was never a fever. I killed him. And Benjamin—I made certain his inventions never saw the light of day. Don't you see? I am the most powerful of all the Somerset men. That is why *I* am the earl—not Robert; not Benjamin. And now, with the aid of my brother's invention, I shall conquer worlds I never dreamed imaginable."

"Then pay me now, and I will step out of your way, Your Royal Majesty."

A slapping sound made Ari jump.

Rachel whimpered.

"I will not put up with your insolence. And as for paying you…surely you comprehend that I cannot have you traipsing through London with knowledge of my secrets."

Ari could see the glint of Christopher's service revolver through the door. "He's got your gun, Christopher. He's going to shoot her."

"No! Do not kill me! Please! I will be silent. I will do your bidding. You never have to pay me—just let me live!"

Christopher started toward the door, but a large hand shoved him aside.

"Stand back!" A constable shouldered his way past both Ari and Christopher, pistol drawn. He threw the door open wide and aimed his weapon at Cedric. "Drop the gun. I have heard enough from the pair of you to lock you both away and dispose of the key."

"You'll do no such thing." Cedric changed his gun's aim from Rachel to the constable. "You see, this isn't just any pistol, it's a gun from the twenty-first century. With it I can put a hole through you from a great dist—"

The constable grunted, then pulled the trigger, dropping Cedric to the ground mid-sentence.

"Oh, Christopher! You've heard your uncle threaten me and have come to save me." Rachel flung her arms open and ran toward Christopher.

Ari had had enough of this girl. She intercepted Rachel before she was able to reach Christopher and grabbed her by the shoulders. "You aren't going anywhere but prison."

Rachel flailed, screeching and swinging wild arms at Arianna. "He promised to marry me centuries before he even met you. Christopher is mine!"

"He belongs to no one. But I assure you, he'd never marry you in any century."

Rachel stomped hard on Ari's foot, a gleam of victory entering her eyes. "We shall see. I believe the constable will have something to say about this." She attempted to wiggle out of Ari's hold.

A surge of strength gave Ari the power she needed to keep Rachel in her grasp. She loosened one hand enough to probe around Rachel's collar until her fingers snagged on a chain. The locket. Pulling it from beneath Rachel's dress, she gave it a hard yank and threw it across the room. "Consider the promise broken." She shoved Rachel to the ground next to the constable. "She's all yours."

The constable secured Rachel in restraints.

Satisfied that Rachel was out of the way, Ari rushed to Christopher's side. He had stumbled across the room to his uncle and lifted his head from the floor.

Cedric's chest rose and fell in a ragged rhythm. Christopher shook his head.

"How could you, Cedric? How could you?"

The dying man coughed, blood spewing from his mouth. "How could I not?" His eyes rolled back, and his body fell limp in Christopher's arms.

Christopher gently laid Cedric's body back on the floor, studied his face for a moment, then staggered to his feet.

Adrenaline kept Arianna from giving in to her tattered nerves. Where was Josh? They needed to leave. Now. She peered around the room until she spotted the time traveling device hidden behind Cedric's desk. *We need to find Josh, get on that machine and leave this place and time.*

Rachel's whiny voice cut into Ari's thoughts. "He is the man you are after." She jerked her head toward Christopher. "He should not be out of prison."

"Curiously enough, that is what I came here to investigate. Then I argued my way past the butler to find this brabble." The constable waved a hand in the air.

Lund stood in the doorway, his face a chalky white. "I—I had no knowledge of my master's dealings."

"Pray you are telling the truth. You and the entire staff *shall* be investigated." The constable turned toward Christopher. "I will need you to be a witness and testify against this woman."

As Christopher narrowed his eyes and opened his mouth to speak, Ari took him by the hand and led him behind Cedric's desk, where the disc lay. He glanced at Ari and back to the constable. "I'm afraid that will be impossible."

"Wait. Where's Josh?" Ari whispered.

Christopher squeezed her hand. "I sent him home."

"You will land right back in prison if you refuse to testify in court." The constable lunged toward Christopher.

"Not this time." Christopher turned the dial on the device. The room rumbled, knocking the constable off balance and to his knees.

Ari clung to Christopher as the device plunged them into the void of time travel. She sighed in great relief, then closed her eyes and smiled.

Chapter Forty-Five

Christopher's heart beat so rapidly, he feared it might explode. Had they indeed escaped the nineteenth century? And was this beautiful woman in his arms Arianna? Or was she an illusion—another hallucination? He'd had so many while ill, it was hard to discern truth from fantasy. Perhaps he had died, and this was heaven. If so, he would happily remain.

"Ari—" He forced out her name, but it dissolved into space and time. Ah, yes. He knew by now that time-traveling was no occasion for conversation. In fact, it put him and whomever he traveled with in a state of temporary paralysis. Any questions he had for Ari would have to wait. He settled for holding her close.

Waves of gratitude washed over him like the blue sea in July as he recalled the events of the day—the events of the last two months, or even the past five and a half years. Nothing had gone according to his plans. As a young college student at Cambridge University, he'd pictured himself graduating, working as a barrister, marrying a suitable young lady and rearing a family. The picture—which had been shattered by his father—was pleasant enough, yet incomplete.

Ari shifted in his arms.

Like a bolt of lightning striking his heart, he realized more than ever before how she completed his soul, his life, his very being. He tightened his grip on her.

He still couldn't believe she had disguised herself as the priest who'd saved his life. Where did she get the robes? How did she know to use the Benefit of Clergy? Surely Cedric hadn't aided her. Not when his end goal was Christopher's demise.

They arrived in his father's lab. The odor of chemicals immediately assaulted his senses. He felt Ari flinch in his arms. The smell must have evoked some horrendous memories for her. "Are you all right, love?"

She nodded then, clutched him tighter. "Before I lose you to your family, let me look at you. I need to know you are real and not just another one of my dreams."

She must have experienced the same doubts about the authenticity of their situation as had he.

"Will this help?" He lowered his head and captured her lips with his. Even after spending time in the nineteenth century, she still smelled sweet. A powerful energy exploded in his chest and spread through his body. *This is real. Ari is real.*

She kissed him back as if her life depended on it. Finally pulling away, tears washed down her face.

"Ari?"

"I never thought I'd see you again." She wiped the tears with the back of her hand. "I am just so happy."

He looked around for something to dry her face, but found nothing in the lab. He tugged off the cravat around his neck that he'd borrowed from Cedric and gently dried her eyes, then kissed her again. "I love you, Ari."

"Christopher, is that you?" his mother clamored

through the trapdoor.

As happy as he was to be home, he craved more time alone with Ari.

Before he had a chance to reply, his mother was down the ladder and wrapping him in her arms. "My boy. You are safe." She sniffled, then turned to Ari. "You did it. You and Joshua brought him home."

"Josh. Is he here?" Christopher owed a lot to his brother. He needed to thank him.

Beatrice stepped out of Christopher's embrace. "Isn't he with you?"

Cold dread spread through Christopher's veins.

Ari gasped. "You sent him home before us." Her forehead creased as her brows knitted together.

"I did. Right after he brought me Cedric's clothes. He should be here." Now his heart rattled in his chest for a whole different reason—Joshua was lost in time.

Christopher couldn't become a victim of this time trap again. That's what it was. Wandering through time and space was unnatural, and nature had found a way to keep them from it—by trapping them somewhere they had no business existing. He looked at his mother, her concern-filled face drooped with defeat. He couldn't put her through this again, either.

Nor could he leave his brother to wander space and time.

He once again mounted the machine. "I must find Josh. We cannot leave him to the unknown.

"It's too dangerous, Chris." Ari grabbed his hands, pulling them away from the dials. "And you're still so weak."

Warmth from her hand brought him to his senses. He must puzzle out where to look for his lost brother before racing into another time dimension.

"Is that you, Christopher?" Sarah's voice preceded her as she descended the ladder. The room began to vibrate, nearly throwing her to the ground.

Joshua landed hard, stumbling across the floor.

Christopher blew out a breath of relief and dismounted the traveling device. "I worried we lost you, little brother."

Joshua's cheeks flamed red. "I may have gone the wrong direction. If you thought the nineteenth century was primitive, best keep your distance from the seventeenth."

No one laughed at Joshua's attempt at levity. There had been too many failures.

His mother opened her arms. "I am delighted to have both my sons home safely." Big tears rolled down her face as she gathered Josh in for a hug.

Teary Sarah joined in the reunion, embracing each time-traveler. "I cannot wait to hear every detail. Mother and I have worried so about your safety—and about being stranded here in the twenty-first century. I'm happy you have all returned." She tugged on Joshua's fake mustache. "Looks like the superglue held out." She smiled.

"Yeah." Josh grunted. "Now to get it off." His lips turned down in a mock scowl.

Christopher soaked in his family's warmth, but noticed Ari's face had grown pale. The chemicals. They needed to get out of this cursed room. He squeezed her hand.

She sagged against him. "I'm just glad you didn't have to go find Josh."

He cleared his throat. "How about we move the

party upstairs."

After they'd made their way up the ladder, Mother and Sarah demanded to hear the whole tale. Christopher wished to hear it, too. After all, he'd been in prison for much of it.

Josh began and Christopher added details from his point of view.

When Ari recited her portion of the story, everyone sat captivated. "I had to do something," she said.

"So you dressed as a vicar?" Mother's face clouded. "If you had been caught, you *both* would have been executed."

"She wasn't caught. Arianna was magnificent," Christopher said. There was no other word for her valiant actions.

"Wait, wait." Joshua's face was creased in confusion. He pointed at Ari. "You were the priest at the execution? But that priest was an old man."

Ari's cheeks turned pink. "I have hidden talents."

Everyone laughed except Josh, who was still gawking at her.

"Sorry I didn't tell you, Josh. I thought you might try to stop me." She shrugged. "And now that I know Cedric's true nature, I'm glad I kept my mouth shut."

Now Josh looked dumbfounded. He shook his head and shrugged. "What are you talking about?"

"What is Cedric's true nature?" asked Sarah.

"That's another long tale. But it turns out Father isn't the worst of the Somerset brothers." Christopher had everyone's attention as he told of Cedric's deceit and failed attempt at stealing the machine for his own purposes. "I should have never gone back in time to save him. He ended up dying because of the machine anyway."

Several silent moments passed before Beatrice spoke up. "You are much too thin, son. I will cook something wonderful for supper to celebrate your homecoming."

In his still weakened state, he wouldn't argue about his need for nourishment. Bread and tea had only taken the edge off.

"Mother, we've remained at home waiting for this day for so long now, I believe we don't have anything left in the kitchen to cook for a celebration dinner," Sarah reminded her.

"Besides that, twenty-first century women don't usually consider slaving away in the kitchen a celebration. Let's go out to dinner, on me," said Christopher. I'm not certain I still have a job, but being reunited after so many weeks of"—his voice cracked— "loneliness—"

"You mean torture," said Josh.

"Heartache," added Ari.

"Worry," said Sarah.

They all looked at Beatrice. "Despair and hopelessness."

Christopher handed her a handkerchief, then squeezed her hand.

She wiped her eyes and smiled through her tears. "And 'tis about time we celebrated away from that wearisome kitchen."

Everyone laughed.

Ari stood and smoothed her skirt. "I'll need some time to clean up—wash the nineteenth century off me."

"I never knew I could miss running water so much." Josh turned toward the stairs leading to his bedroom. He paused. "I nearly forgot. Sarah, I found the tree and..." He tossed a bundle of letters on the table in front of her.

Sarah's mouth fell open. "These were all inside the tree hollow?"

"That they were. Now I plan on taking a very long shower. See everyone in about an hour?"

They all agreed and headed to their separate rooms.

Christopher caught Ari's hand and walked her to the guestroom. Slipping inside and closing the door behind them, he cradled her face in his hands. His heart galloped as he looked into her aqua-blue eyes. Exhilaration and warmth spread through his body at the tender expression in her gaze. He lowered his head and paused, breathing her in before kissing her.

Her soft lips urged him on, but he had to know the thoughts in her heart. "I love you, Ari," he whispered. "I am so sorry for the travails I have put you through." He paused, unsure if he wanted to know the answer to the question he must ask. "I hope you still wish to marry me."

Her eyes flashed open wide. "If there is anything I've learned these past few months, it's that I don't want to live without you. Traveling to the nineteenth century wasn't a completely unselfish act on my part. Of course I still want to marry you. It's always been you—just you." She tugged his head back down for another kiss.

Her words and her kisses brought his soul the comfort he'd craved. He expelled a breath, relief slowing his heartbeat to a more manageable pace. He honestly feared that after getting a closer look at the Somerset family tree, she might reconsider. "You could have lost everything, including your life, chasing after me." Tears welled in his eyes. No form of a "thank you" would ever be enough to repay her.

"It was worth it."

He kissed her again, enjoying the shivers of energy igniting his body.

She matched his passion, deepening the kiss for several long moments.

He reluctantly released her when she ended the kiss, then glanced beyond her to the bed. "Soon. Our wedding must be soon."

Ari nodded. "Very soon. Before Christmas."

"That doesn't give us much time to plan. What is today's date?" He'd lost track of time days ago.

"I believe it's December seventh. And I don't need much time. Without my family, there's no reason to plan a big, fancy wedding. Just a simple church ceremony will do." Her eyes brightened. "Wait— unless—if your father died for his crimes back in 1814, will my family be alive?"

Christopher's body jerked, struck by the notion. "Look on your phone to see if there is any announcement of his death."

"No service here, Chris. This house may as well be located in the nineteenth century."

"Then we'll check when we're in town at the restaurant." The spark of hope lighting her eyes warmed his heart. However, the more he thought about it, the more he realized the fallacy of the notion. If Father died after just being arrested—yesterday, or two hundred and five years ago from yesterday—could Christopher be standing here with Ari? Figuring out time-travel logic made him dizzy.

"But wait. I guess that wouldn't make sense. Your father was only visiting the nineteenth century from our time." Ari's shoulders sagged. Evidently, she'd had the same realization. "Still…maybe?"

"We will check. And don't forget, I have a warrant for his arrest, should he escape Newgate and turn up."

She nodded. "I guess I should clean up." Her voice had gone from enthusiastic to disappointed.

If only he could somehow resurrect her family.

Chapter Forty-Six

After a wonderful meal at Aldolfo's, the family lingered to talk. Ari caught Christopher's eye and they excused themselves to go for a walk outside. Ari pulled out her phone. The chill air made her hands shake, or was it her nerves? She quickly Googled the London Diamond Emporium—the same source from which she'd found the article about Cedric's hanging. Nothing. No article about anyone paying for the crime. Her heart plummeted. "It looks like your father didn't even hang for his original crime." If Mr. Somers hadn't died for the heist and the murder he'd committed, he likely still roamed the earth—rather, ping ponged across it—committing crimes to suit his pleasure. She'd be looking over her shoulder until the day she died. She couldn't keep a scowl from her face.

Christopher frowned, as well. "I was afraid of that."

"Afraid of what? They had him in prison. What could have happened?"

"The vest. He always wore it beneath his clothes. I'm certain the only way Cedric was able to capture him at all was by catching him off-guard with my revolver, then cuffing him. Very smart move on your part—taking my gun and handcuffs—by the way. Once the guards set him free of his hand restraints, he had easy access to his vest controls. He only needed seconds to transport himself to freedom."

Ari groaned. "Of course. I forgot about the other vest. But how would the guards or your father open the modern handcuffs?"

He lifted a shoulder and shook his head. "He'd find a way. Each time he visited my cell at Newgate, Father assured me he could never be confined and didn't fear capture because of the vest."

All hope gone, she threw her hands in the air. "One more win for Mr. Somers."

"Hey, we'll keep checking. I might be wrong. If we're living in some kind of parallel time-line, he could still be cooling his heels in prison, awaiting his execution date." He shrugged. "I honestly cannot pretend to know how it all works. Come here." He pulled her to him and kissed her, warming her cold heart. "Never give up hope. Had you given up on me, I would be a dead man."

Ari's skin prickled at the thought.

"Christopher, promise me—no matter what— you'll never use the time machines—disc, vest, any of them—again. I can't marry you if there is any chance you're going to risk your life for some altruistic purpose through time-travel. Please." She hadn't planned on the wave of emotion washing over her as it did. But passion for her future with him and only him— unimpeded by shadows of his father—flared.

"I love you, Arianna. I will risk nothing. I promise." He wiped her falling tears away, then kissed her, sealing the oath.

****

It seemed liked eons since Ari had been to Abby's for lunch. It felt right being there today, firming up wedding plans. Abby's had internet and cellular service, as well, which they sorely needed.

She glanced up at Christopher as he popped a bite of Abby's famous meatloaf into his mouth. Country music hummed in the background, as if it were any other day. So much had changed in a year and a half. Christopher had become so dear to her; she'd rather give up a limb than lose him... And she was happy to see him eat. In less than twenty-four hours, his face already possessed a healthier glow.

Picking a date for their nuptials proved trickier than they'd imagined. They needed at least enough time to invite the small company of guests on Ari's list, and the even smaller group on Christopher's. Yet, neither one wanted to wait until after Christmas, which left them with precious little time for preparations. No printed invitations; they would just call their friends. "We must still give them time to make arrangements to be there. How about two weeks from today? That puts us on December twenty-second." Ari tapped the datebook sitting on the table between them.

Christopher consulted the calendar on his phone. "I still can't believe this phone survived the nineteenth century."

"And that they bothered to hand me the bag of your personal effects as we exited the gallows," said Ari.

"Ah, that date's no good. There's a Christmas party at the precinct, which will nearly eliminate my entire list. How about one week from today?"

"My dress won't be ready until the eighteenth." Ari had been thrilled to find a quaint bridal shop with just the perfect gown for sale that morning. She was certain rushing to the altar meant wearing an old dress hanging in her closet. But Christopher had talked her into a little shopping excursion, and they had struck gold. Not only did she find a beautiful dress for her, but the shop rented tuxedos, too.

"December nineteenth, then?" said Christopher.

Ari gave her head a slow shake and squeezed her eyes shut to keep the tears away. This was her wedding—a happy time. Crying would only make them both sad. After she'd tamped down her rising emotion, she swallowed and opened her eyes. "That's the anniversary of my family's deaths." She glanced up to see Christopher's face clouding over.

"Arianna,"—he folded her hand in his—"we don't need to be in such a rush. December is probably the worst month of the entire year for us to get married."

"I thought it might be, but so far it's had the opposite effect. I've been so preoccupied with wedding plans, I haven't had time to think about the anniversary. Who knows? Getting married in December might help me enjoy Christmas again. It's been years since I've even gone shopping. The few gifts I buy, I order online." She managed a feeble smile. "I've always longed for a December wedding."

Christopher rounded the table, scooting next to her on her side of the booth, then pulled her into an embrace. "You are the strongest woman I have ever met." He tilted her head toward him and kissed her.

Ari was strong—she'd had no choice. It was either wilt under the weight of her grief or rise to the challenge and move forward with her life. Just now, however, with Christopher's arms wrapped around her, she felt an added layer of strength lifting a weight from her soul. An overwhelming sense of gratitude swept over her. No more loneliness. Strong or weak, being alone never felt good. She couldn't keep the tears from falling, only this time they were happy tears. "Thank you, Chris." She kissed him again, savoring his spicy-fresh scent and the sparks of his touch. Cleanshaven now and dressed in his own clothing—even though they hung on him—he seemed so much more himself.

She thought he'd go back to his side of the booth, but he stayed put. His closeness usually made her skin tingle, but something was different. More than electricity sparked and sizzled around them; Ari felt comfort, encouragement, happiness and a love she'd never before experienced. She'd marry him on the spot, if he asked her.

"That leaves December Twentieth," Christopher said. "Or is that too close to the anniversary?"

"I think the twentieth is perfect." The burning in Arianna's heart told her that her family liked the idea, as well. "Would you rather find a chapel in Pueblo or Denver?" If it were up to Ari, she'd choose Denver. But she wasn't sure the Somers would want to travel there. Her friends wouldn't have a problem with the commute.

"Denver." He surprised her by saying it so decisively. "This is your wedding, love. It should be held in your hometown."

"Really? You don't mind?"

"I never thought it should be anywhere else." He kissed her. His eyes brightened as he angled his head. "Would you mind if some…unconventional guests showed up?"

Ari narrowed her eyes in question. "Unconventional how?"

"Well, they won't be dressed for a wedding. They won't even smell that great. But I'd love to go by the park and pick up my homeless friends—at least Stewart. Without him, I doubt I'd be here, let alone be getting married."

Ari hugged him close. "I don't care how they're dressed. I'd love to have them at our wedding."

Chapter Forty-Seven

After picking up her wedding dress on December eighteenth, Ari drove back to Denver. There were many essentials a thrown-together-at-the-last-minute wedding needed that only a big city could provide. Such as the venue. Ari had secured a chapel but wanted to walk through it to make certain it felt right.

She tapped on Maggie's front door, wondering what sort of reception she'd receive from her best friend. The only conversation she'd had with Maggie since she'd returned from nineteenth century London was a quick phone call she'd made to invite her to the wedding and ask for her help today. She knew Maggie would be bursting with questions.

"Arianna! It's you!" Maggie pulled her through the entryway and in for a hug. "I have missed you. You leave to find Christopher, then come back ready to marry him?" She threw a hand in the air. "You have a lot of explaining to do."

Ari laughed. "Well, can I do it on our way to the chapel? I really need my matron of honor's help right now."

"The sitter is in with Ryder. I'll let her know I'm leaving."

Ari wasn't certain what to tell Maggie about her time in Regency Era London. Maggie had never said it aloud, but Ari knew she didn't believe her time-traveling stories. The last thing she needed was for her best friend to have her committed to a mental hospital two days before her wedding.

They slid into Ari's still-warm car, and out of the freezing Colorado air. Before Ari had the engine running, Maggie began to talk. "Was Christopher in England? Was he cheating on you? What happened when you caught him?" She fired out questions faster than Ari could come up with a believable fable.

"Maggie. I know you won't believe me, but I'll tell you the truth if you promise to do nothing."

"Do nothing?"

"Yes. Do nothing. Don't react. Don't treat me like I'm crazy. Don't call anyone and tell them you're worried about me. This is just between us." She looked at Maggie with determination.

"I wouldn't do that."

Ari narrowed her eyes at Maggie.

"Fine." Maggie let out a huff.

"I've told you about the time-traveling device before, as well as what era Christopher is from, and I'm sure you wanted to have me sent to the funny farm. So, I'll only tell you if you listen. Nothing more."

Maggie's face fell into a frown and she placed a hand over her heart, a wounded expression furrowed her brow. "Of course I believed you, Ari. And I'll believe whatever you tell me now."

Her condescending tone told Ari everything she needed to know. Maggie hadn't believed a word of it. Ari rolled her eyes. She'd just alter the truth a little. "I did find Christopher in London. He wasn't cheating. In fact, he'd had a little scrape with the law."

Maggie's eyes widened, but she didn't say

anything. Apparently, Ari's lecture had worked.

"Don't worry. He didn't do anything wrong. His father did—a long time ago—and Christopher was blamed for it. Joshua and I just had to figure out a way to…clear his name." She shrugged. She'd leave out the parts about the scorned ex-girlfriend and the crazy gun-wielding, power-crazed uncle. Perhaps one day she'd be able to share the entire story. But she couldn't risk her matron of honor going off the rails today.

"No time traveling, then?" Maggie asked, her expression a mixture of relief and disappointment.

Ari pulled into the church parking lot. "Only if you want there to be."

"What kind of answer is that?"

"The only answer you're going to get."

Maggie let out a harrumph but followed Ari through the church parking lot. "It's probably prettier here during the summer. All the trees are dead."

"The snow is pretty," said Ari.

"Yeah, but not very colorful."

The groundskeeper met them at the door. "Are you Arianna Miller?"

Ari nodded.

"I was told to let you in." He pushed a key into the hole below the large, scroll-style handle and opened the door.

Ari and Maggie entered. "It's perfect," Ari said, scanning the area. The chapel was small enough that her tiny wedding party wouldn't seem so small, and large enough for a few extra guests, should Christopher's homeless friends arrive.

Nothing about the church, besides the small, stained-glass windows, possessed any color. The decorator in Ari wished to go crazy decking it out in wedding décor, but there wasn't time. She and Christopher had ordered a bride's bouquet, a mother's bouquet for Beatrice and bridesmaids' bouquets for Sarah and Maggie. That's all the color they'd had time to arrange for.

Maggie's face puckered as if she'd eaten a lemon drop. "Ari, are you planning a wedding or a funeral? You've envisioned your wedding since you were little. Plain, brown pews won't cut it."

Ari had to duck from Maggie's probing eyes. Her friend was correct; she had been planning her wedding since she was about ten years old. Christopher was the right groom, and this was the right chapel, but she'd pictured it radiating with warmth and…color.

"It's better than getting married by the Justice of the Peace, or eloping. This late, those are our only other options."

"You could wait a few months and we could plan a proper ceremony."

Ari clenched her teeth. If Maggie only knew what she and Christopher had endured over the past year, she'd never dare say such a thing. "We're getting married in two days." She jabbed a finger in the air. "Here at this *plain* chapel. I'm fine with it."

Maggie put her hands up in the surrender position. "Okay, okay. Sheesh, jetlag has made you feisty, girl. I like it." She smirked.

After running two more errands for the wedding, Ari and Maggie stopped at The Grille for lunch. A gleam Ari knew so well entered Maggie's hazel eyes— Ari was about to be pelted with more unanswerable questions.

"You promised. Don't ask." Ari lowered her brows, stopping the barrage before Maggie could begin.

Maggie let out a huff. "You really aren't going to tell me about your trip?"

"I did tell you about my trip."

Maggie slanted her eyes at Ari.

"Okay. I guess I can tell you about Uncle Cedric." Ari gave vague details about how much Cedric had helped them, but in the end, was only helping Christopher for his own benefit. "Once Christopher had been released from prison, Cedric's true colors emerged." Reflecting on the conversation she had unwittingly happened upon still made her angry.

"What did he want, exactly? All of Christopher's money?" She let out a mock laugh. "Does he know how much cops get paid?"

"Not exactly. There were other things I can't really talk about." *Wouldn't* talk about, more like. "We overheard his plan and confession. A constable heard it, as well, thank goodness. Sadly, it turned violent, and the constable killed Cedric."

"What? You've got to be kidding. Is that when you came home?"

Hearing herself recite the tale did sound like she'd had quite the adventure. Somehow, now, it only seemed like a nightmare. But it had happened. She couldn't properly explain it all without delving into time travel and the device. "Uh…yeah. That's when we came home."

"Ari, I'm sure there is a perfectly good explanation for your time-traveling fantasies."

Fantasies? Ari rolled her eyes. "Like what?"

"Don't get mad. I just think that…that maybe those

books you read have come to life for you."

Ari let out a scoffing breath. The books *had* given her a tiny education about nineteenth century London before she experienced it first-hand. And even more importantly, they'd given her a fascination with men from that century, which had caused her to fall hard for Christopher. But they hadn't given her fantasies.

"And between the trauma Mr. Somers put you through and nearly losing Christopher, your mind has gone"—she shrugged—"to a happier place."

Maggie's gentle, comforting voice nearly made Ari laugh out loud. "So, you think I'm fragile? I need to be coddled?"

Maggie eyed Ari and paused, taking a long draw of diet soda before she spoke. "Maybe." She said it more like a question.

Wow. A lot of thought for such a simple non-answer. But Maggie was wrong, Ari had never felt so strong in her twenty-six years. Losing her family at such a young age, then being kidnapped and nearly killed by Mr. Somers, then traveling to the nineteenth century to save Christopher had only served to make her solid to the core—unbreakable, even. She wished she could explain as much to Maggie—or anyone, for that matter. Christopher truly was her only confidante.

They didn't discuss the past anymore. Ari was relieved. Perhaps, someday.

Ari drove the back way to Maggie's house.

"Where are we going? You missed the exit to my neighborhood."

"I just want to see my family's old house. I hope you don't mind." Ari had checked the internet daily in hopes Mr. Somers' status had miraculously changed, but still nothing in print had emerged about him hanging for his century's-old crimes. And, if she and Christopher were correct, even if he did hang, it wouldn't alter her family's status.

"I don't mind at all," Maggie said. She looked relieved that the topic of time travel had dropped. She squeezed Ari's arm reassuringly.

Snow crunched under the tires as they rounded a corner onto the street where Ari had spent her childhood years. Nostalgia clamped around her chest like a vice grip, threatening to yank her heart out. Her beautiful home, still well-maintained, had a red truck parked in the drive. The license plate read, "MR Z." "Looks like the Zimmers still live here," said Ari. For someone who'd just declared herself unbreakable, she sure wanted to break down in tears now. Instead, she rushed to the next street and concentrated on getting Maggie home. She didn't need to give her more proof of frailty.

Chapter Forty-Eight

It wasn't in his nature to lie, deceive or break a promise, but Christopher was about to do all three.

"Forgive me, Arianna, but this is something I must do," he said to the dark, chemical-saturated air around him. He twisted the knob on the disc-shaped device back four years, destination: Denver, Colorado.

The room rattled. He hoped his mother and siblings were still in Pueblo, finishing their last-minute preparations for the wedding tomorrow. He'd completed his to-do list.

All but this.

The transport began and ended within only minutes. Looking around, he realized he was in a park near the Denver Mint. Relief washed over him. He worried he'd land in his family's former house—now, yet four years in the past, their current residence—thus running the risk of being spotted and stopped. He located a secluded area to stow the disc.

His watch read five o'clock. Denver was fully dark—and cold. He tugged out his cell phone. Hopefully, it would still work in the Denver of four years ago. It flashed on. He breathed a grateful sigh. Benefits of not buying a new phone every couple of years. Now to get a car—in a hurry.

He dialed one of his friends who wasn't a police officer, just in case he himself was presently on the job at the precinct. There would be no possible explanation for that. "Mac, Christopher Flemming. We worked together at the carwash. Do you still work on old cars in your spare time?"

"Flemming? Hey, it's great to hear from you. Haven't seen you since you moved up in the world and became one of Denver's finest. Gosh what's it been, a couple months now?"

To Mac it had been a couple of months. More accurately four years and a couple of months. "Something like that." Christopher shuffled his feet to keep warm.

"I still tinker. Gotta beaut I'm working on right now—a '68 Chevy Chevelle."

"Sounds great." Christopher would love to catch up with his buddy from years ago, but time was of the essence. "Do any of your cars run? I mean, I'm in kind of a bind and need transportation for the evening—"

"Say no more. You've helped me plenty of times. My brother is here, and we can bring you some wheels right away."

After giving Mac his location, he ended the call and mentally mapped out the city. Having worked as a cop in Denver, he was familiar with the area. But he wasn't certain where to find whom he came here to find—Benjamin Somers. If he could stop him, the fatal accident would never happen. He'd given himself plenty of time. Hopefully Father had begun drinking early so Christopher could get this over with and transport home in a hurry—be rested for his wedding day.

But what if he couldn't find him?

Snow crunched beneath his feet as he paced. He'd

have to stop Arianna's parents from driving on that road. The thought made him shiver. No. He'd find Father.

Though unwilling to accept the possibility of failure, he had come with a plan B. After some snooping, he'd gotten the general location of Arianna's family's home, and from there, he'd pinpointed the local high school, where the Christmas concert should be starting soon. What he knew without a doubt was the location of the intersection where the accident had occurred, having read and reread the police report. Still, what would he say to Ari's parents, the Millers, if he found them? Traveling through time was hardly believable. He had to find Father.

Mac soon pulled up to the park, his brother trailing him in a truck. The three exchanged pleasantries, then all were off to different destinations. Christopher drove the truck, still unsure of his own end point. A bar, but which one? There weren't many between the high school and the Miller's residence, but who knows how long Father had been driving before the fateful accident.

The streets were icy, reminding him of Ari's journal entry to Sarah about the collision which had turned her world upside-down. *Had it not been for Father, who ran the red light, her life would have been much different.* He winced, thinking about the pain Father had inflicted on Arianna.

He pulled over and spread a map across the seat next to him, which he'd marked beforehand indicating bar locations. Once his course was charted, he proceeded to the first lounge. Early yet, there weren't many customers, making it easy for him to see Father wasn't one of them. Five minutes later, he pulled up to bar number two. He nearly got out before he noticed the blackened windows. The place had permanently closed. He let out an exasperated breath at the wasted time. Next, he drove ten more minutes to a club. Bouncers stood guard at the door, admitting young adults with the proper ID. Christopher knew immediately he wouldn't find his father there—too trendy. After three more bars with similar results, panic began to set in. He could start the circuit again or look for Ari's parents. He chose the latter.

The high school was large, but he located what looked like parking for the auditorium in no time. Schools had a distinct smell, but this one was far different from that to which he'd been accustomed. Of course, no candlelight or fireplaces were present, which changed everything. Wandering through the main hall, he found signs directing him to the auditorium.

He opened the double doors. Only a few people filled the seats. Maybe he'd picked the wrong school. He'd assumed the concert began at 7:00. His watch read 7:23. Maybe the concert didn't start until 7:30 or 8:00. His pulse galloped, and his nerves tensed at the thought of failing Arianna. He exited and scanned the area. Two ladies chatted as they arranged a table near the auditorium's entrance. They covered the table with a bright red cloth, placed a poinsettia in the middle, then fanned out programs on either end. A good sign he'd found the right place. His racing heart slowed to a calmer pace.

"May I?" Christopher motioned to the programs.

"Of course." One of the ladies handed him one. "Who are you here to see?"

"Uh…Seth. Seth Miller."

"Oh yes, he's a great drummer. I'm Chloe Ferguson's mother; she's friends with Seth." Moving her finger down the names listed on the program, she stopped at his. "There he is. His family should be along shortly. The concert begins in thirty minutes. Seth's probably in the band room now, warming up."

"Thank you very much." Christopher reentered the auditorium, taking a seat near the entrance. Hopefully he'd recognize the Millers from their picture he'd seen in Ari's apartment.

Families began trickling in slowly at first. He easily eliminated each one. In Ari's picture, her mother had Arianna's golden hair. Her father had looked tall, darker-haired and just a bit robust.

As if a five-minute warning bell had sounded, the crowd entering the auditorium grew into a mob. Christopher couldn't keep up. Parents hurried younger kids along, rushing to find seats before the concert began. He let out a breath. He'd never locate them now. There were too many people, and several fit the picture he had in his head.

"Just save me a seat. I feel like I need to call her," a woman whispered to the man tugging on her arm behind him. They were taking the two unoccupied seats on the aisle in front of Christopher.

The man, clearly irritated, replied, "Why in the world would Ari need to hear from you now? The concert's about to begin."

Christopher snapped to attention. The blonde woman threw her hands in the air. "I don't know. I just have a feeling she needs to talk."

She does. She needs to hear your voice one more

time before your life is snuffed out. Or, perhaps Christopher would change all that.

The man pleaded with the woman to call their daughter after the concert. "Fine. But my premonitions are usually correct," the lady said.

"Ari has a night class tonight, anyway."

"I suppose you're right." She took the seat directly in front of Christopher.

Fate had handed him a miracle. If only he knew what to do with it.

Leaning forward, Christopher cleared his throat, getting the couple's attention. "Excuse me, are you Mr. and Mrs. Miller?"

They exchanged confused glances before nodding. The conductor had just mounted the platform and was about to start the concert.

"My name is Christopher. I'm a friend of Arianna's. I have something I need to speak with you about." *Think, think, think.* He must find a way to convince them without sounding foolish.

"Now?" Mrs. Miller tilted her head and lowered her brows. "Is Ari okay?" She shot an I-told-you-so look at her husband.

"She's fine." The Millers exhaled in unison. "It's you two and Seth whose lives are in danger." It sounded crazy, overly dramatic even, but it was true, and he knew no better way to get their attention—if they didn't have him hauled away in a straight-jacket, that is.

"What?" Mr. Miller said a little too loudly. "Are you threatening us? What have you done with our daughter?"

"Nothing." Christopher shook his head. This

wasn't going the way he'd planned. But time was short. "Could I please just speak with one or both of you"—he motioned to the door behind him—"outside?" He pointed to the program. "Seth's first number isn't for a while. You won't miss a thing."

"How do you know Seth? Never mind." Mr. Miller stood and patted his wife's shoulder. "I'll handle this, Ann."

"Oh, no. If something has happened to Ari, I need to know." Mrs. Miller followed behind as the men exited the auditorium.

Thank goodness the main hall was deserted, since the Millers all but exploded. "What have you done with our daughter?" Mr. Miller stamped his foot.

Christopher wished he'd brought his police badge or maybe even his gun, to be more authoritative—or persuasive.

"And what do you want with us?" added Mrs. Miller. "We aren't wealthy, if it's money you're after."

"Money? No, I don't want money." Christopher had expected a reaction, but he couldn't exactly explain his motives while they hollered at him. Music swelled in the background, competing with the Millers' voices. He willed a calm demeanor, even though his mind ran from one explanation to the next. He really should have given this scenario more consideration beforehand.

"Well?" Mrs. Miller had her hands on her hips and tapped her foot.

Christopher nearly smiled. He could picture Ari reacting the exact same way. "I don't mean to alarm you, Ari needs...I mean, my father..." He couldn't think straight because the truth sounded ridiculous.

Mr. Miller glared at him. "Which is it? Does Ari

need something, or is this about your father?"

"Neither. Both." He shifted his weight and shook his head. "I have come from the future to save your lives," he blurted out. It sounded lame, even to him. He blew out a frustrated breath. He needed them to believe him, but feared he'd gone about it the wrong way. There was no right way to explain time travel.

"Good grief." Mr. Miller turned toward the auditorium. "Come on, Ann. He's crazy."

"Please. Look." Christopher pulled a picture from his pocket. "These are your graves. See Ari sitting next to yours, Mrs. Miller? And here is a piece I tore from today's newspaper. Look at the date."

Mrs. Miller took the photo and the newspaper clipping. She seemed like the one to appeal to. Mr. Miller—an accountant, if he remembered correctly—was all about logic and numbers.

"I'm not here to frighten or extort anything from you. I love your daughter. We are getting married tomorrow—in the future, that is. I would dearly love to have her family there to celebrate. She has missed you immensely." His voice cracked. He truly wanted nothing more than to right this wrong. Ari deserved it—she deserved the best life had to offer, or in this case, death.

"The headstone says December nineteenth of this year." Mrs. Miller wrinkled her forehead. "How can that be? And Ari's getting married? She never said anything." Her voice, high and wistful, sounded strange, eerie.

Christopher held his breath and prayed for a miracle.

"This is imposs—"

"Oh, Ann. You know kids these days. They can photoshop anything." Mr. Miller barely glanced at the picture or the newspaper.

Mrs. Miller kept touching Arianna's face. "Ari looks so much older—so mature." She didn't take her eyes off the photo. "What if he's...telling the truth?" She raised her gaze to meet her husband's.

Mr. Miller let out a huff. "Unless you have anything else, Mr."—he threw his hands in the air—"whoever-you-are-from-the-future, we're going back in before we miss our son's portion of the concert. Come, Ann."

Chapter Forty-Nine

Christopher's gut twisted. How could he convince them? He looked at Mrs. Miller and let the words tumble out. "Your favorite color is purple and you're a nurse. Mr. Miller is an accountant and enjoys the outdoors. Seth loves sports, especially basketball, Ari is an interior designer—the best one in all of Colorado. She learned of your accident from a school counselor. Please, Mrs. Miller, I'm telling you the truth. At least take a different route home tonight. Your car will be hit by a drunk driver." He stopped there, unable to admit the driver was his own father.

Mrs. Miller stood with her mouth agape.

"Ann," Mr. Miller interrupted, "he could have learned those things anywhere. Now come. It's Seth we're here for tonight." Pinning Christopher with a threatening glare, he turned his stunned wife toward the auditorium. "I'll be calling the police if we see you again," he said over his shoulder as he gently guided her back through the door.

Christopher ran a hand through his hair, his desperation mounting. He really didn't expect the Millers to believe him, but it would have been so much easier if they had. Now it was imperative he locate his father.

His watch said 8:17. He had an hour. A race against time.

Google still worked on his phone. A blessing. He punched in "bars in the area" to see if any showed up that hadn't appeared on the map he'd brought from the present day. Some of those seemed to be new—not in operation four years ago. The establishment had to be nearby. Ari had recorded in Sarah's journal that witnesses saw the drunk driver come from a bar down the street. Now that he knew the exact location of the concert, he could narrow the search to bars and lounges in the area. There were two possibilities—if the witnesses had gotten it right. Easy enough to check out; they were positioned in a triangle from where he was— not far from the school, but opposite directions from each other. Not conducive to his time constraints.

Driving as fast as was safe on the slippery roads, Christopher located the closest one. It fit the location description. How he'd get Father out of there, he still didn't know. He'd use physical force if he had to. A quick scan of the room yielded nothing—nobody resembling Father. Disappointed, he headed out, wasting no time trekking to bar number two.

More of a sports grill, the second bar—positioned in the middle of the room and surrounded by several tables with diners—was harder to take in with only a glance. He slowly circled the area, trying not to get too close, but close enough to spot his father in the dim light. He knew the concert wouldn't last much longer. If he struck out again, he may as well go home— defeated.

"What are you doing here, Christopher? I told you to get outta my house and outta my life."

Christopher spun around, and there he sat, bleary-eyed, pointing a beefy finger at him. "You're drunk,

Father. Let me take you home." Christopher moved toward him.

"Another one." Father hollered at the barkeeper, thumping his fist on the counter.

"Maybe you should go home with your son, Mr. Somers," said the bartender.

"Yes, come." Christopher held out a hand to help him up." With so many people dining, he couldn't force his father out, or use violence to disable him. That might result in a call to the police. He'd have to talk him out of the room.

Benjamin swatted his hand away. "He's not my son. My son is dead. Go on, get away from me."

Christopher laid a hand on his shoulder.

Father sprang from his seat, jabbing his fist into Christopher's ribcage.

He doubled over in pain. When he got his bearings, another fist connected with his jaw. Everything went dark for a moment.

Security guards hauled his father out before he had a chance to stop them. Good. Hopefully, they'd put him in a taxi and send him home.

"Are you all right, sir?" the bartender hovered over Christopher with a rag. "You're bleeding. I've called the paramedics."

"No need. I'm fine." He struggled to get to his feet.

"Sir, you blacked out for at least five minutes. Mr. Somers—your dad, is he?—really whaled on you, even after you were down. He won't be allowed back in here. I'm sorry we don't have a bouncer. This is only a sports bar. I tried to stop him, but he just threw me off." The bartender rubbed his red elbow where he'd obviously landed.

"Where'd they take him?"

The waiter shrugged. "They just kicked him out. He wasn't slurring his words yet. He gets far more drunk than that most evenings. We figured since you're his son, you wouldn't press charges." His face clouded with a look of uncertainty. He tilted his head and lowered one eyebrow. "Did you want to press charges?"

Of course he'd want to press charges. Anything to get the man off the streets. Before Christopher could answer, however, two men came up behind him asking where the patient was. The bartender motioned to Christopher, who had managed to pull himself onto a barstool.

"I'm fine. Just a bit of a headache, is all. Sorry you came out for nothing," he said to the paramedic. He really needed to get out of there and make sure Ari's family was safe. Since Father hadn't been taken home, he'd likely just found another watering hole—like the bar down the street from the school. Urgency clawed at him.

"Sir, if you refuse to go to the hospital, you'll need to sign this waiver, releasing us from any liability." A woman—she must have been the manager—thrust a page lined with a blur of single-spaced writing in his face.

He signed without reading a word.

"He can go," she said to the paramedics.

Christopher stumbled to his car. Perhaps he should have gone to the hospital. Father had done a number on him. He glanced at his phone—9:05. The police report had stated that the fatal accident had happened at 9:15. Supposing he hadn't altered the Millers' future as much as he'd hoped, he still had time to do…what? He didn't know, but he had to do something.

Despite every inch of his body screaming out in pain, the cold air cleared his head. He drove to the intersection where the accident might or might not take place and pulled into the gas station on the corner.

The clock on the dashboard read 9:13.

The Millers would be approaching the intersection from the south any minute now. He got out of his car and walked to the road. He could hardly identify any of the vehicles' occupants in the dark, but he'd been to the salvage yard and had seen the Millers' car when he'd investigated the crime last year. He'd never forget the mangled heap. The thought made him shiver. He must stop the accident.

There. He spotted the Millers' car. His gut clenched.

As it approached the intersection, he walked up to the car and stood in front of it, forcing the Millers to stay put.

Mr. Miller lowered his brows and mouthed, "What are you doing?"

Christopher just held up a finger, telling him to wait.

The light turned green. Mr. Miller glared daggers at Christopher, looking like he might blow a gasket. He pounded on the horn, then threw his hands in the air, but Christopher didn't move.

Cars behind the Millers honked.

Christopher didn't move.

Just then, a red car barreled through the intersection, running the red light, narrowly missing Christopher, as well as two other cars coming from the opposite direction. The Millers stared, horror-stricken. Christopher limped out of their way, so they could pass. They seemed too stunned to budge.

Finally, they pulled into the gas station lot in which Christopher had parked. He had just closed the door to his truck when Mr. Miller tapped on the window, his pale face screwed up in a question mark.

Christopher rolled down the window. Blood dripped into his eye and he could feel his lip swelling. He must look like a monster. "I'm sorry I had to do that, Mr. Mill—"

"You saved our lives. Who are you?"

Chapter Fifty

If Ari could capture time and save it in a bottle, today would be that day.

Butterflies turned somersaults in her stomach as she sat in a salon chair. The hairdresser took meticulous care following Ari's instructions—an updo, but not so fancy that it had to be plastered with hairspray. The best sensation in the world was Christopher's fingers running through her hair. *I take that back. His kisses are even better.*

"How we doing on time, hon?" the stylist asked, her hands too full of golden locks to be able to check her watch.

Maggie, who seemed more nervous than Ari, spoke up. "It's nearly nine. The ceremony begins in just over an hour. How much longer will her hair take? Ari needs time to dress, too."

"Relax, Maggie. We'll be fine. Selena knows what she's doing." Ari waved a hand in the air.

"I've been doing this for fifteen years," Selena said with a chuckle. "Give me ten minutes, and you'll be set to go." She began gently tugging curls down to frame Arianna's face.

"Your hair looks beautiful, Maggie," said Ari.

Maggie lightly touched her auburn hair, coifed up in a fancy knot. "Thank you. Have you spoken with Christopher this morning?"

"No. I sent him a text, but he hasn't replied. I'm sure he's just rushing to get his family here on time."

"Didn't you say his friends from the precinct in Pueblo threw him a bachelor party last night?"

"Yeah."

"Then do you really wonder where he is this morning? He probably got plastered and is spending time with his head in the toilet."

Ari shook her head. "Do you even know him? I don't think I've ever seen him take a drink, let alone get plastered. He decided long ago that he didn't want to turn out like his dad."

"Hmm. I suppose you're right."

"There you go, hon." The stylist handed Ari a mirror and spun her around to inspect the back of her hair. "How do you like it?"

Ari turned her head to the right then the left. The bulk of her hair gathered into a cluster of curls in back, secured with invisible hairpins and a beautiful pearl comb. She'd expected a fancy bun, but this was so much better. "It's perfect. And I think Chris will like it."

"Christopher will like taking those pins out of your hair tonight, that's for sure." Maggie pumped her brows.

Ari rolled her eyes, then paid the hairdresser. "Thanks for doing this on such short notice, Selena. It looks amazing."

Twenty minutes later, Ari and Maggie arrived at the church. Ari could hear organ music already playing. Nervous excitement zinged through her veins. Soon she would be Mrs. Christopher Flemming. Married to the man of her dreams.

Snow crunched beneath their feet as they crossed the parking lot. The fragrance of Blue Spruce hung in the frosty air. Cars in the lot indicated that a few people had arrived already.

"We need to get you in there and into this amazing wedding dress." Maggie patted the bundle draped over her shoulder. "It's a gorgeous day for a wedding."

Ari couldn't agree more. The sun shone down from a cloudless sky, reflecting light from the snow-covered earth. "It's beautiful. The ground is covered in crystals."

"You couldn't have planned it better—even if you'd actually *planned* it." Maggie nudged Ari and winked.

"If we hadn't expedited our wedding, something else would have happened to delay it. I don't want to wait even one more day to marry Christopher. And who says I didn't plan? This church is perfect, the weather is perfect, the man I'm marrying is perfect. It's as if we'd been planning all year long."

"If you consider a plain brown chapel to be perfect, that is." Maggie reached for the door handle.

Ari paused before entering. "Are you sure Jason doesn't mind walking me down the aisle?" Countless daydreams she'd shared with her mother about becoming a bride one day surfaced. Conversations about what colors she would choose, where they would hold the ceremony, what her future husband would look like and where they would honeymoon. But never had she wondered who would walk her down the aisle and give her away. It was always Dad. Ari willed away sudden tears. She'd promised herself not to think of her losses today. Only what she would gain—a wonderful man and his kind family.

Maggie's voice cut into her thoughts. "Yes. Of course he's okay with it. He's waiting inside. Without a rehearsal dinner, he felt a bit unsure of himself and came early to practice." She laughed. "I told him the aisle isn't very long, and there's only one man to give you away to, but he's a little nervous." Maggie's hand still clutched the door handle. She peered at Ari, a question in her eyes.

Ari nodded. "I'm ready."

Tasha immediately greeted them. "You're here. I was getting worried. Is Christopher with you?"

"Well, that wouldn't do, Tasha," said Maggie. "He's not supposed to see the bride before the wedding. Bad luck, you know. Anyway, the hair stylist took longer than we'd planned, but we'll—"

Tasha's face creased with concern. "But his family is here. The ceremony is supposed to begin in"—she glanced at her watch—"twenty minutes."

Ari's heart seized. Something went wrong. Why would it go right? After all, their whole relationship had sailed on mostly choppy waters. But she'd thought they finally reached their destination—at least the first major triumph—in which they'd proven they had conquered all odds and remained in the same boat—wearing life jackets, yes, but in the same boat.

Tasha squeezed Ari's arm. "I'm sure he'll be along any minute."

She had to say that. Ari blinked back tears. Her history with Christopher had proven over and over that nothing was a given. Perhaps fate was trying to tell her something. Maybe she should listen... No. No way. That sort of self-doubt only got Ari into trouble. "Of course he will. Let's get this wedding started, girls." She forced a grin in her attempt at confidence.

Tasha motioned toward a small room to the left of the inner chapel. "There's the bride's room. Maggie, do you need help getting her into the dress?"

Maggie shook her head.

"I'm just going to take a peek inside the chapel. I need to see for myself that Christopher's not here." Ari broke away from Maggie and pushed the double doors open. Her jaw dropped. The plain brown chapel had been transformed into a magical, Christmas wedding wonderland. "Ahh!" Forest-green garland woven with thick, red velvet ribbon hung in swags lining both sides of the aisle, ending in two huge bouquets of red and white roses. Three steps up led to an arch covered in white roses. And beyond the arch but behind where the pastor would stand, a Christmas tree decked out in silver, red and white ornaments stood gloriously erect. Arianna sucked in a breath and let her eyes dance from one side of the room to the next, taking in all the beautiful decorations.

"Surprise," piped Maggie.

"We all pitched in," said Tasha.

Trust her interior decorating friends to make her special day beautiful. Tears splashed down Ari's cheeks. "I've never seen anything so pretty. It's perfect."

Maggie emitted a tsking sound. "We're going to have to touch up your make up." She tugged Ari's arm. "Come on. Now we're in a hurry."

"I'll let you know when Christopher gets here, and everything is ready." Tasha shooed them into the bride's room.

Ari slowly turned in front of three full-length mirrors. Her A-line wedding dress didn't have flouncy ruffles, but instead shimmered with satin beneath a layer of tulle, creating a subtly glamorous effect. Lace-appliqued sleeves ended just above her elbows and pearls adorned the gentle curve of the neckline.

"Wow. Just wow. I think that dress was designed just for you. I don't know how you managed to snag it in such a short time. When I got married, I shopped all over Denver before I found one that I could *live* with. I thought my mom would kill me before we were finished."

"Thanks, Maggie. Will you check with Tasha? I hope Christopher is here. The ceremony is supposed to start"—she glanced at a clock on the wall—"right now."

Maggie disappeared.

Ari needed to pace, but her long dress made it difficult. What could have happened to Christopher? Second thoughts? An accident?

When would time ever be on her side?

Chapter Fifty-One

"The chapel is full, but Christopher isn't here yet. Ari, I'm sure there's a logical explanation." Maggie closed the door behind her and sat on a puffy chair next to the mirrors.

"He's the most punctual man I know, Maggie. If he's not here, something has happened." Ari twisted her fingers together. Willing herself to remain calm, she closed her eyes and tried to think of anywhere Christopher could have been detained.

"Do you want me to start calling hospitals in the area?"

"Not yet. I need to talk to his mother. See if she knows where he is."

"Tasha already did. His mother thought he'd spent the night here in Denver."

Cold dread penetrated Arianna's layers of satin and lace. Then she remembered Christopher's homeless friends. She let out a breath. "Christopher had some…unique friends when he first moved to Denver. I bet he's stopped off to pick them up."

"You mean the vagrants sitting in the back? They're here. Why in the world did he have homeless friends, anyway?"

"You wouldn't believe me if I told you." And she had more important things to worry about right now than recapping Christopher's time-traveling past.

Again.

"Try me."

"I already did, and you didn't."

"Are you talking about time travel again? I thought you were past that. Next you'll say Mr. Somers came back from the future or the past—wherever you said he ran off to—just to stop you from marrying his son." Maggie smirked.

Ari clapped a hand over her mouth. "That's it! Benjamin Somers! He's got to be behind this." She nearly spat out the words. Her heart began thudding out of control. Of course Mr. Somers would find a way to ruin her perfect day. What had he done to Christopher?

"Are you kidding right now? How could Mr. Somers have anything to do with this?" Maggie threw her hands in the air. "I'm calling the hospitals." She picked up her phone, mumbling under her breath.

Ari barely heard what she was saying, and when Maggie began speaking with hospital operators, Ari raised her voice and started citing a list of evidence—everything that pointed to Christopher's father as the killer of her dreams. "No, listen, Maggie." She walked in small circles as she spoke. "He was in prison when we left London, but my parents and brother are still dead, which means Mr. Somers didn't hang for his crimes—the jewelry heist and murder. He must have found out about our wedding and has come back to the future and kidnapped Christopher. Or worse." She gasped and felt a rush of blood drain from her face.

"Unless, of course, traveling back to 1814 as just a visitor didn't change my family's status—which is more likely the case. At any rate, I'd bet anything Benjamin Somers is responsible for Christopher's absence this morning." A chill thinking about the monster made her shudder. She turned to face Maggie.

Maggie stared at her, mouth agape and brows furrowed.

"Hello, are you there, ma'am?" said a voice on Maggie's phone.

"I've got to tell the congregation something, Maggie. Then go find him." Closing her eyes, she began frantically digging for a plausible excuse. Would this game of cat and mouse never end?

"What's that?" Maggie said to the phone. She put a finger in the air. Probably wanting Ari to wait a minute before making a fool of herself by telling a church full of people her groom was kidnapped by his evil father, then transported to another time.

Ari wouldn't say that, but she had to say something. She left the bride's room with Maggie hot on her heels, still talking on the phone.

Tasha nearly ran into Ari. "I was just coming to get you." She smiled. "Your groom has arrived and we're ready to begin."

"What? But I thought—" Ari shook her head. "Never mind." She let all her doubts and fears dissolve like ice melting in the hot sun. *Breathe*. Her heart resumed a less reckless rhythm. Christopher was here. Christopher was here.

"Wait for me!" Maggie nearly yelped. "I'm supposed to walk in first."

Bach's *Jesu Joy of Man's Desiring* began on the organ—the wedding party's cue to enter. But where was Jason?

Maggie walked in and started down the aisle. Ari didn't know if she should wait for Jason, or just follow her.

"Sorry I'm late." Whew, Jason had made it.

She turned to thank him. "Jas—" Ari stood motionless, rooted in place. "Dad?"

Her father kissed her on the cheek. "It's been a long night, and you're late for your wedding, kiddo. I'll tell you all about it after you marry that knight in shining armor you managed to snag." He winked and tucked his hand through her arm.

"You've met Chri—?"

"Shh. Later, sweetheart," her dad whispered.

Thoughts in a tangle, she forced her legs to move forward.

It wasn't the most graceful walk down the aisle. With so many tears, Ari could barely make out Maggie's form moving in front of her. Someone reached out and handed her a tissue.

Mom? More tears. She looked back fleetingly. *Yes, she's real.* And there Seth sat beside her.

By the time she and her father approached their destination, she thought she had her emotions under control. Then her eyes landed on Christopher. He stood tall, so handsome in his black tuxedo. He must wonder who was about to give her away… But Dad had acted as if they'd met. Perhaps in the parking lot?

Christopher smiled, his dimples creasing his perfect face—except it wasn't perfect. Peeking out from under his hair loomed a large bandage on his forehead. And did he have a black eye? A million scenarios bombarded her mind. She looked at him, then at her father. As they nodded to each other, a sparkle lit Christopher's eye. She turned to see her father's response. More than just a sparkle; an enormous smile spread across his face as he acknowledged Christopher.

She sucked in a breath. Christopher. What had he gone through to get her parents back?

"Dearly beloved." The ceremony began. Ari would have to tuck all her questions away for now.

…Nope. Impossible. No way. She couldn't concentrate on what the pastor was saying. Not with this huge mystery staring her in the face.

She had to know what had transpired last night and this morning. Clearly, the bachelor party had been a ruse. It looked as if Christopher had fought through a combat zone to rescue her parents. It hit her like a wrecking ball, and she smothered a gasp at the realization—Christopher must have gone toe to toe with his father—even worse than a war. Her heart melted. Oh, how she loved this man.

The pastor continued until the "I dos" were said, with Ari barely able to listen and respond. "You may now kiss the bride."

"I love you, Ari." Christopher said. He pulled her close and placed a sweet kiss on her lips.

Ari couldn't think of the right words to express her love—there were no words for someone as selfless as Christopher. She caught his face before he raised it up and poured her emotions into another kiss. Her heart vibrated as their lips met again and again, sending sparks shimmering through her veins.

Cheers resounded through their perfect, romantic moment. Ari stepped back, remembering they weren't alone. But only for a moment. *Who cares? We're finally married.* She let him pull her close again and kissed him as if no one else existed. At this moment in time—they didn't.

Chapter Fifty-Two

"Wait, wait, wait. You're telling me Christopher traveled back in time and saved your lives?" Maggie looked across the wedding luncheon table at Mr. and Mrs. Miller.

They nodded. "Incredible, right?" said Mr. Miller.

Christopher chuckled. Perhaps now Ari could finally confide in her best friend and she'd believe her.

Maggie turned her gaze to Ari. "And all of those time-travel stories you've been feeding me—they're true?"

Ari blew out a breath. "I knew it, Maggie. You were one phone-call away from having me committed."

"I—I thought you were delusional." Maggie looked pale. "But who could blame you after everything Mr. Somers put you through?"

"Oh, Maggie, you don't know the half of it. I'll fill you in after the honeymoon." Ari smiled at her friend whose mouth had fallen agape.

"Mr. Miller, you said Christopher blocked your car, so you couldn't drive through the light? what happened next?" Josh asked between bites of grilled chicken.

Beatrice leaned in, directing her comments to the Millers. "Yes, please continue telling us what happened last night. We were so worried."

"Of course," Mr. Miller said. "I was getting pretty

ticked by now. The light had turned green, but here was this crazy man standing in our way." He paused to take a sip of his water.

Seth jumped in. "And I didn't have a clue who he was or what had happened during my concert." He shrugged. "Then this red car ran right through the light! We would've all died if your new husband hadn't saved us, Ari!" Seth beamed at Christopher, as if he were a superhero.

Christopher smiled back at Seth, so grateful he'd finally gotten them out of harm's way and to the wedding.

"But why did it take you all so long to get here this morning?" asked Ari. "And if Christopher saved you, Dad, why don't I have any memories of you since the day you died?" She pushed food around her plate.

"Let me finish the story, sweetheart." Mr. Miller reached across the table and gave Ari's hand a gentle tap. "We followed Christopher back to his truck. We needed to thank him—"

"And apologize," added Ari's mom, Ann.

"Yes, apologize. I'd nearly called the police on him at the high school." Mr. Miller shook his head, a look of remorse turning his lips down. "We didn't know what he'd been through with his father during the concert—"

Ari and the Somers let out gasps.

"But we could see he was injured and needed to be seen by a doctor, so we insisted on taking him to the hospital."

"ERs take forever," said Seth. "And it was super crowded because of accidents caused by the icy roads. But they finally got to Christopher, who, by the way, kept saying he was fine and needed to get home for his wedding."

Ari gave Chris a sidelong glance. She swallowed hard, then bit down on her lip.

Christopher hoped she wasn't angry with him for taking such a risk. He noticed her food had barely been touched.

Seth kept talking. "At least all that time in the waiting room gave him a chance to fill us in on what had happened during the last four years. It was crazy to think he'd come from the future to save us, and then to learn he was born over two hundred years ago." His voice rose with excitement. "You really go for older men, sis." Seth pumped his brows at Ari.

She rolled her eyes in response.

"We were still iffy about the time travel," said Ann. "But we decided to go along with just about anything Christopher told us by this point. He'd saved our lives."

"That's right," said Ari's father. "So once the doctor had bandaged him up and said he could go, Christopher asked us if we wished to stay put or travel to the future with him and come to your wedding. We all agreed that we didn't want to wait. So we squeezed onto that contraption—"

"Who wouldn't want to ride on a time machine?" Seth said. "I had to sit on that box thingy."

"Then we arrived in"—Mr. Miller glanced at Beatrice—"I guess it's your basement."

Beatrice flushed and nodded. She glanced at Christopher, a twinge of pain in her eyes.

"More like a dungeon," Christopher overheard Sarah whisper to her mother.

Beatrice gave her a quick, comforting hug.

Ann smiled. "It's good we were dressed up for the concert last night, so we were at least presentable for your wedding. Christopher showered and had his tux on so fast, our heads were still spinning by the time he led us to the car and drove us here."

Ari's gaze roved from her mother, to her brother, to her father, then to Christopher.

"Arianna." Her mother folded Ari's hand into hers. "Now that we are here, memories are trickling in." Her eyes filled with tears. "I never left you. I've always been in your heart. Time couldn't tear me away." She pulled Ari into a tender embrace and said, "Do you remember the nightmare you had about us in the morgue? Or Seth's baseball suspended in air? How about the same TV commercial playing on every channel? None of those came from your imagination. They were warnings—warnings from us."

Ari buried her head on her mother's shoulder, clinging to her for several long moments. "I'll never forget those supernatural occurrences. Somehow, I knew they'd come from my family. Don't forget the quarter I found on your headstone. I have felt your guidance so many times. Thank you."

The background music changed in volume. "It's time for the newlyweds to take the floor for the first dance," the DJ said into the microphone.

Christopher stood and extended his hand to his new bride. "May I have this dance, Mrs. Flemming?"

Ari beamed up at him as they stepped onto the dancefloor.

He reflected on their dance at this very restaurant, the beautiful Palace Arms—wow, it seemed like eons ago—when he and Ari had impressed the crowd with their fancy steps. *That was the night I knew my heart belonged to her*. Pulling her close, he had no desire to repeat the performance. He only wished to hold Ari in his arms as his wife. He'd never seen such a beautiful bride.

As they moved together to the music, swaying and turning, a magnetism pulsed between them. Christopher couldn't take his eyes off hers, their aqua-blue depths swallowing him up.

"Chris," she whispered, "What you did for me…" A tear escaped from those enchanting eyes. She shook her head.

Tempted to kiss her, he resisted the urge, knowing once he started, he'd not want to stop. With an audience, now wasn't the time. "Do you forgive me for using the machine? I know I had promised—"

"Shh. You're forgiven. I can't thank you enough."

"Sweetheart, you should know I would move heaven and earth for you."

More tears splashed down her cheeks.

Her emotion brought tears to his own eyes.

"How long do we have to stay?" she asked.

"What? I thought with your family here you might want to skip the honeymoon." He sure hoped not. They'd waited so long.

"Will they still be here when we get back?" Ari's face shone with hope.

"They have arranged to stay with my family in Pueblo until they figure out living and working arrangements in Denver. I think they are getting on quite well, but I understand if you wish to—"

Ari placed her fingers over his lips. "You are the only family member I want to spend the next week with."

He kissed her forehead. They needed to get out of there quickly, but without offending their guests.

She ran feather-light fingers down his arm as the song they danced to came to an end.

Chills ran the length of his body.

The audience clapped, but he barely acknowledged their existence, so captivated was he by his bride's touch.

Holding Ari's hand, he spotted the microphone. "Ladies and gentlemen, thank you for attending our wedding ceremony and celebrating this happy occasion with us today. As you may have noticed, I was involved in a minor accident last night." His hand moved to his bruised face.

Sympathetic groans rippled through the audience.

"I assure you I am well—just tired. Arianna and I have a long drive to Vail and would like to get on the road. We invite you to stay and enjoy the party. Thank you again for coming."

He glanced down to see if Ari approved of his brash move.

Her eyes glittered with excitement.

"Come on, love. Let's go."

A few minutes later they pulled up to the Four Seasons Hotel.

"Chris, what are you doing? This is a long way from Vail," she said.

"Vail can wait. I cannot." He helped her from the car and led her into the posh lobby. "Are you okay with the small adjustment to our plans?" He stopped and looked at Ari, worried that he should have cleared the detour with her first.

"Absolutely." She squeezed his hand.

After carrying her over the threshold, he hung the "Do not disturb" sign on the knob and locked the door behind them, then scooped Ari into his arms again. Gently laying her on the bed, he gazed lovingly down at her. His wife. His companion. "I will love you forever, Ari." He sank down beside her and cradled her in his arms, relishing in the electricity pulsating between them.

"I never knew I could be so happy. I love you for all time." She nuzzled her head next to his.

He trailed kisses along her jaw, then found her lips. Fireworks exploded in his heart.

No matter the time or place, he had found his true home.

If you enjoyed *Time Trap*, you will want to watch for the next book in the Somerset series, coming soon from The Wild Rose Press, Inc. Here's a sample:

TIME TORN
Somerset Series Book III

Chapter One

If she could not go backward in time, she *would* not move forward.

Sarah Somers emptied a bottle of sleeping pills into her hand. This was not her first attempt to end her life, but it would be her last. Soon she'd be with Hudson, if not in life, then in death. Images of the night she had tried to plunge a dagger into her heart several years past pierced through her brain. *And because I am so weak, the blade left little more than an ugly pink scar.* Self-loathing enshrouded her like a tomb. Perhaps Father had been correct; her childhood sweetheart Hudson would not want her even if she had remained in the nineteenth century. However, in his letters, she found hope—*a fruitless hope, since we live centuries apart.*

Father's haunting words reverberated through her. "You look like a trollop, throwing yourself at the boy as you do. You are no longer his equal. When my status fell, yours did, as well. He will soon take his father's place as Earl of Alleyne and have his pick of young debutantes."

She'd refused to believe his words six years ago in London. Hudson had assured her he could never love another. "But Father took care of that when he irreversibly severed my connection with Hudson by forcing our family onto that unearthly time-traveling device." Her heart spasmed at the memory. She knew Father had had his own reasons for what he'd done— forced Sarah and her family onto a large disc and plunged them forward two hundred years, into an uncertain future in America. But in the back of her mind, she suspected her father had derived a perverse satisfaction from her unhappiness, for which she resented him more each day.

The journal she had kept fastidiously lay open beside her on the bed. Her latest entry explained all. She read through it once more, making certain she had made her feelings clear.

Dearest Beloved Family,

After heeding much counsel and advice from each of you, I still find I can no longer abide in this futuristic world in which Father has thrust us. I have taken classes at the community college, volunteered at the homeless shelter, even attempted employment—at which I failed miserably. Perhaps I should have given the job longer than one month, but interacting with so many people coming and going at the market exhausted me. I've not always been so shy and insecure; however, I find it difficult to play the part of a twenty-first century maiden. For she I am not, and I fear all whom I meet see through my pretense instantly. I long to be with Hudson. And because we are now living two hundred years in the future, he is surely dead and living in Paradise. I am writing this journal entry so you will know that I love you, but I cannot love this life I did not choose. Please forgive me. I go to dwell with Hudson now in the heavens above.

Sarah's hopeless circumstances were no one's fault but Father's. His cruelty toward her, coupled with his actions—taking his family off to another place and time with no thought for anyone but himself had caused irreparable damage. Mother, Joshua, Christopher, and especially her sister-in-law Arianna had done everything they could to help Sarah, but in the end their efforts had been futile.

"Cease your incessant brooding, Sarah," Father had sneered at her. "You are just a chit, after all. Females will never amount to anything beyond bearing offspring in any century. And women residing in London's east end fall to the bottom of the heap. Had we stayed, you'd have ended up working in a life of servitude, or worse, a light skirt." His lip had curled into a scowl.

Father's words had stung worse than the lashings he'd doled out whenever things hadn't gone his way. Before he had become a drunk and a failure to his peers—a lethal combination—had Sarah not been his little bluebell, because of her intense eye color? Memories of such compliments coming from her father were fuzzy now, but she distinctly recalled him also calling her his raven-haired princess.

Tears gathered in her eyes.

"This ends now." With too much force, she grabbed a glass of water from her nightstand, dripping onto a bundle of letters nestled in her lap. Letters from Hudson. "No!" She set the glass and the pills down and sprang to her feet. Locating a cloth to dry her precious notes, she dabbed at the paper. She breathed out a sigh of relief to see that only one letter was marred. It was illogical to care about the running ink on a note she'd not see after tonight, yet her heart could not bear it if anything happened to the last vestiges of her lost love.

"Perhaps I will read them one last time." She took meticulous care ordering the jumble of letters. Every night before bed since her brother Joshua had delivered them to her, she'd read each one, savoring Hudson's words. "It has been months, and I am no closer to finding my way back to you now than I was then. I am sorry I left, Hudson. We will meet again soon in the world beyond." She kissed the letter in her hand, then began to read.

Dearest Sarah,

I found no letter from you in tree hollow today. Then I heard reports of your father possibly committing a jewelry heist and even murder. Oh, my dear Sarah, how I long to console you. Wherever your father has taken you off, I will find and rescue you. We are destined to be together forever.

All my love,

Hudson

She read several more letters, Hudson's concern for her progressively increasing in each. His determination to find and protect her intensified, as well. *Little did he know I was far beyond his reach— anyone's reach but Father's.*

A word about the author…

Jeanie Davis and her husband, Rick, live in Gilbert, Arizona. She loves peach ice cream, shopping, a clean house…oh, and chocolate, of course. She has traveled extensively—from Fiji to Africa and Europe to Costa Rica—but prefers being at home creating new adventures on her computer.

Her four daughters have left her nest empty, but they return often with grandchildren who bring the real fun and adventure to her life.

A good romance will always capture Jeanie's attention; add suspense or historical ties and she's totally hooked. She's the author of an historical fiction novel, *As Ever Yours*, based on the lives of her grandparents, a children's Christmas book, *I Don't Know Why I Did It*, and a romantic suspense novel, *Time Twist*, book one of the Somerset series.

She is passionate about writing, and always has a new story to delve into or an older one to revise. She began by writing poetry and music, which she still enjoys.

When she's not spoiling her grandchildren, Jeanie spends her free time curled up with a good book or typing away on her most recent mystery, adventure, or romance.

Thank you for purchasing
this publication of The Wild Rose Press, Inc.

For questions or more information
contact us at
info@thewildrosepress.com.

The Wild Rose Press, Inc.
www.thewildrosepress.com